QUEEN OF THE NIGHT

QUEEN OF THE NIGHT

THE BLACK TULIP CHRONICLES

2

KAYLEE JARVIS

Contents

For those learning to trust themselves.

KINGDOM OF MONEYRE
THE BLACK TULIP CHRONICLES
SHIFT FOREST
FAE
LOW KINGDOM
OBSID
DESE
LUCENT
KIVAN
SHIFT CITY
NESTBUSH VILLAGE
BLACK CANYON DESERT
MERCENARY CAMP
ABYSMAL DESERT
FARLOW
LOW KINGDOM
Oc
R

OCEAN OF
ROGUES
LUCENT
DEEP
FARMLAND
HARBOR OF
MONEYRE
MONEYRE
HIGH KINGDOM
LUCENT
MOUNTAINS
NYMPHS
ORLET
LOW KINGDOM
MIDON
LOW KINGDOM
N
W
E
S

Prologue

Four hundred years ago...

The king treads warily into a cavern of shadows so deep the torch in his hand hardly lights the ground beneath his feet. To his knowledge, no one has yet attempted to approach Gloam, the god of shadows. The rush of pride that he will be the first, mixed with desperation, propels him onward. The shadows grow so thick the flame flickers violently, the chill air numbing his fingers... and then before him sits a man so dark that shadows seep from within him in writhing black tendrils.

Renton immediately drops to a knee before the black stone throne where the man sits, the silence deafening.

"Rise," Gloam drawls. "What can I possibly do for a *human?*"

The king grips the torch tighter. "My name is Renton, and my throne has been stolen by my twin brother, who plans to exile me and all those who know I truly deserve to be king into a land filled with tainted water and too barren to grow crops, where we'll be left to die. In the fight to regain my rightful place, my soldiers are dying so quickly that soon I'll no longer have an army to fight with."

Gloam's brow rises in interest. "Go on."

"Then my brother," he spits, "had the gall to approach Lucentia, and she blessed the vile man with *magic*. I stand no chance without your help."

Gloam's eyes seem to darken even further. "What do you expect *me* to do?"

Renton squares his shoulders. "Are you not Lucentia's brother?"

Gloam sneers. "Unfortunately."

"Then I ask for magic. Just as she gifted my brother, Ricard, with hers, I ask you to gift us with yours, to give me a chance to retake my rightful place as king and provide a better life for my people."

Renton shifts uncomfortably as Gloam appraises him with one arched brow, aware that the god of shadows could merely kill him on the spot, as it appears he's considering to do based on the steely glint in his dark eyes.

"I have one condition," Gloam says slowly.

"Anything," Renton rasps.

"You have heard of the Black Tulips Lucentia forced on the king of Moneyre?"

Renton nods, confusion causing his brows to furrow.

"I believe they are her weakness. There is no other reason she would force the king to protect them the way he does." He says it as if he's already considered it many times.

"Must I kill them?" Renton asks, more than willing.

Gloam chuckles. "So quick to violence, king." A slow smile spreads across his face. "No. You must bridge with one."

Renton's brow furrows. "Bridge?"

Gloam smiles. "Yes, connect the magic I gift you with one of Lucentia's Tulips. My dear sister, in her compassion for mere humans, has put a piece of her very magic within those women, creating a weakness I plan to take advantage of."

"Why would bridging with a human be dangerous for Lucentia?" Renton asks doubtfully.

Gloam's shadows grow so dark, encompassing his body until only his eyes glow from within, and Renton instinctively shrinks back. "Trust me when I say that even one piece of her power destroyed will dim her light enough for me to destroy her the moment you bridge."

"And if I'm not able to find one of these... Tulips?"

"Bridge with a Black Tulip and you will rule forever. Fail... and disappear as if you never existed."

Renton nods firmly, and immediately shadows engulf him until it would seem that a man had never stood there.

Chapter 1

Vera

I've heard Moneyre is a beautiful city—too bad it's the home of the high king and I'll be stuck there for the next two days.

I'll admit it: I messed up.

I kick a pinecone off the slightly overgrown forest path, cringing as I think about attempting to explain my recent choices to Tatania, the leader of the Black Tulips, but if things go well from here on out, I won't have to. I still won't need the dratted bracelet that costs an exorbitant amount of money to keep me hidden, and no one will know that I took a very lucrative contract offered by a man that I was eighty-five percent sure wasn't a criminal before he told me he's really a high-ranking officer of the high king.

I peek at Ikar who walks beside me. I was angry when he told me that he's an officer, but I soon realized that anger would only make me look suspicious. Now, I've settled on reluctant acceptance. While his profession would make most women feel safe, I would have preferred he admitted he actually *was* the Class A criminal I believed him to be.

A smidgeon of guilt blossoms as I recall the oath I spoke with the Black Tulips to never work for the high king, his officers, or anyone close to him because of the danger it presents to the Tulips... but there's no going back now—the contract is signed. Besides, while I may not be planning to pay the Black Tulips any longer, I still need money, and this job will pay more than I've made in two years combined. All Ikar and I have to do is find a simple magical flower for the king and survive the Lucent Mountains. Then I'll never have to pretend to be an originator again. I'll finally be *free*.

So, here we are. Friends once more—friends that shared a spectacular kiss the night before leaving Mama Tina's and haven't spoken of it once. I won't be the one to bring it up now that I know for sure we can't ever be together romantically. The thought saddens me more than I care to admit. I've grown so fond of Ikar these past days that I can say for certain I've never felt anything stronger for another man, but I refuse to look closer at those feelings when they're forbidden.

I glance at him carefully, secretly admiring his mussed brown hair, strong jaw, striking blue eyes, and the straight line of his nose interrupted by a bit of a bump that only makes it more perfect... but people like him don't court people like me. He must realize it, too, because he's kept a horribly polite and gentlemanly distance since the night of our kiss.

I'm drawn from my thoughts when Ikar tugs the hood of his cloak over his head, draping his handsome features in shadows. Rupi peeks from within, huddled near his neck, and I purse my lips as she turns her head and one sassy black eye meets mine. She still favors him even after he admitted that he's a high officer, and I can't quite forgive her for that yet.

I frown. "What are you doing?"

"Attempting to enter the city without recognition," he says

as we begin walking again. He makes further careful adjustments to his hood. We're still a good distance from the city, and we've passed maybe two other travelers. Why the need for secrecy?

I lift a brow. "For a supposed law-abiding citizen, you're acting blazing suspicious."

"I'd prefer to reach the castle without being stopped. I'm well known in this city, and the charm I used to hide my identity has likely worn off."

"You really are a criminal, aren't you?" Better that than an officer. A girl can dream.

"I'm sorry to disappoint you, but for the thousandth time, *no*. I am not a criminal," he says in that matter-of-fact deep voice of his.

He continues to adjust the hood until it shadows his face to his liking. When he's finished, all I can see is his jaw covered in a day's growth of stubble. But I think that even if I saw him covered in his cloak, I'd recognize his long stride, broad shoulders, and tall stature. He's not one to be easily disguised, with how his confident presence nearly radiates off him.

I continue to watch him, curious. "So you admit to using a charm all this time."

He looks my way, likely gauging if I'm upset with him again.

"They don't work on me, you know," I divulge the secret. I'd bet all the money I make on this contract that no one knows that small, almost useless, detail about the Black Tulips.

He stops walking. "...and you didn't recognize me?"

"Should I have?" I laugh. "You're just an officer, not the *king*. Even then, I've never seen him, so I guess I wouldn't know." I shrug.

The muscles of his jaw clench—a sign that I've hit a nerve.

Does he really think he's so important that commoners such as myself would recognize one of the high king's glorified soldiers? He needs to leave Moneyre more.

Out of habit, I move to put my hand on my short sword, but it slides off the empty leather sheath. "I don't have a sword," I whisper, followed by a groan as I consider how much it's going to cost to buy one.

I grabbed an extra dagger from Mama Tina's that I intended to sell in my future shop, figuring I needed it now more than my future shop does, but I've never had the funds to purchase extra swords to keep on hand.

Ikar interrupts my worried thoughts. "I'll take care of it."

Of course he heard.

I want to yank the hood off his head so I can see his face. Is this my *boss* talking, or the man I recently kissed offering to buy me a weapon?

"Consider it part of the job," he adds.

Well that answers *that*. I refuse to be disappointed. I can be professional, too.

"Thank you. I'll return it when we're finished," I respond primly.

He doesn't acknowledge my gratitude. "Have you ever used an enchanted weapon?"

I shake my head, refusing to remind him out loud how poor I am, and decide to change the subject. "How long will we be in Moneyre?"

"Two days." He looks my way, then adds, "If things go according to plan."

According to plan. Meaning... if we find Darvy and Rhosse alive and waiting for us, which we both hope for. A wave of worry and guilt washes over me—I never wanted anything bad to happen to them.

Soon, the forbidden city looms before us. Few words are exchanged between Ikar and me as the path becomes neatly laid cobblestones that teem with people coming and going from the high kingdom. My nerves tingle with anxiety the closer we get to the tall gilded iron gates, knowing Tatania would choke if she could see me now. It feels so rebellious.

I carefully eye the soldiers guarding the open gates in pristine uniforms as they watchfully scan the crowds of people leaving and entering. For a moment, I have the habitual urge to twist the bracelet around my wrist, but I stop myself. I don't need the bracelet or anonymity it offers any longer, especially while I'm on a remote mission in the dangerous and gloam-infested Lucent Mountains. What are the chances I'll meet the high king there? I nearly snort right there on the path. It's ridiculous the way Tatania and the other Black Tulips have scared us all these years—I'm over it. The money was due today, so I expect something to happen to my bracelet soon. Maybe it'll break, or maybe it'll just stop working. Maybe it'll rust and fall off my wrist in dry brown ashes. I have yet to find out, since not one of the current Tulips has dared allow their bracelets to lapse.

We're only moments from passing through the gates when Ikar leans close, places Rupi back on my shoulder, and, with a low voice, mutters, "Follow the directions. I'll send word."

With Rupi squawking and flapping her wings indignantly in my ear at being handed off without permission, and distracted as I am by Ikar's sudden nearness and the watching guards ahead, I hardly process his words.

Ikar presses a small piece of folded parchment into my palm. I stop and look down, still getting jostled by the movement around me as I open it. All that's written is "The Dapper Canary" in fine penmanship with "on the royal tab" written beneath, followed by his signature. When I look up to ask what this is about, Ikar is gone. I'm alone. Well, with the exception of Rupi and her quilled feathers, which are currently stabbing into the tender skin of my neck hard enough to make me wince.

I'll admit, I feel a little prickly myself at his behavior.

I look all around, turning in a full circle and bumping into other travelers, stumbling when a man with a cart loaded with summer vegetables shoves past as I try to find Ikar. No way could he have disappeared so quickly, and not only that, why would he leave me? I don't know what I thought, but I certainly hadn't planned on being separated at the beginning of this contract.

In just moments, I find my confused behavior has drawn the attention of the guards who eye me with suspicion. I curse beneath my breath as I stuff the parchment in my pocket, duck my head, and hurry through the gates into the city—I don't need trouble with the high king's law enforcement today.

I'm still miffed that Ikar deserted me, but I'm distracted soon enough. My mouth hangs open in awe as I walk through the large city. Shops of various heights line the winding streets in an orderly fashion. Flowers and vines fill brightly painted boxes and large decorative pots outside shop doors. Ladies in elegant dresses perch on shiny benches, talking and eating pastries purchased from a nearby bakery that emits smells so delectable my mouth waters. There's a shop with a swinging wooden sign that has a spool of thread pictured, and two dresses hanging in the large window. Another catches my eye, this one with a sword on its sign and its front window featuring an impressive assortment of enchanted weapons. Out of habit, I wonder if their weapon enchanter is in need of an originator, but within moments, I catch myself. I don't need to keep searching out contracts any longer; this is my last job as an originator. I mean it this time. Besides, no one will find me working in Moneyre.

A group of originators dressed in the stark white clothing they're so easily identified by comes my way on the already crowded sidewalk. I instinctively pull my long dark-navy jacket a little tighter around me, protecting the secrecy of the mark at the base of my neck. I may call myself an originator to survive, but I'll never be one of them. Originators started the rumors that got the Tulips hunted and killed, and I can't wait until the day I no longer have to pretend to be one.

Rupi offers a disgruntled hum and a slight poke in the neck with her quill feathers as she shuffles back and forth across my shoulder, agitated by the crowds and my own anxiety. The originators pass, one of their stark white skirts brushing against my tall leather boots, and I try not to glare at the way they so carelessly travel the streets of the high kingdom, laughing and joking together.

How nice for them that they don't have to hide. I can't help the resentful thought.

Seeing the group of originators stokes my protective instincts and spurs me to focus on finding The Dapper Canary, which I assume is either an inn or a tavern. But another window full of an assortment of items catches my eye, and I backstep until it's in full view. I enter the shop, gazing all around.

This. This is what I want.

I've just entered the shop of my dreams. I walk down one of five rows of tall wooden shelves. I stop partway down and, with an eye of appreciation, pick up a finely engraved compass, turning and opening it before gently replacing it. Rupi flutters to another shelf and taps a set of dice encased in glass with her beak. I gasp when I see they're made of dragon horn and priced to match.

Rupi has always had expensive tastes.

"I love 'em too, but those cost too much." I stick out a finger and she hops on.

We continue to stroll the aisles, passing a multitude of other items before I come upon a dainty solid-wood box with the most detailed tiny bird perched on the edge of its lid. I pick it up and open it, the small hinges moving effortlessly. Rupi chirps her approval.

I don't think; I simply take it to the counter, where a kind young woman wraps it in several layers of paper and ties it up while I count out the last of my money. Should I be purchasing things for my future shop? No. Do I have room in my pack? No. Am I still buying the box?

I slap the money on the counter. This will be perfect to add to the other items I've collected over the years and extra motivation to keep my head on straight during this contract so I can toss off the mask of originator and open the shop I've always dreamed of... and best of all, be *free*.

Chapter 2

Ikar

Guilt claws at me for leaving Vera the way I did, but it's only a matter of time until someone notices me if the charm has worn off, and I can't have her staying at the castle—not that I think she would even agree to that in the first place. And the fact that glamours don't work for her eyes? The woman grows more mysterious with every detail I learn about her.

I refocus my thoughts. There will be time later to figure her out. For now, she should be safe enough within Moneyre, but even with that reassuring thought, I worry. She has a knack for finding trouble and only has her small dagger to defend herself with—something I plan to fix immediately.

I quicken my pace, making my way through Moneyre and its beautiful winding streets as my thoughts turn to Darvy and Rhosse. Is it possible they're alive? Two of my top commanders and best friends since childhood—they're like brothers to me. *They can't be dead.* But if anything can kill one, or even two, of the best soldiers in Moneyre, it's the Lucent River and the monsters that inhabit its murky depths. I grudgingly try to think of who I'll choose to build a team to head into the Lucent Mountains with if Rhosse and Darvy haven't returned, even though it feels as if I'm giving up hope. But if they haven't returned... if they've died... even mourning can't keep me from the journey to come, not when an entire kingdom full of people depend on me to repair the dying lucent.

While I'm eager to rush to the castle to seek out news of Darvy and Rhosse, I must make one stop first. I glance up at the sign for the weapons charmer and duck through the doorway into the familiar, shadow-filled interior. Weapons of all sorts line the walls and rest on dark-blue velvet cushions as if they display the most priceless of gems. To a man of war, they are.

A bear of a man lumbers from a back room at the ring of the bell on the door, squinting to see who's entered. I lower my hood, curious to see if he'll recognize me.

"Your Majesty." Renoff inclines his head.

And there's my answer—the charm has worn off.

I slide my pack off my shoulders and kneel to find what I'm searching for—it doesn't take long for my fingers to graze its smooth surface.

I stand and hand the enormous ivory bantha claw to Renoff. "Can you craft me a short sword? I'd like this to be the hilt." I can barely suppress the grin that twitches about my lips as I imagine Vera's expression when she sees her new weapon. "I'll need it in two days."

"Two days?" Renoff takes the claw with a frown and carefully inspects its length and width.

I see the doubt in his furrowed brow. "I'll pay triple. I'd like it enchanted as well."

He growls as he considers, still turning it in his hands. I know I ask much. He looks up at me. "As you know, enchantments have become the last of lucent to weaken, but they are wearing off faster than ever. I'll do it, but don't expect it to last longer than a few months now."

Neither of us points out the sad fact that an enchanted weapon used to only have to be enchanted *once* in its lifetime.

My mark seems to burn with guilt at the sight of the weariness on his face. Why is it that lucent seems to be decaying so much more quickly during *my* reign? My chest tightens, reminding me of the likely reason—my *worthiness*. Or lack thereof.

I nod. "I'll send my team's weapons to be reenchanted, as well."

I give him a few other details about the style and length before I lift my hood once more and duck out the door.

———

I finally throw my hood back when I've reached the castle doors.

"Your Majesty." The guard snaps to attention, eyes wide with surprise at my abrupt and unusual entry—no guards, no entourage, no other soldiers at my side... no Darvy or Rhosse.

"My first and second commanders, are they here?" I try to keep my voice even.

"Not yet, but they—"

I don't hear what else he says as the grief I've kept at bay with shreds of hope comes to the surface and tightens my chest until I fear it will never expand again. *My brothers.* I pull my hood back over my head and continue walking, slipping into a hallway drenched in shadows from the angle of the three suns. I don't have the privilege of showing emotion of this depth beyond my private rooms... but my rooms are the last place I want to be.

I lean against the cold stone wall in the shadows with a fist pressed against the pressure building painfully in my chest and will the burning behind my eyes to ease. But waves of sorrow keep building, and suddenly this shadowy hallway feels so suffocating it's as if a tight hand is wrapped around my throat. I turn and stalk toward the training grounds where I know there will be *someone* to spar with.

I grip the pommel of my sword like a lifeline, but I can't summon enough mercy to feel bad for whatever poor soul will face me. Sword fighting has always been my outlet for emotion, and right now I need it more than ever.

I yank my hood off before I enter the training grounds. My soldiers jerk to attention as I walk past, startled by my sudden presence. Groups of soldiers are split up across the grounds in fenced-off areas. Distant cheers and shouts echo from one group along with the clashing of weapons, but in moments, everything is quiet, and I have their complete attention.

I whip off my cloak, hop a fence into one of the arenas, and pull my sword with so much speed it leaves a sharp ring in the air. Emotion causes an impulsiveness I don't usually cater to as anger and sorrow mix into duty-bound recklessness. I want to punch something, fall to my knees alone in the woods and scream to Lucentia over my brothers.

But I have a kingdom to save, and my team isn't going to form itself.

"You will compete to join my team to journey into the Lucent Mountains." My voice carries easily, the challenge clear. I eye the men I grudgingly listed as candidates for my team if it turned out that Darvy and Rhosse had actually d—

I shake my head, refusing to finish the thought.

Donovan, my third commander, steps forward. I press my lips together. He's a worthy fighter, one I put at the top of my new list. He scales the fence easily and swings his sword around, preparing for the fight. He's already drenched in sweat, and it's apparent he's already been training hard.

I waste no time, show no mercy.

Our swords hit hard, the shock of the collision reverberating up my arm.

"Welcome back, Your Majesty," he grunts as steel slides along steel. He steps back and then swings again. I block it easily. In moments I fall into a rhythm I haven't felt since before I left to find a Black Tulip. We go on that way for several minutes, but I know I'll need to pick it up to beat Donovan—there's a reason he's a commander. Before I can, I sense another presence behind me. Probably one of Donovan's tricks to try to beat me as he's tried in the past. I spin around, prepared to take on a second opponent as my sword, already swinging, hits another's loudly.

"I do hope you saved me a spot on the team," Darvy says with a cocky grin as our swords stay crossed at the blades between us. "I think Rhosse'll be hurt if you don't invite him too, even though we know *I'm* the better swordsman."

"You willing to bet on that?" Rhosse drawls as he jumps the fence.

They're alive.

I freeze, the steel of our swords still pressed together, unbelieving that my friends stand before me. "The guard said you hadn't returned yet..."

Rhosse grins. "We left on a training exercise this morning; he probably thought we were still there."

I finally release my stance and sheathe my sword, and immediately they step forward, pulling me into brotherly hugs with several strong claps on the back. I find myself blinking to reduce suspicious burning in the backs of my eyes, but this time triggered by relief instead of grief.

I turn to wave off the many soldiers who I'd just ordered to compete, but Donovan already took care of it. Everyone has returned to training. He offers me a distant salute, to which I nod.

I turn back around. "When did you return?"

Darvy speaks first. "The Lucent River spit us out near Kivan. Didn't take long to make it back."

"Would've been faster if not for the bite Darvy took from the river monster," Rhosse adds. "Took us two days in Kivan to get a healer and originator to help mend him enough to travel."

I look Darvy's way with concern, but he shrugs. "I'm fine. Just a bit of a limp I can't seem to kick."

My brows pull together. "Maybe you should stay home this—"

"Don't even suggest it," Darvy growls. "I'll prove I can fight if I need to."

I shake my head. I trust him. He *is* a healer, after all. "Fine. But I thought the two of you were dead the entire time. Don't ever do that to me again."

Rhosse scoffs. "*You* thought *we* were dead? You've taken twice as long to return as we did! Scared years off our lives, Ikar. You left us to make up stories about why we returned without you, and Jethonan sees right through it. It's a good thing you came back or he'd have thrown us in the stocks."

I chuckle, imagining Jethonan doing just that. "The woman we rescued from the goblins? She was a bounty hunter... of sorts. She arrested me and blocked my magic. And worse, the river chose to take us to the far end of the kingdom."

Darvy snorts. "You got arrested by a bounty hunter?"

"Yes, and now I've hired her to be the originator on our team."

Both men are silent, and after a moment, Rhosse finally speaks. "For a journey such as this... don't you think there might be a better fit? Or maybe even Nadiette?"

"You know I won't ask Nadiette." I see the knowing looks on their faces; I don't have to explain why. "I've spent enough time with Vera to know she's powerful—how powerful I don't know. But I sense it. More than another expert swordsman, we need lucent magic."

Darvy cocks a brow. "Oh, it's *Vera* now? First-name basis?"

Suddenly, I want to punch him in the face.

"That's how it usually goes when you travel with someone for over a week," I growl.

"Of course it is," Rhosse says placatingly, but why do I feel like they can see straight through it all? What did I say that gave away my feelings? What have I done in contracting Vera? I stifle a groan. I hired her because I need her—in more ways than one.

Chapter 3

Ikar

Jethonan watches me closely while I finish writing. I sign my name before I roll the parchment and place it into the waiting hands of a servant. It will be delivered to Vera along with a dress the castle seamstress deemed fit for an originator.

"I've never seen you exert such *energy* on a guest you've invited for a relatively simple dinner," Jethonan casually mentions as he scratches Arrow, my wolf-beast dog, between his two pointed ears. Arrow sits half his large body on his royal blue robes that pool on the floor, but he doesn't appear to mind.

His comment draws the attention of Rhosse, Darvy, and Nadiette, leaving the room quiet. Nadiette sits primly in her usual place on a comfortable sofa to the left of my desk, her eyes narrowing slightly at Jethonan's observation. One of her perfectly shaped brows has risen the smallest bit, and I get the sense she's awaiting an explanation as well, appearing more than curious about the originator I contracted. The tension between her and me is almost palpable. Part of me misses the comfortable friendship we shared for so many years, one that began as children. Naturally, it was assumed we would marry, and I believed I loved her as much as a man could love a woman... but now that I've gotten to know Vera—

No. Don't go there. I ended our relationship before I left in search of a Black Tulip, and she didn't take it well. Not that I can blame her. Guilt fills my chest, though I know I couldn't have done it any differently. And still more guilt for the fact that I don't feel as much for her as she apparently feels for me.

I was born into a duty that rules my life; it will always come first, and duty dictates we can't be together. I *do* care for her as a friend and hope that eventually the pieces of our broken relationship can be put back together into something akin to friendship, but from the look in her eyes I find it doubtful. Still, she is the Head originator for the kingdom. Her originators provide as much lucent magic for my soldiers as they possibly can—which saves lives. We *must* find a way to work together, but right now, with only two days at the castle to plan our next journey, I have no time to revisit our past.

I busy myself clearing the rest of my desk, avoiding eye contact with Jethonan. "She's important to the success of our mission."

Jethonan is much too intuitive, and I sense he already knows there is much more to the story. He wisely says nothing more.

I push back from my desk, standing and stretching my stiff muscles. After speaking with Jethonan and Nadiette earlier, it seems things went smoothly in regard to the workings of the kingdom while I was away and will continue to do so after I leave again. Their capability and well-earned trust lifts weight off my shoulders—knowing I'll return to a kingdom as well as it can be while battling gloam. Hopefully, when I return, it will be with the flower I need. Then I'll just need to find a Black

Tulip, but at the risk of triggering hopelessness I refrain from dwelling on that second thought too long.

I walk to a nearby shelf that holds several tightly rolled maps and sift through them, speaking over my shoulder as I say, "Remember to forgo my title for the duration of the mission. I am simply another soldier until we part ways with Vera."

I find the one I need and pull it from the shelf, unrolling the large map atop my desk and placing weights on corners that attempt to spring back.

Rhosse grabs a large fluffy roll and slices of roasted meat off a tray delivered a few minutes earlier. "Why the secrecy?"

Nadiette speaks before I can answer, an untouched plate of food on her lap. "Why bring home an originator? I thought you were searching for a Black Tulip. I have plenty of the best originators you could have chosen from."

I ignore the hint of betrayal in her words and shake my head. "From the beginning I intended to hire an originator outside those currently employed by me. I need every single one of mine to continue to protect the kingdom. Hiring Vera to help is a step in the right direction. She's powerful enough for the job, and it doesn't take any originators from my soldiers who need them." I hesitate to share the next part. "But she has a great dislike for kings and refuses to work for any of them, especially the high king. Which is the reason we'll be referring to each other as merely *soldiers*."

Darvy snorts. Then the three men laugh so hard I'm sure the sound travels outside the castle walls. Even Nadiette's lips tug up in a hint of a smile, somewhat smug, as she slips a bit of meat into her mouth and chews.

Darvy wipes his eyes. "Leave it to you to find the one woman who wouldn't want to work with you when the rest of them throw themselves at your feet."

I give him a bland look, not finding any of this humorous in the least, and I'm sure Nadiette doesn't appreciate that comment, but I don't look her way to confirm.

"She seemed to like me better when she thought I was a Class A criminal," I mutter, needlessly readjusting one of the weights.

Rhosse chuckles deep and low. "Most women like the soldier types."

I shake my head. "Not this one. In fact, I think it was harder to convince her to work for me as a soldier than it would have been if I'd kept the criminal facade," I muse.

Jethonan evades Arrow's attempt to snatch a piece of cheese from his hand. "So she thinks you're simply a soldier on a mission for the king?"

I nod, watching Arrow as he eyes the rest of Jethonan's plate.

"Why doesn't she like us?" Darvy asks, appearing truly offended at the prospect.

"Keep in mind, it's not *us*; it's the titles we hold." I like to think she rather likes me as a person, and that helps ease my guilt. There's no reason she needs to know.

I take a seat again. "All that matters is she took the job, and I believe once she warms up to the two of you, we'll make a team strong enough to retrieve the flower and survive the Lucent Mountains."

Darvy and Rhosse nod in agreement.

Nadiette sets her plate aside, stands, and smooths her dress. "I must take my leave and attend to other business. I'll see all of you at dinner tomorrow. I can't wait to meet this... originator you found." She looks me in the eye with a challenging stare, and I incline my head.

I look between the three men after she leaves, daring them

to say something about Nadiette and me and the obvious tension between us. The three of them wisely sit silently, chewing their food.

I pull out my grandfather's small leather journal and place it on my desk. "Now, we plan the journey."

Chapter 4

Vera

I've never been great at navigation, so I'm pretty proud of myself when I locate the inn after asking *only* four people for directions. I spot the sign first—a bright yellow bird wearing a hat with a red feather protruding at a jaunty angle atop its head. *The Dapper Canary* is painted in scrolling, elegant script onto the wooden sign that swings above the entrance in the cool breeze.

I frown.

It looks like a fancy sort of place. I hesitantly walk up the stone steps as Rupi flutters to the windowsill, turning an eye to inspect the interior. We can both see the dining area on the main floor is full of well-dressed customers. It's nothing like the rundown taverns I frequent in other parts of the kingdom. I bite my lip. Should I even enter? I know for sure I don't have enough money to pay for a meal here, let alone a room for the next two nights. But the note said to come here, and Ikar is my boss—for now.

I deftly scoop Rupi up and instead of placing her back on

my shoulder, I open a deep pocket and drop her inside. She chirps in indignation.

"Stay quiet. This place doesn't look like the type to appreciate pets," I whisper and give her a placating pat as I pull the door open.

As soon as I step inside, fragrant smells have my stomach rumbling and reminding me that the small buttery scone I bought hours ago wasn't nearly enough to satiate me. Patrons sit at round tables scattered artfully throughout the room, fine tablecloths drape over the edges, and straight-backed hardwood chairs wait for more customers to fill their seats. Small bouquets of fresh flowers grace the center of each table, and scattered sprigs of delicate greenery surround each.

I look down at my boots, almost expecting to see my old pair, but instead, new ones of the softest leather hug my calves with hardly a scuff on them. My nerves ease a bit. I'm more grateful than ever that I accepted Mama Tina's gifts before I left.

A woman in a practical but noticeably expensive gown approaches me with a smile and hands clasped before her. "Welcome to the Dapper Canary; my name is Edna. What can I do for you?"

She doesn't seem overly surprised to see me here, so apparently I don't look *too* much like the dirt-poor, low-class citizen I am. Feeling awkward and clumsy, I pull the rumpled parchment from my pocket and hand it to the woman, fully prepared to be turned away. She reads it quickly and looks at me as her brows raise in pleasant surprise.

"On the royal tab? Always room for a friend of the king." She smiles brightly. "Follow me."

I'm certainly no friend of the king's, but I don't correct her assumption. If it gets me a room for the night, I'll go with the ruse even if it's further from the truth than anything could ever be. But it *is* concerning that Ikar has permission to use the royal tab... how close are he and the king anyway? Right now I should feel happy. I've never taken a contract with such fine amenities, but a pit forms in my stomach. Ikar has enough sway to purchase a room in the king's name, and it's obeyed without question? What does *that* mean? Do all officers do that sort of thing, or is Ikar a favorite? I sigh. I assume he's a favorite. He seems to be that type, and that just makes everything more dangerous.

Edna leads me up a set of stairs, and we leave behind the low hum of conversation as we enter an elegant hallway lined with beautiful wood doors and a plush rug that travels the length of the space.

She procures a gold key and inserts it into the lock, opening the door effortlessly. She gestures for me to enter and drops the key in my hand. "As a guest of the king, we are at your service for any needs you might have. I'll have a private dinner and hot water for a bath sent up."

I thank her quietly, half in awe, as I step through the door and hear it click shut quietly behind me. I find myself standing in an elegant sitting room, albeit a small one. A door to my left must lead to a bedroom, but before I investigate, I take in the space before me. Two small settees face each other, a tiny table with fancy legs and scrolling woodwork along its sides settled between them. I walk carefully between the two couches along a finely dyed rug I can't wait to sink my toes into later and over to the large window that overlooks the busy street below.

I pull aside light curtains to find the second sun has almost set, the sky set afire in deep orange, and in the not-so-far distance I spy the top of the ivory stone castle rising far above even the tallest of Moneyre's buildings. My eyes roam over the spires and turrets outlining the sky. Even from this distance, it's clearly beautiful.

This is closer than I should ever be, but here in this fancy inn, having spent a day shopping and traversing a new and very beautiful city and seeing little evidence that gloam exists, I feel a sense of safety I will readily admit is false.

I spot the first groups of originators walking the streets with lucent orbs in their hands to provide light to patrolling soldiers, and I snap the curtains shut. I don't need any further reminder that I will be sleeping amongst a great number of enemies tonight.

I turn, ready to investigate the bedroom. When I open the door wider, Rupi soars to one of the bedposts on the elegant four-poster bed, perching on its tip, where she eyes the space with a critical eye. Ever since Ikar left us, she's been jumpy. I don't blame her since I've felt the same, which is *outrageous*. I've always been happy on my own and always believed in my innate ability to figure any situation out. But I'd be lying if I said I don't miss him, and we've only been away from each other less than a day. I have excellent reasons to worry for the state of my heart when I leave for good after this journey.

I wearily ease my pack from my shoulders and drop it on a fancy sort of sitting chair with a plump cushion as a seat. I fear the delicate piece of furniture might collapse beneath the weight, but after watching it with narrowed eyes for a moment, it seems it'll hold. I turn my attention to the head of the enormous bed that sits against one wall, covered in an array of fluffy pillows in all shades of green and a lovely blue comforter. A claw-foot bathing tub occupies the corner to the right, calling to me like a siren, and a wood dresser with fancy gold knobs stands opposite the bed. It's all very perfect. So perfect that I'm not sure I'll be able to get comfortable.

Rupi finishes her inspection and coasts back to my shoulder, using her beak to nip my earlobe affectionately. I pull out a small handful of her favorite birdseed and spread it across the polished wood dresser. She wastes no time fluttering down and begins to peck happily, hopping here and there as she picks through the seeds. Her gentle cracking and crunching soothes my nerves, providing the sense of normalcy I need.

I begin to relax as I shrug off my cloak and drape it across the back of the chair my pack occupies. I eye the tub that has yet to be filled, and a smile begins to turn my lips up. Who knows when I'll get to bathe again? I plan to make the best of it.

I sit on the edge of the bed to begin removing my boots, but there's a knock at the door, and I freeze. Rupi shoots back to the tip of the bedpost and quills up, looking much larger than her actual size.

A muffled voice comes through the wood. "Delivery for Vera."

I didn't order anything. I stand and pull my knife from its sheath, hiding it slightly behind my thigh as I open the door and peek out. An elderly man with bright-white hair who's dressed in royal-looking clothing holds up a garment bag. A petite woman with hair as dark as ink stands behind him. I'm instantly on edge.

"Wrong room." I begin to close the door.

The old man is faster than he looks, and he sticks a polished boot in before I can get it closed. "Are you Vera?"

"Yes, but—"

"Then it's for you."

The castle folk sure know how to make sure their deliveries are made. This man is persistent.

I sigh, deciding he's no threat and slip the knife back in its sheath before opening the door a bit wider and sticking my hand out resignedly for the garment bag.

I snatch it, and I'm about to close the door again when he places a large white scroll in the space and speaks again. "Meredith is here to take measurements for armor."

"Armor?" I ask doubtfully.

He shakes the scroll at me.

I eye him suspiciously and hesitantly reach for it. He keeps his shiny boot wedged in the door to ensure it doesn't close, and I purse my lips at the fact he assumes correctly. I snap open the scroll and scan it quickly. It appears armor will be a requirement for this journey and Meredith has, in fact, been sent by Ikar. The signature at the bottom matches the one on the parchment he left in my hand earlier.

I sigh. "Fine."

In no time, Meredith is whisking around me, measuring and recording numbers, but she's much faster than the dressmakers Mama Tina forced me to endure, so I can't complain. Within minutes she's finished, speedily rolling up her measuring tape and tucking away her notes.

"Watch for a black carriage, unmarked," the man says before he gives a sharp nod, and the two of them are out the door.

I watch as he marches down the hall with Meredith scurrying behind him. I waste no time shutting and locking the door before laying the bag across a settee in the sitting room. I quickly open it and find a *stark* white gown—whiter than that old man's hair and as blinding as what the originators wear.

I don't know what kind of fabric it is, but there's a lot of it. It's smooth and shimmery, and when I pull it from the bag, it spills out like water from a pitcher, puddling on the ground. Hand-stitched half-suns are embroidered throughout the fabric, catching in the candlelight and sparkling like real shining sunrays. The details are fine and intricate—I'm sure the dress cost a small fortune. But it's *white...* and the *suns.*

My face twists in disgust. I put it back in the bag and reach for the rolled parchment. I've never felt parchment so velvety soft and thick. The quality is a blatant reminder of where it came from, and it sets my nerves on edge. I pull it open and Rupi flutters down to my wrist, turning her head to eye the letter with me.

In the same neat hand that had written the note to the owner of *The Dapper Canary,* Ikar informs me that I am invited to dine with him at the castle tomorrow evening to meet some of his close friends and team members. Then, in the next sentence, he tells me that Darvy and Rhosse are alive.

I let the parchment roll up as I sag into a nearby chair in relief.

"They're alive, girl," I whisper to Rupi who shuffles up and down my forearm, bobbing her head excitedly. I let the relief wash over me as I close my eyes and the guilt over their possible deaths seeps away. Rupi allows it for only a moment before she shuffles back toward the letter and prods it with her tiny black beak.

I pull it open again and scan the rest quickly. Ikar goes on to say that he hopes I like the dress, and mentions the unmarked black carriage that will arrive to pick me up. He gives no other information, including whether or not the king will be there, and it leaves my nerves in tangled knots. Is this the type of invitation where a person can decline, or is this the type that's a requirement disguised as an option?

Just like this room being paid for, I assume the dinner is considered part of the job as well.

I set the parchment on the table where it snaps back into a

roll and fiddle with the end of my braid as I consider the situation. But with that motion, I spot the bracelet on my wrist and drop my braid as I tug on it to test its strength. Still works, as far as I can tell. If it can just hold through tomorrow, then even if the king is there, dining only feet from me, he won't know what I am. Still, the thought of it stirs nausea in my belly. I attempt to talk myself down from rising panic.

It's just one meal. I only have to evade the horrid man for one night.

I can do this.

After several deep breaths and some encouraging chirps from Rupi, I find myself calming down. If I want to be free, I have to finish this job. So while the situation isn't ideal, I can do it.

I have to.

Chapter 5

Vera

The thought of seeing Ikar tonight has butterflies stirring in my stomach mixed with a wallop of guilt, since I shouldn't feel that way about an officer. It's a feeling very similar to indigestion. That and the fact that I'll be venturing to the castle this evening, entering the lair of the high king himself—for sure breaking a rule of the Black Tulips by doing so. If Tatania knew what I'm about to do, I'm sure she'd faint dead away. All I can hope is that the king won't be joining us tonight.

I tug on the bracelet again—still secure—and step into the dress with a grimace. I find it's a style that could fit many sizes with so much fabric and a fancy belt about the waist, but when I finally look in the mirror, I find it drapes over my every curve. Add to that... it's *white*, blatantly marking me as an originator— I simply *cannot* get past the color.

I tilt my head to the side with a frown. It also sort of reminds me of the lusty everwisp that stole my looks in an attempt to seduce Ikar in Shift Forest, especially with my hair curled and hanging long as it is tonight.

I wrinkle my nose and stare a moment longer. The bodice is an intricate wrap style with two gold half-sun pins on either shoulder that hold up a sweeping bow of fabric that reveals my back. I turn to the side a bit and eye the unacceptable design. Originators are known for showing off their sun-shaped marks like badges of pride, but I think they'd be rather surprised if I were to reveal *my* mark. I'd probably be arrested—or killed on the spot.

I pull the curls aside and inspect my mark, a black tulip, stark against my fair skin. I'm fairly confident the volume of my curled hair will be enough to keep it hidden for the night— there's a reason I went to such lengths to style it this way. Rupi chirps loudly from the window, and I assume the carriage has arrived. A sudden rush of nerves leaves me feeling jittery as I peek through the curtain and find a carriage so black and shiny it gleams waiting below. It looks very... terrifying.

I sigh, unable to believe I'm actually doing this.

Rupi flutters atop my finger, intent on not being left behind.

"No silly antics tonight. We're entering the high king's residence and need to avoid any more attention than a woman in a white dress with a bird already draws."

She tilts her head, the epitome of innocence, and blinks twice. She's not as blameless as she likes to appear, having gotten me into plenty of trouble over the years, but I take the blinks as agreement. And having her near gives me comfort, so I lift her to my shoulder.

"For freedom," I say as I yank open the door and make my way to the doom carriage.

The ride isn't nearly long enough. In what seems no time at all, we've already crossed half the distance, and I can see more and more of the castle as we travel the busy streets. Even from a distance, its presence is imposing. I know because I was staring at the despicable towers that knifed through the sunrise from my window this morning, and now I'm drawing ever nearer to entering its treacherous doors. At the thought of actually stepping inside, the interior of the carriage grows horribly stuffy. Moisture begins to bead along my brow as the castle comes into view a few streets ahead, and as expensive as this dress feels, it does nothing to absorb the sweat that begins to gather beneath that fabric.

"Completely impractical," I mutter to Rupi as I clamber to fiddle with the latch of a small gleaming window in an almost panicked motion.

It gives way with a refreshing burst of cool air across my face. I sigh with relief. But having it open increases the noise from outside. We round a corner onto a road that leads straight to the yawning, fancy gates of the castle, passing closely by a group of women. I freeze when I hear their words float innocently through the window. "...the king returned home just yesterd—"

Their voices fade and are replaced with other snippets of conversation from people we pass—none of which I care to discern as my ears buzz with dread. The king is *at the castle?* I mean, I shouldn't be surprised. It *is* his home.

I try to calm my breathing. I already assumed he'd be there, didn't I? Somehow, having it confirmed makes it one hundred times worse. I don't know how many times I've twisted my bracelet, but Rupi pecks my hand, telling me to stop with a tiny scolding eye. "Right. I gotta pull myself together." I sit back against the cushy bench with a huff, eyeing the redness around my wrist. It'll draw unwanted attention, so I force myself to leave it alone.

We roll through the gates and a full view of the massive structure fills my vision. The castle is built of smooth, creamy stone, with architecture so elegant and graceful it appears to be something out of a vivid dream. Large balconies grace its outside walls, dripping with beautiful flowers and greenery, and I imagine they lead to grand ballrooms. An enormous set of steps leads to an entrance made up of three sets of wood doors so large I guess it would take three men to open one. Six stoic soldiers stand guard before them, covered in intimidating armor and a variety of weapons. None move when our carriage stops and the door swings open. A serious young man dressed in dark-blue royal clothing, seeming to appear out of nowhere, stands with one hand outstretched—I assume to help me out.

I lift Rupi to my shoulder and glance at her dubiously, but she only offers a *cheep* and prods me with a quill-feather in the neck. Apparently, I'm not the only one who wants to see Ikar.

"Into the lair we go," I mutter.

I clasp the servant's gloved hand and step out, feeling more like an imposter than ever in my life. I don't belong here. I'm not royalty or even a member of the high class. I don't belong in this color, or this fancy dress, or on the palace grounds. I don't even know if I'm good enough to belong on this team for this journey. But here I am, and it appears I'm stuck.

I watch the black carriage pull away with the clip-clopping of horse hooves and turning wheels on cobbled stone, the road it travels framed by the exquisite gardens full of tall hedges, flowers, shade trees, and gurgling fountains. While I'd love to allow my eyes to linger on the gardens that extend as far as I can see, my attention returns to the castle where I stare at the rows and rows of windows sparkling in the sunset along its walls... And those rounded towers I thought looked so tall from my room? Now they appear even higher, so high I have to crane my neck to see the tops of their pointed turret roofs where small flocks of birds perch. Does the king keep his prisoners locked in there... or in the depths of the dungeons I imagine are hidden beneath this beautiful nightmare?

I'm pulled from my thoughts when Rupi ducks her head and peeks beneath my chin to look at something, and I follow her attention to find a young woman coming our way. I straighten my shoulders. Time to be the imposter I am, and I better make it good if I don't want to end up in the dungeon...

I glance upward once more... or in one of those towers.

She gives a slight bow and offers a kind smile. "I'm Belinda. I'll be your escort."

Her eyes catch on Rupi within my curls, and a slight frown pulls at her brows, but she doesn't say anything. A bonus to pretending to be upper class, I suppose.

"This way." She motions away from the front entrance and toward a path I wouldn't have noticed on my own.

Tall hedges are shaped in a way that creates a covered-arch path draped in fanciful shadows. I saw well-dressed men and women traversing other parts of the grounds, but there's no one but us on this path. What does that mean? *It can't be good.* Secret paths aren't for the normal people... they're for kings. I gulp so loudly Belinda looks over her shoulder as if she's worried I might be choking. I muster up a tight smile to assure her that I am, indeed, as fine as I can be.

We reach a double door with two guards who step aside in the darkness to allow us passage, and I try not to show how terrified I am by lifting my chin the smallest bit. Belinda is quiet as she leads us through a gorgeous interior garden that rivals the beauty of the fae's green thumbs. I look up to find open balconies overlooking all of it, with rays from the suns above adding a brightness and warmth that invites me to linger. That is, until I remind myself the high king resides here. And as quick as the snap of fingers, the garden becomes a mirage to hide the wickedness that goes on behind these walls.

We enter another double door, once again blocked by two guards who step aside as Belinda nears. I'm proud when I don't hesitate to step over the threshold. Then, just like that, I'm in the depths of the high king's home. If I weren't so blazing anxious, I could actually enjoy this moment. I'm not sure how long we've walked, distracted as I am by the slick, polished white marble floors that spread before me and the intricately crafted, light-colored woodwork that graces every wall. A large chandelier—in much better shape than the one we have at our Black Tulip headquarters—hangs in a dome-shaped room we pass through; the sunlight that shines through the enormous sparkling windows reflects off the crystals and sets it afire. It's all very beautiful. Dangerous. The high king's lair is all I imagined—and more.

Rupi brushes against my neck, and I'm surprised I don't feel her trembling or her feathers beginning to quill. She usually gets anxious when we're in danger, but I look down to find that she leans her body forward, tiny beak and fluffy white face jutting out between strands of my hair as if she's an arrow intent on her target, who I *know* is Ikar.

I don't see anything particularly *evil* here. It's actually quite cheery, clean, warm, and bright... and the servants appear pleasant and well. It's odd when I know the atrocious acts the kings have committed. Just another indication I must be on my toes. This all has to be a facade. Fake. The best villains *are* experts at hiding.

We pass through long hallways, two of which have statues

of men I assume are past kings lining their walls. I wonder which one it was that murdered the Black Tulips. I have only a chance to cast a quick glare at a few of their cold, hard eyes as we pass. Belinda keeps up a rigorous pace that I have difficulty maintaining between the desire to take in the castle and trying to take a proper step in this dress. Large tapestries and paintings grace the walls, and tall windows allow evening light to warm the light-colored halls. Passing servants, nobles, and soldiers give me slight nods of respect, eyeing my gown, and groups of two or three originators at a time pass me in the hall, inclining their heads toward me as if I am one of their own. So this is what it feels like to dress as an originator. I don't like it.

I'm on edge, not just with the extra attention and large numbers of originators who seem more than comfortable in these halls, but waiting for a procession of soldiers to walk by with the king in their midst. Would I be required to curtsey before him? The thought has me disturbed. Partially because I have no idea how to perform a proper curtsey, but mostly because I have no respect for him. And my heart beats double time when I realize that maybe I haven't seen the king in the halls because he's attending dinner tonight and he's already *there.*

I swallow tightly and touch my bracelet still wrapped securely around my wrist, then instinctively make sure my hair hangs full over my back. Even if the king attends, he'll think I'm an originator. *I'm safe.* I repeat that mentally, three times, until I fool myself into believing it.

I take a deep breath as Belinda stops before two tall wooden doors with complex vine designs engraved into the wood panels that are fitted with enormous gold handles. Rupi appears unconcerned with the entire situation, keeping her tiny eyes fixated ahead on the doors and who she knows is on the other side. I'm slightly irritated. She's the one who usually keeps me safe, and here she is, not warning me *at all*. There could be a *king* in there.

Two guards stand before them and one opens the door wide.

"Here we are, my lady." Belinda curtsies again.

I nod in thanks as the door swings open, and I try not to fidget with my hands or the folds of my dress while a servant in the room announces my name.

I take another deep breath and enter. Before me is a lavish dining room with a table draped in deep-blue cloth, set with fine dishes and shining silverware, with mounds of flowers and greenery arranged around tall brightly glowing candles. A row of tall windows framed with dark-blue curtains that reach from ceiling to floor shows that there is, indeed, a beautiful balcony outside. The table is only set at one end, though it appears to seat at least thirty along each side. Soft music drifts from a harpist perched on a small corner stage surrounded by more flowers. It's all beautiful, picturesque really, but my eyes search for just one thing: a fat, shining crown.

Chapter 6

Vera

I search for a crown... but the only people I see are speaking near the head of the table and I immediately spot Ikar's familiar face—no king in sight. It's only been a day since we've been apart, but I savor his presence as if it's been months. He's clean shaven, and his hair has been freshly trimmed. I imagine that when I stand a little nearer, I'll see that the storminess that's usually only a mere hint in his blue eyes will be drawn out by the dashing gray suit he wears. I find the cut of it seems to enhance his broad shoulders and trim waist and looks much too fine. And somehow I just *know* he smells as good as he looks. My mouth suddenly feels uncomfortably dry.

Rupi flaps her wings against my neck impatiently. I gather my wits about me and make my way toward the group, shoulders back, careful to shove all signs of worry beneath the weight of this awful white dress.

Halfway there, Rupi loses patience and soars from my shoulder straight for Ikar. He grins as she flutters to his shoulder and comfortably shuffles up close to his neck, settling in as if she plans to never leave. I just know she's going to carry his scent on her when she returns to me, leading to a torturous night. We're going to have a chat, she and I.

"Welcome, Vera. Thank you for joining us." I see the flash of appreciation in his eyes as he takes in my appearance, but I'm disappointed when he doesn't move to stand by me, though I know I shouldn't be. He's my boss now, and apparently, one of the king's favorite officers.

If I thought he looked comfortable at Mama Tina's, he looks completely at home and more at ease than I've ever seen him here. Other than Mama Tina's house party, where I still believed he was a criminal, I'm used to seeing him with some type of gore on his clothing, dirty, and at times, injured. It was easy to believe we were equals, but now I know we never were. I don't know this side of Ikar, the side that's not a criminal and one who is at home in the high king's castle. I find myself curious and more than a little unsure.

He begins introductions with a beautiful brunette to his right. "This is our head originator, Nadiette."

Her smile is warm, but her green eyes are cold—like a viper. I plan to avoid her at all costs. She sidles up beside Ikar, close enough that I'd assume there's something between them except he steps away, putting an extra inch or two between them. Ikar has never said anything about a significant woman in his life and isn't indicating she is one, but a flash of jealousy I have no right feeling stabs me in the gut. I'm irritated that I want to know every detail of their history.

I smile in what I hope looks a mature and confident way even though it feels like I just sucked on a lemon, and nod at her. Then I turn my attention to the man Ikar introduces next.

"This is Jethonan, Head Advisor."

Jethonan smiles and bows grandly in his deep green robes. His long hair swings forward with the motion, and when he rises again, he says brightly, "It's truly a pleasure to meet you, my lady."

A genuine smile turns my lips up as I nod. I like him already.

Ikar gestures toward the next two men. "And, of course, you know these two, unofficially. Darvy and Rhosse."

I nod to both with an embarrassed sort of smile. I mean, it was my fault they almost got devoured by a river monster.

Then Ikar gestures toward me. "Everyone, this is Vera, the originator who will be joining us on our journey." He reaches a hand up to where Rupi is still snug against his neck. "And this is Rupi. She'll be joining us as well."

Nadiette lifts a brow as if she thinks it's ridiculous. I sort of want her to have the opportunity to experience one of her quill stabs, but Rupi appears more than content to stay with Ikar, so I ignore her and turn my attention to Darvy and Rhosse.

"I'm happy to see the two of you alive. I'm sorry for what happened." My cheeks flush.

Darvy speaks up. "No apologies necessary. Neither of us were too badly hurt, and it's given me another story to add to my repertoire." He smiles in a charming manner, and a dimple appears in his cheek.

I laugh. "I'd like to hear your version of the story."

I notice Ikar cast a quick look at Darvy and the dimple quickly disappears.

Rhosse chuckles. "We hear you and Ikar have quite the story to share as well." He motions with a hand to the waiting table. "Shall we hear it over dinner?"

We move toward the table, and I'm giddy when it appears it will only be the six of us dining. I breathe a sigh of relief—the king won't be hovering over us with his heavy, wicked presence during dinner after all. I immediately feel myself loosen up, my smile widening and my lungs taking what feels like a full breath for the first time today.

We take our seats in the plush, luxuriously cushioned chairs. Ikar pulls Nadiette's chair out like the gentleman he is, then seats himself beside her. Darvy pulls my chair out with another charming smile, minus the dimple, and sits to my left. I end up across from Ikar at the end of the table, nearest the head seat that sits conspicuously empty, but I certainly won't be the one to comment on it.

Rupi hops to a small silver tray filled with a fancy variety of seeds, fresh berries, and other fruits she favors. Ikar had to have planned this. My already softened heart melts further. He's apparently going to make himself as hard as possible to resist. The scoundrel.

I look up from Rupi happily pecking through the tray to find Ikar watching me. Our eyes meet, but rather than a quick glance, something about the way he looks at me forces me to hold his gaze and takes me straight back to the dim hallway at Mama Tina's where we shared our first kiss just days ago. Does he think of that night as often as I?

Heat stains my cheeks, more pronounced by the color I wear, I'm sure. *Another reason to avoid white.*

Servants bring out the first course, and I take the interruption to dip my head and gather myself.

Darvy turns toward me slightly after our food has been placed before us. "You arrested our highest commanding official, you know. That's not something I think most people would have the bravery to do. Very commendable." He smiles in such an endearing way I can't help but grin in response. He's handsome with his mussed light-brown hair, cropped on the sides and longer on top, and green eyes brimming with mirth. He's filled with boyish charm. If I weren't still battling feelings for Ikar, this man would be dangerous.

"I was told he was a Class A criminal." I shrug in an unladylike way before I can catch myself. "Work is work."

Rhosse chuckles, and I notice a glint of what looks like approval in his eyes before he takes another bite. Rhosse is also handsome, in a dark and rugged sort of way. He's taller and broader than both Ikar and Darvy, which is impressive. At first glance, his black hair, size, and the broody looks, combined with the scar across his eyebrow, all lend a dangerous air about him, but I'm beginning to see that beneath it all he's kind. Admittedly, he would also catch my eye if I passed him on the street. I'm not sure how I'm supposed to manage on my own with three magnificent-looking men for the next who-knows-how-many days, but I suppose I can do it. For the kingdom, of course.

"I can't imagine being in such a... *rugged* line of work; it must be so hard," Nadiette says with a velvety voice. I know it's intended to be an insult. No decent originator would choose to work with hunters, roaming dark, dangerous forests for criminals—they're too busy clambering for the top.

"I rather enjoy it," I drawl with a confident half-smile, knowing it will annoy her. I don't usually fall into these petty games with other women, but something about her irks me.

I meet Ikar's eyes again and catch another glimpse of open attraction before he shutters it away—as if it escaped and I wasn't supposed to see it. Feelings I shouldn't be feeling curl in my belly.

"You two." Nadiette suddenly speaks again, drawing our attention. With effort, I mask my irritation. She looks between Darvy and Rhosse. "How did you survive the river?"

Darvy finishes a bite, uses the fancy linen napkin to pat his lips, and, with a humorous light in his eye, begins. "It all started with a list of Black Tulips that Vera ruined..."

Nadiette's spoon clatters into her soup, and my wide eyes betray me by jumping straight to Ikar's before I realize that was the last thing I should have done. His gaze holds mine like a vise. I *feel* the promise of questions to come, and I swallow with a throat so tight I nearly choke. Drat Darvy for reminding him.

I pull my eyes from Ikar's, busying myself by lifting a spoon of warm broth to my lips, which was a mistake. The spoon visibly shakes in my grasp, and drops spill over the sides. Ikar watches intently. I've already committed, so I sip it ever so slowly, more relieved than I should be that it goes down without causing more of a scene.

With the break in eye contact, I can actually listen to Darvy's regaled story, and I can't help but laugh over his detailed and dramatic retelling of the goblin situation that has me relaxing until, soon, thoughts of the Tulip list have once again been tucked safely away. I hardly have time to eat before the course is cleared and the next placed before us.

Darvy turns to Rhosse when he finishes the tale. "Anything to add?"

Rhosse smirks. "Think you covered it all, and more. All that matters is we're alive."

Nadiette laughs as she catches my gaze, as if we're the best of friends just because we're both women. She's wrong. "Men. Always downplaying the most dangerous things." Then she changes the subject rather abruptly, keeping her attention on me. "So you arrested Ikar after that? And it was just the two of you?" She acts nonchalant, but I see the tips of her fingers whiten around the delicate fork she holds.

I take a sip of wine in a fancy glass with the tiniest stem I've ever held between my fingers. I'm afraid I might break it clean in half. "Yes, and yes." I set my glass down and dip my head for a bite, but I spy Nadiette's lips pursed like she drank something sour and nearly laugh into my soup.

Ikar and I take turns sharing the story of our journey, prompting more laughs and disbelief from our group as we argue lightly over details. Warm tension tugs between us after recounting our journey together, heightened by flashes of eye contact when we're both silently aware of the parts we intentionally skip to keep to ourselves.

Dinner has long since been cleared from the table and my cheeks ache from so much laughter, and Rupi has made a second and third trip to her tray, always returning to Ikar after. I find myself feeling something very close to camaraderie with this group, aside from Nadiette, who looks irritated and distant. But everyone else? I feel as if we've been friends for a very long time. And most impressive, I hardly remember I've been dining in the castle for the past two hours. Rhosse and Darvy start speaking with Nadiette about an incident between a group of soldiers, two originators, and a gloam creature that happened three days ago. Nothing interests me there, so I turn my attention to Ikar and Jethonan.

"I must say I'm glad to have you back, Your Ma—Commander... ship," Jethonan stutters momentarily. "I've been working on a new weapon, but it's quite difficult to find the time when I've taken on so many duties." He looks at Ikar pointedly.

Ikar chuckles. "Yes, there are many of them. Will it be ready for me to take when we leave tomorrow?"

Jethonan appears to do mental calculations for an extended moment. "It *should* be. I'll try to finish it tonight. There are other matters to discuss, as well, before you leave."

Ikar nods and sits back in his chair. "We leave early, and it's growing late. We should head to your office now."

Before they stand, I can't help but jump in, curious. "Jethonan, you make weapons?"

His eyes light when he sees my apparent interest. "Some say I'm a wizard, of sorts. But really, I simply enjoy experiments, and that includes creating weapons. Come with us if you'd like."

"Enter at your own risk," Ikar says with a smirk.

I laugh. Surely he's joking.

Chapter 7

Vera

Ikar was most definitely *not* joking. A wave of putrid blue air belches from the large keyhole of a door down the hall. Jethonan hurries ahead of us to insert the key and turns the lock with a click.

I slow my steps with a frown, unwilling to go any closer until I know what that smell is coming from. Ikar comes from behind me, places my hand on his arm, and clasps his larger hand over mine in such a gentlemanly way that I wouldn't have known he was teasing if not for the look in his eye. He guides me toward the rolling mounds of blue-tinged air now escaping the room before us through the wide-open door.

He leans down and whispers near my ear. "I *did* warn you."

He smells incredible, like I knew he would. I'm suddenly flustered and feeling too warm to think properly.

"As good friends do," I say, attempting to get my mind and body on the same page.

Friends.

And there he is, still too close. "Is that what we are?"

Jethonan saves me from becoming a blubbering idiot by

opening the door wider and summoning us into the room. I step away from Ikar, acting unaffected, while I wonder what he meant. Did he sound pleased that I called us friends, or was he implying we're *more?*

I cough as I enter Jethonan's office, then hold my breath as I wave a hand before my face to try to clear some of the fog away. It does nothing. I have no choice but to inhale or pass out—on the bright side, maybe it'll dye my dress blue.

"Is *this* the weapon?" I ask. "'Cause I think it's ready."

Jethonan laughs. "No, no. This is simply a byproduct of the chemical process." Clinks and clanks come from the far side of the room, followed by what sounds like a book thudding on a wood desk, but everything's fuzzy through the fog. I turn to find Ikar forcing open a window and leaning slightly out for clean air before he moves to the next. Rupi makes a sound that I can only describe as a tiny sneeze before she flutters from his shoulder to one of the now-open windows, searching desperately for fresh air.

"You know, the temperature in this room is a delicate balance. You never ask before you swing those open, and you may one day ruin one of my projects," Jethonan scolds, even as he's bent over something on the table.

"You may one day ruin *me* if you don't find a way to clear this room on occasion," Ikar responds dryly. "How do you know this blue stuff won't hurt us?"

Jethonan waves that question off with his hand. "I've been breathing it all week, and I'm still alive."

I look toward Ikar with concern, but he's busy making himself comfortable in a cushy armchair near a bookshelf, settling into its back with his legs spread wide and relaxed. He sighs so deeply that it causes the blue air to billow around his face temporarily. He doesn't appear too worried.

Finally Jethonan finishes tinkering with a glass contraption I have no name for and calls me over, proceeding to give me a short tour of the many projects he has in progress. They're interesting, to be sure, but I'm more entertained by Jethonan's antics and the passion in his expression as he explains details I'll never actually understand. When he's finished, he leaves me to browse while he speaks with Ikar about someone's journal. Rupi joins me on my shoulder, and I stroke her soft white fluff as I tune out their voices and return to one project that caught my eye during his short tour.

I lean down until my eyes are level with a glass vase-like container with a lid that contains a portion of misty gloam. Rupi leans forward, same as I, as I reach a finger up and tap it. It reacts by swirling furiously, and swiftly begins to form the shape of a tiny deathstalker. I tap it again, and it viciously attempts to attack me against the glass, snarling and clawing. Deathstalkers are terrifying creatures. But feeling brave with that wall of glass between us, I touch it again. It feels cold as ice now, and frosty. I've never actually tried to attack gloam—I merely defend myself while sending magic to whatever hunter I'm currently working for—but my lucent orbs have deterred gloam creatures before, and I'm curious what this little guy will do.

The protection of the glass jar between us boosts my confidence as I bend closer, come a little nearer, and align my nose with its face. I lift an inquisitive finger and pull lucent, tapping where the tiny deathstalker snarls against the glass. The moment my lucent finger and its snarling form meet against the glass, the miniature deathstalker implodes, and I instinctively jerk away. All that's left are shreds and bits of gloam that are already fading.

I look at my finger, then back at the now-empty jar. That

was unexpected. I look at Rupi who stares at me with wide eyes. I silently curse and spin around with the jar behind my back, instantly becoming the epitome of innocence. *I ruined Jethonan's project.*

I bite my lip, trying to decide what to do. *Act normal.* I sidestep and hurry to another project I'd seen that looked interesting, promising myself I won't mess with this one.

From the corner of my eye, I see Jethonan grabbing a glass vial filled with what looks like purple sand. "Here is the weapon I've been preparing for you. It appears small, but I assure you it is quite powerful." He begins walking toward this side of the room, and I stand, clasping my hands behind my back like I should have been doing all along.

Jethonan stops before the vase-jar and motions for Ikar to join him. "Come, I'll show you how it works."

Ikar stands and makes his way over while panic builds.

No. Not that one. I cringe a little as he bends down to inspect it and finds the gloam gone. He taps it, just like I did. But this time, nothing happens.

I killed it.

"Very strange, but my gloam specimen is missing." Jethonan inspects the lid and finds it secure, then leans down to search the glass again, tapping here and there. He stands, and now he's tilted his head to the side and looks at me like *I'm* a project. He looks at me so long that I start to fidget with the fabric of my dress.

"Everything okay?" Ikar asks.

Jethonan startles as if the deepest of thoughts were interrupted. "Yes... Yes, fine." He speculatively eyes me once more.

I will myself to stay calm. He can't know. That would be crazy. No one can just *know* what I am like that. I didn't even tell him I'm the one that killed it. But I know when it's time to take my leave, and that time is *now*. Before anything else weird happens.

"Well, I'll be going. Need to get plenty of rest before we leave tomorrow. Meet at the stables, right?" I smile gingerly.

Ikar nods with one brow raised as if he's confused by my abrupt departure. I bow awkwardly and rush for the door.

Chapter 8

Ikar

Vera fairly runs from the room, and I look Jethonan in the eye when the door shuts behind her. He smiles like a smug cat.

"What was that about?" I ask, perturbed at his behavior.

"You should thank me for producing such an astounding plan to save the kingdom. It's going better than I ever imagined." He bends to inspect the empty jar again, tapping the glass twice before he stands with a gleeful smile.

I lift an eyebrow. "I'll give you credit for finding the information, but until I've accomplished the mission—to find the flower *and* a Black Tulip—I don't think we should bask in our success."

"Oh, we'll be successful," Jethonan says, as if it's a known fact, as he tosses me the vial of purple sand. "It pains me to say that I don't know if you'll need that. It's one of the best weapons I've come up with to fight gloam to date, but I think the *originator* you found just might be better."

"Is there something I should know...?" I ask, frowning over his antics.

"No, no. Press on, Your Majesty."

It's not the first time I've been left confused by his behavior, so I let it go. "How do I use this?" I shake the bottle a little.

"A few pinches thrown at gloam creatures should obliterate them."

"And have you created anything to make me a *worthy king*?" I ask somewhat sarcastically to hide the actual doubt and fear I feel as I walk toward the door. It's the one thing that could ruin this entire plan. If Lucentia doesn't deem me worthy, no matter how long and far we search, no matter if we find the Field of Tulips... no flower will be given to me. I was raised to be a king. Confidence isn't something I lack when it comes to my knowledge of the kingdom, weaponry, or even how to rule my people. But my worthiness has been in question since my mark began to turn black years ago, and I can't seem to get past the constant visual reminder.

"I could try, but it's unnecessary," Jethonan mumbles as he grabs an armful of ingredients from a tall cabinet across from his desk. I'm about to lunge forward to catch them when one begins to slip—who knows what sort of smell or potion might be released if one of those breaks? But he catches it just in time and returns to his desk. I take a deep breath. The man stresses me out like no other. If he wasn't so blazing brilliant...

"I am confident you will return with a tulip." He raises his brow at the same time he lifts a finger as a thought comes to mind. "On that note!" I watch as Jethonan scurries across the room with robes flying behind him and pulls a long, aged wood box with intricate tulips engraved all around it from beside a nearby shelf and hands it to me. "I was forced to dig this out of the royal archives amidst piles of dust and old tomes in the depths of the castle. An adventure I hope to never repeat."

I smirk. "So glad to hear you survived."

"As am I, my lord," he says ever so seriously. "It will keep the flower healthy until you're ready to use it. At least, that's what the records say."

I take it in my hands, rubbing a thumb across the engravings. "About that worthiness potion—"

"Unnecessary."

"Just look into it," I say sternly. It pains me to sound so under-confident.

Jethonan sighs in an overly patient sort of way. "I will attempt to come up with one, but I've never heard of such a thing."

I nod once and head for the door, but I hear him mutter, "The things he asks of me," beneath his breath, and I can't help but smile.

I close the door behind me, only to find Nadiette waiting in the dim hall.

"You mentioned we could speak before you leave," she says quietly.

I incline my head. "Walk with me."

We stroll down the dim hallway, and I notice the way her eyes latch on to the box in my hands.

She frowns. "What's that?"

"It will keep the flower safe until I'm ready to use it."

The crease between her brows deepens and she purses her lips. Part of me misses the comfortable relationship we had before, so easy and natural. It's gone now, replaced with a somewhat forced and stilted tension. I know it's my fault. But what is a king to do? I'm duty bound to my kingdom, and my people will always come before my own personal interests or desires. Still, there's a sort of sadness that comes with realizing the feelings I had for her all this time were little more than a strong bond of friendship. Vera taught me that. My feelings for her are stronger than I've felt for any other woman, but it can't be love. Heavy attraction and infatuation is all it is, I'm sure. It doesn't matter either way; she's yet one more woman unavailable to me.

I pull my thoughts back to Nadiette and remind myself that she has been a friend since childhood, one who stood by my side in many battles and will for more in the future. That alone inclines me to listen.

She clasps her hands together in front of her as we walk and takes a deep breath, as if gathering her courage. "Please reconsider our relationship, Ikar. I've had time to think while you've been away these last weeks, and I realize how much I truly care for you. I missed you dearly."

Missed me dearly? Did I miss her dearly? I feel guilty that she didn't cross my mind nearly as much as she should have for someone I thought I loved romantically. I miss Vera to the point of distraction and the urge to leave all responsibility behind to ensure she's safe. To hear her laugh. To just *be with her...* has it ever been that way with Nadiette? I frown.

We continue walking the lonely halls, empty besides the guards who salute as I pass, and the stray servant here and there. Everything else is quiet now that most of the castle has bedded down. I have no desire to hurt her more than I already have. But only one thing matters.

I start slowly. "I explained to you that I need a Black Tulip to restore lucent magic—to repair my kingdom." I look at her apologetically, only to see her looking at the ground and blinking quickly. *Don't cry.* I grit my teeth. Guilt presses on my chest, uncomfortable and hot.

She seems to gain control of her emotions after a moment, and I visibly see her shoulders set. She lifts her slightly watery gaze to mine. "You don't see though, Ikar. I know we can fix this together. We are both magically powerful individuals. Any children we have, I'm sure, will have the power to fix this. Your father married and quickly sired an heir—you. Adding more lucent to the mark and extending lucent magic for the kingdom. You must do the same. We're running out of time. Marry me and ensure the kingdom continues. Give us time to figure it out together," she pleads.

For a moment, her plan is tempting. Though I've come to realize that I never *loved* Nadiette, we've always had a strong friendship. She's beautiful, capable, respected by my people. We get along well. What *if* I chose that route? The thought sours quickly.

"My kingdom will likely fall before an heir has a chance to be born. And even if it didn't, you cannot guarantee me a male heir. But none of that matters because while your plan *may* delay complete devastation, it doesn't fix anything."

"It's Jethonan, isn't it?" I see the anger in the set of her mouth. "He doesn't know *everything*, Ikar. He doesn't know that the low kings are worried about you. That they could... mutiny, if you don't..."

I shoot her a livid look, and she stops speaking.

"Listen to them?" I finish her sentence with a deadly note to my voice. "I'm not a child, Nadiette. This is *my* kingdom, *my* responsibility. I was born into this position, raised to be the high king, and I am duty bound to protect my people. I will do whatever I have to for my people. The low kings are nothing. I'm aware that they don't agree with restoring Black Tulips to their rightful place in the kingdom. They're cowards, unable to see that there's no other way."

Her eyes are wide with surprise and a hint of defiance. One of the low kings, Waylon Orlet, *is* her uncle, but she must understand.

"Your position as high king is in danger!" She shouts, her hands fisted at her sides.

I finally stop and face her. "No more than before... unless *you* told them my plans."

She looks as if I slapped her as guilt floods her features. I have my answer.

"I *will* marry and bridge with a Black Tulip to save my kingdom," I grind out.

If I can find one, that is, but I don't add that. I also don't mention what the backup plan is. No one knows that but me.

I stride away, leaving her in the shadows, but I hear the sorrowful tone in her words behind me. "You're too stubborn, Ikar. Too noble. Don't let it be your downfall."

I continue walking.

Chapter 9

Ikar

I wake before the first of the three suns rise, imparting last instructions to Jethonan and other advisors before I leave. There is no end to the weight and guilt on my shoulders as I prepare to depart. Not only do I feel horrible about Nadiette, but my absence will put the majority of my responsibilities on Jethonan's shoulders *again*. For the hundredth time, I remind myself that this is for the kingdom and my people. They need me to do this.

There's just one last thing I need to do before Vera arrives at our meeting place. I make my way to the royal stables where my horse, Champion, awaits, snatching a carrot and a few sugar cubes from a cart nearby. The stables are bustling with activity, as usual. Servants and castle folk are everywhere, pulling carts, mucking stalls, brushing down the many horses, and more. Sunshine through the open doors illuminates small dust motes, and the smell of fresh hay and the nickers of content horses calm my nerves. That is, until I see who stands before my horse.

"Are you being ignored, big guy?" Vera coos to him, her

pack and cloak resting against the stall door and Rupi perched on her shoulder, looking more than a little jealous as she side-eyes Champion.

I take a moment to appreciate the perfect fit of Vera's new armor before I pull a bit of lucent to hear better from where I stand. Champion nuzzles her hand and neighs in indignation, wholeheartedly accepting her unwarranted sympathy. She laughs and shifts to rub his neck before he snuffles her hair and sets Rupi to quilling, and she laughs again, dodging the worst of her prickly feathers. Something about the scene sets my heart ablaze. A rush of affection has me envisioning a future where she's my wife, and every morning I would walk up and put my arms on either side of her, balanced on the solid wood of the smooth gate, my lips finding that sweet spot below her ear as she tips her head back...

"Champion, is it?" she asks, and it startles me from the vision. But she's not talking to me; she's still fawning over my war horse.

"The king's favorite," I say impulsively, my voice slightly rough. Harmless enough words. She won't know I mean her.

Vera startles away from my large horse and looks at me, unsure, as if caught, but she recovers quickly. "I see why. He's *darling*," she says affectionately as she reaches a hand up to stroke his jaw again, and he leans into her touch.

Much as I would like to.

I redirect my thoughts. Did she just call Champion... *darling?*

My eyebrow lifts. "Most wouldn't agree. And I don't know that he appreciates being called darling. Perhaps strong, or maybe magnificent would be a more appropriate description?"

"Look at him. He needs more attention." She ignores me,

and her voice is sugary again as she holds Champion's face in her small hands. He blinks his large brown eyes at her.

My horse snuffles in agreement, reaching for her hand, lips searching gently for a treat.

I snort and shake my head, incredulous. He's like putty in her hands. My horse and I have much in common. I step forward and rub his neck with the manly sort of affection and familiarity that we're used to while whispering, "behave yourself," in his ear and offering a carrot that he happily snatches from my hand.

Vera looks around, and I can sense that she's about to ask questions, worst of which would be asking which of these horses is mine. I quickly throw her pack over one of my shoulders, grab her cloak, and tug her out of the stables. Champion's is the only gold nameplate in the stable, and I just told her he's the king's favorite. I'd give everything away if I answered truthfully. I make a mental note not to talk about him on our journey.

I lead Vera to a fenced-off field quite a bit farther out than the stables, where three saddled horses wait. She frowns at there being only three. Darvy and Rhosse are near, conversing with one of my horse trainers, an expert at training my soldiers to fight in battle atop their mounts. When they see us, they quickly nod their goodbyes and join us.

Vera gestures to the horses. "Which one am I riding?"

I use my chin to gesture over her shoulder with a wicked grin, watching her expression carefully. "That one there."

Vera turns slowly. Across another set of fences and somewhat hidden behind the bulk of another set of smaller stables stand three sharp flyers. The massive creatures—a mix between dragon and scorpion with six insect-like legs, razor-edged wings, and each with a sharp stinger that dangles above the saddle—wait patiently. She curses under her breath, forgetting that I can hear every word. I smile even wider.

"Such language, Vera," I mutter near her ear. I don't look down, but I can imagine her fine brows tugging into a frown.

"Where did you get those?" she asks in disbelief.

"We have connections in high places," Darvy says with a wink.

Without another word, she yanks her pack from my shoulder, throws it over her own, and marches toward the giant flying creatures.

Chapter 10

Vera

"Looks like two of you are riding together," I call over my shoulder, cackling to myself as I slip a foot in the high stirrup of the one I've claimed.

Rupi lands on the pommel of the saddle above me, confident in my abilities as she fluffs her feathers cockily. We'll show Ikar that I can handle this big guy on my own this time.

"That would be us," Ikar says from behind me, so near my ear that a delightful shiver runs down my spine. I don't have time to react before he quite simply tosses me astride and smoothly climbs up to seat himself behind me, his muscular legs snug around mine, and pulls me back against his chest as if he has permission to do so. Apparently he does, because I'm more content than ever to stay right where I am.

The flyer sidesteps with our weight, and I don't think I'll ever enjoy the sound of its joints, but I'm proud of myself when I don't panic. I quickly glance around to see Darvy and Rhosse astride their own, appearing to get acquainted with the creatures and hardly paying us any mind.

"I can handle a sharp flyer on my own, you know," I tell Ikar in an attempt to redeem myself.

"Never said you couldn't."

He leaves me sputtering with questions and feelings I'm having difficulty sorting through as he turns his attention to giving last orders to Darvy and Rhosse before we take off. Rhosse appears completely at ease, but that makes sense, given his hunter magic. He takes off smoothly and circles in the air as he waits for the rest of us. Darvy, on the other hand, can't seem to get his beast to even walk in a straight line.

Ikar shouts further instructions amidst attempts at smothering his laughter as Darvy grows more frustrated when the flyer he commands begins turning in slow circles rather than running for takeoff. But my attention turns to Rupi who is still perched on the pommel. I'm certain she can't fly as fast as a sharp flyer and I'll lose her if she doesn't ride in my coat. I reach a finger out for her, intending to drop her in my pocket, but she flutters over my hand and onto Ikar's upper thigh to my right.

I turn the smallest bit and open a pocket wide, right in front of her, careful not to touch him more than I already am with his strong legs so tight around me, and motion her to hop in. She refuses with an obstinate ruffle of her feathers.

"You're going to blow away during takeoff if you don't obey," I warn with a whisper.

She turns one tiny dark eye my way and blinks as if I'm ridiculous.

I huff. "Fine."

Ikar is shouting something at Darvy, and while he's distracted, I muster the courage to scoop her up myself, my fingers brushing across his trousers as I'd wanted to avoid. He stops shouting mid-sentence, and I *feel* the way I've caught his awareness at the contact.

"Did you need something?" he asks, perfectly still behind me.

I almost die at the question. *Of course I need something. I need him to be a criminal instead of the blazing officer he is so I can run away with him.* I'm grateful I'm seated ahead so he can't see the deep blush tingling in my cheeks. I make a show of plopping my misbehaving bird into my large pocket to show that I wasn't *trying* to do that.

"Just grabbing Rupi is all," I mumble, trying to ignore the sudden, warm tension between us.

I sense his eyes on me for another moment, then he seems to accept my answer and returns to shouting instructions to Darvy. I glance at Rupi in my pocket with narrowed eyes. She appears smug as she snuggles comfortably into the shadowy depths. I purse my lips at her before I button it shut.

Darvy whoops and draws my attention as he finally gains a shaky sort of control over his flyer and takes off, dipping and weaving, but flying all the same.

"And that's why you're not riding with Darvy." He chuckles again as Darvy's flyer continues to dip and weave. I refrain from asking why Rhosse wasn't an option, but he answers for me anyway. "Neither of them has ridden one before, so I figured your chances were better with me."

Does that mean this decision was completely practical then? That knocks a little of the wind out of my sails. He acts as if he's always known how to fly one of these even though I know for a fact the first time was only several days ago. But I don't argue. I'm choosing to look at the silver lining, and that is having Ikar's warm chest at my back and his strong arms around my waist as he holds the reins and guides our sharp flyer into a smooth ascent.

The wind tugs at strands of my hair that I braided so tightly

I feared it would cause a headache this morning, but pieces still come free. Ikar seems unbothered, so I try to ignore it. I watch below us as Moneyre grows smaller and smaller. *Things are looking up.* I unexpectedly get to ride with Ikar, we're leaving the high king's lair behind, and best of all? I never had to meet the wicked ruler. With that thought I relax against Ikar as if it's the most natural thing in the world. How can it feel so right to be close to him when he's a person I should never feel safe with? A high officer for the high king? He's too good of a person to be that.

Back at Mama Tina's when I decided to work for him, I was still highly suspicious that he was anything other than a criminal. Now, after dining at the castle where he looked more comfortable than ever, I can for sure say I know he's not a criminal. But I still wish he was, because then at least he wouldn't be some sort of high-ranking official. The thought has me wondering if I could convince him to retire... eventually. The problem is, whatever role he carries as an officer seems to be engrained in him in a way that can't be left behind by simply retiring. He hasn't shared much about his role, or what exactly he does, but I'm not overly familiar with the way an army works and probably wouldn't understand if I asked anyway.

The air grows colder the higher we fly, until my nose and cheeks are red and I shiver even with my coat. But my attention is pulled from the uncomfortable chill when I take a moment to really *see* our kingdom from this height. As we fly over its expanse and toward the Lucent Mountains, I find myself sickened by the shadows covering the land. Rather than rolling hills, patches of farmland, and vibrant green forests, darkness engulfs and spreads like disease. Clouds of gloam hover like swarms of hornets over what could have once been prime grazing land, sparkling lucent river, and lush trees.

"I didn't realize it was this bad," I say loud enough that Ikar can hear me over the wind roaring in our ears.

"It's multiplied considerably, especially recently. We do everything we can to push it back, but people are suffering. Our success on this mission could change that."

I nod, but I still don't even know the entire plan. It's never been shared with me, whether on purpose, it's just on a need-to-know basis, or it's simply been overlooked. These capable men trust Jethonan, and I trust them... enough. All I know is they search for a magical flower of some sort, but there are many. How a simple magical flower is supposed to remedy an enemy this destructive is beyond me. My job is to provide lucent magic, not ask questions that could encourage them to ask questions of their own, something I need to avoid at all costs —especially after that pesky conversation that I'd locked in the recesses of my mind... where Ikar handed me a list of all but one of the Black Tulips and asked if I knew anyone on it... was brought up by Darvy over dinner last night. I get the feeling Ikar is simply biding his time until he asks me about that again.

I attempt to calm my rising concern, reminding myself that we'll be so busy fighting for our lives in the Lucent Mountains that there won't be time to fall further for him, or for him to bring the topic of Black Tulips up again before I can disappear. That thought is both comforting and terrifying, but at least if I die on this journey, I die with my secrets safely intact.

Chapter 11

Vera

The Lucent Mountains sit at the Eastern edge of the kingdom. Originally named after Lucentia, they used to be brimming with lucent. I've heard fantastical stories of magical, lucent creatures who lived there, of forests so colorful and vivid they looked right out of a dream. Those who were weak and had difficulty pulling lucent magic for themselves could go to the rivers in these mountains and soak up pure lucent. It was also told to be teeming with nymphs—powerful magical creatures connected to the earth—who lived in small communities throughout the mountain range.

I've *also* heard that people stopped traveling these mountains years and years ago because gloam had overtaken them and they were much too dangerous, which is why I balked when Ikar initially told me he intended to travel them to find the magic flower the king needs. It's funny how desperate life situations and large amounts of money can change things.

Just after we pass into the mountain range, dark clouds roll across the sky, and within moments, it begins to rain. Our visibility reduces to almost zero with a gray fog so dense I can hardly spot Rhosse and Darvy on either side of us. What might have been a chill drizzle on the ground stings harshly against the exposed skin on my face with the speed and height of our travel. The weather is always unpredictable and drastic, going from hot and sunny to forceful winds and snow in less than a minute at times. While I'm not at all surprised, I *am* irked at the moisture that sneaks beneath my cloak and begins to dampen my clothing beneath. I'm relieved when Ikar finally motions with his hand, and the three of us circle a few times around a misty meadow before landing.

Once the sharp flyer touches down and its skittering comes to a stop, I take a moment to look around. We may be some of the first magic users to travel these mountains in hundreds of years, and it feels very... eerie.

"You sure this is where we're supposed to start?" I ask Ikar as the chill rain beats down on us. It looks blazing creepy to me.

"As good a place as any," he says matter-of-factly as he dismounts, jumping to the dirt and leaving my back and legs immediately chilled without his solid, warm presence behind me. I want to pull him back into the saddle and fly away together, but whether by duty or contract... we're both stuck here.

I can tell he's about to turn toward me to offer help, but I catch Darvy and Rhosse watching, so I slide off on my own. It may not be the most graceful dismount, but I don't fall, and I consider it a win. I already shared a saddle with Ikar for half a day; it's time to show that I can hold my weight on this journey. Especially for Darvy and Rhosse who don't know me as well. I'm no delicate lady. I've assisted hunters for years now, and though I may not be the best with weapons, tracking, or directions in general... and I'm not even quite sure why Ikar hired me when he has an entire selection of royal battle-trained originators at his beck and call... I *can* offer lucent, more than any originator, though this team will never know that—and I believe I'm capable of handling most things. I wouldn't be a very good assistant if the hunters were so worried about treating me as a lady that they couldn't focus on their jobs. Ikar grins a little, as if he sees what I'm trying to prove, but he wisely says nothing before he turns and calls the others over.

I'm used to it just being Ikar and me, but with Darvy and Rhosse here now, I sense the brotherly camaraderie between the three men stronger than ever, and I'm left feeling out of place. I find I'm also hyperaware of my feelings for Ikar with his two friends around. Will they notice? Am I revealing too much? I don't know how to be normal around him. I nearly groan.

They converse a few feet away, and I catch a word every now and then as they discuss directions and other important details I can't help with. Instead, I busy myself by patting the sharp flyer on its long scaly neck in thanks. It leans into my hand. Surprisingly, I'm finding comfort beside its large form as I stare at the murky forest that surrounds the field we landed in. I snort. The first time I saw a sharp flyer, I was terrified and refused to mount—which almost got Ikar and me recaptured by the shifters. Look at me now, friends with one of the large beasts.

My eyes drift back to the forest that awaits us, and I swallow hard. Gloam curls like black fog along the ground and claws its way up the trunks of the tall fir trees. I even see wisps of it lingering higher above, a growing monster attempting to devour everything it can reach. And in a sense, it is.

I unbutton my pocket and Rupi pokes her rumpled head out, her feathers quilling as she turns her head to eye what awaits us. I stroke her tiny head with two fingers to settle her, but the action also serves to comfort *me*. What have I gotten us into this time?

Just as quickly as it began, the rain stops and the clouds part to reveal the three hot suns that will dry and warm us quickly. That is, if it doesn't start raining again. The lack of lucent magic creates havoc with the weather as well as everything else. For now, though, I'm grateful for the warmth and the way the light cuts through some of the gloam around us making it not look quite so scary—even if it's temporary.

"It'll be a quick journey, Rupi. I hope." My voice comes out in a whisper.

I admit it doesn't sound convincing. Rupi's tiny fluffy body trembles even through the layers of my clothing. I notice the men pulling out weapons, which had been stored in their packs for the flight, and strapping and tucking them across their leather armor. How many weapons do three men need? Soldiers will be soldiers, I guess. I only ever carry two weapons, my dagger and my trusty old short sword.

I instinctively move to pat the hilt, but my hand smacks empty leather sheath, and I frown down at it with concern. *I have no sword.* I'd meant to ask Ikar for one to borrow before we left, but when he'd found me in the stables... *How could I have forgotten?* I blow out a deep breath. Admittedly, he distracts me. What sort of adventuress who contracts with the high king's best soldiers heads out with only a somewhat dull dagger? I nearly groan beneath the weight of feeling even more the imposter than I was before.

I quickly wipe my expression of any self-doubt as Ikar heads my way, a swagger in his stride and a confident set to his lips. I step back beneath the steadiness of his gaze as he comes closer. He looks like he's about to slide his hands along my jaw and kiss me senseless against this sharp flyer—or maybe it's just my inappropriate imagination wishing he would.

"I have something for you." He reaches around me, and for a moment, it seems as if he truly is going to kiss me, and butterflies burst into flight in my stomach. But it seems he's merely inflicting torture upon me as the saddle bag opens behind my head, and his scent tickles my nose as his arm brushes my ear. I realize I should've moved, how this must look, but before I can step aside, he finds what he's looking for. He steps back and lays a blade flat against both palms and bows in a gentlemanly way that forces a smile to my disappointed lips.

I catch Darvy and Rhosse glancing in our direction with curious gazes and admit that it would have been horribly awkward timing for a kiss anyway. And what happened to my intention to create space between us? I've already failed.

"My lady, your sword." He stands up straight and offers it to me with a heart-stopping smile.

Rupi offers a short trill of approval from my pocket, perking up immediately with Ikar so near.

I look closer at the sword he holds, and my gaze immediately locks on the hilt. It appears to be made of a smooth ivory material, like the tusk of a beast or...

"The bantha claw?" I can't help the laugh of wonder and delighted surprise that bubbles up as my eyes caress the smooth hilt and the gleaming silver hand guard engraved with intricate vines and tiny birds that look very much like Rupi.

The blade is sharper than a deathstalker spike with those same beautiful etchings traveling midway down. It's obviously brand-new, and of higher quality than I've ever owned. My eyes burn, and I blink to clear the blur of moisture as I stare at the sword in awe. It's the weapon of my dreams.

"It's yours, and it gets better." I finally look up to see his blue eyes eager and his hand outstretched, waiting for the sword. "Lend me lucent."

I put it in his hand and he steps back, tossing it in the air and snatching the hilt, readying the exquisite weapon before him. When I hesitate, he simply nods for me to go ahead. I can't help but laugh and shake my head, but I send him lucent and watch as the blade immediately glows. He smiles as he watches it, and the enthusiasm so blatant in his expression makes my heart stop for a moment. I've known he loves weapons, and I've come to realize that his sword is basically a revered companion, but now I'm reminded how much. While my eyes want to linger on his face, I force myself to drag them away and take a good look at my new sword held firmly in his grasp, the blade bright with lucent magic.

I frown. "It's enchanted?" I ask, a little breathless at this lighter side of Ikar I've only seen glimpses of. I like it.

"You need an enchanted weapon for this journey," he says matter-of-factly.

As if it wouldn't cost me an entire year, or more, of savings to pay for.

I wrap my hand around the smooth hilt, still warm from his grip. "But I know how expensive these are. I've contracted with a weapon enchanter before—"

"Don't worry about the cost." He stares intently into my eyes. "Your safety is the kingdom's highest priority."

The moment grows warm between us as his words run through my mind. He makes it sound like a sensible, logical sort of gift... but the look in his eyes tells me it's more. Not only that, but I see the fine details—the sentimentality of the bantha claw as its hilt, the way he watches to see if I'll love it, the pleasure that lifts the corners of his lips as he waits for my reaction... and I *do* love it, though it feels ridiculously extravagant.

I run a finger across the gleaming, flat side of the blade, almost blinded when it hits the sun and reflects into my eyes.

"It's beautiful, thank you. Now I need to learn to wield it," I say with a smile, feeling extra clumsy with it all of a sudden even though I've carried a sword for years.

It just feels so *fancy*.

"Rhosse is an expert." He gestures with a thumb over his shoulder in Rhosse's general direction as if he, himself, is not also an expert. "He'll be working with you in the evenings. Whenever there's time," he adds.

I don't know what to do next. I mean, we've kissed... but just once... and now I'm working for him, but he just gave me a *very* expensive gift... then told me it was meant to be a sensible gift that certainly doesn't *feel* sensible. What's a woman supposed to do? I figure a hug is *friendly* enough, if I don't linger—and that's a big *if*.

I carefully sheathe my new sword, then smile at him before I throw my arms around his waist, intending to release him quickly after. *Half-second hug*. But just as I'm about to pull away, his strong arms come around me, and he smells so good, and even through his leather armor against my cheek his heart beats strong beneath the solid muscle of his chest. I melt. Purr. Sigh. However it can be described, it's all of the most content feelings summed into one.

"I wondered what you'd think of the hilt," his voice rumbles deliciously in his chest, and that just deepens my contentment. It feels so natural to be in his arms.

"It's sort of gross but really sweet," I mumble into the leather of his armor. I hear his laugh against my ear as I recall the bantha claw that almost killed him, the one I pulled from his leg and is now the hilt of my new sword. It seems too intimate a gift for a simple friend. Someone you've only hired to work for you temporarily.

I breathe in deeply once more, then muster up every ounce of self-control I've developed over the past twenty-six years, and step away while trying to pretend he doesn't affect me and my bleeding heart hasn't begun to hemorrhage with the addition of this moment to my memories.

He steps back with a relaxed smile, as if he's not nearly as affected as I am, but he can't hide everything. I see something I can't quite describe in his eyes. *Friends, Vera.* It's then I notice that Rupi left my pocket while we hugged, and she now nips affectionately at his earlobe before settling onto her broad, muscular perch looking more comfortable than she should for being *my* bird. I narrow my eyes at her. If I can't have him, she can't either, but before I can snatch her back, Darvy comes up beside Ikar and rests a forearm on his opposite shoulder.

He smiles boyishly, looking between us. "From the looks of it, you like your gift." He grins wickedly at me.

Does he mean the sword or the hug? The hug wasn't *that* long.

I pat my new sword twice, smiling and trying to hide all evidence of my feelings. "I've never been gifted anything like it. Ikar is a very thoughtful friend."

Darvy's snort is so loud that Rupi squawks and quills up. Ikar irritatedly jerks his shoulder from beneath Darvy's arm. Was it what *I* said, or what *Darvy* said? I look between the two of them, unsure how to proceed and worried I've said something wrong.

I take the chance to escape the suddenly tense situation when Rhosse approaches to pull more gear out of the saddle bags, and I need to move out of the way. I grab my pack from the ground several feet away and throw it over my shoulders, huffing beneath its weight. A few minutes later, I watch as the men send the sharp flyers flying back in the direction we came. I sorta wish I was going with them, and take a moment to watch them longingly as they become smaller in the distance. Then I remind myself that I want my freedom—and that freedom requires money—even if it means I pretend to be good enough until I am. I steel my shoulders.

"This way," Ikar calls, and as a group, we trudge across the field and into the gloamy treeline.

Chapter 12

Vera

It feels as if we journeyed into a painting where the artist's palette consisted of only gray, black, and dark browns with a little watered-down green. It smells of moist dirt and rot, and many of the plants, though living, look wilted and half-dead. We walk through a particularly spindly copse of trees—their spidery, fragile leaves dangle loosely on their branches. I imagine if I were to take a deep breath, I could blow all around me in a circle and the leaves would come spinning off. It would be quite magical, but I don't. We don't need any extra attention drawn toward us. I already feel as if we're trespassers—lucent magic users crossing into the depths of gloam. I catch a glimpse of a deer in the shadows who watches us pass with curious dark eyes. It appears even the animals know it.

The drizzle has begun again, but we're partially protected from its chill by the forest that tangles and knots above us. With no idea what to expect in these mountains, we stick close together. The men appear relaxed, but I see the way their hands rest on their weapons, how alert and quiet they stay.

Every crack of dead forest debris beneath my boots is magnified compared to how quietly my companions tread; it seems I'm the loudest of the group, though I'm the lightest by far.

The sounds of a normal forest are there, the animals are there, the trees and plants are there; it's just... weak. Several different animals pause and watch us closely as we pass, most of them thin and appearing more tired than the faded leaves crunching beneath our boots. Various birdcalls come from the trees above, paired with the whisper of dry vegetation when a soft breeze blows, but none of it is *normal.* I spend much of my time in the forests of our kingdom traveling with hunters, and none of them feel so haunting.

I position myself strategically between Rhosse and Ikar, who are in the lead, and Darvy, who brings up the rear now.

"Anyone else feel like we're being watched?" I ask.

Even with our kingdom's best soldiers at my side, the eerie pressure of unseen eyes pressing into my back makes me want to run.

"There are a lot of curious animals out," Rhosse says in as comforting a tone as a man as dangerous-looking as he can manage. As a person gifted magic that allows him to track and work with animals, he is especially intuitive, but this feeling doesn't feel like animals.

"There's also a lot of gloam, and with gloam comes creatures, and you better believe they'll be watching for a moment of weakness," Darvy warns from behind me. "Stay alert."

An unnecessary reminder. I stuff all of my sarcastic responses down my throat and focus on visualizing the way Ikar showed me how to quickly pull my short sword in our training sessions, over and over. But then I decide I should focus on keeping lucent at the ready, because it's not likely I'll be any sort of help with my sword. I frown, thinking back across all the days that have passed with Ikar... have I *ever* actually shared lucent with him? Of course, when he was passed out from the bantha claw, he wasn't aware when I healed him that my magic works in a much more comfortable fashion than normal healers, so that doesn't count. My mind spins as I search my memories. There was the time I powered the enchanted arrows when we battled the shifters, and he didn't notice, but we were also battling high above the earth while riding foreign creatures. Ikar is more watchful and aware than anyone I've met... will he notice that my magic runs cooler than the originators he's used to working and training with? What about Darvy and Rhosse?

I nibble at my lip. I'm always careful to control how much I send, and in all my years of assisting hunters, no one has commented on it, but can I limit the lucent enough here? Or will the amount of gloam require lucent so strong that these warriors will question me? The thoughts remind me that this is why I shouldn't make snap decisions.

On top of that, I've only ever contracted for work with individuals, not groups. I haven't trained like the originators to lend lucent to groups of soldiers. In fact, I've never attempted to send lucent to more than one person at a time. I'd ask to practice with them, but that's basically blurting out that I'm a complete amateur when I assume they believe they've hired an expert. Except, Ikar knows my abilities quite well after our journey together. Why exactly did he want to hire me? I warily eye each of the men around me. *What have I done?*

Darvy interrupts me with a friendly shoulder bump, pulling me from the downward spiral. "You appeared so comfortable on the sharp flyer that I almost don't believe Ikar's story." His eyes are light with humor, and I know he's trying to help me relax. For a man who appears a somewhat lighthearted rogue, there's an intuitive depth behind his green eyes that I can't deny.

"Ha. Ha." I roll my eyes. Ikar, unfortunately, did *not* leave out the fact that I almost sabotaged his rescue and escape attempt by refusing to board the creature until the shift king was almost upon us when he retold it at dinner the other night. "Ikar exaggerated, I'll have you know."

Darvy chuckles. "I'm sure."

He doesn't believe me one bit. Ikar isn't prone to humorous dramatics like Darvy is, and we both know it.

"Cheer up, Vera. You're going on a fantastical journey with three strapping soldiers," he says, tossing his knife into the air and catching it with a bit too much swagger in his stride.

"None of you are merely *soldiers*," I remind him blandly while eyeing Ikar's broad shoulders, trim waist, and long legs with attempted disdain.

For a moment Darvy's eyes widen in surprise, like I've learned something I shouldn't have.

I quirk a brow. "What? You're all officers, aren't you?"

His quick smile is back. "Oh, right. Yes, of course. But that's even better." He raises his eyebrows twice in quick succession.

"No, it's not."

I see when his expression turns from teasing to genuinely curious. "What is it, then? I thought this is what you *do*. You're a bounty hunter. Adventuress extraordinaire."

I snort. "You do know I hardly know how to use this, right?" I pat my sword. I'm no delicate flower, but I'm also not going to pretend I can hold any sort of weight in a battle.

"Like I said, strapping soldiers."

Darvy's smile is infectious, and my lips can't help but turn up. "My correct title is much closer to hunter *assistant*. And it's what I've *had* to do, not always because I wanted to. All

I'm saying is don't depend on me to save you from a death-stalker."

He cuts away some foliage to better clear our path and presses more of it aside while I step past a particularly thick section. I quietly thank him as I pass, hoping he'll let the matter drop.

He smirks. "Lend us lucent and you won't need to." With another flip of his knife, it's expertly sheathed. "Why did you contract for this job? It sounds like you don't feel you're qualified."

I curse inwardly. I didn't intend to sow doubt in my abilities. "I'm more than qualified to share lucent. I can send you as much as you want."

He has no idea how true it is.

"The pendulum swung from under- to overconfident." His eyes are still light with teasing, like he doesn't believe me but knows I can do enough.

I shrug. That's better anyway. "I'll show you when I need to."

He leans in a little and whispers. "Careful, or Ikar will want to hire you on permanently."

We both know Ikar can hear it, but there's no indication in his posture or stride that shows he intends to answer.

"You evaded my question," Darvy reminds me.

"Which one?"

"Why'd you contract for this journey?"

"I want to be free, and to be free I need money." I'm unable to keep a bit of weariness from coloring my tone.

"Free from what?"

I struggle to come up with a response. The conversation went from light to deep in half a second, and I'm kicking myself for my choice of words. I'll have to be more careful around

Darvy; it seems he has a way of tricking people into getting personal—fast.

"What I *meant* is that I want to retire."

Darvy laughs. "You're all of what... *twenty* years old?"

"Twenty-*six*."

I frown at the smile he attempts to smother. "What will you do in your retirement?"

"I've always dreamt of having my own shop, selling things I've collected over the course of my travels."

He nods. "Okay..." A slow smile turns his lips. "Do you want to know what else I'm really curious about?"

I almost audibly sigh in relief. "What?" I play along, more than happy to move on to a different topic.

He lowers his voice. "I'm wondering what happened between the two of you." He arches a brow as he uses his chin to gesture toward Ikar ahead of us.

"Do you mean the fact that I arrested him under the assumption he was a Class A criminal and just a few short weeks later, he's my contractor?" I smile sweetly. "We do have *quite* the history."

He grins. Apparently, he thinks I'm funny. I have no idea how he and Rhosse became friends. Darvy is handsome in a boyish way, his honey-brown hair long on top, brushing his forehead and slightly mussed; the sides are short like those in the Moneyrean army keep it. His green eyes are lit with humor almost constantly, he has a dimple to die for, and his smile is quick. Rhosse is almost the direct opposite.

I decide to turn the tables on him in a strategic sort of way. There's a question I need answered. "Do *you* plan to ever retire?"

"When I can no longer do my duty to my king, yes."

I press him further. "But *can* you retire early, if you choose?"

He laughs a little at my persistence and shakes his head. "It's not done by the highest officers. Traditionally, the king chooses them, and he also decides when their service is complete."

I glance at Ikar as disappointment washes over me. I guess hoping that he might retire is off the table. I've considered it before, and I can't quite put my finger on it... but something about his duty runs in his veins, and I don't think he'd leave it by choice—even for love. It appears less and less likely we could ever be together.

"So the three of you are stuck." I try not to sound disappointed.

"If that's the way you're inclined to see it, then yes. But I see it as a privilege to work with the king as a close friend. He's one of the best men I've ever known." A sly smile tilts his lips. "I could introduce you, you know. You simply need to ask."

"No! No. That won't be necessary. I'm not interested in meeting him," I say quickly. "That is, in fact, one of my worst nightmares."

Darvy has just opened his mouth—I assume to ask why—but Ikar must have heard at least part of our conversation because he throws a thunderous look directed at Darvy over his shoulder. Darvy ducks his head with a smile, and I find that the mischievous glint in his eye has me smiling too. It's in that moment that being in these secluded mountains with these men, knowing that we only have each other to rely on for survival... There's a comfortable camaraderie between us that I've never experienced before on a job—as if we've always been friends, even though it's only been a day. If it could just be me and them, taking jobs like this forever, I might not want to quit. I imagine they could teach me much about navigation and weapons, and I'm sure I would get better at offering lucent... *A Black Tulip friends with the high king's officers?* If they knew who I really am, the mark I bear, I can guarantee they wouldn't see me as a friend. A small voice reminds me I've also kissed one of them.

I glance at Ikar and scoff under my breath at how far I've fallen, but somehow, alone with them in this dark and very eerie forest, I can't bring myself to care about the rules I've broken. I want to be free, and this job will pave the way... Now I just have to survive, and I know these men are my best bet. If that means I find forbidden friends along the way, so be it.

We continue our trek through the forest, and it's not long before we begin to see evidence of life long past. An aged axe stuck in a tree, skeletons left of what were once people's warm homes, and gloam-infested wells that I try not to look too closely on. It appears we pass through the remnants of what was once a thriving village. Several large buildings lean to the side, walls crumbling with roofs fallen in and filled with trees and tall grass. I'm afraid to look for fear I'll find something, but afraid to look away in case I miss it—the worst sort of feeling.

We walk over mottled pieces of a once-cobbled road as we make our way through the abandoned community. Some of the stones have crumbled to gravel, leaving the path uneven, as if it aims to purposely trip us and requires us to watch our footing closely. But that's impossible, because none of us are willing to keep from constantly scanning the buildings that line the path.

Shortly after the larger buildings end, there are smaller ones that, based on their size, must have been more homes. Their walls still stand, acting as a shell of what they'd been, now overgrown with vines and brush. Broken, foggy windows, and yawning, dark doorways fill my eyes. They're blazing creepy, if you ask me.

I find myself sidling up beside Ikar, walking so close I bump his arm with my shoulder every once in a while, but he doesn't seem to mind. I'd like to think I'm quite courageous—I *did* agree to journey through this death forest—but right now I'm feeling anything but courage... more akin to regret in the form of cold sweat and fear-induced nausea. I'm not so proud that I can't admit my chances at survival aren't much better with him near. I'd rather be clinging to his bicep and I'm not, so that's got to count for something in terms of bravery.

Though we appear to be alone, it seems wrong to speak loudly right now—as if doing so might get us killed.

So I lower my voice and ask, "Did you expect this... village to be here?"

He eyes a structure to our left carefully. "The journal mentions it, but we didn't know the state it would be in." I don't like the fact that his voice is just as much a whisper as mine. It means he feels the same.

I think I'd like to study more of this journal to find out what's in store for us on this joyous journey, but now's not the time. He's still focused on a partially collapsed house, and my heart picks up in pace. *Did he see something?* I warily eye more empty windows. This is the type of place where people die— I'm sure of it. Something creaks and I jump, squeezing the straps of my pack, but I only spot a lean squirrel bound from within an empty house, staring at us for a moment before scampering away.

It's then that I'm positive I hear a whisper that nips my soul, one that calls my deepest doubts and fears to the surface and forces me to gaze at them with eyelids pried open.

I'm not strong enough for this contract. I'll fail and kill these men. I'm not capable enough to be part of such a mission.

Chill air bites at the skin of my face, reddening my nose. Whispers grow in volume and my vision blurs in and out. I'm positive I see small black forms in the shape of squat humans, but with only wispy gloam for appendages and oddly blank faces fleeting and skipping around us. I attempt to focus on one, or is it five of them? More?

I should never have taken this job. I'm not good enough. My magic is weak. Nonexistent. Why do I even try? I'll never be free. Never.

A feeling I can only describe as that of ultimate failure seeps through my body, traveling my veins like thick poison. All will to continue onward, to live, is numbed and slowly devoured by... *whispers.*

Rupi quills up and her feathers stab into my neck, giving me a moment of painful clarity as I reach up and wipe away warm beads of blood. My vision sharpens, and I find Ikar with a distant look on his face, eyes filled with despair that matches what still reverberates through me. We no longer walk, and I don't know when we stopped, but I watch as each of the men relaxes the grip on their weapons as if they just lost a battle they desperately needed to win.

Their shoulders gradually lose strength... dropping beneath the weight of defeat in their eyes. I fight to keep my coherence even as I spy the shadowy appendages stretching out, wrapping around my comrades, only to look down and find one with wispy arms wrapped around my thighs and crawling up my body with glee. I attempt to step back, but my legs won't move.

I grab Ikar's arm and shake it. "Ikar!"

But he doesn't regain focus. He mutters something about worthiness beneath his breath that I can't make sense of. My eyes widen as the hilt of his sword begins to slip from his fingers and look over my shoulder. "Darvy! Rhosse!" Panic and an unexplainable sorrow I still can't shake tinges my voice.

No one so much as blinks in response, their gazes remaining distant and sorrowful, and I begin to lose the sharpness around me when my vision begins to blur again. The whispers grow louder as they drown out Rupi's panicked chirping near my ear.

You are nothing. Your lucent is powerless. What's the use in having it? Give it up...

The despair grows, drowning out all other feelings until I'm positive my soul will suffocate beneath it, until, out of sheer habit and instinct, I reach for the one thing that's always been constant in times of darkness. It fills my body so easily and naturally; it's as if it was intended to beat through my heart, the same as the blood coursing my veins.

I pull an orb of lucent in my hand, and I'm shocked when, immediately, the whispers cease around us as the light bathes us in its glow. I watch with shaky relief as the shadows are forced back, their wispy appendages shrinking back as if stung. Ikar, Darvy, and Rhosse snap out of the odd trance, blinking and frowning, regripping their weapons and looking around, the despair and pain still evident in the creases of their eyes. I don't blame them. Having all your deepest doubts and fears played upon, that depth of despair... it does something to you. It still prickles beneath my skin.

"Whispers," I tell them, refusing to douse the orb just yet. I may just carry it like this the rest of the way.

"They really sneak up on you, don't they?" Darvy attempts a joking tone, but it falls flat.

I don't miss the disconcerted look on Ikar's face as he runs a hand through his hair, and Darvy blinks his eyes as if he attempts to blink away the entire experience.

I jump when Rhosse claps a firm hand on my shoulder, and with a somberness in his voice, says, "Glad to have you with us."

I offer a tight smile. I try to be confident. I really do. But what if this was just a lucky chance? I pulled lucent without thinking. I nod anyway, accepting his gratitude with as much grace as I can muster after nearly dying of despair. Rhosse doesn't seem the type to offer it freely, and I know I should feel honored. But really, I feel as if I just accidentally set a bar so high I'm not sure I'll be able to reach it again.

I meet Ikar's eyes and find warm admiration there, shadowed by something I can't define. He's always seemed to carry a weight on his shoulders that I don't quite understand, but it seems as if what we just experienced made it even heavier.

He begins walking again, and I step close.

"They were all lies," I whisper in an attempt to help him feel better.

He glances down at me for a moment before he looks straight ahead again, and a muscle in his jaw flexes. "That remains to be seen."

I frown. That's too cryptic an answer to respond to without prying, and while I crave to know more about him, I know it's not my place to ask, so I press my lips shut.

We continue forward in silence. No one seems inclined to talk much about what just happened, and now that I know how sneaky this forest can be, I'm even more on edge. But instead of a hand on my sword, I pull a near-constant amount of lucent through my veins. Though they can't see it, I'm as ready as they.

Chapter 13

Vera

Rupi sits perched atop a golden arrow that sticks from a half-dead tree, as smug as a pirate who just found a treasure, patiently waiting for us to see her as it comes into view.

"Well, it's not three arrows... but it's *one*. Does that count?" Darvy asks as we circle around the tree in the dwindling light of the three suns.

The arrow has seen better days. It's dull as an aged coin, but with a little love, I see its potential to shine again. Ikar frowns, and I watch as he reaches within his armor and pulls out the small brown book. He flips through a few pages and begins to scan its pages quickly, as if he's read it so many times he only needs to double-check.

I've learned over the past day that this is usually the moment where navigation discussion ensues to make sure we're headed in the right direction. When I assisted hunters, I never worried much about the direction we took; I just knew they'd get us home since we both wanted the pay. I'm the first to admit that I'm not helpful with map reading, seeing as I'd probably lead us off a cliff unintentionally with my lack of talent in regard to navigation, but I *might* be able to help with something else. I'm tempted to take the easier route, fall into habit, take a seat, and let them handle it as I have the past two days and all the contracts I've ever taken before this... But this contract feels different, and I can't say why, but I'm beginning to feel like maybe this time I should step up and attempt to be more a part of the team.

I watch as the small book that I'm beginning to grow more and more curious about is passed around between them. I bolster my courage and step forward. No one comments on my joining their conversation; they merely shift so that everyone can see the book Ikar holds out for us to see. Warmth floods my chest at their inclusion.

I listen as they discuss the path we took and flip pages back and forth. Rhosse points to one section of the aged writing, and Ikar angles the book toward him. "We traversed that path yesterday."

"We *might* have," Darvy chimes in. "It's been hundreds of years, and the field of pink flowers with all the boulders it mentions? We didn't see that."

"Of course we didn't. There's nothing pink in this forest anymore," Rhosse mutters.

"But what about all the boulders?" Darvy questions.

A muscle in Ikar's jaw works and I can tell he's thinking. "We *did* pass the engraving in the mountainside this morning. So whether we saw the boulder field or not, we know that, as of today, we're on the right track. And if we're right, that means we're at least halfway there."

My eyes dart between the three of them as the discussion continues. I have nothing to offer, but my eyes continue to snag on the book that I haven't quite gotten a good look at yet. I lean over a bit to see if I can catch a better view of the page so I can read it myself the same time as Rupi lands on Ikar's hand that holds it. She tilts her head toward it, then pecks at the page before sidestepping backward and forward along his forearm. Ikar attempts to assuage her with a placating pat on her tiny head, but she quills a bit as she ducks from beneath his touch and pecks at the page again until he finally turns it. She tilts her head again and eyes it closely, then chirps happily as she bounces across his forearm. She can be quite forceful when she wants to be. I smirk, having experienced the same. But when he sees the page, he pauses.

"The nymphs..." Ikar mutters as he runs a hand through his hair, mussing it delightfully. "We discussed bypassing them to save time... a shorter route..." He frowns as he rereads the page that I can't quite get a clear view of without leaning any farther into him and being obvious about it.

Darvy takes the book to reread the passage. "Remember, though, the nymphs might be dead. The shorter route might still be the best option."

Rhosse folds his arms and glances at the page Ikar and Darvy are so interested in. "But if they're alive, and they can lead us straight to it... might be worth it. Who knows what has happened to the alternate route. It's a risk either way."

Straight to *what*? I'm ready to tear the book out of Darvy's hands and satiate the curiosity that is killing me. *Stay professional.* I open my mouth to politely ask if I can take a look, but Ikar takes the journal and snaps it shut so decisively I feel stray pieces of my hair blow out from my face. He tucks it within his armor before a word leaves my lips. "We'll find the nymphs first. Keep an eye out for another set of three arrows. The nymph cave should be nearby."

I purse my lips. I gathered a whole lot of *nothing* from that conversation.

I jog to catch up with Ikar, leaving Rhosse and Darvy slightly behind as I try to get the answers I'm craving, but Ikar beats me to it.

"Do you have lucent?" Ikar asks, looking my way.

"Of course I do." I can't help the offense in my voice. If there's *one* thing I can contribute with confidence on this journey, it's lucent. I pull a small lucent orb in my hand closest to him and show him just to ease his worry. "Plenty."

He stares at it for a moment, then brings a hand up and cups my smaller one in his. "I don't know how you're doing it. The lucent is so sparse here that it almost feels like I'm cuffed again at times." His laugh lacks humor.

My orb flickers, reflecting my fear... Should I have been more careful? Should I have pretended it's harder than it is? I silently curse and snuff the orb out, and now it's just his hand cupping mine. He adjusts his hold, now moving his calloused thumb across the palm of my hand where the lucent orb just flickered.

"If you ever feel like you don't have enough, you'll tell me?" He ducks his head to meet my eyes.

I stumble with the intensity of his focus, and his hand grips mine tighter while I gain my footing.

"Rhosse, Darvy, and I all know how to fight and having lucent is helpful, but it's *your* greatest weapon... If there's not enough..." He pauses and swallows. "Sometimes I feel guilty for contracting you for a journey so dangerous—"

My chest grows warm seeing his concern. "I'll tell you," I agree, just to appease him, but somehow, I know I'm not going to run out of lucent. Ever.

I glance at his face, getting the perfect view of his dark

brows, blue eyes, the hard line of his nose, his strong jaw, and lips that I know from experience are exquisite—

His thumb runs over my palm once more, leaving it tingly and warm. "Either way, stay close."

I force myself not to cling to his hand even as he lets mine drop. *Stay close?* That's one order I am more than happy to obey. For survival reasons only, of course.

We keep a pace that nearly has me jogging to keep up with these longer-legged officers while I try to warn away the turkeys that have been trailing us off and on for the last few hours with shooing motions when the men aren't watching. But I fear they'll likely become dinner—it's always harder to eat them when they're friendly.

I can't worry over them for too long, though, because a crawly sensation that prickles at the back of my neck prompts me to look over my shoulder, searching for the cause, and I know it's not the turkeys. *More whispers, or something else?* The view is the same as always—ailing forest and gloom. A hint of a shadow catches at the corner of my gaze before it disappears, and I stare hard at the spot until my vision grows blurry.

Rupi turns on my shoulder, looking over my back, her head jutting forward suspiciously as she searches the depths of the forest the same as I. She's a guard at heart, even if she does look more like a fluffy wad of cotton. I pat her tiny back in comfort and force a small smile to Rhosse who turns his head to find what I'm looking at.

"Did you see something?" he asks, still searching the shadows behind us.

"I thought so... but maybe not." I bite my lip.

Nothing materializes, so after a few more moments, I turn my gaze ahead and try to ignore the feeling. It seems Rupi is picking up on my anxiety, and now so is Rhosse—I need to control it better. I still feel like someone, or something, is watching us, but I don't bring it up because, of course, something *is* watching us. The gloam is so thick it looks almost solid at times. But aside from that, I'm still catching sight of the dark shadows, always in my peripheral, that I started seeing weeks ago, and I don't know what they are. It's likely too much stress.

I take a deep breath to calm my racing heart and wipe my sweaty palms on my trousers, worried if the gloam doesn't get us, my paranoia will.

Chapter 14

Vera

We survived our first day and night in the Lucent Mountains, but between the chill gloam so thick it felt as if I might suffocate and listening to every creaking branch and leaf crunch in the forest, I didn't fall asleep once. It appears I wasn't the only one who struggled.

I watch as Ikar runs a hand through his hair again, Rhosse attempts to smother another yawn, and Darvy has been much quieter today as we continue our trek through the forest. Ikar continues to keep up a pace so rigorous it's hard to hide my heavy breathing and the sweat beginning to drip down my face, but I'm not complaining—I want to be out of this forest as much as they do.

The third sun is about to set when Rhosse easily catches the turkeys for dinner—I tried to warn them. He leaves them nearby, and we work to gather materials for a fire while Rupi hops amidst coarse field grass nearby, pecking here and there for insects. After getting a warm fire going that helps ward off the chill of the darkening sky, I overhear Darvy and Rhosse unsheath their swords, and the sound of metal on metal sounding behind me. I'm just relieved it's not me fighting this time. I haven't said a word about it, but I'm terrified of training with Rhosse, and I'm hoping they'll all forget about it.

"You really should leave some women for the rest of us," Darvy says.

I look over my shoulder, grinning at the way he taunts Rhosse. I can't tell if Rhosse's face is red from exertion or embarrassment.

Darvy blocks a hit and twists his sword to redirect Rhosse's with effort. "Who were those two barmaids again?"

Another blocked hit. From Rhosse's darkening expression, I'm beginning to grow concerned for Darvy's safety, but he continues as if unconcerned.

"Melinda and Ashe?" He jumps out of the way and swings toward Rhosse's exposed side, but Rhosse blocks it just in time. "No, that was the other tavern. Maven and Abigail."

Rhosse swings harder, and Darvy's sword flies from his hand. He puts his hands up in defeat, laughing.

With his sword tip at Darvy's throat, Rhosse growls back. "Maybe if you weren't so comfortable gambling, you'd catch a few yourself."

"You sound like my mother," Darvy says, pushing the blade away as he laughs.

"You should listen to her; she's a wise woman." Ikar smirks.

I try not to stare as he begins rolling the sleeves of his shirt up, then picks up the birds and heads toward a small creek burbling several yards away, hidden by trees and gloam. I've been waiting for a moment to ask about the journal, and this feels like it might be it. I jump up and jog after him to catch up, careful to make sure to walk on the side opposite the one that holds the swinging, very-dead birds.

"If you wanted to clean them, you could've just asked," he drawls, looking straight ahead.

"And take the opportunity from you?" I joke sweetly. I'm secretly pleased when I see the relaxed smile on his lips.

"You should learn. It's a skill you need in your line of work. I don't know how you've survived this long." I don't like the serious note in his voice, which usually comes before an order.

"No thanks. I've done well enough without it." Not only does the thought of it make me gag, but I'd rather eat gloam leaves than kill my friendly forest animals.

Ikar lifts a brow. "Fine, not today."

I let out a breath of relief.

"But soon."

The gag threatens my throat again. I just *know* he'll do what he says he'll do. My only hope is we finish this journey before we get time.

He kneels down near the water and begins to prepare the turkeys to be roasted over the fire. I look away, having no desire to watch. Instead, I make myself comfortable on a large rock nearby. I'm sure he's wondering why I tagged along, so I get straight to the point.

"Ikar?"

"Hm?"

I resist the urge to look his way. "I'm wondering... what flower does the king need? Maybe I can be more helpful if I know what to look for?"

"Inside pocket of my vest."

The book. I whip my gaze around and find that he hasn't looked up from what he's doing. Does he intend for me to grab it myself? I sit there on the rock, unmoving until he looks up at me.

"You'll have to get it." He lifts his hands, and I swallow

with difficulty. I've never done well with blood, hence why I didn't assume the title of healer.

I hop off the rock. "Get what?" I act innocent, as if I haven't been driving myself crazy wondering what's inside those pages all this time.

"The journal." He turns to face me, holding his hands wide and chuckling as I give them a wide berth with a disgusted look.

I step closer, telling myself not to make this more than it is. I'm simply snatching the journal and backing off. I've seen him tuck it away easily, so I assume it won't take long to find. I tentatively reach inside the warmth of his armor. Immediately I feel the defined muscles of his chest through his shirt. Not only that, but I feel an assortment of knives, a folded piece of parchment, and what feels like a compass. How many things can he be hiding in there?

"Other side." His voice is deep and holds a note of humor, and my cheeks warm.

I avoid his gaze and purse my lips. I try to not be awkward as I fumble around the other side before feeling a small book beneath my fingertips. I yank it out as if he's burned me.

Ikar returns to cleaning the birds as if he wasn't affected by our nearness at all. It appears I'm the only one who struggles to maintain a professional relationship at this point. That sour thought has my lips pressed together.

Tufts of feathers poof into the air as he says, "I figure I can share more detail now that you're officially on this journey with us. But remember that included in the contract was a confidentiality notice. You agreed not to tell anyone what you helped us find, where we found it, or what it's for."

I nod, feeling a little nervous now. The journal feels like a hot coal in my hands.

"Good. Turn to the page I've marked—its corner is bent. Two pages after that is a drawing of the flower we search for."

Bent corner. I open it to find scrawling aged handwriting filling every bit of the pages in neat, faded lines. *Flip two pages.* I suck in a breath and almost die. A drawing of the flower that is clearly marked at the base of my neck stares up at me.

Ikar glances up at me momentarily, still busy with the birds. "You found it. Do you know what that is?"

Do normal people know what these are nowadays?

I swallow. "It looks like a... flower" —my voice catches— "... of some sort."

"A black tulip," he says in a no-nonsense way.

I'm screaming inside. I close the book shakily, slowly, trying to act cool—bored, even. But it's hard when I can hardly draw a breath as panic squeezes my lungs.

"It's pretty, but what's it for?" I ask, my voice a little higher than it should be.

Ikar smiles sardonically. "What you really want to ask is why would a king risk some of his highest officers and a powerful originator's lives to find one?"

"Yeah, that." I try to smile normal, but it feels unnaturally tight.

"You've heard of the Queens of the Night." He looks up as he states it. It's not a question.

"Everyone has." I shrug a shoulder and act like it's common knowledge, but it doesn't relieve the suspicion in his blue eyes.

For a moment, I worry he suspects *me* of being a Black Tulip, but then I remember he has always suspected I know something since I destroyed the list of names. Now I've unknowingly reopened that awful conversation. I *knew* I shouldn't have asked questions.

"Well, finding one of them is the next step on our mission.

The king plans to bridge to restore lucent. He'll need the black tulip flower and a Queen of the Night to do so. It might be the only way to save our kingdom."

I freeze inside while the words he just spoke sink in, pushing me past the point of coherent thought as the world around me blurs.

The Black Tulips' worst nightmare comes to pass, and I'm supposed to help with it. Somewhere far away, I hear a splash in the river, birds calling, Rupi tugging at my earlobe. *When did she arrive?* Ikar's standing now, the birds cleaned and ready to cook, lying nearby. His hands are washed clean with his sleeves still rolled up and revealing his forearms—one of my favorite looks on him. I float on the distracting thought, staring at his corded arms, allowing shock to dull my senses.

"—list?" he asks.

"What?" I jerk my gaze to meet his.

He smiles, somewhat confused by my behavior. "I asked if you can tell me what you know about the list of Black Tulips, the one you ruined when we first met? Do you know any of them?" He smiles casually, but the look in his eyes reminds me of a stealthy predator.

The dratted list that started all of this.

I still haven't spoken, so he continues. "Now that you trust me and know my mission, I'm hoping you'll share what you know. It could make a big difference."

Now my hackles rise, his assumption stretching too far, my emotions too battered.

"I know *you*, but I don't know the king and I don't trust him or—" I almost say *originators*, but that would blow my cover, so I press my lips shut before the word comes out—barely catching myself.

"—or who?" Ikar asks.

"Anyone. I don't trust anyone," I say flatly.

"Except me."

"Sort of—you." If I'm being truly honest. I cringe a little as I say it.

He throws his hands up in the air and mutters a curse. "You are the most—"

"What? Most *what?*" I challenge with narrowed eyes as I walk toward him.

I practically shove the journal at him. He takes it slowly and slips it back inside his armor. We're close enough now that I can see the small gray specks in his eyes, surrounded by a ring of darker blue, and the small scar that infringes on his perfect upper lip. We stand there for one moment, then two.

Then we're both leaning forward, an invisible pull between us. His hands slide up the back of my arms as I feel the barest touch of his warm lips against mine—

"The birds ready yet?" Rhosse growls from the forest behind us.

I startle so hard Ikar has to steady me for the briefest moment before we abruptly step away from each other.

Ikar rubs a hand across the back of his neck, avoiding looking at me. "Yep. Coming."

We walk in awkward silence the rest of the way back to camp.

"Have fun *cleaning the birds?*" Darvy asks with a glint in his eye.

Ikar mutters something to him that has him immediately quiet, but it doesn't wipe the mirth from his eyes.

I gingerly take a seat before the fire. *What in the blazes is wrong with me?* I just told him I didn't trust him... and to prove it I almost kiss him? I silently groan. There is something wrong with my taste in men. He might not be a criminal, but he *is* a favorite of the high king and I consider that even more danger-ous. Now he's distracting me from the fact that the high king wants a Black Tulip to bridge with for the first time in two hundred years. He says the king wants to bridge to restore lucent, that it might be the only way to save the kingdom, but why should I trade the safety of my Tulip sisters and myself for lucent to be restored to a kingdom full of people who hate us? It's a selfish thought... and maybe it makes me a little wicked, but we don't owe these people anything. There's no way to know if the king is kind and genuine, or evil and twisted. But my biggest fear? That after we've restored lucent a future king will end up having us tracked down and killed under the guise of *what's best for the kingdom* again. History tends to repeat itself, but, in this case, it can't if the Tulips stay hidden.

The inklings of true regret flicker to life as I recall my deci-sion not to pay the dues. I tug on my bracelet twice, and it still holds, so I assume it continues to work, but it's only a matter of time until it stops. I stare at it with the growing realization that I *do* actually need it. Tatania was right all these years, and I ignored her. But here in the remote mountains I'm safe... from the high king, at least. It's the time between when I return to the kingdom and get Tatania paid that I'm worried about.

My cheeks heat at the thought of groveling before her to take me back, but knowing what I know now, I have no choice. To ease my panic, I remind myself that I've never seen the king in my life, so it's not likely it'll be an issue at all, and I'm worrying over nothing. I can't help but wonder, though, what will happen when my bracelet stops working? Will it simply fall off? Turn to dust? Or will it show no change and I won't be able to tell at all? The questions surrounding it are a bit unnerving.

Rupi lands atop my wrist and turns a curious eye toward me. I twist the bracelet again.

"I should've paid the dues, girl," I whisper.

She chirps once and pecks the bracelet as if it's a bug she'd like to eat. I take that to mean she doesn't agree with me.

And what do I do about this job? I can't help the king's extremely capable officers find a flower that could destroy my sisters and me... but I signed a *contract*.

I bite my lip and continue to turn the bracelet around my wrist as I mindlessly watch Rhosse turn the turkeys over the fire. I come to the decision that, until I know the king's true intentions, which are probably horrid, I'll only offer magic as I contracted to do—as little as necessary, only enough to keep these men and myself alive. But if I see that flower, I'll do everything I can to make sure it doesn't return with us. My conscience is satiated with that compromise. I'm not betraying my sisters, and I'm not betraying Ikar—fine line though it is. I'll just have to walk it carefully.

Chapter 15

Ikar

"This turkey acted like it wanted to be caught," Darvy says as Rhosse turns it over the fire.

"I'm sure it did," Rhosse says with sarcasm.

"You're just jealous I saw it first. Tell you what, I'll let you have the next one," Darvy responds in a placating manner.

Rhosse's brows raise. "You'll *let* me?"

I smirk. We all know if he really wanted to catch the meal, he would, and could, beat all of us to it.

Vera smiles across the fire as she listens, her hands pressed between her knees to avoid the chill bite to the air. How is it that I feel guilty for getting caught about to kiss her... and it's still the only thing I want to do? I run a hand through my hair and duck my head to keep my eyes from continually drifting her way. She draws me like a moth to a flame, and I fear I'm going to end up scorched. To make it worse, I've already been worried about Lucentia deeming me worthy, and here I am pining for a woman I can't have when I may very well be married to another in a matter of *days*. Part of me wants to enjoy this time with Vera while I can, knowing that the rest of my life will be spent with an unknown woman, a relationship not of love but built on duty. It's what I've been raised for... but now that I've tasted what I can't have—

Rhosse hands me a large piece of meat, pulling me from my thoughts. Then he directs his gaze to Vera, who avoids looking my way entirely. "Do you hunt?"

Vera shakes her head and swallows the bite she was chewing. "No, I'm not great with weapons in general... or blood."

"Have you had any weapons training?"

"Actually, we were just beginning her training before we were separated," I glance at my friends. "You now have two more expert soldiers to train with."

The smile she offers is tight. "Wonderful," she whispers and hurries to take another bite of meat.

"I can work with you after we finish," Rhosse states.

It's more of a command than an offer. She nods hesitantly, looking at me for half a second like she's hoping I'll intervene— but I don't. I'm in search of a Tulip to bridge with and being near her is torture. I can't train her. But she might not be able to rely on lucent forever, and I want her to have the skills to protect herself when I'm not around—a painful thought. I'm amazed she has the power she does, but all the originators, even Nadiette, are now struggling to pull enough... here in the Lucent Mountains, it only makes sense that she'll begin to struggle too.

I give an affirming nod, smothering a smirk—if she thought I was scary to train with, she's in for a surprise.

Vera's been so quiet for most of our meal that when she speaks up, she has all our attention. "At the dinner we had... Jethonan and Nadiette. I didn't get a chance to know either of them, but you all seem... close."

Her unspoken question has me immediately on edge.

There's a beat of silence, and I get the feeling that Darvy and Rhosse are waiting for me to speak.

When I don't, Darvy clears his throat. "We are. Have been for a long time." He takes a large bite of turkey.

"Jethonan... what's his story?" she asks, looking between the three of us to see who'll answer.

Rhosse laughs, relaxing a bit now that the conversation has turned toward Jethonan. "He's a puzzle to everyone. He showed up at the castle as a teen and at first he was..."

"Avoided," Darvy says bluntly.

"Many people don't know how to handle his personality." I attempt to phrase it nicely.

Vera nods with the smallest of grins, and I'm reminded of the night she met him and the way she practically ran from his office.

Rhosse continues. "But his knowledge and skill with magic made a place for him in Ikar's circles, and Ikar didn't seem to care so much about how different he was. They quickly became friends, which led to Darvy and I becoming friends with him as well. We got into all sorts of trouble in our younger years." Rhosse chuckles, and I find myself grinning as I remember too.

"Ikar may seem frustrated by him at times," Darvy says, "but he trusts Jethonan to the point that he made him his top advisor and leaves the kingdom in his hands when he's away. People have suggested that Jethonan came from another continent, holds a different sort of magic... no one knows, well, maybe Ikar does." Their gazes swing to mine, but I keep my expression flat, and Darvy continues. "But Jethonan doesn't talk about his past, and I don't think we'll ever know for sure as he's unwilling to share anything, but that's when people began to name him a mage."

"And... Nadiette?" she asks, hesitant. Why does it seem like she's nervous?

I keep my answer simple and to the point. "She's the head originator. She's been trained for the position since she was a child and is one of the most powerful originators in the kingdom. She joined us on many of our escapades."

I take a bite of meat so large I'm hoping it ends the conversation because I can't speak with my mouth this full. It doesn't.

"So you've always been close to her as well?" She leaves the question open to all of us, but I feel her gaze linger on me even though I won't meet it.

Darvy just took a bite as big as mine which leaves the uncomfortable topic to Rhosse. I watch his face closely as he considers her question. He's being much more careful now, and I'm curious what he'll say.

"Ikar more than us, but yes, friends since childhood."

I'd punch him for his comment, but I figure I better get it out of the way. The turkey travels painfully down my throat as I swallow. "At one time we considered marriage, but no longer."

I don't want her to think there's anything between Nadiette and me, though I shouldn't care.

Vera swallows so tightly it seems as if she almost chokes. Then she smiles, but it doesn't reach her eyes.

"So sorry to hear that," she nearly whispers.

I've never enjoyed a lie so much. Something in my chest warms at the thought that she might be jealous, and I have to work to hide the grin that tempts my lips.

Then Darvy jumps in. "Yeah, it's unfortunate. Ikar isn't in a position to court anyone."

I clench my jaw so hard I'm sure my molars will crack as I stare at him. My hand itches to rip my sword from its sheath and battle him until he takes the words back. But even as he stares back at me, challenging me, reminding me of my duty... I know his words are true, and I hate them. That near-kiss that just happened? It's forbidden.

"Vera, are you ready to practice?" Rhosse asks, breaking the tense silence.

She nods and stands, catching my gaze and looking away quickly as she rounds the fire and follows him to a small clearing nearby.

I watch as Rhosse instructs her, testing her skill to find out where to begin. Jealousy that it's not me adds to the frustration I already feel. We didn't have much time to train while I was cuffed, but I'm proud of her when he pulls a wicked-sharp knife, and her eyes simply widen before she steels herself. At least it's not the battle axe. That weapon even scares *me*.

Darvy and I are quiet for a moment, the only sounds the crackling of the fire and Vera and Rhosse's training that holds my attention.

"So she's an originator *and* a healer," Darvy states thoughtfully, watching the two of them.

"Apparently. I've experienced both."

"Never heard of such a thing."

It seems odd to me too, but I don't say that.

"What's her story?"

I try to sum up what I know, which now seems like very little. "She most often works with bounty hunters and lives with her best friend, Renna. And, it seems that Drade is her ex-boyfriend."

Darvy laughs out loud. "Low king Drade?"

"Yes, that Drade."

"How—"

"I have no idea. All I know is she's half-fae and spent her teen years living with her aunt there."

"She's pretty," Darvy says.

I jerk my head toward him with a scowl before realizing I played right into his hands.

He nods slowly. "Thought so. You like her."

I press my lips together. She's been with us for less than three days, and Darvy already figured it out. My feelings must show more than I realize. I've got to do better.

"Doesn't matter how I feel about her. I'm on a mission to save my kingdom," I force the words from my lips.

"So do I have permiss—"

"No."

He uses a stick to move the wood in the fire and sparks shoot up, illuminating the smug grin on his face. Imagining Vera in Darvy's arms has a foreign sort of rage building in my chest.

"You know, I think I can use some sword practice tonight myself. Let's go." I stand angrily and stalk toward the open field, drawing my weapon.

"It was just a joke," he mumbles from behind me while he sets the stick down and follows, pulling his sword in resignation.

Chapter 16

Ikar

Another portion of my mark turned black, waking me in the night with its horrid burn. I caught Darvy's attention with the sound of my curse while he took his turn keeping watch, but he said nothing. He already knows what it means. It's a physical indicator for me to know the state of my kingdom. It wasn't good before, but now it's worse.

Since I'm up anyway, I volunteer to take my turn at watch, early. I feel antsy as I wait for the suns to begin their trek back across the sky. The dark lingers too long, and I find my knee bouncing before I promptly still it. I get irritated when those around me fidget, so it's alarming to find myself doing so. But the further darkening of my mark and the vast amount of gloam in these mountains has me feeling close to panic—as if I'm stuck watching sand fall through an hourglass with only the smallest bit left, unable to turn it over when it runs out.

I cannot fail.

My people have been resilient these many years, but they are weakening—dying, even. I've lost some of my best soldiers just for attempting to pull lucent when there was none during battle. It's something I don't think anyone considered when they decided to do away with Black Tulips and their bridging all those years ago.

I watch Rupi work her way out of Vera's blankets, tumbling out before she rights herself and flutters to perch on my knee. She may not be Arrow, Simon, or Champion, my own pets, but I've come to love her all the same and appreciate her company. I stroke her soft feathers as my thoughts turn to the Black Tulips I search for. Jethonan says he has no idea where they might be, though he certainly believes they still exist. Do *I* believe they still exist? The question tugs uncomfortably, and I rub my tight chest with a frown. Lucentia wouldn't just *stop* sending Queens of the Night, would she?

I shake my head. It does no good to wonder since this is the only good plan we have. Besides, there was an entire list of them—if it's to be trusted. I frown as I'm reminded that I *did* win it in an illegal fight ring.

The other plan, the one where I find Lucentia and offer her my life in exchange for lucent for my people, I've kept to myself —even from Jethonan. It's doubtful my life would be worth enough to trade for my kingdom's well-being anyway, so it has become Plan B though I feel selfish for making it so. Wouldn't it be faster to just offer myself up and see? Maybe my family line isn't worthy enough and a new one needs to start fresh. But something in my soul, a fire within, pushes me to make this all right—it's my duty.

Rhosse's quiet movements as he rises and proceeds to wake the others draw me from the thoughts that plagued me. I savor the distraction—especially Vera. I allow myself one lingering glance as she runs her fingers through her long wavy brown hair as she prepares to rebraid it, and think of how soft those strands felt beneath my hands when we kis—

No. Don't go there.

I move Rupi to my shoulder and stand. I need to busy myself. I begin packing up our camp, but my eyes rebelliously find Vera once more, and she meets my glance with a soft smile that tempts me to linger.

I duck my head and run a hand through my hair with an inward groan. How much can one man take?

We finally escape a field of prickly plants that stand taller than even Rhosse. Their light-green stems as wide as a grown man appear soft to the touch, topped with large spiky purple balls that had me concerned for our safety if one happened to drop. But we found rather quickly that the true weapon was the facade of the softness of their stalks that clawed at our clothing as if they attempted to keep us trapped within their clutches.

Darvy finishes tearing a bit of his sleeve from the last of them before we break free. I'm surprised to find that I'm so relieved to be out of the prickly plants that I'm somewhat happy to be back in shadowy, gloamy forest again.

Here and there I see patches of color, and it catches my eye —bright-green moss on a portion of a fallen log, a lone flower yet to wilt and lose its luster, a tree every now and then that retains its health. It hints at what this forest was once like and gives me a small bit of hope that maybe the nymphs still live.

Rupi's happy chirps on my shoulder don't seem to belong in a forest such as this, but I'm grateful for the sense of normalcy it brings. After a moment, she flutters over to Rhosse where she sidesteps along his shoulder, having become quite taken with him these past days.

I glance over my shoulder, and my eyes meet Vera's, and

before I can think about it, I'm slowing my steps until we walk nearly side by side, allowing Darvy and Rhosse to take the lead.

Our hands brush, and I sense her awareness. It would be easy to snag her fingers in mine, and if it were just she and I, I would. The attraction we share hasn't dissipated—if anything it continues to burn stronger, but we both resist its flame. Darvy and Rhosse's presence also reminds me of my duty.

Do I appreciate it? No.

Is it needed? Very much so.

I shouldn't care, since I have to find a Tulip to marry soon. Still, it bothers me like skin with a splinter snagging on cloth, and I wish things could be different.

Vera smirks. "Rupi has found a new favorite." She eyes the way Rupi nips at Rhosse's ear in an attempt to gain his attention.

"You jealous?"

She smiles. "Nah. She might act like she has other favorites, but she always comes back to me."

When she speaks again, her voice is somewhat hesitant. "I'm wondering... about the journal, er—the flower..." I lift my brows as I wait for her to get the rest out. "What happens if the king doesn't find a Queen of the Night to bridge with?"

"Do you have suggestions?" I ask, truly curious. Desperate for another option—one where Vera and I can be together.

She shrugs a shoulder. "Don't have one yet, but since no one knows if the Queens of the Night even exist, it might be good to have a backup plan."

"There is *one*. A last resort," I answer impulsively, and immediately regret it. I'm too comfortable around her. It's dangerous.

She looks at me expectantly, but I hesitate to say it—it exposes the selfish side of me. But there's part of me that is truly curious about what she'll think. I find that I value her perspective.

"Can I trust you'll keep it between us?" I ask, voice quiet. She nods, her expression matching my serious tone. "If no Queen of the Night can be found who is willing to bridge, the high king has considered finding Lucentia and offering his life in exchange for the restoration of lucent. Allowing her to choose a new, worthier line of kings who will keep the oath originally given Lucentia for the magic given us."

Vera considers for a moment, nodding. "It's not a bad idea, you know. That family line has really botched things."

My face pales, and my jaw tightens at her blunt words. What did I expect? Her opinion matches mine; it's just painful to hear it spoken aloud.

She bumps her shoulder against my arm teasingly. "Maybe she'd choose *you*."

Her words ease the sting of her previous honesty, but I can't find it in me to act as lightly as expected.

She continues, unperturbed. "What? You'd be a worthy replacement. You're already a respected High Officer and, from the looks of things, well-versed in royal rules and such. And, as an extra bonus, you seemed right at home in the castle."

Now I can't keep the grin from my face. "Royal rules and such?" I chuckle and shake my head.

She nods again. "Yeah, I think that plan B should become plan A. It would save us a whole lot of trouble, and I'm positive Lucentia will choose you. You'll make a great king."

I'm unsure how to respond. "I'll take that as a... compliment. Though it sounds a rather treasonous opinion."

"You won't tell the king, will you?" She says it with a lilt of sarcasm and a somewhat dramatic whisper. Her shoulder brushes my arm with unnoticed familiarity, and her gray eyes are bright in this moment of unguarded lightness. She's not making it any easier to put distance between us.

"I'll not speak those words aloud. You have my word." I place my hand across my heart, and while it's there, I rub the tightness from my chest caused by the ever-building guilt I feel for continuing to hide my true identity from her.

Vera laughs, but it fizzles out like steam from water-drenched fire as a snarl sounds, raising the hair on my arms. I instinctively step in front of her while simultaneously reaching for my sword. Rhosse and Darvy both turn back, unsheathing their own weapons.

"We'll be needing that lucent now," I mutter.

Chapter 17

Vera

I freeze. My veins are full of lucent, pulsing beneath my skin, eager to be used and tested. I push lucent toward Ikar, focusing on the amount I send, not too little but not too much. In less than a second, his enchanted sword glows bright. I curse, having forgotten about Rhosse and Darvy. I quickly separate two more channels, controlling the same amounts, but I find that my focus is strained between the three men and the enemy before us. Darvy's sword glows as brightly as Ikar's, and Rhosse uses an enchanted battle axe, glowing with lucent, as well. I nod to myself; things are going well.

Then the wolves attack.

I pull my sword, my back to Ikar's, and fight off a smaller wolf that has targeted me—if you can call any of them *small*. They stand as tall as horses, their shoulders rounded, with sharp, bony spines that run the length of their back and down their tails. Add to that their fierce, enormous faces and mouths full of razor-sharp teeth ready to rip our bodies to shreds.

Gloam whispers around them, giving them life and making them appear even larger than they already are. The wolf snaps its jaws at me, backing off and moving forward again as if testing me. I swing my sword like I know what I'm doing, but it won't be long before it realizes any skills are practically nonexistent.

Immediately my mental focus wavers as the wolf lunges. I lift my sword, targeting its chest, but its jaws clamp down around my blade and wrench it from my grasp, tossing it into the forest beyond. I certainly don't have time to clamber around searching for it, so instead I pull my dagger, but it seems woefully small. Somehow, I know if I survive this Rhosse is going to *kill* me in our next weapons lesson.

It stalks toward me as if it has already won—drat myself for agreeing. I back up, realizing that Ikar's back is no longer against mine, stumbling a bit over the forest floor, searching over my shoulder for help only to see Ikar, Rhosse, and Darvy wrapped up in fierce battles of their own to my right.

How could I have thought I was capable enough for a job like this? The dark whisper eats at my confidence.

The wolf continues toward me—I know I'm being cornered, but I have nowhere else to go. I continue to stumble backward, farther and farther away from my comrades. I yelp when I trip over a jagged branch and end up forced to scuttle backward like a pitiful crab.

The wolf prepares to spring forward, but Rupi dives from the treetops with her feathers quilled larger than I've ever seen them, straight at the monster's eye. I don't let her bravery go to waste, scrambling to my feet even as the wolf roars so loudly my ears ring. The wolf easily shakes her off and charges at me, its mouth gaping so wide I can see down its gloam-filled throat, just a breath away from tearing out the soft flesh of my neck. Rupi prepares to dive again, and I instinctively pull an orb and thrust it out ahead of me at the same time I jab at the wolf with my dagger. For a moment, the orb seems to stun the monster, then Rupi makes contact again, and the wolf rears up in rage before slamming down before me again. I cringe and hold my hand steady, waiting to feel its jaws clamp down around my forearm, but instead the nauseating sound of a sword plunging into its form fills my ears.

"Vera, lucent!" Ikar shouts, reminding me.

My orb flickers badly, and I realize I've forgotten about the men and the lucent I was hired to offer them. Feeling a rush of guilt, I pull more and send it rushing out in somewhat erratic waves toward each of them. Ikar's enchanted sword pulses in the wolf's chest, and the beast falls to the ground at his feet, lifeless.

Ikar wastes no time pulling his sword free and running back toward Darvy and Rhosse to finish off the other three wolves. Grunting and shouting and the awful sounds of gruesome fighting assault my ears as I scramble through the brush in search of my sword. All the while, I'm sure to keep up the lucent. The odds are fair, three wolves to three men and a mostly unhelpful *originator*.

Rupi soars to a spot in the long grass and flaps her wings, catching my attention. I spy a glint of steel and run toward her, finding my sword and pulling it from the dirt and grass.

I give her a rushed pat of gratitude. "Thanks, girl."

I turn and view the fight, worried I'll do more harm than good if I go rushing in. One wolf lodges its claws in the back of Rhosse's armor, taking him to the ground, its wide jaws going for his neck before Darvy jumps in and stabs the beast through the side at the same time the second wolf locks its teeth on Darvy's forearm and throws him to the ground as well.

Ikar finishes off the one he'd been fighting and runs to help. It's then that from my outside perspective, I see another wolf creeping from the shadows of the forest, eyeing Ikar's exposed back as he stabs the wolf that intended to maul Darvy.

I don't think—I run. I pull lucent through the newly enchanted blade and hold a lucent orb in my other hand as I sprint. The wolf lunges, and I force myself not to close my eyes as I brace my sword arm. I feel the moment my blade makes contact, and the beast's heavy form lands atop me, sending us both crashing to the ground.

I lie beneath its weight with my eyes squeezed shut, waiting to see if it got *me* before I got *it*. It's unnaturally silent as its last breath leaves its lungs. I can't see anything besides thick black fur, but apparently my sword hit its mark. I might not be skilled, but with a hefty dose of Lucentia's luck and a little bravery, maybe I *am* capable enough. I'd laugh, but I feel as if my lungs have been pressed to my spine. I struggle to breathe, and my head aches from the impact. Even as darkness encroaches in my vision, I force myself to continue sending lucent for the men, though I no longer hear any sounds of fighting.

Ikar shouts my name, but my hearing is growing fuzzy with the lack of air, turning to a high-pitched ringing. The next second, he lifts the wolf off me as if it weren't twice his size, and I realize he used my lucent to increase his strength. I'd forgotten he could do that...

Did I know he could do that? I wonder dreamily as I stare at his handsome face and suck in lungfuls of air at the relief. My lucent orb flickers, and I finally let it fizzle out as I lie in the dirt, exhausted and still battling darkness at the edges of my vision.

Ikar sheathes his sword and kneels, looking over me with concern. "Are you hurt?"

Rupi hops worriedly atop my chest, gently nudging my

chin in an attempt to get my attention and ensure I'm okay, but I'm still gasping for breath and wheezing in a manner that I'm sure is attractive, making it impossible to answer.

A moment later, I see Darvy lower to his haunches beside me on the opposite side. He takes the sword from my limp grasp, scoops Rupi up to his shoulder, and begins running his hands skillfully down my limbs before I can tell him it's not necessary. I see none of the carefree Darvy now; he's all battle-field healer in this moment, and according to Ikar, the best of the best. Still, healing magic burns like a branding iron, and I don't want it.

Ikar watches his every movement like a hawk, but I'm so distracted by Ikar's profile that I don't realize what Darvy is doing until he finds the rock my head hit, which he promptly tosses away before he probes the tender spot it left. I flinch and lift a hand to push him away, but Ikar snags it before I can.

"Let him help," he says firmly.

"I'm fine. I'm awake, aren't I?" I force more strength into my voice now, though it still hurts to breathe. I don't need to be coddled.

Darvy places a steadying hand on my shoulder, and his searching fingers move from my head to my neck, brushing my mark and causing me to instinctively jerk away in panic which causes matching concerned looks on both his and Ikar's faces. I instantly regret the reaction. The situation is going from bad to worse. If I have to fight like a feral cat to keep my mark hidden, I will. The movements are causing the back of my head to throb worse, but when his fingers return to the skin of my neck I force myself to stay calm. If it's not injured, and I were a normal person, I wouldn't care. *Act normal.* Problem is, I don't know how.

I think as fast as my throbbing thoughts will allow. I need to get their attention back to the injury on my head to keep attention from my neck.

"My head," I spit out, hoping they'll go with it.

It works. Darvy's hand returns to my head as he turns it to the side, and I let him as I grit my teeth and hope no sign of my mark is visible. There's a reason I wear the clothes I do, and I hope they do their job now more than ever.

Darvy moves some of my hair away. "I'll need lucent."

I wince and feel a trickle of warmth trail through my hair. *Is it bleeding?* I attempt to investigate, but find both my hands now captive in Ikar's. When did that happen? I scowl, knowing there's only one way out of this situation. *Fine.* I let lucent rush through me, wishing more than ever I could heal myself before I send it to Darvy.

Immediately, I feel hot tingles begin to prick at the back of my head that quickly turn to what feels like open flames. It's only half a minute, but it feels like a very long year. I let my cheek press into the cool dirt and grass and focus on deep breaths so I don't pass out and cut off his magic supply. Finally, the horrid heat stops, and the burning begins to cool. I keep my eyes closed for a long moment as I let the tingling fade, and I realize how hard I've been gripping Ikar's hands. He doesn't say a word, though I'm sure his fingers are numb by now.

"Done." Darvy reaches to feel along my neck again. "Are you sure your neck is okay?"

"Never better, thank you," I practically shout as I sit up faster than I should have, leaving my head spinning and taking both men off guard while putting my face very near Ikar's. His eyes meet mine, only a mere breath away.

Darvy chuckles. "Ok, it looks like Rhosse might need me, I'll let you know if I need lucent."

I nod slowly, hearing him walk away, but my thoughts are

elsewhere as I look into Ikar's eyes and try to keep my focus off his tempting lips. I can't help but think that if I were to lean forward just a bit, and he were to meet me halfway—

Ikar's thumb brushes along my jaw ever so softly as he lowers his voice, and his eyes darken. "Don't ever do that again." His tone is commanding and deep, and I feel inclined to obey just from the sound of it.

But I frown, genuinely confused. "Do what?"

"Sacrifice your life for mine." If possible, his eyes darken even more, and my mouth goes dry.

"We're supposed to be a *team*," I argue.

"I didn't contract you to fight. I contracted you to give us lucent," he nearly growls.

I could never let him die, but I can't say that because although the thumb trailing across my jaw is soft as he speaks, I can see frustration in the depths of his blue eyes.

He stands and offers a hand to help me up, and I take it, pleased to find that he doesn't step back when I come to standing so near that my nose nearly touches his armor. With difficulty, I rein in my feelings because I have something I need to say.

I cringe as I imagine further disappointment in his blue eyes as I apologize for my erratic lucent... the job I was hired for and practically failed. I don't want to be the one that puts it there, but before I can stop myself, I'm bumbling an apology.

"I'm really sorry. I should have told you that I'd never trained for this. I'm underqualified and—"

"Vera."

I continue, unwilling to stop. "I guess I thought it was more like being a hunter assistant, you know? But I realize now that this is a whole different situation... I don't want to kill you guys—"

"Vera." He says it loudly this time, and I look at him. "Stop."

I press my lips together and nod once, firmly. He still holds one of my hands in his, and it feels like he's my criminal again, that comfortable sort of companionship we had when it was just he and I. For a moment, I allow myself to appreciate his hand engulfing mine. I can feel the calluses and rough skin that come with years of hard work and regular weapon handling.

I look down and take in his long strong fingers twined with mine. Such a simple thing eases my fears, instantly makes me feel safe. I swallow carefully.

He ducks his head so he can catch my eyes, forcing me to meet his gaze. "You only started true training with your sword a couple weeks ago, and we'll keep working on it for your own protection. But like I already said, I hired you for *lucent*." Then I see a gleam in his eye that looks a lot like admiration. "I haven't seen lucent so powerful in... I can't remember how long. Maybe ever." He looks at me curiously, and I try to appear extra innocent, which isn't difficult with how surprised I am at the turn the conversation has taken. Wide eyes, small smile, slow blinks.

"What's your secret?"

I tuck a piece of hair behind my ear. "My secret?"

Oh, if he only knew what he asked.

"To pulling so much lucent," he says. "You just provided three men enough lucent to power enchanted weapons for a prolonged amount of time." With a slight frown he mutters, "I don't know if Nadiette can even do that anymore, and in the Lucent Mountains, no less."

I lift one shoulder in a casual shrug. "It's a gift."

I smile weakly, kicking myself for possibly offering *too* much lucent now.

"Well, it's more than I ever expected. I'm glad you're with us... But if something happened to you..."

I can't make myself meet his eyes, so I look at our twined hands instead.

He sighs. "Just don't do it again."

"I can't promise I won't," I argue softly.

"How did I know you'd say that?" He chuckles. "I'll just have to do better to ensure you don't have to." Then he adds, his voice firm. "And we'll be training every night. You can practice sharing lucent with the three of us until it feels more normal. If you don't feel comfortable fighting, that's okay; we just need to adjust our technique. Darvy, Rhosse, and I have fought side by side for years, so it comes naturally. It'll get better, I promise."

I nod and look into his eyes. For a moment I feel the warm tension build between us, and wonder if another kiss might—

He pulls his eyes from mine as he plucks a leaf from my hair. I immediately bring a hand up to feel it and cringe as my fingers run over an assortment of small twigs, pine needles, pieces of dried leaves, and a bit of blood. *Lovely.*

Ikar smirks as I drop my hand. There's nothing to help it right now. *Definitely no kiss.*

"We'll be able to clean up once we find the nymphs, I'm sure." He eyes my hair once more, grinning a little wider now as his thumb caresses my hand distractingly. Then he pulls his fingers from mine and turns toward Darvy and Rhosse, leaving my hand uncomfortably cold and lonely.

Chapter 18

Nadiette

King's Council

The low kings sit around the table. The head chair, as old as this kingdom and empty as it should never be, draws my eyes. I can't deny that it feels wrong to meet here without Ikar. I begin to fist a hand in the fabric of my white jacket, but I catch myself and force myself to relax. I ignore the pang of guilt about my part in this council and promptly remind myself that if not for my intervention, there would have already been mutiny in Ikar's absence.

The low kings are antsy. I can feel it. Their eyes shift between each other, their shoulders taut—unrest thrums in the room. Well, except for Drade. He slouches in his chair as if this is the last place he cares to be. I purse my lips, irritated by his uncaring attitude.

Waylon eyes the empty head seat with a hint of calculation before he turns his attention to the others. "I have called us together to discuss our high king's decision to pursue marriage and bridging with a Queen of the Night. It has been made known to me that our dear king is, at this very moment, scouring the Lucent Mountains in search of a flower. We are all in agreement that his mission is reckless, that it puts our kingdom in danger?" His gaze sweeps the table, waiting for nods of agreement. Then he turns his eyes to me. "Nadiette, any progress regarding marriage before he left?"

I'm annoyed he asks. If Ikar left to find a blazing flower, then it's easy to assume things didn't go well. Adrian's chin is already dipping in a steady bob, soon to rest on his chest. Drade is unreadable and relaxed, as usual, but I can tell by the awareness in his dark eyes that he observes the proceedings closely.

"I have not been able to gain an answer from King Ikar thus far," I say, keeping my chin high and clasping my hands confidently on the table before me while trying to forget about our last conversation. "But I believe with time and continued effort on my part he will agree to marriage."

There's a prolonged silence.

Rhomi shifts uncomfortably in his chair before finally speaking up. "How long should we wait before acting?" He asks no one in particular, but his eyes meet mine with question.

I answer with all the confidence I've ever portrayed as being the kingdom's highest originator. "It won't be long. As soon as he returns, I'll speak with him. I'm sure I can change his mind."

Waylon shakes his head. "We've waited long enough, my dear. You have three weeks to marry, and no longer."

My clasped hands tighten around each other on the table. "That's hardly enough time. He's away again, as you well know."

"I don't disagree, but while we've been waiting, our dear *king* is gallivanting about the kingdom in search of a Queen of the Night, endangering our entire kingdom, and you dare ask us for more time?" He raises his brows in question.

I clench my teeth, but say nothing.

"Three weeks."

I nod, ignoring the silent stares of the other kings around the table.

Jethonan slides a parchment from one stack to the other with a heavy sigh. "I must say, I look forward to the day our king returns." He frowns at the remaining stack of parchment waiting for attention.

I stare out the window, thinking, and only slightly aware that he watches to see if I'm listening. He slides a new parchment before him and begins to read, preparing to sign his name at the bottom, when I suddenly speak.

"I've just returned from the King's Council. This fool mission may irreparably damage our kingdom." Anger seeps into my tone. I can't help but blame Jethonan for his part in all of this.

Jethonan raises his head, curious. "Why do you say that?"

Everything seems to be going well in Ikar's absence— the gloam as awful as ever, but the ins and outs of the kingdom running as they should under Jethonan's direction. Nothing the other kings should be concerned about. In all, the high king had only been away for a few weeks, and Jethonan had handled all of this easily many times.

He narrows his eyes as he thinks about what I've said.

"The low kings are not happy that Ikar is set on bridging with a Tulip," I say with spite.

Jethonan leans back, frowning. "So you told them—behind his back, I might add."

I spin toward him, triggered by the judgment in his voice. "He presented his idea himself. I merely gave an update. I had to, though it should have been him, if he was acting responsibly."

Jethonan purses his lips and nods. "It's apparent you have no trust in your king."

I jerk as if he slapped me, my face as red as if he had. "No, I don't trust *you*. This is *your* fault. You're the one who planted all the ideas and sent him away." I point an accusing finger at him. "You're the one who made him leave me."

He simply shakes his head. "No, Nadiette. You know Ikar. He never allows anyone to *make* him do anything." He readjusts the paper on the desk, making the angles straight before continuing. "I urge you to stop this. For the kingdom. For Ikar."

I scoff. "It's out of my hands now. The only way I can stop it is by marrying him in three weeks. I was able to convince the low kings to agree to that, to keep the peace. Otherwise, they'd be on their way here *now*."

Jethonan considers me for a moment, the youth of his face belied by the wisdom and age in his eyes. "This is the first I've seen you act the enemy, my lady. It doesn't appear to be a good fit for you."

My cheeks flame before I turn and leave the room, slamming the door behind me.

Chapter 19

Ikar

I lean back against a fallen tree, sitting in sparse grass and dirt before a crackling fire as I repair one of the many tears in my leather armor and deliberate over the next day's direction. According to a journal kept by one of my grandfathers many years ago, if all goes according to plan, we should find the nymphs in a day or so.

I tuck the journal safely in a pocket of my trousers. Even with the gloam, we've made good time. I pull a sturdy thread through the largest of the tears, neatly stitching it back together. Vera sits across camp rebraiding her hair while watching Rupi hop about in the dry dirt, her beak moving in quick, jerky movements as she devours a small spider. She hops again, leaving small puffs of dust as she goes in search of another. For a moment I allow my gaze to linger on Vera as she tilts her head forward to braid the back before she brings the tail of it forward to finish. I smother a grin. We've spent enough nights together that I know that no matter how tightly she braids it, by morning it'll be loose.

I drag my gaze away, feeling too warm as I watch her

prepare for bed. Instead, the thought that has occupied my mind for the majority of the day returns to the forefront. I recall the moment I met her, the way she reread the list of names. I know in my soul she knows something. I've been biding my time, knowing that as long as she believed I was a criminal I would never get an answer. She trusted me enough to uncuff me and sign my contract. And now she knows I'm an officer. I don't know what else to do to earn her trust. Will she ever answer my questions? I have a feeling the answer is no... but why? She still refused when it came up a couple days ago, and that conversation led to a fight, and then, somehow, a near-kiss. The stubbornness in her gray eyes, the set of her perfect lips...

I silently groan and clench my jaw. I can't do anything to mess this up, including falling in love with her.

Correction: Falling in love with her more than I already have.

I swallow uncomfortably as I remind myself that the reason I hired her is to help me get closer to finding my future wife.

"When do you think they'll be back?" Vera asks, looking around our small camp with a crease between her brows as the shadows thicken.

"If there's anything to hunt in the vicinity, Rhosse'll find it quickly," I reassure. But even I don't like our group separated in this forest—especially after the encounter with the wolves.

Vera nods and begins a game of catch with Rupi and her favorite seeds. I find myself so distracted by the openness on her face that I look down to find my last two stitches are now quite crooked. I flex my jaw in frustration and begin the work to fix it, but before I can even get the first one out, I feel the tingle that ushers in the molten hot burning when another piece of my mark turns black. I suck in a silent breath and hold it for the duration—sweating and tense when it finally stops. I won't be able to see how much of it has turned until we get back, and I don't usually keep track of when this happens, but I feel like it's increasing.

"Your shoulder pains you again?" Vera asks, tilting her head and eyeing me closely.

"I'm fine." I force my shoulders to relax and hope she doesn't press the subject.

I'm reminded of how she caught sight of my mark paining me when I was her bounty, and it seems she's more aware than ever. She looks at me a moment longer, then appears to accept my response and returns her attention to Rupi.

I stare through the spindly tops of the trees, catching sight of the second sun beginning to set. With the further blackening of my mark, my thoughts turn to my kingdom and my father. He was a good man, an honorable king, and well-loved by our people, but the way he did things won't work anymore. I recall the disapproval shown by the low kings at the last council and cringe when I think of how they'll react when they hear of my wedding and bridging with a Black Tulip. All I can hope is that they will see the needed changes and the good a Queen of the Night will bring our kingdom and offer their support—same for the citizens who've been taught to hate the Black Tulips. It will take time, I'm sure, for my people to adjust, but if things go according to plan we'll have plenty of time after we bridge.

I find myself habitually scanning the forest between stitches. My magic usually alerts me when gloam creatures are near. I sense them, but it's difficult in a forest such as this where gloam is, literally, everywhere. So when I hear a few quiet clicks that don't fit with the forest around us, I tense, listening. My first instinct is to protect Vera, but I hesitate to alert her unnecessarily. What if it's nothing? Many of the sounds in this forest are concerning and don't amount to anything.

After hearing nothing further, I relax the smallest bit and return to repairing my armor—a little faster now with the urgency to get it back on. Vera is still distracted, now sitting in patchy grass while Rupi hops over her legs, appearing oblivious to my concern.

A series of unsettling clicks meets my ears, and my eyes rest on the shadows just behind Vera. Do they appear deeper than they should? I squint as I search the darkness. It only takes seconds for me to recognize what it is. Is it too much to hope that we aren't its target? My heart drops. *We* are not the target; *Vera* is. The deepening darkness of the twilight sky helps hide its large form in the trees. It seems as much as I can sense *it*, it seems to sense my recognition, and immediately eight long legs skitter across the earth, the only sound the popping of its over-sized joints as it scuttles toward us. I attempt to pull magic to increase my eyesight, but find that there's no lucent to pull without Vera's help. I curse. For some inexplicable reason, the woman attracts trouble like no one I've ever seen, and I feel the strongest drive to keep her safe, to sacrifice myself for her, even. More than I've ever felt for an individual person.

I regret tossing my armor to the side, but if I have to choose between armor and sword, it'll always be my sword. So when the velvet widow jumps, without a second thought, so do I, brandishing my weapon and blocking Vera with my body as my weight falls on her. Her yelp of surprise is muffled beneath me, combined with a smothered smatter of panicked *cheeps* from Rupi. I feel the instant when my sword and the spider's pincers simultaneously find their mark. I pull the magic that Vera offers as my sword slides into its underbelly at the same time its venomous pincers strike the vulnerable flesh at my neck.

The spider hisses in pain, and I shout as an excruciating burn runs through my bloodstream while the venom does its work. I yank my sword out, attempting to get another stab in, but within seconds, my grip loosens without my permission. My arm falls to the ground, limp, my sword hitting the dirt with a dull thud. In mere seconds, I'm completely paralyzed. My throat tingles and numbs, and I try not to panic when it feels like I may even suffocate.

The spider backs up for a moment, and I think that maybe my single stab took care of it, and I only need to wait for the paralyzing venom to wear off—I thought wrong. The spider visibly regains its strength and returns, this time with rope-thick spider silk wrapping efficiently around my ankles, feet, and calves.

Vera squirms out from beneath my dead weight with a rumpled Rupi perched on her head, her feathers askew, eyeing the spider's backside with wariness. She promptly flutters into the nearby treetops while Vera kneels beside me and holds my face in her hands.

"Why aren't you moving?" I can sense her panic, and her high-pitched whisper-yell has caught the spider's attention. It pauses its wrapping of my limbs.

I can't respond. My vocal cords won't work. But my eyes still do.

I attempt to look to the side to motion for her to run before the spider turns around. She must get the message because she's up and running in a second, disappearing into the darkness.

The spider continues twining her rope silk in layers until it reaches the backs of my knees, then I'm hoisted into the air by my feet, dangling like a lifeless piece of bait. I swing from the widow's thread, arms swinging uselessly above my head, and watch our camp disappear from view while hoping that Vera makes it without me.

Chapter 20

Vera

I scan the deep shadows of this dark, inky cave, crouched down and creeping as silently as I can with Ikar's enormous sword in my grasp. Rupi chirps disapprovingly when it bangs against the wall for the fourth time.

"You try carrying it. It's blazing heavy." I defend myself, feeling sweat gather beneath my clothing. "He'll never know if we don't tell him." I raise an admonishing brow at her where she perches on my shoulder.

She narrows her eyes the smallest bit, and I'm struck all over again how devoted my bird is to a man who's much too close to the high king.

"You shouldn't care for him like you do," I warn.

By the way she looks at me, we both know the words aren't just for her.

I refocus on the path ahead, stepping across the moist floor carefully. I debated for about thirty seconds if I should wait for Darvy and Rhosse to return to camp to help, but I decided that if I didn't follow the spider we might never find Ikar, and I'm not willing to risk losing him. Now I'm glad I did. The entrance is nearly impossible to find, and I never would have located it if I hadn't trailed the spider. I never got close enough to actually catch sight of it, but I could hear the popping of its legs far ahead, which are ridiculously fast for its size. I lost it once it entered a hidden hole through a grassy hillside, and now I'm left to pick my way through the dark, echoing cavern on my own.

I hold an orb of bright white light in my hand, but it casts eerie shadows off every bump and crevice. The scent of wet rock overwhelms my senses, and something else hovers on the edge—like rot. I gag. Rupi tried to stay behind when I found the entrance, perching in a tree and attempting to wish me good luck with a couple of firm chirps and a ruffle of her quills, but I finally convinced her back to my shoulder, where she currently trembles in all her spiky splendor against my neck. I wince when she shuffles and my neck gets stabbed, again. I'm still grateful to have her with me, though—this place is beyond creepy.

The cave eventually widens into an open space filled with all lengths of strange rocky growths growing from the ground and dropping from the ceiling in odd shapes. Chilled drops of water cling to the tips, growing heavy before falling on my head and shoulders as I walk beneath them. The drips echo around me, amplified eerily by the cavern walls.

I follow iffy rock paths that grow thin, bridging gaps between endless deep-black recesses beneath. An instinctive scream tears from my throat when I slip and reach out with my free hand, grabbing the only thing that seems likely to hold my weight and that of Ikar's sword—one of the long slimy rocks. The sound of the thinnest part cracking as I pull myself up and away from the cavernous space below leaves my heart racing and my breath shaky. I eye my situation warily while wiping my free hand along my trousers. The other clammy hand grips Ikar's sword like a vise. *Maybe it didn't come this way. Would these fragile bridges even hold the weight?* I eye the thickness of one across the way. *Doubtful.*

I almost turn back, but stop, positive I heard something besides the incessant dripping. I turn my head and focus completely on listening. Rupi lifts her head from where it was tucked beside a wing, her trembling easing.

"You hear that, too?"

She shoots from my shoulder in a blur of white and takes off down the dark cavern. I didn't think her night vision was that great, but half a minute later she comes flying recklessly back through. She flaps around my face, and I can't tell if she's overwhelmed with panic or excitement, but I figure either one means she's found Ikar.

I set my shoulders and forge ahead, more aware now of the slippery, occasionally sloped, surface beneath my boots. I reach the opposite end of the cavern and find two paths leading in different directions. All I can hear is the same steady dripping now. I stop for a moment, but Rupi continues flying down the cave to the right, and I follow.

"Ikar?"

It comes out sounding like I shouted with how my voice bounces off the walls. I cringe, crouching a little lower on the dark path as I wait for a pack of venomous bats or some other sort of horrid creature to come flying at me in irritation for the disturbance. I don't even know if there are such things as venomous bats in these caves, but there's *something*. There always is. Or, with my luck, the spider will hear. Nothing comes, but I do get a response.

"Vera?" The echo of Ikar's voice seems to come from every direction, all at once.

I readjust my grip on his heavy sword and forge ahead. Best be more careful not to hit the stone with it again as he'd likely hear it echo and never forgive me. I skirt around gaping death-holes and dodge the scattered growths trailing throughout the cave. Then I round another corner and stop. The narrow walkway opens into an enormous cavern, the ceiling shaped in a reverse-funnel, with a small opening allowing weak sunlight from the first of the three suns rising—enough to light up the scene before me.

Ikar swings upside down from what I am sure is a velvet widow's thread, only instead of swinging behind a spider, it's attached to the very high ceiling of the cave. Widows prefer their food... unalive, and are known for their patient waiting while their meals die a slow and miserable death. I shiver as my eyes dart around at the hundreds of other threads hanging empty around him. From what creatures, or long-dead people, I don't know.

"You shouldn't have followed," Ikar scolds. "But since you're here anyway, toss me your knife."

"Did you try magic?" I ask.

"Of course." He sounds even more irritated now. "There's none."

Naturally, Ikar's face is red from the position the spider left him in, and I would have laughed at his irritated expression—the painfully handsome, untouchable Ikar hanging upside down from a widow's thread—but my teasing smirk fades as my gaze is drawn to the way his shirt has slid up, revealing his remarkably muscled torso. I've never appreciated the force that holds us to the ground more than in this moment. My attention must be too obvious. He quickly tugs his shirt up and tucks it into the front of his trousers. It immediately slips back out. I'm not complaining.

"I'm going to need your *focus* because the spider is going to be back any minute," he whispers as he once again jerks his shirt up toward his trousers and shoves it into the waistband.

My eyes rebelliously dart to where he holds his shirt to keep it tucked, then back to his face. "I'm completely focused." I raise my brows innocently.

He works to keep his shirt tucked in. "Mmhmm."

I stride forward like I have nothing to be embarrassed about and toss my knife up. Without hesitation, he snatches the handle with one hand. Rupi soars up to perch on the sole of his left boot and proceeds to offer him an assortment of encouraging chirps. I stand several feet beneath him, my attention now diverted to the shadowy, dark edges of the cavern. I really don't want to wrangle with a velvet widow today.

"Anytime now," I call up, still watching the entrances warily.

I turn as I hear a scuffle from somewhere beyond my line of sight, angling my body toward where I think it came from. The only problem is, Ikar's sword is too heavy for me to fight with, even with both hands, so I slip my smaller sword from its sheath.

Ikar curses and grumbles something as his shirt continues to slip.

"Forget the shirt already!" I hiss, keeping my eyes on the slowly emerging shape to our left.

I hear the telltale popping before I see its giant black pincers. It steps into a ray of weak light and millions of intelligent, reflective eyes stare at me, followed by a body of deep violet that looks soft as velvet. A spider aptly named—a velvet widow. It approaches slowly, and I realize it's eyeing me as bait, exhibiting a complete lack of concern for the swords in my hands.

I glance up at Ikar for a split second, hoping he's almost free. He has pulled himself upward with his torso in what can only be described as an impressive ab hold, slicing through the thick rope that winds around his ankles and lower legs. In his effort, his shirt has once again slipped, and my eyes do an immediate double-take. Not because of his impressive build this time—though there's that—but because I spot the edges of a scrawling black mark that reaches almost to his mid-back on the left side, and if I am correct in my assumption, snakes its way up and wraps around his left shoulder, then crawls down the upper left of his chest. Only a select few have a mark like that, and I know exactly what it means.

"You're a king," I whisper.

My grip relaxes on the sword handles as numb tingles travel throughout my body, and everything grows fuzzy. *I arrested a king. I was alone with him for over a week. I'm stuck on this journey with a king.* The weapons clatter to the ground. *I kissed the high king.* How did this happen?

I shake my head in horror. I am a Black Tulip. I do not associate with kings, or become friends with them, and I definitely do not ever kiss them. Ikar is good. Kings are bad. *Ikar is a king.*

I press my hands to my temples as I attempt to process what I've learned, but my world has tipped, and I have no idea which way is up.

"I kissed a king," I whisper.

Chapter 21

Ikar

I curse when I realize she's seen my mark, but I have no time to consider the implications now, and neither does she.

"Can we not do this right now?" I ask through gritted teeth as I strain to hold my upper body high enough and simultaneously force the dagger through the fibrous, surprisingly dense thread that has seemingly been wound around my lower legs at least a billion times.

I tried to pull magic to tear it apart with strength, but not one of the thick ropes broke. There's not enough lucent here without Vera's help. I've never been caught in a velvet widow's thread, but it's worse than I ever imagined.

"A little lucent might help," I call sardonically.

"I can't believe you didn't tell me when I arrested you!" she hisses from below, unwilling to wait for this conversation.

And apparently unwilling to lend me lucent.

I continue sawing at the threads feverishly. "*Why* would I have done that?" I grunt as I press even harder, and a thick bunch finally loosens.

"I think that's obvious," she spits.

"You don't understand any of this," I growl.

"On *that* we can agree." Her voice is as cold as an ice-crusted lake.

Finally, I cut through the largest portion, leaving only my ankles still wound tight. Rupi still perches on the edge of my boot, quilled up and looking ready for a fight. The ominous popping sounds closer. I give an extra push and grab on to the hanging bit of thread, my muscles resisting like flames beneath my skin at the deep stretching I'm unaccustomed to.

I thrust the knife quickly into the last section, slicing through the remaining thread, and keep a firm grip on the thread now hanging loosely above me so I don't fall on my head. Rupi takes flight as I let go and land in a crouch beside Vera, grabbing both our swords from the ground and shoving hers into her hand. It takes a moment for me to gain my balance as the blood rushes from my head, and when it clears, I glance at Vera to make sure she's prepared to battle our way out. But instead of choosing a defensive position, her weapon before her, she looks at me like I'm a deathstalker and she'd rather side with the velvet widow in front of us.

The spider lunges, and Vera finally does something besides stare at me with abject horror. She darts to the right, her movements mirrored in the numberless reflective eyes.

I take a swipe at one of the jointed legs, and the spider hisses and comes at me instead, grazing my arm with its pincers, but I move quickly, and finally feel the rush of lucent magic from Vera. I pull it quickly to increase my senses and speed while seeing it as a good sign she doesn't want me dead, at least.

I scan the length of the spider, calculating the best way to kill it when I hear smaller skitters—many of them. Vera shouts from somewhere in the cave and whatever she's done draws the widow's attention once more. It shifts its velvety body to investigate, and I spot her swinging wildly, slicing through wave after wave of baby velvet widows. Rupi swoops down to attack, her feathers still spread out in her quill form, and punctures the tiny arachnids until they stop moving. I'm impressed by the tiny bird; she's more formidable than I'd have ever guessed.

The small purple spiders rise almost to Vera's knees, pincers opening and closing ferociously, but their attack can only be described as disorderly. I take advantage of the widow's distraction to use one of its long thin legs to swing onto its back, then waste no time thrusting my sword through the top of its head. It jerks, skitters from side to side momentarily, then falls in a quivering heap. I jump down to the cave floor, intending to help Vera and Rupi with the continuing wave of miniature widows swarming her.

"I don't need your help!" she shouts as she stabs one, flings it against the wall of the cave, and goes for another.

From the look in her eyes, it's what she'd like to do to me, as well.

"I know." And I mean it.

It appears she can be quite fearsome when she's angry, but it doesn't stop me from jumping in to help. As I do so, almost methodically swinging my sword against these small enemies, I also battle confusion. One of the first conversations we had was about her dislike for kings... but she knows me now. We've traveled together for weeks, even visited her family. I have to believe that her reaction is simply born of habit. If we can just get a chance to talk, she'll understand. I hope.

Chapter 22

Vera

The three of us leave the cave covered in widow blood and bits. It's gooey and it smells, but it's not as bad as knowing that Ikar is a king. I shoved that fact aside for survival while we fought the widows, but now that we're out, I'm done. You cannot simply *arrest* a king. Or kiss one, for that matter. I mean, *I did*, but I most definitely shouldn't have. I know for a fact now his story is true, but I wish he could be a criminal instead.

I could definitely fall in love with a reformed criminal... I can never be in love with a king. My breath hitches with a painful tug. I need to get away from him, end whatever this is between us. *Escape.*

My eyes meet Ikar's with fiery accusation. "I still can't believe you're a blazing *king*," I spit out as if it's the most disgusting word I've ever spoken.

He stares at me, eyes hard and a muscle in his jaw flexing. I want to cry when attraction still burns bright beneath the all-encompassing betrayal.

I fist my hands, force all emotion from my face, and keep

my voice flat. "I'm done. Whatever this was"—I motion with my hand in the air between us—"it's over."

I need to get away from him, find another job, forget about his smile, his presence, his draw… that glimpse of bare torso and his muscled back. I shove it all down and begin formulating a new plan for my life. I pat Rupi in all her sticky widow-blood glory, but she quills her feathers out to prevent me from stroking her, as if she's upset with *me* and what I'm doing. I ignore her silent argument. She gives me a short, angry chirp and flies into the trees at our right. I'll smooth things over with her, just as soon as I escape the king at my back.

Ikar calls from behind me. "What about my contract? You're going to take off on your own in the Lucent Mountains?" His tone is challenging.

I hate that he's right. I fist my hands and stop, which gives him time to catch up to me. My mind packed the last few weeks into a neat, tidy box labeled *mistake* and was ready to run. But here in these mountains, I'm well and perfectly stuck.

I turn toward him with ice in my voice. "Why did you let me arrest you in the first place? Why didn't you say something?"

My eyes burn, and my voice is louder than I intended. I feel like a fool.

He's in front of me now, appearing just as frustrated as I and somehow still achingly handsome covered in widow-battle gore. To make it worse, there's a guarded vulnerability in his eyes, and I don't like how it tugs at my heart. He runs a hand through his hair, making it stand up in places, always perfectly mussed.

"I couldn't just tell you. You don't understand the pains I took to stay invisible, what my mission truly is."

A bark of laughter rises in my throat. Ikar? Invisible? He

was doomed from the beginning if that was what his plan was built on.

His eyes fill with accusation. "Don't forget that when I dropped the biggest hint I ever could have, you rejected it and called me a murderer."

A memory of the night in the tiny cave, the image on the badge in my hand. Ikar and I waking together—I shake it away.

"I can't trust criminals, or I'd have been dead long before now. I'm sure at any of the villages we stopped at you could have found a way to verify—" I stop myself. "Actually, you know what, this argument is pointless. I don't work with kings." I raise my chin to solidify my stance.

He frowns. "That's an absurd rule and you know it."

"You lied to me. You hid that from me even after I shared" —I bite my lower lip, fighting back emotion—"everything."

Tears are burning behind my eyes, and my chest feels heavy, and I know I need to get away before I fall apart. He's no longer *my criminal*, or my friend, or someone I could love... he never really was.

"Everything?" His tone is almost mocking. His icy blue eyes drill into my soul, as if he senses what I've held back and is ready to force it out. Hold me to my word. Wait for me to spill, literally, *everything* right here, right now.

I turn my back, unwilling to meet his gaze, and stalk away. I want to run, but the way my eyes have filled with tears I'd probably biff it and land on my face in my escape, and there's no coming back from that. Instead, I set my pace to a wide stride and rapidly work to blink back my emotion. I run my sleeve across my nose. I don't care if he sees. I sniff loudly, and it's then I notice how still the forest has become—almost too quiet. We must have frightened away the animals with the tension strung tight between us.

"Wrong direction," he calls, finally breaking the silence.

I look up at the sky and curse before I slowly turn around. "Lead the way," I grind out.

He pulls the journal out of a pocket in his trousers and flips it open. I openly stare at him as he turns the pages and studies the book, frowning as I try to grasp the reality that Ikar is the *king*. Maybe it's shock, maybe it's my traitorous feelings, but my mind begs for me to keep him safely labeled as my criminal again.

He glances up and catches me staring, but I refuse to look away like a coward.

Our gazes war for a moment before he finally speaks. "Darvy and Rhosse likely have my armor and pack and have left in search of the nymphs. That was our plan in case something like this happened. We need to meet them there as soon as we can."

I frown deeper. "You're the only one with the journal."

He closes it and tucks it safely away. "They have a copy of the most important notes and a guide for the journey in case we got separated. They'll know to meet us at the nymphs."

"Wait, why don't I?" I ask vehemently—nothing like finding out my love interest is my greatest enemy to make me feel all sorts of argumentative.

"I've seen you try to read a map; it's more dangerous than if you didn't have one at all."

I sputter as he comes closer, his challenging gaze holding mine. What am I supposed to say when he's right? *He's always right.* Blazing king.

I step back when he comes too near, wondering what he'll do to me now that I know his secret. Is this when his wicked side will come out? The side I've always been taught to fear? I try not to cower when his fingers graze my shoulder as he reaches for the strap of my pack. I attempt to pull away, but he snags it and leans in closer.

"When are you going to learn that you have nothing to fear from me?" he whispers, his rich voice so low and deep that my body traitorously freezes as he gently tugs the heavy pack from my shoulders.

He effortlessly throws it over his own and begins to walk away with his long, confident stride. The action leaves me scowling so deeply I'm sure it's etched a new wrinkle that will grace my forehead forevermore. This is a manipulation tactic of some sort. *It has to be.* He's the ruler of an entire kingdom, which means he's an expert at that sort of thing. It's to be expected, isn't it?

It makes me cringe to admit that I'd rather stick with a *king* than brave this dark forest on my own. I've never felt so traitorous in my life, but I grudgingly follow him while still drowning in shock. A reasonable voice in my head questions how I can justify being angry with him for hiding something like that when I still hold my secrets close. But I shut it out, in no mood for logic or fairness.

I blow strands of hair from my face angrily as I continue marching, hands too sullied to rebraid my hair. The quick pace helps cool the burn behind my eyes, helps me think. The thing is... I'm not sure if I'm more hurt or afraid. All my life, I've been lectured by the Black Tulips, specifically Tatania, that I should take precautions, that I should never work with anyone close to the king, including soldiers of any rank. Oh, and, the biggest, most important one? To never remove my bracelet. Don't mind me, breaking every blazing rule. I couldn't have created a worse situation in my imagination if I tried. Here I am, a Black Tulip whose bracelet is going to quit working at any time, in a remote mountain location with the high king, who I've kissed. *Of all people.*

It's all suddenly so clear... the sense of power that seems woven into his very veins, his manners, the way he holds himself, his skill with weapons, his magic. All of it. I feel like an idiot for not realizing.

I grip the pommel of the sword at my side as we walk, the solidity of the handle an anchor to reality, until I remember it's the very bantha claw I pulled from Ikar's leg mere weeks ago. I yank my hand away and sigh heavily. How has he become so much a part of my life in so short a time? In the last three weeks, I've done more to mess up my life than in my entire life combined.

I kick an errant pinecone into the brush alongside the path. Bounty hunting assistant was always risky, but paid so well for my magic that it seemed to be my only option to ensure my Tulip dues got paid. Aside from that first bounty job where I almost died, I didn't realize until I arrested Ikar how much danger I've evaded all these years. But even though I took part in dangerous work, I always had the Black Tulips behind me. No matter that I was a misfit. Now, even that's gone. A sense of isolation yawns before me, waiting to swallow me whole as soon as my bracelet stops working.

I'm on my own now.

A pit grows in my belly as I realize the depth of my trouble. I may not have known that Ikar was the high king, or even that he was a high-ranking officer, when I signed the contract, but the only person I can truly blame is myself. I scoff inwardly, thinking of the job title he gave me. *High-ranking officer.* I mimic the words with attitude beneath my breath. I'm frustrated that I can't even call it a lie. I acted as a naive fool, driven by greed and fanciful dreams.

My eyes burn again. All I ever wanted was a simple life. Just me and Rupi and a small shop where I get to sell strange treasures and not have to be an originator. That's it. I thought it was reasonable... now I know I should've just been happy with surviving. It appears that some dreams are better left alone.

I *will* my bracelet to keep working. Beg it, even. I send it good thoughts and make sure nothing jostles it too much as we journey mile after mile. By the end of the day, I'm a mess of anxiety and worry because I know as soon as it stops working, *I'm prime bait.*

Chapter 23

Ikar

For a while, I leave Vera alone in her anger. I didn't even try to attempt to speak to her after what happened last night, and even this morning, I kept my distance. Today, she walks behind me, and besides quickly looking away if our eyes meet, she blatantly ignores me. I swear all she did last night was twist that bracelet on her wrist around and around while she stared at the fire. Her fidgeting belies her... Anxiety? Fear? Anger? I'm confused, considering her behavior a vast overreaction.

A wry smile overtakes my lips when I recall a time my mother taught me to never tell a woman that, so of course I've kept my mouth shut.

So I'm the king. What does she think I'll do to her? Haven't I done enough to earn her trust? I've saved her life more times than I can count, gave her a weapon, we've kissed, and it seemed she enjoyed it as much as I... and Rupi loves me, though that fact seems to irk Vera more than work in my favor.

I'm left frustrated and wondering what else I can do to fix this. I've tried to figure out what to say, talking to myself as I practice a proper apology for a situation such as this, but even after a morning filled with repeated lines in my head, none feel sufficient. But I have enough experience to know our journey won't be successful with a group at odds with each other, and the success of this journey greatly affects my kingdom. There's really no way to prepare myself more than I already have, so I stop and turn, waiting for Vera to catch up, hating the spark of fear I catch in her eyes when they meet mine.

I swallow and begin. "Vera, about hiding my identity... I'm sorry." I truly mean it. There's a part of me that's relieved to not have to hide who I am from her any longer.

She seems to battle with herself, and I almost see her soften, then her eyes harden. "I don't accept apologies from kings."

"You are the most stubborn woman I have ever met," I grind out.

"Good." She turns her petite nose up. "At least you won't forget me."

"I couldn't forget you if I tried," I mutter impulsively.

My words hang between us—sparking in the silence. I see her hands grip the ends of her coat sleeves tighter, turning her fingertips white, and she blinks a little too quickly. My chest tightens with discomfort—I hadn't intended to make her cry.

"You have nothing to apologize for... Your Majesty."

She makes my title feel like a hot knife sliding between my ribs.

"My friends only use my title under official circumstances. No need here," I say tersely.

"We're not friends, so I'll continue to use it."

Frustration claws through my patience, but I force it down. She'll rise to it, and I don't want a worse fight and need for further apology on my hands. I turn and begin walking again, neither of us willing to speak—silence taut between us. I'd intuitively felt the need to keep my identity close when I met her, and for good reason it seems. I found out soon enough that Vera is wary of kings... but she's more than wary. The look in her eyes when she realized who I am was closer to horror and disgust than mere wariness.

I rub a hand along the back of my neck, then let it drop to my side. She has still offered no response, no questions, nothing. She seems almost apathetic, which is concerning.

"I had to keep my identity a secret," I say, making one last attempt at helping her understand.

Her hand drifts toward her sword hilt like it does when she's stressed, but when her fingertips brush it, she pulls them away and shoves her hands into her coat pockets instead, saying nothing. Does she avoid the sword because I gifted it to her? I try to ignore the hurt and remind myself that at least she's still wearing it—for now. I wouldn't be surprised if she tosses it at my feet when we finish this contract.

She doesn't argue, so I continue. "It would be dangerous for me to travel the kingdom without more soldiers for protection, and not only that, but it would take much, much longer. My presence garners attention, people want to meet, talk... I don't have *time* for any of that." I run a hand roughly through my hair without thinking. "My kingdom is suffering—"

"I get it," she says flatly. "You don't have to explain anything to me."

She may be walking right beside me, but I've never felt more distant from a person. Rupi offers me a commiserating side-eye from Vera's shoulder.

I clench my jaw, quickly losing patience with the stubborn woman. "Why does it matter so much? You didn't know yesterday, and we got along more than fine. Now you know and suddenly we can't be friends? It doesn't make any sense. Friendship is based on trust and respect, not what titles one may or may not have."

"It should be that way; you're right," she whispers so quietly that I almost miss it.

"It *can* be that way, if you'll allow it."

She smiles sadly. "You say I don't understand why you hid that from me, but *you* don't understand all of my story either."

"Then tell it. Help me understand. I'll listen." I can't help the exasperation that colors my tone.

"Since my story isn't mine alone to share, I can't. It seems we are at an impasse, but I think we should agree to continue our acquaintanceship for this journey, then we'll part ways. I'll fulfill the contract as I said I would." She appears to nod to herself, more emotionless than I've ever seen her.

I scoff, stuck on one word that irks me more than it should. "*Acquaintanceship?*" I lean closer and lower my voice. "Do you often find yourself *kissing* acquaintances?"

I know it was a low move. She double steps but catches it smoothly enough. Still, her posture is stiff and her cheeks pink. I'm not sure why I brought it up. Probably because I feel her pulling away, and I'm not ready for it.

Sometimes it feels like I'll never find the elusive magical flower, the missing Queen of the Night—that it's all tragically doomed to fail anyway, and I'll be left watching my kingdom be consumed by gloom. Dangerous thoughts whisper through my mind, tempting me from my purpose.

Why not marry a woman I love to end my days with, however soon that comes?

I rest my eyes on Vera's profile, tracing it as I fight the urge to tuck stray hairs behind her ear, resist running my thumb along the smooth line of her jaw. But then I remember my duty dictates that even if I don't find a Queen of the Night, I'll have to attempt to sacrifice myself to Lucentia, and I'd end up breaking Vera's heart, if I ever gained it. I press my lips together and back off, realizing I've taken things too far. It's clear I haven't put enough effort into distancing myself from her. I chastise myself for the weakness I've shown in hiring her in the first place—she's a drug I can't resist. So, my identity being revealed... well, it seems this is the best for both of us.

Chapter 24

Vera

Fat white flakes of snow pile up across Ikar's shoulders and hood where he walks ahead of me. My limbs are as frozen as my feelings. The tension of my discovery has eased to a dull numbing sensation—matching the state of my mood. Panic over the knowledge of Ikar's identity comes in waves, bringing high-pitched ringing in my ears, lungs gasping for breath, heart racing, and bouts of heavy sweating that are borderline embarrassing. The waves come more sporadically now, instead of being constant as they were the first day. Now I am merely set on avoiding Ikar and finishing this journey as quickly as possible. I know it seems ludicrous, but I feel as if he's betrayed me in the worst way though he has no idea he has.

Since my thoughts and feelings have begun to calm, a persistent and uncomfortable realization has settled into the cracks of my heart. I may feel betrayed by him, but I'm now forced to face the fact that I will now have to betray someone I care for, no matter which side I choose. But it's not actually a question—I'll choose the Tulips over the kings every day. I don't care about the kings, but if I take the title away... I'd be lying if I said I don't care for Ikar. I don't want to betray him, even if I *am* blazing angry and hurt right now. The snowflakes increase in size, falling cold and heavy and turning the already soft, moist dirt to squelching mud that leaves my boots covered in a solid, thick layer. At first, I was grateful for the snow and the excuse it provided to pull my hood forward and avoid Ikar, but now it's so cold my muscles spasm and my teeth chatter. I clench my jaw off and on, in a failed attempt to quiet them.

I'm distracted from my discomfort when I see a familiar-shaped snowball bobbling toward me in a somewhat erratic flight pattern, as if the weight is too much. I catch Rupi in my hands, and instantly the snow that has conglomerated in layers begins to melt as she offers a near-frozen *cheep*. I immediately pull her within the confines of my cloak where she soaks the front of my jacket and makes it impossible for me to retain any remaining warmth as she trembles against my chest.

"Am I forgiven, then?" I ask her lightly as I rub the accumulated snow and ice from her feathers, leaving them sticking out sporadically and extra fuzzy as they dry.

"I told you he was dangerous; you need to stay away from him," I can't resist whispering.

I've always depended on Rupi to guide me, warn me... but I want her to know that *I* was right about things this time. I feel her feathers begin to quill at my words, and she pokes her head up, side-eyeing me with a single blink. I'll take that to mean she doesn't agree, even as she proceeds to take advantage of my warmth and begins to clean her feathers snuggled up beside me. I can't help but smile, though it hurts to know how much she loves him.

I return to my cold trek behind Ikar with nothing to look at but *him*. There's tension that simmers between us even though we haven't spoken more than a handful of words to each other in over a day. I hate it because there's nothing to distract me from being constantly aware of him, constantly attracted to him, constantly mourning over the loss of *my* criminal and the easy conversation and companionship we shared—not even being half-frozen.

The snow stops in the late afternoon after leaving several inches for us to hike through. Only a single flake falls here and there, now, but it's not even pretty. What should be white and sparkling in afternoon sunlight appears dull and gray covered in gloom. And as the clouds above us clear and the suns sink, a new depth of chill begins to creep into my frozen bones. I fill my mind with visions of all my favorite warm things—steaming baths sprinkled with bright flower petals at Mama Tina's, sitting before a crackling fire, a cup of warm tea between my hands, the warmth of sunshine on a hot summer day. The thoughts keep my feet moving when all I want to do is curl into a ball and sleep.

When Ikar finally stops for the night, I nearly cry with relief.

He eyes the rock wall of a cliff that rises above us. "It'll provide a little protection, at least."

He looks my way, and I nod. I try to ignore the disappointment that flashes in his eyes at my lack of response. I can't feel bad about it. I know if I start talking to him again it will be harder than it already is to hate him.

Thanks to Ikar's skill, it's not long before warm firelight casts long shadows that reach and flicker up the cliff wall. As I stand near, holding my hands over the flames, tingling and aching as they thaw, Ikar drags a small tree trunk close to the fire and brushes off the snow. He gestures for me to sit. My teeth continue to chatter as I eye the situation warily. I can either share the small log that looks much too cozy with Ikar, or attempt to warm my behind on the large, cold, snow-covered boulder several feet away from the fire. It feels like a mean trick. But I'm so cold I can hardly imagine I'll ever be warm again, and the heat calls me. I feel my heart soften the tiniest bit at his thoughtful actions, and I silently nod my thanks. I leave my stuff in a heap and take a seat on the log, a hand's width from Ikar—as far as I can get without sliding off the end, and hunch forward as I press my hands between my knees to warm them.

He turns the rabbit he hunted over his hard-earned fire—it's no small feat finding wood dry enough to build one in weather such as this. The growing flames illuminate his handsome profile, and I get frustrated when my eyes are continually tempted to trace its outline.

Rupi pokes her head from the folds of my cloak, testing the warmth to see if she's able to leave its protection. It appears the heat of the fire is acceptable because she hops out and perches on my knee. Her fluffy feathers stick out in disarray, and I stifle a laugh as she settles herself on the edge of my knee, as near to the fire as she can get. Her gentle movements as she puts her feathers in order and the gradual thawing of my body have me feeling sleepy and more relaxed than I've felt since I found out Ikar is the high king. As long as I ignore that, I enjoy the warmth he offers from where he sits beside me.

But the peace doesn't last long.

I feel the very moment the bracelet comes free and slips from my wrist, so soft it could have been one of Rupi's feathers brushing across my skin. It falls lightly to the wet dirt near my boots with hardly a sound, and I freeze. Just like that... I'm *free*.

It's what I wanted, isn't it?

Rupi appears to sense it and peers down at where it lies on the ground, then back up to me, as if waiting for my reaction.

Her bright eyes and feathers puffed up to make her appear almost twice her size show me she's pleased. My fingers graze the bare skin of my wrist in shock.

I'm free from the rules of the Black Tulips and their expensive dues that plagued me for so long. For one long moment, I ignore the panic and let every single one of my bad decisions be worth it. I revel in my recklessly earned freedom. The reprieve from guilt over my actions feels like a weight lifted from my shoulders... until my magic begins to twist and curl in a way I've never experienced. I still for a moment to attune to its movement and sensation with curiosity, feeling it move throughout my body as if I've freed a piece of magic that was tied to the depths of my very soul. But the curiosity turns to dread as I realize what's happening. I'd hoped my lucent would be too weak, as Tatania said it should be, but it feels as if some foreign part of my magic stretches itself out and flexes its claws like a lazy, warm cat waiting for a mouse to pounce on—or a high king. *Ikar.*

His heat calls to my cool like never before, and I snatch my wandering magic back in horror, hoping he didn't sense anything. This is undoubtedly what Tatania meant when she spoke of the way a Tulip and king are drawn together, except it's stronger than I ever imagined—and worse, something traitorous within me whispers that I should allow it.

No.

"Vera." Ikar's deep voice captures my attention. "Your bracelet."

I jerk out of my frozen trance to find him much too close, my magic curling in traitorous delight. He leans down as he reaches for it, his arm brushing my calf in the process. He holds the dangling piece of jewelry out for me to take. I don't miss the irony that the king I was always supposed to be hidden from holds the very thing that kept me concealed from him in his fingers. All those days ago I imagined I would feel a lot... *freer*.

I brave a look up and meet his eyes for a long moment. I can't help but notice the small crease that forms between his brows.

Does that mean he feels something?

I resist the urge to bite my lip and offer a small nod as I shakily take it from his fingers, then, just to check if it's truly irreparable, I hold up the two ends... and find no clasps to reattach it. My shoulders fall, though I expected no less.

I see a hint of compassion in his eyes as he watches me. "I'm sorry about your friendship bracelet. I'm sure it can be repaired when we return."

Friendship bracelet. I almost laugh. That's what I told him it was back when he was a criminal and I a bounty hunter—I let the half-truth stand.

I smile tightly. "Yes, I'm sure you're right."

I only say it to appease him. I already know that no simple jeweler can repair this bracelet, only the copious amount of funds I need to pay the Tulips can do that—and that's only if Tatania is willing to overlook my rebelliousness and take me back. The last layer of safety I've been relying so heavily upon since learning who Ikar is... is gone. I'd always wondered what would happen if I didn't pay the dues—now I know. It was rather anticlimactic, but I really don't need more excitement in my life at this point anyway.

Rupi pecks at the bracelet, tugging it from my fingers as if she wants to play, but I have a feeling she'd really like to drop it somewhere in this horrid forest where I'll never find it again, hoping I'll forget its existence. I tug it from her beak with a look of warning. She shoots me a saucy glare as I slip it into my pocket and grapple with feeling more trapped than ever. Another failed choice of mine.

I'm on a roll.

Ikar removes his heavy cloak, and I side-eye him, seeking further signs that he feels something different, but he acts as if nothing has changed. Does that mean it's just me? He offers me some of the meat, and I take it with a nod of thanks as he returns to tending the fire and digs into our meal.

I chance another look as my magic continues to twist and curl and reach for him, but he appears as at ease as ever, simply taking another hearty bite and chewing as if he's enjoying the best meal of his life. I allow my gaze to linger a little longer, knowing he's distracted. On hunting contracts and journeys such as this, etiquette is necessarily set aside—looser manners, eating with our fingers, no napkins in sight... He seems too normal, too reachable like this. Just another soldier. My friend. No, more... he's someone I could fall in love with. Doesn't help that he's so handsome it makes my breath hitch on a regular basis. He doesn't seem at all like the image of the king I've had in my mind.

The thought triggers memories of a specific afternoon when Renna and I were teens, giggling over a harmless game we played as we waited for the annual Black Tulip meeting to begin—we'd never seen a king, nor did we intend to, so what harm was there in imagining what the king might look like?

I smile as I drift into the memory.

"I'm sure he has a huge throne with a massive pillow to cushion his behind," I say.

Renna giggles. "Clothed in satin and velvet, with gold trim. Oh, and black boots that are shined every hour."

I snort. "And long, thick gray hair, because I'm sure he looks distinguished."

Then Renna adds, "And a thin, wiry beard that he twines around a finger in his boredom."

I laugh so loudly it catches Tatania's attention from the side of the room. I muffle it with my hand and whisper, "With hands softer than a noblewoman's, and his back as hunched as an old man with the weight of the gold crown on his head."

Renna snickers. "And plates of five-tier cakes and bowls of fruit surrounding him."

"Don't forget the sneer on his lips," I whisper.

The memory ends there. I blink, my eyes readjusting to the reality around me. Rupi hops to my shoulder, and she follows my gaze to Ikar, where I consider him carefully with narrowed eyes. There has to be *some* indication I missed that gives away his status, the awfulness that goes hand in hand with being king—aside from the mark he's kept hidden as well as I've hidden mine... until the widow cave. At first glance, I notice nothing awry, but maybe with the perspective I have now, I'll be able to see what I've been told kings always are and what created the picture in my mind: an aged man, slouched in a gold throne, a heavy crown settled pridefully on long, thin hair, luxurious clothing and boots that have never seen a speck of dust, selfish to the core. I admit I've been quite judgmental, but all I've had to guide me all these years was this mental picture and the words of warning from Tatania. I intend to prove it right in some way—prove to myself that he's not as good as he seems.

So I peer at him with a critical eye. He's obviously not aged. In fact, I'd say he's in his prime—I'd guess his late twenties—but I try not to linger on that thought as it goes against the image in my head. *Focus.* I start at the top of his head, but unfortunately, I don't have to think hard about the crown. I've never seen one grace his tousled brown hair. In fact, he runs his hands through it so often it appears he's in the habit of *not* wearing one more often than not. I frown at that and move on to the next thing on the list.

His jaw is rough with thick, days-grown scruff, lending an air of danger to his features that isn't as visible when he's clean-shaven—though I prefer him that way. Another difference to my long-pictured king.

I chide myself for having a preference for his appearance. *Inappropriate, Vera.*

I move to his shoulders next. I've walked behind them for so many days that I know they're broad, filling out his shirts in a way most men envy, and indicate the opposite of lazing away on a throne. His arms, included. His hands are calloused and rough, an obvious sign that he is no stranger to hard work and weapons... and which, admittedly, I find incredibly attractive.

Aloof perusal, Vera.

My eyes drop to his waist—no overabundance there. I've seen it myself. I swallow, my mouth dry. Along with all that, he takes turns hunting, cleaning the meat, starting fires. He's carried my pack the last day and stitched my arm when we were in the Shift For—

"Yes?" I find Ikar looking at me with a questioning brow raised, and I pull my gaze from his trim torso with surprise.

"Nothing." I scowl as if he did something wrong and return to the meat that has grown cold in my fingers.

Rupi practically coos with approval from where she perches on my knee.

From the corner of my eye, I see him continue to watch me for a prolonged moment, that small crease reappearing between his brows, before he turns away again and resumes his meal. I resist the urge to wipe my sweaty palms across my trousers.

I realize then that I *must* do better to act normal—completely innocent. But I accept the trickle of relief at his ignorance of any change in his or my magic. Tatania always warned that the king would know us by our magic drawing to each other, whatever that means. But maybe right now it's only mine that's changed. I don't know what to expect now that I no longer have the bracelet's protection, but it seems for this minute, maybe this hour... maybe even this night, I'm still safe.

I'll take it.

My thoughts drift back to my perusal and judgment of his person—which doesn't help. If anything, it proves my entire picture wrong, reminds me how attractive and likeable he is, and leaves me confused, as if I'm picking up pieces of a puzzle that simply cannot be completed. No matter how I try to twist it, Ikar doesn't fit who I envisioned the king was. And it scares me. Even with the magic firmly in my grasp I feel the tug, the way it *yearns* for him, and I realize with deepening sorrow that now not only is it my heart that's broken, but my magic will be too... because one day, I *will* run. I *will* fix the mistakes I've made. I *will* get a new bracelet and commit to being a better Tulip, and one day, I *will* be safe and hidden again. Broken-hearted, but safe—a trade I'll attempt to convince myself is best. There will be no bridging of magic between me and this king.

The thought seems to trigger my magic to rebel, pushing at its bounds, and snapping me from my thoughts with a frown. I clutch my magic tight, frustrated that it's misbehaving as badly as my bird. How exactly am I to keep track of *both*? The initial wonder has worn off, and reality is beginning to hit like one too many cups of a shady fae drink, and a sordid mixture of feelings rise to the surface. In a moment where I expected to feel empowered and independent, I feel like an animal who just stepped in a hunter's trap.

Now the true danger begins.

Chapter 25

Ikar

I work to bind my wildly misbehaving magic up within me, careful to mask any surprise on my face so Vera doesn't notice. I've never had difficulty controlling my magic, but as soon as I handed Vera that bracelet last night, it felt like the once-continuous and dependable rope of lucent within me began to unravel. It's as if my magic snapped. *Broke.* It moves in a foreign rhythm through my veins, which is concerning in and of itself, but to make matters worse, it's acting more than eager to reach out of its own accord toward *Vera.* I don't know what to call it or how to describe it, but it's not normal. At this point, I can't tell if it's me or my magic that wants her more, and neither one can have her.

My first thought was that this is what Jethonan meant when he said my magic would draw toward a Tulip, but that thought was quickly extinguished. To know that my magic is drawing toward Vera is like rubbing salt in an open wound. I know she's not a Tulip, and I know I can never be with her, which means something is horribly wrong.

I enjoyed a slight reprieve from my magic's pull while filling water a short trek away before we continue our journey this morning, but as soon as I walk back into camp, Vera turns quickly—as if I've startled her. And worse, I catch a hint of wariness in her eyes as she waits for me to pass before falling into step behind me. Is it still because she fears me, or does that mean she felt it too? I nearly groan as I rub a hand along the back of my neck and shake my head, frustrated. Just what I need when she's barely had time to accept the fact that I'm high king.

Now what? She feels some sort of odd magic from me bombarding her? I feel like a complete creep. I wind the wayward magic up tight again, unsure what exactly I'm supposed to do with it to keep it away from her—I have to find a way to control it better. And as soon as we find Darvy I intend to ask him about it; maybe he can even heal it. I'm left wondering if the velvet widow venom or something else in this long-forgotten forest broke it. No matter the cause, I know my magic needs to be working properly to recognize a Tulip when I find one, and if my magic is lunging at every woman I come into contact with, it'll be impossible to find who I'm looking for. Besides, I imagine it'll create all sorts of offense toward ladies at court when I return.

I clench my teeth—just one more thing to make this mission of finding a flower and a Black Tulip to bridge with even more difficult.

Rupi settles on my shoulder, seeming extra chipper this morning despite the heat that scorches us from above. Still, she puffs her tiny chest up and trills birdsong, that, on another day, I might appreciate. Instead my thoughts wander back to last night. The look of stark fear in Vera's eyes when I handed her the bracelet is like a knife in my gut. Her anger, her stubbornness... I can handle that, but to have her fear me?

I run a hand through my hair in frustration. I'd thought we trusted each other at the start of this journey, that we were friends, of a sort. But she fears me now that she knows I'm high king more than she did when she thought I was a violent Class A criminal, and now that my magic is after her, it's going to make it even worse. Still, there are things about her that simply don't make sense. In fact, not much makes sense when it comes to Vera. She supposedly has healing magic *and* origination magic, which I've never heard of before. She refuses to dress as the other originators, preferring darker colors over bright white. And her fear of me as king? I don't know where to start with that since she refuses to discuss it.

She's tantalizing, and I can't resist trying to figure her out. I should just let her be mysterious, do her job, pay her, and send her on her way. That's what my ever-practical self recommends. But something about her draws me, and she has parts of me wrapped up so tightly in her grasp that I quite simply don't want to be just friends or *acquaintances,* as she so aptly calls us. Just thinking of those words on her lips has my jaw clenching again. In the end, though, there's nothing for us. I work on feeling grateful for my wayward, broken magic forcing me to keep my distance, even if it does leave me feeling like an unseemly cad in the meantime.

The thought reminds me that I should clear the air about the... magic issue. I cringe just thinking about it. I know I need to speak with Vera. I can't tell if the looks she gives me are based on her dislike of me as the king still, or because my magic is broken and she can sense it—maybe it's both. I can't do a thing about either, but I can at least explain that I'm not *trying* to make her uncomfortable. I'd rather lead the front lines of my army into battle against a horde of shard beasts than broach this topic with her, but I need to ensure this mission succeeds, and we have a better chance if I clear the tension-filled air between us. No matter if I feel ready, I'll speak to her tonight.

Chapter 26

Nadiette

"You must try harder." I walk through the groups of originators struggling to pull lucent. "The soldiers you're assigned to depend on your strength, your magic."

Sweat marks the white uniforms beneath their arms and down their backs at the effort to keep up a sufficient amount of magic—until suddenly, the lucent is gone. The orbs of light snuff out in their palms, leaving every originator grasping at nothing. Several faint, falling to the floor amidst shouts. I frown with concern as healers rush across the floor to help those who have collapsed. I look down at my palm, void of any lucent though I try to pull it. Lucent has been weak for years, but never *gone*.

"Nadiette."

I lift my head to find Tryn waving me over to the side of the room.

After ensuring no one has been seriously injured, I smooth out nonexistent creases along my close-fitting white breeches and paste a smile on my face that hides the concern for my originators.

"We are finished today. Take the afternoon off to rest. We'll begin again tomorrow," I say before I take my leave and meet Tryn in the shadows of the hallway she drags me into.

"Renton is here to speak with you," she whispers. The worry in her eyes fills me with annoyance. She gives the man too much credit.

"He's a simple mercenary, Tryn. You've battled far greater than *him*," I chastise as we walk down the hall and turn a corner, where I see him leaning against the stone wall, one boot crossed over the other.

"Good day, Renton," I say as we approach, ignoring the chill draft that suddenly wafts down the hall.

I notice he's dressed in costly buckskin breeches, soft leather boots, and a jacket that would rival the quality of any of Ikar's. He stands and bows low, then rises with a grin so handsome I find my smile wavers. This impeccably dressed man is much different than most mercenaries I've encountered, but I chastise myself just as I did Tryn.

He's just a mercenary.

If anything, it proves he's worthy of the job he's been given, doesn't it? He appears more than capable and has the confidence to match.

The air around us cools drastically, and I resist rubbing my arms to warm them; it's odd for the castle to be so chill on such a warm day, but I shake off the distracting thoughts. Focus is necessary around a man like Renton.

We enter an empty room nearby with two small settees and a delicate table with a large vase of fresh flowers atop it. "Please, sit. I'd like an update on your search for the Tulips."

His gaze darkens, and do I spy gloam about him for just a

moment? That's impossible. I blame the strange thought on my fatigue from training this morning and Tryn's irritating anxiety.

He relaxes lazily onto one of the small settees, legs wide and arms stretched out, resting along the back. "You act as if I answer to you."

"Don't you?" I tip my nose up the smallest bit as I sit beside Tryn on the other settee, unused to being questioned by anyone but Jethonan, Ikar, and Waylon.

I remind myself he *is* working for Waylon and may be deferring to him. That is neither here nor there—he is here, and I expect answers.

He smirks, but neither confirms nor denies my assumption.

I forge ahead, fighting to stay in control. "We have a deal. You'll take care of the Tulips, and you'll return the king and his friends to me."

"Yes... but wasn't your precious king just here?" He makes a tsking sound. "If you can't keep him here longer than three days, what makes you think he'll want to marry you?"

My neck flushes red, and I narrow my eyes at the man.

He begins again, that annoying smile still on his face. "We've been tracking, and I think we may have found a lead on a Tulip. I think you'll be surprised... if she is who I think she is."

I clench my jaw, unwilling to play into his drama like a dog after a treat—I don't care who the woman is. I just need Ikar. "Wonderful. I'm sure you'll have Ikar back to me in no time. I have three weeks."

"Oh, there's a time limit now?" He narrows his eyes.

"Hasn't Waylon told you?" I lift a brow. "He takes the throne in three weeks if we haven't married. That won't happen though, will it?" I ask as if it's a question, but my tone is threatening.

"No, it won't."

Chills race across my skin at the promise, or is it from how cold the room has become?

He smirks darkly, and why do I feel as if he laughs at me behind the blue of his eyes? He stands and straightens his jacket, and I'm sure I see a flicker of gloam about his shoulders. I blink quickly to clear my vision, and it disappears.

He bows once more, a mocking grin twitching about his lips. "Three weeks, then."

Chapter 27

Vera

If I thought I was drawn to him before, it's nothing like this. I feel as if I could find him anywhere—eyes closed, with only my magic to guide me. The feeling is startling, overwhelming, and one I'm not sure I'll ever get used to. After some trial and error throughout the day, I discovered that the closer I am to Ikar the more unruly and pushy my magic is. I figured out how far he'd let me hang behind, and then we found an unspoken, acceptable distance. Once that was settled, I spent the day sharing dried fruit with Rupi and tried to keep my eyes off Ikar's broad shoulders and long, muscular legs as we trekked through dense, gloamy forest.

He acts as if nothing has changed, beyond my being angry with him. Does he truly not feel *anything*? No one has ever explained how this is supposed to work, and I find myself mildly angry with Tatania. All she ever cared about was telling us to pay the dues and stay away from anyone close to a king. That's it—entirely unhelpful for the situation I find myself in. I remind myself that Ikar is the type to face issues head-on, unlike me, and I'm positive he would've confronted me about it by now if he'd felt something. The thought gives me a measure of relief.

But that relief is short-lived because there's no reprieve from the pull while we're together. Even here, sitting across the fire from him where we camp tonight, I can still feel the way my magic reacts to his. It's practically drooling, and it irritates me because my magic is a perfect match for my feelings and now it all feels amplified.

I look down at my hands and focus on trying to get better at tying up the loose threads of new lucent. I finally get what feels like a strong knot set, then risk a glance up only to see clear intention in his eyes when they lock on mine across the heat of the crackling fire. I don't know what he intends, but it's something, and it has me feeling both warm and panicked. The flames flicker and snap, sending sparks as he stands. I resist the urge to cower as he makes his way around it and stands before me as the entire lucent knot I worked so hard for unravels. I feel a mere touch of his hot magic that my cool magic yearns for, and I suck in a breath. It was only a moment. So fast that if I wasn't hyperaware I may have missed it. I wonder for a moment if I possibly imagined it.

"I need to speak with you for a moment." His voice is low, as if there are others listening and it's meant only for me. He looks all shades of serious, which ignites both physical attraction and a fiery pit of fear in my belly. Even Rupi looks up from where she forages for insects in the dry grass close by. Does he realize what I am? Have I been found out?

I give a curt nod, because what else am I supposed to do? He takes it as permission to sit beside me as I shove my trembling hands between my knees to hide the show of emotion. For a moment, all I can hear is the crackling of the flames and the weak chirp of crickets in the gloamy shadows around us.

His shirt sleeves are still rolled up from the heat of the day, revealing forearms that are entirely too distracting for such a serious situation. I try not to fidget or stare as I wait for him to speak, and I can't help but feel a wave of sadness at the distance between us. He appears guarded and uncomfortable, and sweat beads on my skin as I wait to see what horrid topic he feels the need to discuss with me—none of them can be good.

He starts slowly. "You may have noticed. Or not. I don't know. But... my magic... it... it's..." He pauses while he clears his throat and runs a hand roughly through his hair, leaving it delightfully messy. He seems to be looking everywhere but at me. I've never seen him this uncomfortable... except for maybe when we were choosing a mate bond potion...

My fear dissipates as I suddenly realize what's happening.

"It's what?" I prompt.

If my assumption is correct, I plan to use it in my favor.

"Well, it's..." He hesitates for another moment and looks into the trees. His jaw clenches as if he can't make himself say it.

I lift a brow, which seems to make it worse. "It's coming for me?"

"No," he nearly growls. "I was going to say that it's *misbehaving... broken...* something is wrong with it, and I don't know why."

I feel slightly wicked for enjoying his discomfort. The ever-confident, unflappable *king,* Ikar is stuttering for words before me like a schoolboy, and I find it entirely too irresistible. "So it *is* coming for me."

"Can you *not* say it like that?" he finally snaps.

I fight the smile that tempts the corners of my lips, feeling like the worst sort of scoundrel for leading him to believe his magic is the only thing misbehaving.

"Apparently you've noticed. Just... ignore it." He stands and stalks back to the other side of the fire without waiting for me to respond.

Rupi sends me a scathing look from the forest floor with a narrowed eye turned toward me, but I ignore her attitude. She doesn't understand yet, but this couldn't have gone better. Not only does Ikar believe his magic is *broken*, but he must not recognize mine either, which means I'm hiding it well. I almost pump a celebratory fist in the air. *Finally*, something goes my way.

Ikar refuses to look my way the rest of the night, just stares into the flickering fire, occasionally using a stick to stoke the flames. He remains there as the darkness deepens, and I prepare for bed. I notice the frown he wears when he's deep in thought, the way his forearms are braced on his thighs, and his shoulders appear as if they carry the heaviest of weights—good thing they're broad and very muscular. I assure myself he'll be fine, but guilt burns at the knowledge I've added to that load tonight.

I spot Rupi perched on one of his thighs, side-eyeing me beneath his arm as if *I'm* in the wrong. I narrow my eyes at her. What does she want me to do, spill all my secrets, break my promises, and get my sisters killed? *Absolutely not.*

I flip over on my bedroll angrily. Sometimes I wonder if she'll stay with me or Ikar when all of this is over. I toss and turn restlessly, trying to be quiet so Ikar doesn't notice, but I know it's pointless. He's the most observant man I've ever met, which makes my restlessness even worse.

Finally, once the fire has died low, I drift off.

Tatania stands before me, my Tulip sisters spread out on

*either side of her, facing me, as we recite the Black Tulip
oath in echoing tones:*
*"We will never remove the bracelet and will always pay
our dues on time. We will never reveal our Tulip identity. We will never work with soldiers, armies, or kings
in any way. We will always attend the annual meeting.
We will never bridge with a king."*
*Everyone claps after, except me. I'm crying because now
the past Tulips, the ones who were murdered, rise up
behind them, begging me to keep the Tulips safe,
reminding me in eerie tones, "Kings are murderers. They
can't be trusted." Over and over again. I see the blood on
their bodies and squeeze my eyes shut and clap my hands
over my ears. I try to shout that Ikar isn't a murderer, but
their voices grow louder and louder... and louder...*

A hand shakes me gently within the fog of dreaming.
"Wake up, Vera."

My eyes flash open in the dark with a gasp, and I find Ikar
crouching beside me with a hint of concern in his eyes and a
warm hand resting on my shoulder. I don't know when it
happened, but my hand grasps his wrist so tightly I feel his
pulse beneath my fingertips. He waits for me to make the first
move. For a moment we stay there as images of the dead Tulips
hover on the edges of my vision, the fear and horror of it making
me want to curl into his warm chest and allow his solid presence to block the memory, but I realize painfully that the one
person I want to turn to for comfort is the one I can never ask.

"Sorry for waking you," I whisper.

"No need to apologize. We've all had nightmares."

I force myself to let go of his wrist, even though it feels like

I'm letting go of a lifeline. His fingers slip through mine and he squeezes them gently before he stands and heads back to his bed. I pull my blankets up to my ears, my fear of kings deeply renewed even as I battle confusion over how safe I've always felt with Ikar. As my eyes grow heavy again, I remind myself that not all dreams carry meaning... but deep within, I still hear the echoes of my dead sisters, and I can't help but feel that that nightmare carried a message I'd better pay attention to.

Chapter 28

Vera

I yank the sleeve of my shirt from the grasp of a scraggly bush with pursed lips as I follow Ikar up a rocky, weed-infested incline. Maybe it's the lack of sleep, or maybe it's the nightmare that still nags with images of dead Tulips whenever I close my eyes, but I'm in no mood for the gloamy forest today. What would I give to see the bright color of a healthy butterfly... even just a few patches of soft grass rather than the spindly, spiky twigs that claw and scrape at my boots? I have a stash of items for my future shop, and I occupy myself by mentally examining each one, debating which I would, in fact, trade to see something other than gloam and half-dead vegetation.

We reach the top and Ikar's deep voice breaks me from my contemplative musings. "The arrows."

We stand beside what I can only describe as a never-ending, tightly woven fence of thick, gnarly, unnaturally bent and twined trees that grow as tight as a twisted rope and climb high above us. Ikar points ahead, and I'm tempted to rub my eyes to see if it really is the three gold arrows glinting in weak evening sunlight.

Ikar picks up the pace, motivated by the sign that we're not actually lost. "We should be close. Just need to cross this somehow." He eyes the tight-knit trees with a frown as he continues forward.

"Wonderful." Forced cheer in my voice belies the rush of nerves racing through my belly. We're one step closer to finding the nymphs, who will likely lead us to the dreaded flower. On the other hand, we're also one step closer to escaping this blazing forest—I'm going to choose to focus on *that*.

As we search for a gap wide enough to accommodate Ikar's breadth, I stop and peer through a small opening, curious what awaits us on the other side. The forest looks *healthier* somehow, if we can get past this tree border.

"This look like a fence to you?" I take one last look through the opening before I follow him as he examines the tight weave for a place to pass.

Ikar shrugs. "Of sorts."

"Usually when there's a fence, it means you shouldn't go through it," I say dryly.

"We have to. The velvet widow set us off course, and we don't have time to find a way around. Besides, the three arrows indicate this is the right direction."

"This part does seem to look a bit healthier..." I observe the rich brown colors of the trunks and a few flowers sporadically springing from forest grass with bright color that appear even more beautiful because of the lack these past days—looks like I don't have to trade one of my trinkets after all. I'm tempted to pluck one of the tiny flowers from the soil and keep it, but I can't; this forest needs all the life and color it can get. So after reaching down to touch the soft petals, I continue moving along the treeline.

There's still gloam around us here, but not as much. It reminds me of the forest in Moneyre that I'm used to, well, aside from this tree fence that doesn't seem to end in either direction. Never seen one of these before.

Ikar's expression is pensive, as usual. It's entirely too attractive, so I do my best to keep my focus on our surroundings instead of him—which is a feat in itself. He can be difficult to read when talking isn't an option, which reminds me of the ache I feel over the absence of comfortable conversation we once shared. I'm aware of him walking several feet ahead of me, and at times, I wonder if I feel the whisper of his magic that runs so much warmer than mine. It makes me skittish and grumpy as the day goes on, trying to maintain a facade of perfect indifference when it's the complete opposite of what I feel.

Ikar's mood doesn't seem to be much better than mine. I maintain the necessary distance between us, always responding politely when needed, but it seems as if he's even more broody than he usually is. Whatever the cause, it seems both of us are frustrated.

Why does he have to be the high king?

A rustle nearby pulls me from my thoughts, and I'm positive I catch movement from the corner of my eye. "I think that branch just moved." I eye a long, twisty branch suspiciously, but all I see is Rupi hopping from tree limb to tree limb, happy and completely carefree, above us.

"Oh, look, that one did too," Ikar says dryly, then in a more serious note, adds, "I know you want to find another route, but this is it."

I stare at the branches cautiously. "No, really though."

"You're going to scare yourself if you don't quit," he warns.

I want to assure him that I am not, in fact, scared. But that would be a lie, and my self-imposed distance I'm suddenly beginning to regret keeps me from sidling closer to him for protection, so I keep quiet while I eye the trees warily.

Ikar is already focused on something else as he stops and eyes the width of a space in the trees. "This spot should work."

He removes my pack from his shoulders and pushes it through the gap easily, then turns to the side to squeeze between a space barely wide enough for his broad chest, but he makes it through just fine, aside from a few bits of bark left on his shirt from the tree. If he can fit through, my petite frame should be a breeze. I turn my shoulders, left side first. It should only be a couple of side steps, but as soon as I begin to step through, my right wrist snags on something behind me, and why does it seem the gap is more narrow than it should be?

I wiggle my right hand—it feels as if I accidentally slipped it into a hole, but I don't recall feeling one. I twist and pull, but the friction of tree bark only serves to scrape the sensitive skin of my wrist. I tug a bit with my body weight a few times and only feel my wrist joint click uncomfortably. There's not much space between these two trees where I'm stuck, and it's difficult to maneuver in a way to free myself.

"What's wrong?" Ikar asks. He steps closer, and my magic reacts. I imagine he's already reaching for his sword—it's what he always does at any sign of danger. I'd be irritated at myself for knowing him so well, but right now all I'm concerned about is getting free.

"I'm fine. Just a bit stuck." I'm proud of the absence of panic in my voice.

But it doesn't *feel* fine—somehow it feels as if my hand is more stuck than before. I don't have enough space to turn my shoulders to get access to my arm so I can investigate, and I'm unable to see anything in the near darkness. If I were prone to claustrophobia, I'd begin feeling it about now. How is it that *I* got stuck and Ikar made it through just fine? I can't even turn my head to look at him without scraping a few layers of skin off the tip of my nose.

"Where?"

I wiggle my fingers even though he can't see them. "My right hand."

He steps near my right side. "I'm going to reach across and see if I can loosen it."

I offer a strangled gasp when his chest presses against my shoulder as his hand and arm slide past my stomach, searching for my stuck hand on the other side. He finds my wrist easily, and his fingers gently search for a way to free mine. He smells really good. Too good. And why does my mind jump straight to considering how close this is to a lover's embrace? He's bent rather awkwardly, but still. It doesn't help that my magic is sizzling with him so close.

I force myself to keep my thoughts straight and go back to trying to slip my wrist free, but it still doesn't budge. My magic is raging against the wall of my control, and I feel it all beginning to waver.

"I don't think it's working." My voice comes out sounding a little breathless because I can feel his face very near my neck, and it reminds me of the kisses he left there just days ago.

"It's not." His voice near my ear sends delightful, traitorous shivers dancing across my skin.

We stay in this near-embraced position for another moment while I question all of my decisions to stay away from him. *Is being the high king really all that bad?*

I gather my dignity and coherence, along with my traitorous magic. "Too bad it didn't work. You can move away now."

"You didn't mind being so close a couple weeks ago," he reminds me with a voice so low and deep I just *know* he's trying to torture me.

It's working. Drat him. Why does he insist on reminding me as if I've forgotten? Suddenly I'm grateful my face is stuck between two trees and hidden from sight as a hot blush colors my cheeks. I push a shoulder against his muscular chest, fighting my desire to stay close to him.

He doesn't budge.

"I'm *also* stuck." I can just imagine the roguish glint in his eyes as he says it.

He tries to shift to give me space, but with one arm snug between me and the tree and him bent at an awkward angle, it's not happening.

I panic. His nearness is too much for my resolve, and a feral need to escape rises within me. If I can't have him, I can't be near him. Also, this tree may be trying to eat my hand, and I'd like to keep it. I continue pulling, more forcefully now, jerking my arm like a cornered animal, but in the process, my shoulder knocks his chin upward and he curses.

"That is *not* helping," he growls.

He's right. It seems like he's always right. Drat him twice.

I pull at my wrist again.

"Can you be still for *one* moment?"

I can, but not because he asked me to. He's a king, and I don't take orders from him. But I'm positive I feel the tree move, and I freeze. It doesn't release us, but slowly changes shape, twisting and creaking all around us.

"Ikar..." My voice rises several octaves as I look down and see nothing but the forest floor growing farther from us as we continue rising with the twisting and growing tree trunk. We end up surrounded by branches in a basket like enclosure in the tree tops, bits of much-missed sunlight filtering through the loose weave of crisscrossed branches and fluttering green leaves. Our hands are freed, and I find myself tucked beneath his shoulder, my hand clutching his solid waist. We stand silently for a long moment, waiting to see what the tree will do next, but nothing happens.

"What do we do now?" I whisper, worried the tree will hear me.

Ikar tries prying apart the weave around us with his free hand, but it holds strong. He slams a fist against it.

I pull magic and offer it to him—pure lucent. "Try again."

He slams it again; this time, it cracks a bit with the extra strength he's gifted with. But the crack disappears quickly, and a new leaf sprouts from the same spot. *That's odd.*

"What about your sword?" I suggest it only because his is much bigger than mine.

The affronted look Ikar gives me tells me that it was a horrid suggestion. "It's not an *axe*."

I roll my eyes.

After over an hour of trying to pry the branches apart, we sink to the floor of our branch prison as far apart as we can get from each other. Even with the effort, our shoulders remain only inches apart. After a while, Ikar begins to sprawl out, lying back and crossing one leg over the other. I pull my knees to my chest and wrap my arms around them, attempting to keep my distance, but it's difficult when his large form takes up most of the small space.

I spend two hours spewing random guesses at magical keywords that will make the tree move.

"Dragon's blood."

I count five seconds under my breath. Rupi gives an encouraging chirp from outside the tightly woven branches.

Nothing.

"Nestberry."

Nothing.

"Blackipor."

Ikar snorts.

I give him an affronted look. "I'm running out of ideas."

He appears completely relaxed with an arm thrown over his eyes as if he's about to sleep. "Thank the blazes."

I would smack him in the arm, but I need to keep my hands off him.

I scoff. "Do you have a better idea?"

"Nope."

He looks so calm and unflustered while I struggle and appear to be the only one affected by our proximity, and that irritates me. After days of doing everything I can to keep my distance, it seems all of it was for naught.

We don't say much as the suns descend. This is complete torture.

Ikar is both the first and the last person I want to be stuck in a tree with. Even if we wanted to do something, like kiss, we couldn't because he's a blasted king. The only option is to talk, and I'm about to lose my mind, so talk it is.

"What does a day in the life of a king look like when you're not adventuring for magical plants?" I ask, somewhat blandly and with a hint of sarcasm. I swallow my pride like a hot lump of coal to be the one to act like things are fine first.

"It doesn't seem like you actually want to know."

"I actually *do*, or I wouldn't have asked." I soften my voice. "I really would like to know."

He finally drops his arm from his face and looks up at me.

"No two days are alike. When I'm at the castle, on any given day, I have to meet with several different advisors and leaders, those meetings can take hours. I also join my army in training and on expeditions, visit with the people, tour the kingdom, oversee the low kings, write correspondence, meet with delegates from other countries... all sorts of things."

"And what do you do in your personal time?"

He scoffs and mutters, "Personal time?"

"You must have *some*."

He thinks for a moment. "A little. I often read in my rooms, hunt with Arrow and Simon, and I do enjoy training. I spend time with Champion, my horse..." I'm about to ask about his horse, but he adds, "I also often sneak food from the kitchens after supper."

I laugh. He says it so seriously that I can't decide if he's joking. "You're the king. You don't need to sneak food; they're your kitchens."

"You've never met my cook."

"She must be terrifying."

There's a humorous gleam in his eye. "Very."

"What is worth the danger of sneaking past this terrifying cook, then?"

"There's these pastries..." He closes his eyes as if he's savoring one right now.

I laugh loudly, and Ikar grins. For a moment, all is well between us.

We're just two regular people who feel for each other, who are stuck in a tree. We talk late into the night, and I let myself revel in the feelings of normalcy between us, even though I know it can't last. This is all temporary. *It has to be.*

A low thrumming sound, as if a hummingbird is hovering nearby, wakes me from sleep. My eyes flutter open for a moment, then sleepily close again, the pillow far too comfortable to face waking. *Pillow?*

"Vera," Ikar whispers, but I hear the pleasant rumble of it beneath my ear.

"Hm."

"Wake up." He jostles me gently, and I force my eyes open only to find my head settled comfortably against his broad chest, and his arm wrapped around me.

I'd take a moment to die of embarrassment, since it's apparent it was *me* that moved toward *him* at some point in the night, but there's no time when I see what's before us. I scramble to sitting as a small being that appears to be a mix of tree bark and fairy hovers above us, standing the length of one of my hands, wings beating as quickly as the hummingbird I thought I heard.

"What are you?" She tilts her head to the side inquisitively as she hovers before us.

"Soldiers sent by the king of Moneyre. We're in search of the nymphs," Ikar says.

"Nymphs, you say?" She spins and swoops down before she comes so close to Ikar's face he nearly has to back away. To his credit, he doesn't even flinch.

"They don't like outsiders," she whispers. "And neither do I."

"So they still exist," Ikar says with satisfaction.

She backs away so quickly she becomes a blur before my eyes, then stops. "Never said that." She eyes us carefully. "It's been a very long time since I've seen humans here. You *are* humans, aren't you? You're very entertaining." She swoops near me and pokes me in the arm. "And this one has lucent." Her wings seem to beat twice as fast, which I wouldn't have known was possible.

"What are *you*?" I ask, ignoring her comment about my lucent.

"A nymph, of course. Can't you tell by the beauty of my tree? My name is Endri." She eyes us closely, and I get the idea we may offend her if we don't tread carefully. I look to Ikar, at a loss for how to respond to this odd creature.

He steps in. "Can you take us to Odella?"

She tilts her head and thinks for a moment. "And what shall you do for me?"

Ikar and I glance at each other. *He's* the king here. I'm sure he'll find a way out of this.

"Restore lucent." He's never sounded more confident.

The flying lady laughs so hard it nearly sounds like high-pitched squeaking.

Ikar remains expressionless.

"Impossible. But you can give me the woman. I need lucent."

I'm sitting so close to him that I feel his muscles tense, but you'd never be able to tell from the easy smile that turns his lips.

"The woman is more trouble than she's worth."

I'd balk at that, but if it keeps me from becoming a nymph's plaything, I'll go with it. The branches around us shift and wind a little tighter, and I find my hand wrapped around Ikar's upper arm. Rupi appears unperturbed as she watches from outside our prison, eyeing the nymph with curiosity. Either that means Endri's not dangerous, or something is terribly wrong with my bird who's usually very protective—given that she loves the king I'm currently clutching, it could most definitely be the latter.

"I must speak with Odella," Ikar reminds her, and the little being frowns at his tone.

"It's been a very long time since Odella allowed anyone entrance. I think you'll likely be killed," Endri says. "Even *I* have not been able to gain entrance since she locked her doors."

"Odella won't kill me." Ikar has never sounded more sure. "She'll want lucent restored as much as I do."

She tilts her head thoughtfully and stares at him for a moment. "You truly believe you can restore lucent?"

Ikar nods, confidence unwavering. If not for the creases at the corners of his eyes that I've come to realize belie his worry, I'd believe him too.

She comes closer, her interest piqued. "I'll show you to the entrance and Odella can decide... on one condition."

"What's that?"

"You must take me with you. When Odella closed off the passage, I waited too long. I didn't realize that the forest would die so quickly... If you're so sure you won't be killed, I'd like to return with you."

Ikar agrees with a nod. "If Odella allows it."

Immediately the tree twists and turns until we're standing on the forest floor once again, and the limbs that surrounded us silently draw back. It's then I notice that I still hold tightly to Ikar, and it pleases my magic, so I grudgingly pull my hand away and hold to my pack straps instead. They don't offer the same effect as gripping his bicep, but they'll have to do, I suppose.

The fluttering woman takes off ahead. Ikar and I look at each other, then follow after her. But before we get much farther, she spins around quickly.

"I forgot to mention... my tree caught two others. Do you know them?"

Chapter 29

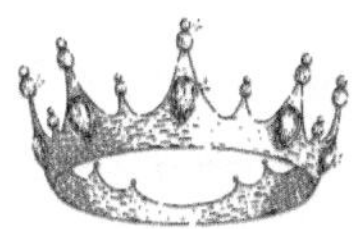

Ikar

We follow Endri quietly, taking in our surroundings. To go from dead, gloamy forest to this—a forest where the branches and trees are twisty, but look healthy, and where there are only small bits of gloam in the shadows—is almost shocking. There are bright flowers and long, dewy blades of grass, and bushes heavy with dark berries that Rupi stops to peck at, staining her white feathers purple as she hops within the bushes. I've known that nymphs are connected to nature by their type, but I didn't realize the extent.

I frown, confused. "Are we already within the land of the nymphs?"

Endri laughs and looks over her shoulder with a grin. "Oh no. Wait until you see what's within. I'm sure they've fared better than I."

"How have you survived this long?" I ask.

Endri drops back a bit to continue the conversation. "Odella, of course. Her magic has lasted much longer than any other, and she supports those of us who are left. We aren't far from her, and her magic sustains me, but my tree has been weakening... It's time to join the others before it's too late. Though without lucent, I guess we all die eventually." She spins around in the air and faces us, forcing me to stop abruptly so I don't crash into her. "But I told you I can only take you to the entrance. Whether you're admitted or not is up to Odella. If she denies you, you'll be killed."

"All I ask is to get to the entrance," I remind her.

I just have to hope that Odella will listen before attacking.

I glance at a wide-eyed Vera. She leans closer. "That other route is sounding really good about now."

"We don't have time."

"Better than being killed!" she hisses.

"She's not going to kill me."

I hope.

"She doesn't even *know* you."

"She will soon."

I hear her mutter something about stubborn, cocky, arrogant rulers, and I smirk, which prompts an even deeper frown that tempts me to smile wider. "Just trust me."

"It would be easier if you weren't the *king*," she whispers, glancing at Endri ahead to make sure she's not listening.

"Most trust me because I *am*. Why don't you? You'd be the plural wife of the shifter king if not for me," I remind her with a raised brow.

Vera snorts, but it quickly turns into a laugh that warms my chest as the scowl on her face softens. "I admit, I'm grateful you returned"—I see the lighthearted challenge in her eyes before she continues—"but I think I was doing pretty good on my own."

Now it's my turn to laugh. "If you consider being stuck

beneath the edge of a tent wearing a dress of animal heads *doing pretty good,* then, yeah, sure."

She frowns. "I merely needed to get Collette's head unstuck."

I shake my head in genuine disbelief. "I still can't believe you named them."

"You almost ripped her ear off."

"Got you out, didn't I?"

"Barely."

"Just admit it. I take good care of you."

She presses her lips together, but I take it as a win that she doesn't deny it.

"They're just ahead," Endri announces.

I quicken my pace, but I can already hear Darvy and Rhosse. I smother a grin as they come into view. Both men are wrapped in smooth branches high above the ground, their feet dangling in the air. But the relief on their faces to see us alive tells me they believed the worst had happened.

"You can let them go; these are my friends," I tell Endri. She flies up to hover before Rhosse's face.

"This one took an axe to my beloved tree." She pokes his shoulder with her other hand fisted on her hip as her wings beat even faster.

Rhosse growls with frustration. "How was I to know it was yours? It came for our weapons."

"We'll not do anything to harm your tree or any of the nymphs. Release them," I say.

Endri glares at him with narrowed eyes, then the tree lowers them to the ground and lets them loose. Darvy stumbles out and groans as he stretches his neck from side to side.

Rhosse eyes Endri with dark eyes. "I'll be needing my axe back."

Endri huffs, and suddenly Rhosse's enchanted axe comes hurtling from the tree branches and lands before his feet with a thud, sharpened edge planted in the ground. He grabs the weapon and inspects it with a critical eye.

"This is Endri. She's taking us to the nymph entrance," I inform Darvy and Rhosse. "How far is it, Endri?"

"Less than half a day's walk and we'll reach the entrance to see if Odella will grant you entrance... or kill us all for trying."

Chapter 30

Vera

I don't know what I expected the entrance to the nymphs to look like... a waterfall? A beautiful tree path? Something... not like this.

Endri leads us inside an enormous cave. It's blazing scary if you ask me—all dark and echoing and cold with odd engravings on its walls. Rupi doesn't appear to like it either, given the way she huddles beside Ikar's neck. I would also love to huddle against him, but he's the blazing king, so I keep my distance like I know I should, watching him walk ahead while I feel irritated by the situation all over again.

I bring a small lucent orb to life in my hand, just enough to light the ground beneath our feet, and follow grudgingly. Unlike the velvet widow cave, the ceiling of this cave is high and the ground solid and unnaturally smooth. I eye the engravings on the wall, looking for violent images that would warn us away, but I don't understand any of them... I'm not sure whether to feel relieved or more concerned. There have been no turns to take, so surely, if we need to escape, we can.

I'm sure if Endri hears that I doubt her as a guide she'll be offended and decide not to show us the way, so I lean closer to Darvy and lower my voice to a whisper. "What happens if this cave ends up going nowhere?"

"We'll turn around, of course." He says it so jauntily I want to smack him in the arm.

I envy his carefree spirit and the fact his magic isn't lunging for a forbidden lover. I'm not sure how many more days I can keep my sanity intact with the way my magic yearns for Ikar.

Eventually Rhosse and Darvy take the lead, following Endri around the twists and turns of the cave. I eye their backs, confused by feelings of relief to have found them again, but resenting that they were in on the *worst* of secrets. I can't help but admit I feel betrayed by them, as well, but I don't have it in me to bring it up with the two of them. What good will it do? I just need to finish this blazing mission and disappear. I ignore the rebellious ache in my heart at the thought of never seeing the three of them again and remind myself that it's for the best.

I can't linger on those thoughts long because Ikar walks behind me, and I'm highly aware of how my magic so badly wants him now that we are in this quiet, dark space, and there's nothing to distract myself with. I try to fill my mind with thoughts about the nymphs, which is a mistake because now I have to ask questions. I tell myself it's only because I want to be prepared, that I don't *need* to hear the sound of his voice or walk beside him, but my magic and I both know it's a lie.

I look over my shoulder and slow my steps until Ikar catches up. I meet his questioning gaze as he comes to walk by my side.

"I've heard you discuss the nymphs, that they should be able to lead us to the"—I clear my throat and force the next word out—"flower. Why are they so special?"

"As far as I know, a king hasn't visited the nymphs since the last time a black tulip was retrieved from the Field of Tulips, which was hundreds of years ago. But at that time, there was a queen named Odella who was a seer and a powerful magic user. Sort of like the fae... the nymphs have always existed in their own realm, mostly unseen by humans, then lucent magic drew those creatures to our realm, and they settled in—there are benefits to having them here."

I snicker. "I won't tell Drade you consider him a creature."

Ikar grins, and for a moment I sense normalcy between us, and I savor it.

"The fae have their own realms that I have no authority over," he explains, "but here in Moneyre I do, since some of their people choose to live in the human realm—and that means Drade and I have to do our best to get along."

"He doesn't seem to like you," I say bluntly.

"He doesn't like *anyone.*" Ikar looks down at me with a thoughtful expression. "Except you."

Our hands brush as we walk, and I can't help the twitch of my fingers that gives away the instinctive urge to have them entwined in his...

"Don't think he likes me much either, actually," I muse. It's true. How could he after how I took off the way I did?

Ikar shakes his head. "You're wrong. I've thought about it for days... and I think I know what you did to him, Vera."

I can't tell if he's joking or not, but the sound of my name on his lips has my heart skipping beats. My mouth opens, but no words come out. *What does that mean?*

"Did you love him?" he asks, not waiting for a response.

"Love hi—What?" I sputter.

Rupi bounces back and forth across Ikar's shoulder, apparently sensing the tension between us.

"So you did."

Why do his eyes darken in the shadows when he says it, as if he's jealous? I can't think straight and my words come out like an uncontrollable avalanche.

"No. We were young. We had a lot of fun." I glance up to see a scowl on his face. "We got along, but it never would have worked. It was nothing like—"

He raises a brow, and I realize our steps have slowed.

"Nothing like what?"

Nothing like this. He and I.

I frown at him, done answering his questions. I stuff my feelings into a manageable corner of my heart and remind myself that I've never actually *loved* anyone, so how should I know? I can't love a king, especially the one standing beside me. And if we're going to step into past relationship territory, I have questions of my own.

"Nadiette. Did you love *her?*"

A slow smile turns his lips in the shadows as his gaze holds mine. "I thought I did, but I've learned recently that what I felt was never more than friendship. She'll always be a good friend, but never more."

Why does my heart pound with delight at those words? Why do I assume he's implying feelings for me when that can never be? I force myself to look away, and I finally see warm light ahead, beginning to light the cave and stealing our moment of shadow-shrouded privacy.

Ikar looks my way. "Does Drade still have a chance?"

"Well, he did win the challenge..." I laugh at the affronted look on his face.

"That was a *draw.*"

I offer a one-shoulder shrug. "Was it though? No one actually saw. You looked pretty beat up." *And incredible.*

I remember that night well.

The look on his face when he's about to argue with me is so attractive my breath hitches, but before he can say anything, Rhosse and Darvy stop behind Endri.

Her high-pitched voice carries through the cave. "It's just around the corner. When you walk beneath the light, it will alert the guards."

She gestures with a hand for us to move past her. The way Ikar's hand goes to his sword doesn't escape my notice.

"I thought the nymphs were supposed to be our friends. You were confident Odella wouldn't kill you," I whisper, alarmed at his reaction.

"She won't if she gets a chance to meet me... the guards, I don't know. They were friends two hundred years ago. We'll find out soon if they still are. Prepare to defend yourself, and be grateful if you don't have to."

Spoken like a true warrior.

I sigh and prepare to grab my own sword while pulling lucent just in case. Ahead, I spot what appear to be ancient soldiers sculpted out of the stone walls, their bodies half-protruding with swords and shields grasped in their large hands. I lean around Rhosse to get a better view of what's past the stone guards and find it's merely a sealed off wall that ends the cave. I almost moan at the thought of having to turn around. I thought Endri said this was it.

"This looks like a dead end," I whisper, though I don't know why I'm worried about anything hearing me because it's merely us stuck at the end of a torturously long tunnel.

Endri points to the ceiling with an overly patient look, and my eyes are drawn upward. "Like I said, you must walk beneath."

Gentle streams of light enter through intricate, swirling cutouts in the stone above us that brighten the stone walls, illuminating the faces of the stone soldiers. We step forward, but I'm very aware that Endri hangs back in the shadows—it's apparent she doesn't have much confidence in our survival. My chest tightens with nerves. Just as the warm light touches our skin, the cave walls that hold the soldiers crack and transform, and six living men step forward. I blink quickly several times to ensure I'm not going insane. They move faster than men who were just encased in stone should be able to and form two lines before us, blocking our way. Their bodies are sculpted muscle, and they appear to wear ancient armor over clothing of twined vines, holding swords at their sides with shields raised. Their features are perfectly chiseled and unmoving. They stand so still that they once again appear as statues.

"Go no farther," one of them commands, his voice echoing so loudly off the walls around us that it hurts my ears.

We freeze where we are. I shift my weight and prepare myself to sprint in the other direction, but instead, with an almost unnoticeable nod, Ikar indicates for Rhosse to proceed.

"We are here on behalf of the High King of Moneyre." Rhosse says. "We request a meeting with Queen Odella."

While he speaks, I take a moment to glance at the cave walls around us. Are there other warriors waiting to step out? And what happens if they refuse us entrance? Will they let us leave... or will we be killed before they step back in their walls, as Endri warned?

I swallow tightly and shift closer to Ikar, not caring at the moment how my magic curls in delight and pulls toward his. Better that than being sliced by a cave man.

"Queen Odella will grant passage to one who proves he is the high king."

Rhosse looks back at Ikar and there's a long moment of silence before Ikar steps forward.

I grab his arm without thinking, eyes wide. "What are you doing?" I hiss.

He's gone to great lengths to keep his identity a secret. Why would he blow it now? Besides the fact that those warriors look ready to slay someone at a moment's notice. I don't care to think about why I feel so protective of him.

"Trust me." He looks at the hand on his arm and back to my eyes, and almost tangible heat simmers between us.

I drop my hand instantly, as if I were burned. His eyes linger on mine for a moment longer, then he offers a finger for Rupi to perch on and lifts her to my shoulder, where she happily hops off, before he steps forward.

Blazing impulsive, Vera. I shove my hands in my pockets so I don't make that mistake again.

Ikar steps forward and Darvy and Rhosse step to either side of him, swords drawn. I send lucent their way, not waiting for a fight to start.

"I'm High King," Ikar says, his voice clear and confident.

The tension is tight, and I find myself sweating. This cave may be large, but to battle within these walls? It suddenly seems far too small.

"Your mark," the warrior demands.

My jaw drops at their audacity, but if Ikar is surprised, he masks it well. I notice nothing other than a muscle in his jaw flex as he drops his pack on the ground behind him, takes time to remove his outer armor, hands the pieces to Darvy, then pulls off his shirt in one fluid movement. I wasn't prepared for this, and I fight for my life while breath refuses to fill my lungs.

Let Tatania's rules burn. I need him in my life.

Endri emits a high-pitched gasp of surprise behind me. The mountain warriors bow their heads and speak something in another language, and Ikar inclines his head.

I find my mouth as dry as the sands of the Obsidian Desert as my eyes lock on the scrolling designs of his mark that should still trigger anger, disgust, even fear... but if I were to describe how I feel right now, it most certainly wouldn't be with words like those. I try not to be entranced by the muscles moving in his back as he puts his shirt back on, but I fail miserably.

The warriors part, lining up with their backs against the walls as they wait for us to pass.

Ikar turns to grab the pack he set behind him and meets my eyes... and maybe it's just me feeling guilty about drooling over a man I should hate, but I see knowing in his eyes and the slightest hint of a cocky smile on his lips before he turns forward once more, takes his armor from Darvy, and leads the way out of the cave, no hesitation in his confident stride. *He knows what he does to me.*

There are no shadows beneath the rays of sunshine to cool the fiery heat in my cheeks, so I lift my chin with all the dignity I can muster and pass by the guards after the stone wall slides away. Ikar may have taken his armor from Darvy, but he doesn't take the time to don it, opting for his loose-fitting shirt alone instead. I wish he'd put his armor back on, though; he's too trusting of these foreign people. But maybe that's the message he intends to send—I don't know the way these diplomatic things work.

I keep a steady stream of lucent flowing through my body, just in case it's needed. Endri flies past so quickly that Rupi's fluff blows in her wake as she passes near my shoulder in a blur, not stopping until she reaches the open space beyond the cave as if afraid she'd get left out again.

I can't blame her, and I hurry to catch up.

She immediately approaches Ikar with a dramatic bow, then she meets his eyes with a quirked smile. "I thought you were lying when you told me you were trying to restore lucent just to escape my trap... Now that I know you're the king, I hope you're successful. Thank you for gaining entrance for me."

Ikar nods, but before he can say anything, she's speeding away toward one of the most beautiful sights I've ever seen in my life—a forest alive with lucent. I'm ready to skip into the treeline and spin in circles at the scene before us. It teems with sunlight—no gloam to be seen. Towering trees with huge trunks and thick, healthy bark reach into the sky. Soft grasses grow from rolling hills and bend in a whispery breeze, and flowers of every color and variety dot their expanse. A blue sky with wispy white clouds above us reveals the three suns, and I savor the feeling of warmth on my face. A river runs through, its water sparkling and clear, almost rainbowish in its reflection.

My jaw drops in awe. The Lucent River... as it's supposed to look... but *how?*

We walk through a tall grassy area that leads down from the cave and into the giant trees, and I pick up my pace to catch up with Ikar. Specks of gold float in the warm air, and a soothing feeling washes over me that makes me want to drop my pack and nestle into the soft grass, dip my toes in the river, and nap beneath these towering trees. Rupi is just as ecstatic as I, fluttering from branch to branch, trilling a song I've never heard but that exudes perfect joy, keeping pace with us from above.

"How is this place here?" I ask Ikar quietly.

"The Queen of the Nymphs, Odella. There's a reason this small portion of the forest remains alive with lucent, and it's because nymphs are directly connected to the earth and their magic is powerful. If a nymph's tree dies, the nymph will die. A river nymph, or naiad, will die if their river dries up," he says. "So if Odella had succumbed to the gloam as we feared..."

"This would all be dead too," I whisper.

I've grown so used to a world filled with darkness that I didn't realize how it might have been before.

Another nymph appears from behind a large tree trunk in front of us. I try not to stare, but I've never seen anyone with light-pink hair, green skin, and leaf ears. Even with the differences, she radiates pure beauty. She wears a pink flower as a dress—upside down with its petals forming a bell skirt that reveals her bare feet beneath, with a lone petal as a bodice. A choker of twined vines encircles her neck to match the twined crown on her head. Her appearance is so fragile and delicate that I'm afraid to breathe too hard, worried my breath might cause the petals of her dress to blow away.

She curtsies to Ikar. "Your Majesty, allow me to lead you to Queen Odella."

Ikar nods and we follow along, but I can't stop staring at the little forest nymph and the way her hair flows down her back, brushing the ground behind her, waving back and forth gently as she skips ahead of us. She leads us on a winding path deeper into the forest.

"It seems we're not alone," Rhosse says so low I nearly miss it.

I immediately look closer at our surroundings, and my eyes widen when I notice a tiny face that at first glance appears to be a leaf... Another could be mistaken as the boulder it trembles behind, and another miniature one rides on the back of a small red bird, who circles us once before racing for the treetops again.

We follow a meandering path that weaves in and out of thick forest, at times traveling right alongside the rushing

Lucent River that I can hardly keep my eyes from. The path eventually splits, one side going to the right, deeper into the forest, and the other is a bridge, of sorts, made of intricately woven vines and stretching across the rushing, sparkling depths of the Lucent River. I press my lips together. Bridges and I don't always get along, and I don't swim well enough to risk falling into the Lucent River.

Ikar tests the vine bridge first, and when it holds beneath one of his boots, he looks back at Rhosse with a shrug and continues forward. Rhosse goes next. I watch how the vines give a little beneath their boots warily, but it holds.

Darvy gestures with one hand for me to go next. "Lead the way."

I wrinkle my nose. He gives me a gentle nudge to get my boots moving.

"I'm going," I grumble.

"Isn't it beautiful?" Darvy asks from behind me, sounding overly cheerful about the situation.

"Quite," I mutter.

"I enjoy the unimpeded view we get without a handrail."

"Aren't you scared of *anything*?" I ask with a growl as the vines bounce with the movement of so many who are heavier than I.

I envy the nymph who continues to skip ahead without fear.

"Of course I have fears."

"So nice to hear you're normal."

"—Just not very many of them."

I roll my eyes. "Tell me *one*. Help me feel better."

"Let me think for a moment," he says so seriously I almost laugh. But I don't because I'm still angry with him.

"An animal?" I ask, trying to help.

"No..."

"Dying?"

"Not really."

"Water?"

"No."

"Spiders?"

"Nah."

"Deathstalkers?"

"Everyone is afraid of those."

I can't help but laugh this time.

"Women?" It was only supposed to be a joke, but his hesitation piques my interest.

"*One* woman."

I look back with so much surprise that I almost topple off the edge. Darvy grabs my forearm and sets me back on the path while I exclaim over his admission.

"You're afraid of a woman? *Why?*"

He smiles somewhat tightly. "I think I've given enough of an answer for now."

He's right—I should be glad he admitted as much as he did, but I can't resist digging a little deeper. "Just one more question."

"Ask it, and I'll decide if I answer."

I step carefully along the vine bridge, trying to focus on keeping my balance while also sating my curiosity. "Family member or love interest?"

He doesn't respond for a few moments. "Fine. *Past* love interest."

I look back to see his expression guarded, and I know I won't be learning anything else today. I send him a commiserating half-smile over my shoulder. He might not know it, but I sort of understand. My heart is in the midst of breaking—only held together with the temporary glue of being in Ikar's presence.

I'm pulled from my thoughts when we finally leave the bridge and are led along another shorter path and up a set of beautiful smooth rock steps. When we reach the top, my eyes widen at the small clearing that spreads before us. In the center is a smooth wood throne covered in flowers and vines, where a woman so ethereally beautiful sits that I reach up and gingerly touch my dirty hair, feeling extra grungy. Somehow being covered in dried spider blood and layers of dirt didn't matter so much until now. I tuck a few stray strands behind my ear as if it'll make a difference.

Her skin is green, like the nymph who led us here... I nearly envy it. Her hair falls in dark green waves around her, making her light blue eyes that sparkle like the Lucent River even more pronounced. Flowers adorn her hair throughout its long length, and intricately woven vines make up her dress where more bloom. I watch as a small flower slowly unfurls within her hair and try to keep my mouth from hanging open. Another blooms along the length of her vine-woven dress. She appears to be a literal, growing part of the forest.

She rises from her throne and curtsies deeply to Ikar. I step back even further, aware that I'm nowhere near royalty and feeling like a complete outsider. I bump into Darvy behind me, who steadies me with a gentle hand.

"It's been one hundred twenty-five years since a king visited last," Queen Odella says in a voice as light and beautiful as the whisper of leaves rustling in the wind.

Ikar nods. "My apologies. There are many things I attempt to make right."

She smiles slowly. "Come."

Chapter 31

Vera

Odella waits a moment to walk beside Ikar, all grace and peaceful elegance. They immediately fall into quiet conversation, leaving the rest of us to follow. I feel a nasty sting in my core at the sight of the two of them. Her beauty matches his effortless good looks, and from the appearance of their easy conversation, they get along well.

But I can't focus on that for long because right before us are large flat leaves wrapped around a large tree trunk that create a set of steps that look too fragile to actually use, but Ikar follows Odella without hesitation. Darvy follows next, and Rhosse motions me to go before him. I tentatively step on the first leaf, and even though I've seen three others use the steps before me, I still expect it to fold beneath the weight of my boot... but it doesn't. So I step on the next and the next as we circle the trunk upward. Above, I continue to hear the occasional word and the deep timbre of Ikar's voice, and the uncomfortable feeling in my belly continues to grow. I'm so distracted by Odella's light, tinkling laughter that I miss a step, and my foot falls through a gap.

Rhosse snatches me by the arm and sets me back on my feet.

"Careful there," he growls.

But as I steady myself, Darvy whispers over his shoulder. "He means... quit being jealous and focus on not falling out of the tree."

I whip my gaze to his, finding a completely unapologetic look on his face. "That is *not* what happened."

The commotion has Ikar and Odella peering down through a gap above to see what's going on, and my cheeks heat. Ikar eyes me closely. I'm reminded that with plentiful lucent here, he can surely pull magic to increase any of his strengths without my help—including his hearing. I inwardly groan knowing he likely heard everything.

"Continue on," Rhosse says, but he watches me as if he's waiting for me to fall through another gap.

I try to ignore him and pay extra close attention to these stupid branches so I don't draw further attention to myself while I seethe. I want to rage at Darvy. Scream at him that he's wrong. Punch him for suggesting it. I am *not* jealous. This feeling is simply stress curdling like sour milk in my belly knowing we are close to finding out if the Field of Tulips still exists.

Everyone but the cozy couple ahead is silent as we follow them through twisty treetop paths. The humidity and warmth of this little piece of lucent land has my hair springing up into fuzzy fly-aways that refuse to be poked back into my braid or stay behind my ears, making me feel extra frustrated as we trail behind a stunning forest queen. The leaves above us form a canopy roof, and within those leafy branches, I spot numberless colorful birds of all varieties whose songs blend and mix in ways I've never heard—it would be calming if I wasn't so riled up.

Just as I begin to feel the first waves of dizziness from the height of our ascent, we reach the top. Odella walks forward across space between trees that's empty—one that would have me free-falling to the forest floor, but solid wood grows and reaches outward from beneath her feet with every step, creating a gleaming balcony that spreads out around us, long and wide. I watch with continued amazement as a table and chairs fit to grace a royal dining room arises, growing from the wood itself.

Once everything is still, Odella gestures to the head seat, and Ikar nods his thanks. He seats Odella to his right before he seats himself, and she smiles kindly as she waits for the rest of us to sit. I have the urge to race Rhosse for the chair second to Ikar's left, not wanting to torture myself by sitting right beside him and unable to say it out loud since his blazing hearing is so good. Instead I hang back momentarily, trying to get Darvy or Rhosse to sit to Ikar's left, but to no avail. They're both too gentlemanly to let me have my way.

They usher me toward the table, and Rhosse pulls out the chair for me.

"Thank you," I offer tightly.

I scooch up to the table, feeling flustered, and suddenly find my knee pressing straight into Ikar's solid thigh. I make the mistake of glancing up to meet his blue eyes that are just as aware as I feel. My lucent hums with pleasure, rushing toward him as if I've given it permission with the accidental contact. I snatch the rebel magic back.

Odella didn't appear to make enough space at her table for the height of these men. I attempt to move to the left toward Rhosse, but it only bumps my chair into his awkwardly, and I realize if I attempt to scootch anywhere else, I'll be drawing attention. I finally give up and slide back in my chair until my back is straight against it, leaving my knee a whisper from Ikar's leg, and sigh, causing all the fly-aways to float out around my face. I accept that this isn't my best moment.

Ikar shifts just then, relaxing into his seat and allowing his long legs to stretch out, appearing without care as his thigh presses more firmly against my knee now—with nowhere for me to go. I see the smallest hint of a grin on his lips, but he turns his attention to Odella when she says his name in a magically soft way that makes me tense.

I direct my gaze to the edge of the balcony so I don't do something ridiculous, like leap over the table and throttle her. It's then I realize there is no edge or railing to this balcony; it just simply... ends, offering a full and unimpeded view of the healthy, vast forest beyond. I admit, it's incredible in a way I can't describe. I even spot a waterfall in the distance that I would love to investigate.

Rupi flutters to the edge, perching alongside a flock of vibrantly-colored birds in hues of red, blue, and purple. She hops excitedly amongst the bunch, appearing to have made friends easily enough. For a moment, she meets my eye, and I can't help but smile at the way her fluff blows in the gentle breeze and how relaxed she seems. It makes visiting the nymph queen worth it, even though it makes me feel like a raggedy pauper.

Rupi and her gang take flight a moment later, and once again I'm left staring at the blunt edge of the fancy wood floor beneath us. If this woman wanted to kill us, would she simply tilt the floor and slide us off? It's a morbid thought. But better to think of that than the heat I feel from Ikar's thigh still pressed to my knee. I try not to move. At all.

A nymph dressed in similar petals to the first sets food before me. What looks to be fresh roots, seeds, perfectly ripened fruit, and fresh-caught fish lay within a large vein-covered, green leaf. I sigh in relief. No bugs—this, I can handle. The fae eat in a similar way, but they do enjoy their insects. I think of my teenage years with Mama Tina and the variety of insect dishes she served at her fancy parties: sides of queen-ant eggs, salted grasshoppers with a dash of lime, cocktails garnished with worm salt among others. I gag just thinking of it.

I lift a crunchy root to my mouth and chew, but when Odella lowers her voice, I wish I'd chosen something softer so I can listen better.

"Your mark is black," she says bluntly, her vivid blue eyes flashing.

Ikar smiles in a self-deprecating way. "Your guards told you."

A fiery urge to defend him rises to my lips. She should know how much weight and guilt he carries, how he worries about his people... but I keep quiet. What am I going to say? He's doing everything he can, and I care about him... except I also want him to fail, and I hate him? I cringe as I realize that's the truth of my feelings. It doesn't sit well. I've never been more emotionally confused in my life.

"They don't have to tell me," she says softly. "I'm connected to everything here."

"Then you know it's not completely black."

She nods. "Which means we still have time, short though it is. The shadows have been devouring my nymphs, sucking the life from them as it spreads. It's only this small portion of the mountain left." She looks out over the forest that spreads before us. It's difficult to think that this part of the forest is struggling when it appears so vibrant and full, but apparently she considers this *small*, and it makes me wonder what it used to be like.

"I can't maintain it forever." The tone of her voice tells me she has accepted her fate as she turns her wrist over, and my eyes widen with shock at the black that darkens her veins and crawls up her arm.

Chapter 32

Ikar

I eye the black streaks traveling up her lower arm with concern. "That's why we're here. We search for the Field of Tulips."

"Have you found a Queen of the Night?" Odella asks.

I force calm into my voice. "Not yet."

Her eyes hook on Vera, curious.

"That's our originator," I add, clearing up any confusion.

Vera looks up, and Odella tilts her head to the side, meeting her gaze.

"Your hand?" Odella gracefully extends one light-green hand midway across the table toward Vera, who looks at me, unsure.

I offer an encouraging nod. She hesitantly stretches her hand out. I watch with interest as Odella folds her fingers around Vera's. I'd mentioned that Odella is a seer, but it is rare to receive knowledge from one. Seer visions can't be requested—only offered. I wonder if Vera understands the gravity of the moment.

The vines that are settled in a fancy crown on Odella's silky hair loosen and glide down her arm, twining around both their hands, then traveling up Vera's arm and around her neck. I can hear her heart pounding from here as she watches, but I know Odella won't hurt her. Vera stiffens when they reach the back of her neck, fear pronounced in her gray eyes.

I'm about to call Odella off, but suddenly she speaks, her eyes flashing gold. "Lucentia favors you greatly. Out of many who are weak, you are strong. Do your duty, and you will help in restoring lucent to our kingdom. Beware of one whom you're inclined to trust..."

Her gold eyes hold Vera's as if silently communicating with her, and I clench my jaw in frustration that I don't know what's being said.

The vines retract, and Vera sits back against her chair almost violently, fear lighting her eyes.

Lucentia favors her? Her duty? It makes sense, I guess. She is a gifted originator—the best I've ever seen, if I'm honest. Her help on this journey *will* help in restoring lucent if I retrieve the flower. Which it sounds like I might from Odella's revelation—that thought brings a hint of relief. But what else did she share with Vera?

Odella stares with open curiosity at Vera from across the table. "You have secrets."

"Don't we all?" Vera responds simply.

Her gaze is challenging and guarded, and she doesn't seem to realize how hard her knee digs into my leg. Odella triggered something, and I'd like to know what it is, but somehow I already know Vera won't be telling me a word.

Odella glances at me but speaks to all of us. "The Black Tulips will either save our kingdom... or be our downfall. There is a formidable enemy after them. Ensure that enemy doesn't get one of the Tulips, or all could be lost."

How am I supposed to ensure that when I can't even find *one* of the blazing women?

I frown. "What enemy?"

"Gloam, the god of shadows, and his people."

They were banished long ago, and I haven't ever seen one, but my firm nod seems to appease Odella.

She continues. "I can tell you where to find the Field of Tulips, but the rest you must do on your own." She looks pointedly at Vera, but I'm unable to decipher what she might be communicating, and Vera's gaze reveals nothing. She appears so bored that I *know* she's hiding something. I'm left completely confused—it irritates me when so much depends on the success of this mission, and I appear to be missing details that could help.

"The Field of Tulips, can you help us reach it?" I ask.

Another flower begins to bloom on her dress as she smiles, distracting me slightly. "One of my Naiads will help you."

"Naiads?" Darvy asks, glancing around to see if he's the only one who doesn't know what she's talking about.

"River nymphs," I say.

Darvy still looks confused, as does Vera.

Odella simply nods. "They, and I, are the reason the river is still lucent here. But once it passes my boundaries, it will return to its poisoned state. I will provide a boat and a Naiad to guide you, but only so far as she is not in danger."

I nod. "That's all we ask."

"I recommend you leave the river as soon as possible once you've left lucent waters," she advises with warning in her voice. "And if the boat makes it in one piece,"—Odella and I both glance at Vera with concern as she chokes on her drink before Odella continues—"leave it for your return journey. I'll leave the border open for two days."

"Your kindness is appreciated," I say.

"We need lucent restored as much as you do, King Ikar."

I nod, then the same nymph that led us here appears as if from within the tree itself.

She curtsies. "I'm here to show you to your places of rest for the evening."

"Darvy, I need to speak with you. Rhosse and Vera, you can go ahead; we'll be along soon."

Rhosse nods, and Vera scoots her chair back and offers Odella a polite smile. I feel the stark absence of her knee pressed against my leg when she stands and walks away with Rhosse without a backward glance. My magic aches uncomfortably as I watch her go, and I find myself wondering with a clenched fist if I am doomed to feel this way for the rest of my life.

"You have feelings for her." Odella speaks so softly that if I didn't have excellent hearing, I would've missed it.

I jerk my gaze away from Vera's retreating form and laugh dryly. I'm not inclined to lie to this ancient ruler, so instead I deflect her comment. "Any advice on how to fix broken magic?"

Odella laughs, and it feels like listening to a warm summer breeze. "Magic does not *break*. If you learn to listen, it will teach you much."

It will teach me more self-control than I ever wanted.

"I'll work on... listening... then." I nod, though I have no idea what she means, and I still intend to speak to Darvy about it.

She merely smiles. "I will see the four of you tomorrow."

With one last nod, I catch up to Darvy who waits near the path that Rhosse and Vera disappeared down. Odella may believe that magic doesn't break, but mine *has*. I've gone back and forth over whether I should mention it to Darvy. His healing is for the physical, as far as I know, but maybe he can help, and this is the first chance I've had to ask.

We walk along the wide vine-woven path through the trees for a while in silence, and my jaw works as I try to figure out how to begin. "Darvy."

"Yeah?" He looks my way and sees my dire expression. "What's wrong?"

I flex my hands and wipe my palms on my trousers, then run a hand through my hair, almost tugging at the strands. "I think my magic is broken."

Darvy laughs until he realizes I'm completely serious, and quiets immediately. "What's wrong with it?"

"Maybe the widow venom did something to me—"

Darvy interrupts, all healer now. "What's happening?"

I've been thinking about it for a few days now, but it's difficult to put into proper words.

I lower my voice, aware that there are any number of nymphs hiding behind every leaf and branch in this forest, and try my best to describe it. "My magic has always just been *mine*. It was content that way. Then a few days ago, out of nowhere, my magic reacted to Vera. It was as if a piece of magic I've never known about rose from the depths of me that wants to... *bond* with her. It's desperately trying to do something that feels far too intimate with a woman I have no right connecting with," I finish in a harsh whisper.

"And your magic has never reacted to her before?"

I shake my head. "No, and Vera can't be a Black Tulip. I've seen her use originator and healer magic—"

"But didn't Jethonan tell you they're similar to both of those factions?"

I stop, caught off guard at the reminder, and a smidgeon of hope blooms in my chest before I quickly squash it. "He did, and I see where you're going with this, but keep in mind that I have been around Vera for weeks, and my magic has not reacted to her any differently than any other woman until now."

Darvy nods in agreement. "Good point."

"If my magic reacts to every woman I meet, I'll be in an even bigger mess. How will I identify a Queen of the Night?"

"Send out a letter to the kingdom?" Darvy suggests.

"They're in hiding. From *me*. I don't think a simple letter will draw them out," I growl. "Can you fix this?"

Darvy frowns. "I've never tried to heal *magic,* so I don't believe so. Never even heard of such a thing, actually. Have you tried pulling lucent from Vera?"

I frown. "Yes."

"I assume it worked?"

I think back carefully, but I've had no difficulty using lucent. "Yes, that all feels normal. But the other part, it's still there."

"Has it drawn toward any of the nymphs?"

"No. But they're not human, either."

Darvy nods. "Maybe Jethonan has heard of this before. Talk to him about it when we return."

I plan to—if I don't lose my mind first.

Chapter 33

Vera

I leave Ikar behind. His large frame barely fits the chair that was made for him, but he sits as regal as the king he is. The knee that was pressed against his thigh feels cold as I walk away. It's irritating how much I miss his warmth—my magic agrees.

I follow Darvy, Rhosse, and the nymph through the trees as I think about the seer vision I was just shown that feels as if it will forever be imprinted on my mind. I almost miss when the nymph points down to a magnificent bathing pool where we can wash. It's a scene I normally would have appreciated, but right now, all I can see is the flash of hot white light before my eyes replaced by a faceless Tulip bridging with a man so dark that gloam emanates from his form, and I don't know how to explain it, but I could *feel* Lucentia dying. It seems eerily similar to the seer vision that I've heard of that began the Tulip murders, and I admit that if that's what they saw, then there's part of me that grudgingly admits I understand the fear that led them to violence—still wasn't right, though.

But why show *me*? Why not Ikar? He's the king. What

does Odella want from me, and why didn't she explain it? I'm certainly not planning on bridging with *anyone*, and that definitely includes whatever demon was in that vision.

I'm pulled from my thoughts, having missed the beauty of the entire walk, when we arrive at two rooms that stand side by side, high in the trees. Thick vines have been woven into walls, my room and the men's, which share a wall. Garlands filled with thick, vibrant fresh flowers hang, acting as privacy curtains in place of doors.

I politely thank the nymph before I quickly duck through them. Brushing against the petals carries their sweet scent farther into the room on my clothing, and I inhale deeply, reminded of Mama Tina and the copious vases bursting with flowers she always orders for her parties. I can't help but smile at the thought of her.

The room is furnished simply, but it only adds to its natural charm. A soft hammock hangs from the branches above with a cozy blanket slung over its side. I draw my fingers along its edge, admiring the texture. Nearby, the other curtain of flowers hints at a balcony beyond. There's a small chair with a seat and back made of tightly woven vines and a small wood table with a variety of nuts, seeds, and fruit.

I gently set my pack on the ground near the hammock, afraid to disturb the perfection and simplicity of this space. I can hardly wait to grab my things and rush down to that tantalizing bathing pool, but before I do, I take a moment to part the flowers that curtain the back door and peek through. A small balcony, shared between the two rooms, is surrounded by a fragile railing made of smooth wood that twists and curls into shapes of intricate flowers. It appears more for looks than use, so I keep my distance, but what I see beyond draws me the rest of the way out. Peachy skies from the two suns already set are beginning to spread across and tinge the forest with added warmth and color. The last sun and its dim rays dip below the horizon, accentuating the deepening orange glow. The Lucent River weaves through the forest below, and the sun reflects off its surface in shimmering rainbow hues. I think if I could stay here forever, I would.

Rhosse ducks through the flower curtain of their room, and I grin a little as petals cling to his shoulders after he steps out. I return my gaze to the view before us as he leans lightly against the rail to my left.

"The river is magnificent," I breathe.

I continue to stare at it, completely mesmerized. I've always been terrified of the river and its ability to take me where it wants if I touch it, not to mention all the monsters that lurk beneath its surface. But here... it looks like a dream.

Rhosse nods. "It is. Can you imagine our kingdom returned to this? Being able to travel the Lucent River as Lucentia intended?"

"You believe it can be? Truly? After so many years?" I can't help the doubtful tone in my voice. This is the only way I've ever known it to be.

He smiles wryly. "That's the goal. Why else would we be tramping through a poisoned forest?" He looks out over the forest. "I assume you know the entire plan by now."

"What matters of it, at least," I mutter softly.

He looks at me with a compassionate eye and, for some reason, I dread what he's about to say. "Then you know Ikar searches for a Black Tulip, a Queen of the Night, to marry and bridge with."

My lungs tighten. He's warning me off. I know it. I feel like a girl being scolded by her father, except it's worse because it's

Rhosse. Do *all three* of them know I struggle with my feelings for Ikar? So awkward.

"Yeah, I've been told. What about it?" I ask, feigning nonchalance.

He continues to look my way, and I force myself to hold his gaze. "He'll follow through, no matter if his heart feels otherwise."

Do I spy a sprinkle of *pity* in his eyes? Gah.

"I'm not after him," I grind out through my teeth.

The opposite, in fact, but I keep that to myself.

"I apologize if I've botched this... it's just..." He grips the rail tightly, and I get the sense he's as uncomfortable as I am. Rhosse is usually so calm and collected that I can almost forgive him for bringing this up. Then Darvy swaggers from the flower curtain and plops his forearms on the rail on my other side.

"What he's *trying* to say is that Ikar's magic busted a few days ago, and it's still acting strange. Don't take it personally if it has done anything... *untoward.*" Darvy clears his throat.

I nearly laugh out loud with relief, but I can't let them see that. Ikar already told me he believes his magic is broken, and I have roguishly allowed him to believe it. I feel a rush of guilt and stamp it out—I have no choice.

"But he will also kill us if he finds out we've said something." Rhosse speaks from my left, drawing my attention back to him.

"Undoubtedly," Darvy agrees, more serious than I've ever seen him.

I pat their broad shoulders on either side of me. "I won't say a word."

Finally, a promise I can keep.

I spin around before they can spot the wide smile on my face, more than pleased with how the situation is panning out.

Maybe, just maybe, I'll get my bracelet and anonymity back with Ikar none the wiser.

I pause, carefully wipe the smile from my face, and turn back. "Where is Ikar, anyway? I thought he was with you." I direct my gaze to Darvy since he was with him last.

"He's speaking with Odella."

How nice. I force myself to smile as if the thought doesn't bother me like a sharp pebble in my boot. I escape to my room, listening to the deep tones of conversation between Rhosse and Darvy as I snack on some of the fresh fruit and nuts. By now, the sparkling sky is lit by the first of the three moons, and its dim light reaches into my room between the strands of the flower curtain. But I can't sleep with Ikar still alone with Odella, wondering what they might be talking about all this time—and also, I need to clean up worse than ever.

I don't ask one of the men to come with me, but Rhosse pokes his head out as soon as I exit my room.

He gestures me forward. "I'll walk with you."

"It's safe enough here, isn't it?" I frown, looking around as we head toward the main path through the trees that brought us here. "Did I miss something?"

"You almost fell through the trees today."

"Right." I purse my lips. It's not like I can argue. "Hey, Rhosse?"

"Yes?"

"What do *you* think about all this? Ikar's plan?"

He lets out a long breath. "It's complicated."

We walk down the steps that twist around and around the very tall tree. The steps are even and flat, but there is no rail other than the smooth trunk of the tree to our left, and I feel even more clumsy with him watching me so closely.

We're quiet for a few minutes while we descend, only

hearing the muted thud of our boots on each step, and I try not to look off the edge. The entire way down, I'm wondering what's so complicated. Ikar has decided he wants to improve the kingdom, which is great. Gloam *is* a problem, but it has been for years. I've always thought the kingdom can just keep going how it is—not perfect, but good enough. That's what the originators are for, isn't it?

"How is it complicated?" I ask, appalled with myself for my curiosity.

"The plan has caused a rift between the low kings and Ikar, though they were practically waiting for something like this to happen just to take advantage of it," he nearly growls. "Nadi-ette has said that low king Waylon is leading the beginnings of mutiny."

I frown. Ikar is willing to continue, even with mutiny as a consequence? He's never mentioned any of this.

We've reached the forest floor now, and the roar of falling water grows louder as we walk on a moss-covered path.

"Then... why? There *has* to be a way that everyone can agree on to fix this. Lucentia has to have had another way—"

"If there was another way, Jethonan would have found it in the history."

My brow furrows. "I thought that's why we had originators. Why not just leave things the way they are?"

"People are *dying*." He looks at me like I'm crazy. Maybe I am. I've never felt quite so selfish in my life. "There's not another way, Vera. The originators aren't enough anymore." His tone is final.

"What if he never finds the Field of Tulips, or a Queen of the Night? What then?" I risk the questions, knowing I tempt his patience.

His gaze darkens. "That's not an option."

I almost roll my eyes—these men and their blazing persistence. "I didn't suggest it was optional. I asked *what if?*"

"We will search until we find them or the kingdom is consumed by gloam and we're all dead." He says it in such a cold and final way that chills skitter down my spine.

Before I can argue further, we stop alongside a tall thick hedge, which has a solid wood door embedded in its growth.

"If there's anyone you can trust, it's Ikar." He looks hard at me, as if willing me to believe it.

I offer a weak nod, prompting a heavy sigh from him.

He opens the door for me to walk through. "I'll be waiting here when you finish."

He shuts the door after I enter, abruptly ending our conversation. I try to ignore his disappointment, reminding myself that Rhosse didn't tell me anything I didn't already know... but to hear how determined they are to find the Tulips is chilling enough that goosebumps have risen across my skin.

I distract myself by taking a moment to soak in my surroundings as I approach the bathing pool. The moonlight from the two moons that have risen shines brighter here than I've ever seen, their light reflecting off the water before me in an ethereal way. I don't generally like dark water; in fact, with the dangers that usually lurk there, I tend to lean toward terrified. But here, the water glows luminescent, and it's so clear that I can see every pebble at the bottom with the way the moonlight shimmers through its surface. The magnificent waterfall completes the stunning picture, the mist and foam at the bottom appearing to sparkle with magic.

Small waves lap at the shore, which is covered in small pebbles so smooth and round they could be pearls washed up from the depths of an ocean. One side is the canyon wall from which the waterfall flows, and the other three sides are blocked in by the thick hedge. I spot Rupi's tiny white form soaring over the top, almost glowing in the bright moonlight as she bobs happily through the air. She lands on the round pebbles as I quickly remove my clothing and place the bundle just out of reach of the gently lapping waves. Goosebumps rise across my body as the air whispers across my bare skin. Rupi has already begun to hop in the smallest waves, cleaning her feathers and chirping contentedly. Her fuzzy feathers begin to dampen and cling to her body, making her appear even smaller.

I take a breath and remind myself that this water is safe—nothing lurks in its depths here with the nymphs. I take my time searching for a spot to enter that's not too deep, since I'd prefer not to drown tonight. Even the *thought* of Rhosse, Darvy, or Ikar running in here to my rescue without a bit of clothing on is mortifying.

I wade into the water, and my tense muscles relax immediately—it's warmer than most baths I've taken, and I laugh with surprised pleasure. My toes brush the bottom, filled with more of the smooth pebbles, and I'm reassured I won't drown. I waste no time cleansing the many layers of velvet widow gore, my own blood, and the caked-on dirt and grime from my body and hair. I'm left feeling invigorated, and when I'm finished, I take time to enjoy this beautiful pool, dragging my hand through the water and creating splashes and waves that sparkle. Does all water in this small piece of lucent heaven sparkle and glow? I've never seen a healthy magical river or pool in my life.

I stare at my hand beneath the surface and catch sight of a small fish that darts away from my feet, and as each tiny wave crests toward the shore, a small spray of sparkling water bursts into the air. This little bit of forest is what our kingdom could be like again. No excess gloam, no monsters. I feel my hardened heart soften the smallest bit toward Ikar and his mission. I know he wants this too. He's good. I know he is. But he's not infallible. What about his future opinions? What about the future kings and my Black Tulip sisters? Their safety is in my hands, just as the kingdom is in his.

I keep my hand just beneath the surface and turn in a fast circle, sending a spray of sparkling water into the air, interrupted when another, quieter voice in the back of my mind that I locked up when Rhosse and I spoke, finally frees itself and questions me about the lives of people who are dying from gloam. *What about them?*

I tentatively lie back, attempting to float on the gentle waves as I feel another thought coming to mind. My first instinct is to beat it back into submission, but it feels as if the magic in this warm water, the peace in this beautiful and perfect piece of forest, coaxes me to acknowledge it.

What if I told Ikar I'm a Black Tulip?

Instinctive, deep-rooted fear shoots through me, sending me sinking beneath the surface, flailing until I gain my footing and stand upright again. I wipe plastered strands of hair from my face as images of the dead Tulips in my nightmare come to mind in horrid succession. I waste no time trudging toward the shore, using my arms in the water to speed my escape.

No. Tatania's words echo through my head. The Black Tulip oath. *We will never reveal our Black Tulip identity. We will never bridge with kings.* How many times have I repeated that? I promised. How could I even consider breaking that and betraying my Tulip sisters?

I shake my head and climb out of the water to dry myself. Minutes later, as I cinch my vest tightly beneath my bust, I look over the water with narrowed eyes, wondering if, perhaps, it truly was the magic water that messed with my mind tonight.

I sit back on the round pebbles, waiting for my feet to dry

before I shove my boots back on. Rupi looks like a soggy wad of cotton as she hops toward me, then with one quick flutter, lands atop my thigh, leaving small wet spots on my trousers as she hops and flaps her wings. I smile at her antics, but it slips when my thoughts return to Odella's... advice? The seer vision. I've only heard rumors of the first one that got the Tulips killed, but this one seemed eerily similar. Then she tells me to be careful who I trust... Trust *who*? Ikar or Tatania? It has to be Tatania, my Black Tulip sisters, but how does that help restore lucent for our kingdom? That's why I asked Rhosse if there was another option, but he's certain there isn't. Why didn't Odella just tell me what to do? I groan, feeling stuck.

"Vera? You decent?" Darvy calls over the hedge.

"Decent," I shout, wondering when he showed up.

The door flings open, and Darvy strides through, followed closely by Rhosse, grins on their faces and spare clothing swinging in their hands.

I wiggle my clean toes once more, still reluctant to put my boots on my damp feet. "You kicking me out?"

Rupi's feathers are almost dry, her fuzz beginning to fluff up and become soft again, but now clean and even brighter white.

"Unless you'd like to stay for the show." Darvy winks with an incorrigible grin.

Then Ikar saunters through the door with a grin to match theirs. "Did you bring my things?"

Darvy tosses a small bag of items at Ikar, which he catches easily as he comes closer. I know it's time to leave—I've taken up most of the evening here anyway. And also, they don't appear to have the patience to wait for me any longer. A shirt lands near me in a puddle of fabric, and I quickly grab my boots, unwilling to look up to see whose it was or what other pieces of clothing might have already come off. I hurry toward the hedge door, enjoying the mossy coolness of the path now that I've left the pebbles.

I pass Ikar on my way and meet his eyes. "I didn't expect you to be here; I thought you'd still be speaking with Odella." I hate how breathless and jealous I sound.

He glances over my shoulder, and I can tell he's as eager as I was to use the pool. "We just finished."

"She's interesting."

My comment captures his attention once more, and one side of his lips turns up into a smile. "She is, but also very gifted. She doesn't see something for everyone. It's an honor to have her share with you."

"I just don't understand what she meant." I look down and rub a toe through the cool moss beneath my feet.

"Whatever your first impression was, that's it."

I don't have to think hard about it. The moment she said *Lucentia* and *duty*, I thought of my duty as a Queen of the Night. But betraying my oath and my Tulip sisters and potentially putting them in danger *can't* be the right way. It can't.

I offer a one-shoulder shrug. "I'll have to think about it."

"Don't think too hard. First impression." He casts a knowing glance at me and then looks back to the pool.

I can't agree with him because my first impression is wrong, so I laugh instead. "Go. I'll head back on my own."

It's torture to stand this close to him and speak as if my magic is behaving normally when really it's frantic with want, racing through my veins.

He looks toward the pool again, where I hear Darvy shout, followed by a large splash. "We won't be long..."

"Don't rush on my account. I'll be fine. I won't fall through any holes, okay?" I intend it to be a joke.

But he looks back at me, his brows drawn together into a frown. "It's not funny. Be careful."

I wave away his concern. "Go bathe; you need it." I make a face and brush past him.

It's a lie. Somehow he smells and looks as tempting as ever.

As I walk away, I hear another giant splash and whoops joining with the roar of the waterfall, and I can't help but smile. The three of them are as close as brothers by blood, and their boyish energy tonight leaves me smiling... until I remember how Ikar looks without a shirt on, and it's definitely not boyish. *Stop it.*

I trip up a few steps and wipe all thoughts of Ikar from my mind so I can keep my promise to safely reach my room.

"They'll be so pleased to see I made it here alive," I mutter to Rupi sarcastically as I scoop her from my shoulder and place her on the table. She picks through the tray of food that was left there, chittering to herself as I ready for bed. I take time to rebraid my clean hair, and fall into the surprisingly comfortable hammock. It swings gently beneath me and cocoons me in its center. I snatch the cozy blanket and easily begin to drift off. I'm not sure if I dream in the night that Ikar ensures I sleep soundly, or if the scent of him always hovers around me, but I feel safe.

I sleep better than I have in days.

Chapter 34

Ikar

Though the room is barely lit from the first of the three suns rising, I clamber out of the swinging hammock and shove my boots on, my movements waking Darvy and Rhosse. Though the hammock was unusually comfortable, my thoughts were not.

I blink my dry, fatigued eyes and rub a hand down my face. Worry over the Field of Tulips consumes my mind. So far, the journey itself has kept my thoughts busy with our safety and navigating our way through the Lucent Mountains—not to mention fighting for control over my misbehaving magic—but now that we're safe within the land of the nymphs and haven't had to worry over the next fight or our next meal, I've had too much time to think, and the reality of the situation sinks in.

I duck through the curtain of flowers with my pack on, ready to get on with things. I lean near Vera's curtain and call through the flowers, "Vera. It's time to go."

She responds with a muffled curse and a groan, and I smile. I hear the soft thump of her feet hitting the wood floor a few moments later. Guilt for pulling my companions from safe slumber and comfort nags at me, but we have a journey to complete and a kingdom to save.

I breathe in the fresh, cool air, and try to enjoy the sounds of the forest waking as I wait. I should be overjoyed that we've made progress, that we've traversed a good portion of the Lucent Mountains and survived—an admirable feat in itself. And now we've found the nymphs who can help us find the Field of Tulips. I might even have one of the flowers in my possession this very day. That is, *if I'm worthy*. My most significant concern from the beginning.

How does Lucentia determine if a king is worthy? Does she have a way to measure his care for his people? His willingness to sacrifice for them? His honor and the goodness of his heart? Even then, I'm likely still too selfish, and if it's merely based on the amount of gold left in my mark, then I'll find myself tulip-less and begging Lucentia to take my life in exchange for my kingdom's magic out of desperation—not a comfortable thought.

Rhosse steps out first, placing a hand on my shoulder with a firm, brotherly grip. "You'll be holding a black tulip in your hands soon. It'll be worth it."

Apparently, even a hammock can't mask the sounds of restlessness from him.

"If I'm worthy," I mutter.

"You're the only one who doubts it."

It's always easier to say that about someone other than yourself, but I don't say it aloud because I'm not looking to argue. Instead, I laugh, but it lacks the genuine ring of humor. "Have you asked Vera her opinion on that?"

He inclines his head in agreement with a wry grin. "I'd recommend *not* doing that."

Vera steps from her room, her hair in a neat, loose braid.

She brushes loose petals from her shoulder and firmly plucks one from the tight grasp of Rupi's tiny beak. "You need my opinion? It's free of charge today." She looks up with a teasing glint in her eyes and a saucy tilt to her mouth that draws my gaze, tempting forbidden feelings to grow.

How is it that every morning she's more beautiful than the last? She's a siren made specifically to be the woman of my dreams to tempt me from my duty. It's been a long time since I kissed those perfect lips, traced the curve of her jaw with my finger... and the way she's smiling right now... It feels as if we're back to criminal and bounty hunter. I blink, and anger flares. It's not just my magic that's misbehaving; it's *me* as well. Another mark against my worthiness for my wayward thoughts. I feel as if I'm betraying my future bride.

"Free of charge? I'll take advantage of that." Darvy exits the room and joins us on the small platform. "Tell me honestly, Vera, do you like this jacket?" He holds the seams out wide and turns a little to show it off. But really, it just reveals more of his broad, armor-clad chest.

Vera laughs. "It's very nice." Her cheeks pink prettily, and I feel a rush of annoyance.

"Odella will be waiting," I interrupt. "Let's go."

I catch Vera's eye before I turn and try not to make more of it than I should. So what if Darvy wants to court her? He deserves someone kind and beautiful, funny and resilient. Someone like Vera. But the thought of them together is too painful to consider. I'd see her constantly... I'd be at their wedding and probably godfather to the children they make together.

I resist the urge to retch over the side of the path. I feel as if I was stabbed with my own enchanted sword. *No.* Darvy can find someone else.

Another strike against my worthiness as I wallow in selfishness.

It's not long before we reach the dock, where Odella awaits us. She's just as beautiful and serene as yesterday, though flowers have bloomed in different places along her dress of vines and in her hair. I try not to stare at the woman beside her, who I assume is the Naiad Odella mentioned would help us. Her skin is light blue, and shimmers the same as the water that rushes beneath the dock. She's clothed in a delicate sleeveless dress of what appears to be spider silk—similar to how I've seen the fae use it—but hers has fish, plants, and other designs woven into the fabric. Her eyes are captivating, the color within her irises moving like rushing water, and her dark hair hangs long and wet down her back.

"This is Adara. She will speed your journey and help you to our border. Remember, I'll leave it open for two days. If you're late, you'll need to find another way around."

I nod. Two days. Odella seems to think it will be enough time.

Beside the dock, there is a leaf-shaped boat constructed of gleaming wood with two solid benches that span its width. Two oars rest on the sides, and at the rear of the boat there are two curved handles. Adara motions to the boat, her eyes gleaming with eager excitement. It makes me nervous.

"Vera, take the front." It pains me to order the next part. "Darvy, beside her. Rhosse and I will man the oars."

I stand on the dock and rein in the tendrils of magic that excite when Vera looks up and our gazes hold for an extended moment as she places her hand in mine to step into the boat. She lowers her eyes and slips her hand from mine as quickly as I do from hers. Darvy jumps in next. Adara watches Rhosse with unguarded attraction as he steps in. I grin at his reddening face as he gets comfortable on the small bench. Then there's only me.

I turn to Odella. "Thank you for your help. With it, we will hopefully return with a black tulip."

She nods with a soft smile, and then with a whisper meant only for me, she says, "All depends upon your worthiness, hm?"

I stare at her for a moment, attempting to discern if she's trying to tell me something. She says nothing else, and her expression gives no other indication it was anything more than a reminder—a reminder that I don't need.

I nod sharply and jump into the boat.

Adara slips into the water behind us, her blue hands locking around the smooth handles. "Hold tightly. You won't be needing those oars until the border." Her voice is as clear and sparkly as the Lucent River.

Vera hurriedly tucks Rupi into her pocket, where she chirps indignantly, before she holds to the side of the boat. I grip the wood edge, and then, with no further warning, we're off. We travel so quickly it feels as if we skim across the water. The river's shimmers turn into one continuous bright flash on either side of our boat, and cool wind rushes through my hair and tugs almost violently at my clothing.

Rhosse and I look at each other, brows raised in surprise. This is much, much faster than we've ever seen a boat safely travel the Lucent River. The greenery and forest on either side of us is a blur. I see the flash of a large bear on the river bank, but it's gone just as quickly. And then, the color of the forests disappears, replaced with the brown color of two steep canyon walls. Then we stop so suddenly we're almost spilled from our leaf boat, causing Rhosse to curse loudly while Vera yelps as she goes half over the edge at the front and Darvy grabs her waist to pull her back in.

Adara speaks from the water behind us, her blue eyes still rushing, and her voice so pure it almost hurts my ears. Her skin shimmers with exuberance, and her long hair is carried behind her like a dark stain in the river. "Use the oars to travel until you see three gold arrows embedded in a tree. Tie the boat there and make the rest of the way on foot. There is a path that leads to the Field of Tulips, but I can't say what condition it's in after all this time. Whether you retrieve the flower or not, be back within these canyon walls before two days pass, or the border will close and following this river will no longer take you to the nymphs."

I incline my head with gratitude. "Thank you, Adara."

She waits for us to ready the oars, then she releases the handles and disappears beneath the gentle rush of the river. As soon as she lets go, our boat is carried forward, and Rhosse and I push the oars through the water at intervals to stay on a straight course.

"And there's the boundary," Darvy says grimly, his voice low and his hand on his weapon.

We watch as a clear line of healthy magic river ends and the poisoned, gloam-infested river begins. The murky, muddy water is a stark contrast to the shimmering, clear magical river we've experienced this past day, and I dread navigating it.

Three paces. Two paces. One. The boat rocks violently as we cross. Darvy draws his sword, and Vera grips the edge of the boat with white knuckles. Rhosse and I work in tandem, oaring with focused rhythm learned through years of teamwork and training. On the way *to* the Field of Tulips, the current works against us. On the way back, at least it will be in our favor.

Vera stares at the water as if she expects something to appear on the surface, and I'd laugh, except... it's possible. Other than a soft bump here and there, it would seem we merely travel a filthy river, but we all know what lives in the depths.

I train my focus on the rhythmic oaring and search for the arrows. Odella said it wasn't far from the boundary, but with the stress of awaiting an attack, it seems as if we float on the gloam water for a long time.

Darvy points to a tree just ahead on our right. "Three gold arrows."

Rhosse and I easily adjust our pattern to navigate our way to the shore.

"I've got the rope," Darvy shouts as he jumps from the boat to the bank, slipping slightly on its muddy surface before gaining his footing and knotting the rope expertly around a solid tree near the shore. With quick efficiency, the rope is attached to the boat, and then he's helping Vera out.

Rhosse and I jump to the bank next.

I lean down to grab the boat and glance at Darvy. "You grab one side. I'll grab the other."

We drag the boat as far up the muddy bank as we can get it while still staying close to the river. Never know what sort of gloam creatures we'll find near the Field of Tulips, and we may need a quick escape.

"That's quite the path," Vera states dryly, looking ahead through the trees as she frees Rupi from her pocket. She quills up and huddles near Vera's neck, eyeing the way ahead and rustling her feathers nervously.

"It was considered a bridal path, meant to be beautiful for future queens to traverse so they could bestow a tulip on their king before they wed. All very honorable and steeped in tradi-tion," I say as I check my weapons. "There's a drawing in the journal, put there by a more recent grandfather."

"It looks like the path to certain death, if you ask me," Vera mutters.

Rupi cheeps quietly in agreement.

Feeling pleased with how my weapons are situated, I rest my hand on the pommel of my sword and turn to see what she's looking at. Immediately, I frown. A steep set of rock steps covered in thick, slippery black moss leads upward through what once was a bounteous green canopy of tall ancient trees with thick, twisted trunks. Except now, the steps have begun to crumble, and sharp rocks have knifed through... and instead of branches weighed down with healthy greenery, flowers, and birds, spindly tree branches look like skeletal fingers waiting to stab at passing travelers. To add to the deathly image, there isn't a single ray of warm sunshine lighting the path, as shown in the picture. It's filled with clouds of foggy, dark gloam.

I start forward. "Staring at it won't get us anywhere. Let's go."

Vera grudgingly follows without another word.

I take the first steps two at a time, calling over my shoulder, "Vera, we'll lead, but stay behind me."

She mutters something about how I act like a king beneath her breath, and I know she didn't intend for me to hear it, but I can't help but respond.

"That *is* what I am," I say. "Should offer you comfort, knowing I'm so predictable."

"Must you hear *everything*?"

"It's a gift." I flash a grin I know she'll frown at before grabbing her hand to help her up a particularly tall jagged outcropping of rocks.

My magic rushes against its bounds when she puts her hand in mine... and though it was annoyance I just heard in her voice, her eyes tell otherwise when they meet mine. All at once, guilt for the way I feel for her and dread for the day she leaves washes over me, and that leads me to question my worthiness again.

I grit my teeth as I help her up and release her as soon as she's found her balance, then continue picking my way forward. Neither of us says anything else as we finish climbing the rest of the way up the overgrown path. Darvy and Rhosse follow silently as well, alert and watchful.

The air is brisk at this elevation, made worse by the dense gloam hovering around us, stinging any exposed skin, but the steps improve the higher we climb, and we make good time. My heart pounds with anxiety. There's no way to prepare myself completely for the moment I have feared since this plan came to fruition. If we find the field, if the tulips are still there, my worthiness will be decided. It doesn't seem likely to be successful with the state of my mark—there are only the smallest bits of gold left at the ends.

I consider my backup plan, since I'll likely need it—offer myself up to Lucentia. We'll be at the field already, and it will be more than convenient. I set my jaw. My companions will be confused, probably, but they're resilient, and they trust me. Well, Rhosse and Darvy do. Vera is still yet to be determined. But I know if I told them my plan, they would do everything they could to dissuade me. As king, I often carry heavy burdens alone, and this is one of them.

After the crumbling, overgrown stairs end, we stop. The canopy of naked branches above our heads has ended, but we can hardly see ahead. Patches in the foggy gloam clear for fleeting moments, enough that I catch sight of the thick evergreens the journal mentions far ahead across a rolling field.

I grip my sword and continue onward, my gaze swinging wide as I pull lucent from Vera to increase my vision. It seems if we are to encounter another gloam attack, right before the Field of Tulips would be the place, but we've nearly made it across the field, and nothing appears. All I hear is the crunch of the prickly field grass beneath our boots, a chill breeze whispering through the gloam, and distant howling.

Towering fir trees form a thick border before a small majestic mountain peak that grows more imposing as we approach. I rub a hand against my tight chest, feeling as if I can't quite inhale enough breath. A quick glance at Vera shows that she looks as pale as I feel. Does that mean she doubts my worthiness as much as I? The thought stabs like a knife between my ribs. I don't look at Darvy and Rhosse; if I see doubt in their expressions, it may ruin me and have me heading straight to sacrifice myself to Lucentia rather than attempt to retrieve a flower. The imaginings of my ultimate failure becoming reality is mental agony. I find my steps slowing. No matter how fair a king I try to be, no matter how expert I am at wielding my sword, no matter how much lucent I can pull, no matter the width and breadth of my kingdom, Lucentia is the only one who deems me worthy or unworthy. The unknown threatens to overtake me.

The next moment, I find Rhosse at my side. He doesn't say anything, merely gives me a firm nod and walks beside me, his battle axe in his grip. Darvy is at my right. They may not have been born with the responsibilities that I was, but their friendship eases my burdens more than they'll ever know. Their solidity buoys me up.

I set my shoulders; it will do no good to draw this out. With my friends at my sides, and Vera trailing silently behind, my stride lengthens. We reach the outskirts of the trees as the first of the three suns has set. The smell of fresh pine overwhelms my senses in the best way. The smell of a living, healthy forest is an enjoyable reprieve from dry grass and moldering vegetation. As we make our way deeper into the small forest, the scent begins to mix with another—the first indication that the Field of Tulips is truly there—drawing us forward with dark floral and deep honey-musk fragrance. The branches of the evergreens are thick with strong needles that brush against my armor roughly as we weave between them, and the gloam fades until I don't see any at all—even in the shadows.

Then, through the trees, I spot a dark ocean of gently waving tulips.

"It's actually real." Darvy's voice is filled with awe.

I can tell by the low tone it was intended only for Vera, who walks by his side. He should know better than that. I hear everything.

"Maybe." Her voice is indifferent, bored even.

I've never met a woman who's harder to read.

As I step from the trees and into a small clearing, I'm not sure whether to smile with triumph that we've found the tulips, Lucentia's personal garden, or be consumed with the dread held at bay with only the strictest self-control.

A stark line of tulips marks where the field begins, and it extends acres both long and wide. A garden fit for a goddess.

Chapter 35

Vera

The four of us stand before an enormous field of black tulips. *It actually exists.* It's like nothing I've ever seen. A slight breeze has the tulips swaying in rippling waves. Their velvety petals and intoxicating scent tempt me to reach down and pluck one from the soft earth. I feel drawn to them, but I resist. It must appear as if I don't feel anything special here. *Stay calm.*

My breaths are shaky by the time we reach the edge of the field. We look over its expanse, and my eyes are drawn to the sky, where I see Rupi swooping and gliding as if in greeting to hundreds of birds that look just like her. I've *never* seen another bird that looks like her. How will I explain *that* to Ikar? I have so many questions and no one to answer them. I thought I found Rupi by accident, a chance encounter, a lucky day, but now...

I realize then that I've continued walking when Darvy and Rhosse stayed back several feet. I curse beneath my breath. I should have been more watchful; it would look better if I had stayed behind as well. Now I feel stuck, so after forcing myself to stand with Ikar before the field for a few minutes, I decide that's likely been long enough. It's time to sow some doubt and get out of here before this situation goes from bad to worse.

"Better get moving before it gets dark. Looks like the wrong type of flower," I say as I begin retreating from the tulips and heading back toward the fir trees that encircle this field.

Ikar continues to look out over the field of flowers, unmoving. "Wait, Vera. This is it. I feel it."

I freeze, my hands gripping the straps of my pack so hard my knuckles turn white. I slowly turn around.

"This is it?" I ask slowly, feigning ignorance.

The field before us holds his unwavering gaze. "Don't you remember the drawing I showed you? Do you know what these are?"

I shrug, looking out over the field, using all the talent I have inside me to look and sound completely innocent. "Uh, well. They do look sorta like tulips."

I could kick myself for my response, but my brain feels blank as I fight panic, and I struggle to come up with a new strategy. His bicep brushes my shoulder, and I startle. I hadn't realized he was so close.

"*Black* tulips," he says low as he scans the gently waving flowers. He pulls the journal out and flips to the familiar page, holding it out for both of us to see.

Breathe in, breathe out. What in the blazing deathstalkers am I supposed to do now?

"They look sort of... purple... to me. You sure this is the right field?" I want to slap a hand to my face. How many fields of tulips do I expect us to find?

"It's the right place." He sounds confident as he snaps the book shut and tucks it away, then trades his sword for a small knife he pulls from within his armor. He kneels before the first of the tulips and reaches down. My eyes are as wide as the two suns left in the sky watching his hand grasp the stem. Time seems to slow as he places the blade of his wicked-sharp knife against it and presses.

Nothing.

It doesn't even mar the surface with a scratch. I inwardly sigh in relief.

"Thought so." He shakes his head as he stands. "I can't take one. Only Lucentia, one of her Queens of the Night, or one of those birds can give me one." He adds quietly, "They'll do so only if I'm worthy."

Well, the second option sure as blazes isn't happening. Good thing I controlled the impulse to pluck one from the field, or I would have given myself away without knowing it. A bead of sweat trails between my shoulder blades. It's an uncomfortable feeling, not knowing things I should know in a situation where naivety could ruin everything.

"How do you know all this? The journal?" I ask, doubtful.

He nods. "A small bird gave my grandfather the flower. He was worthy."

The last part comes out sounding like he thinks he's *not*. But how? He's the most capable, respectful, caring, fair, good... *Stop it.* He's the blasted high king, and my heart will not be softened. But he does have my curiosity piqued.

"What did you mean about being worthy?" I ask.

"Only a king deemed worthy by Lucentia herself or one of her Queens of the Night, who will care for the Black Tulips as Lucentia first instructed, will be allowed to take one of these tulips."

That's comforting, but not enough to break an oath. Is it? My heart wants to ache for the hint of desperation in his voice, in the lines creasing the corners of his eyes. I decide I can let it.

I can feel his pain even if I can't fix it the way he wants me to. I can't risk the lives of my Tulip sisters.

Ikar stands, sheaths the knife, and stares out across the flower ocean. I'm not oblivious. I see how tense his muscles are, how rigid his shoulders. I see how his hands grip and regrip his favorite weapon, the muscle tightening in his jaw the longer we wait for something to happen. It's torturous for both of us.

After several very long minutes, he still doesn't make any inclination to move. Since I'm not prepared to break an oath to my Tulip sisters, and I have no idea what to say in a situation such as this, I figure I better get comfortable because I've seen no evidence of the lucent magic goddess around here, and the birds seem content to live their lives as normal.

I sit down in a patch of sparse grass and grab a piece to twist around my fingers, but he suddenly walks up to the first of the tulips that make up the vast field—so close I fear he'll step on them. I sit up straight and watch as they begin to bend away, forming a path that grows and lengthens the span of the field, directly to the face of the mountain. Ikar seems to consider traversing it for a moment as he takes another step, and with dread, I remember what he once told me—that if he should fail in finding the tulip flower and a Black Tulip to bridge with, he'd try to offer himself to Lucentia. That was before I knew he was the king, and it's only now clicking into place.

I find myself horrified by my response that day. I may not be able to give him a flower, but I can't let him *die*. My entire body tenses, ready to spring up, run after him, and snatch him back. I'm halfway to standing, but before he goes any further, Rupi, *of all birds,* comes soaring out of the sky, swoops through the waves of flowers, and soars back into the air with a single tulip clutched in her beak. I don't even know how such a small bird can fly with a flower of that size.

I realize what's happening then. I *will* her to drop it. To eat it. Whatever she needs to do so that she doesn't bring it to Ikar, but I watch in horrified disbelief as she coasts straight to his shoulder and preens at the wide grin he bestows on her as she drops the tulip gently into his hand. I feel a momentary stab of jealousy, wishing it was me who had given him the flower and imagining his reaction. I set my jaw and shove the thoughts away.

He rubs a large hand down her tiny body, whispering his thanks. Rupi has never looked happier. If I thought she was a traitor for liking him before, it's nothing compared to now. *Bad, Rupi*, I scold her in my head. It seems like she hears it because she turns her head slightly so she can look at me innocently with one of her dark eyes. But I sense a hint of reprimand about her that makes me defensive. What does she expect me to do? I used to be able to trust her implicitly; now she's been so swayed—by a *king* of all people—that I've lost my needed guide.

I narrow my eyes at her, but she simply tips her beak in the air with that bit of attitude she always has and continues to soak up Ikar's warm affection.

"You're much more than you seem, aren't you?" He directs his deep voice toward Rupi and strokes her thoughtfully.

After getting her fill of his attention, she takes flight, and Ikar stands there, staring at the tulip reverently resting across both his palms. It's a moment even *I* don't dare interrupt. He eyes the path that leads to the mountain again. Instead of traversing it, he kneels, rests one elbow on his strong thigh, and bows his head, placing his other hand and the tulip in the soft grass. He whispers words I can't hear, but somehow I feel Lucentia does. The slight breeze lifts and blows his hair and cloak around him, seemingly in response. Even in his submission to Lucentia, he's never looked more powerful. I'm left staring helplessly until he stands.

He looks over the field once more, then turns toward me. I try to avert my eyes quickly, so he doesn't realize I've been staring. It seems inappropriate with how important this moment is for him.

I glance at Darvy and Rhosse several yards behind us. They wait, stoic and silent, while their king basks in the triumph of finally securing a black tulip. Hopefully that's the *only* sort of black tulip he'll ever hold. That thought triggers a revolting image of one of my Tulip sisters in his arms. I force the image away with the shake of my head.

When I look back at Ikar, he's digging through his pack and pulling out a long, intricately carved box, before opening it and gently placing the tulip inside. "It should keep the flower healthy until I can use it." He looks at me like he expects a response, but I can't think.

That image of a Tulip sister in his arms has become intrusive. What if it was Petra? Or Tatania? Fina? My stomach twists with jealousy. I simply nod, the piece of grass now crushed in my sweaty grasp.

He looks at the box almost reverently. "Time to get on with the next part of our mission."

If I swallowed a rock, I think this is about how it'd feel. I don't need to ask what the next part of the mission is. It's the part where they find a Queen of the Night—a Black Tulip. If they can find an elusive field of tulips secreted in the dangerous and gloam-filled Lucent Mountains, I'm certain they'll find what they're looking for next, no matter how well we hide.

And if he happens not to find what he's looking for? I think about the way he stared at the path. For a moment, I thought he'd do it. Duty-bound, honorable, and self-sacrificing, as usual.

I feel immediate revulsion, bordering on panic, at the thought of a world without Ikar. With his steady presence beside me, his sure steps and wise gaze—that fate seems unreal. He's too capable to resort to something like that. But images of the gloam monsters, news of more deaths sweeping across every village and city, the way gloam infests the land...

I remember the surety in Rhosse's words when he told me they'd never give up. Maybe he'd really do it—drat his honor. What about that... response from Lucentia, if that's what it was? Does that mean she'd accept his life as payment?

I swallow tightly, imagining him before Lucentia, dying as she sucks the life from him, taking his mark and magic by death. Ikar doesn't deserve that fate. I think back to our conversation and inwardly wince at the way I'd so callously told him his family had botched everything.

"Ikar?"

He's about to start walking toward Rhosse and Darvy, but he stops and looks my way. I'm taken aback at the absolute sureness that emanates from him. If I thought he had a kingly sort of presence before, it's nothing like now. I'm left wondering how simply receiving a flower changed him so much.

One of his brows rises. "Yes?"

His blue eyes delve into mine so intently that I struggle to remember what I was asking.

I have to look away to gather my thoughts again. "I told you that your family line should be ended before I knew you were king, but now that I know the truth..." I let the words drift off because I'm not certain how to say what I want to say.

"Now that you know the truth...?"

"Please don't do it," I whisper, my eyes finally meeting his gaze again.

I've never felt like such a beggar in my life. I see in his eyes that he knows what I refer to, and he immediately throws up walls to block me from seeing any further emotion.

"I can't promise that." His voice is quiet, harsh. "I'm selfish enough to keep my kingdom waiting, suffering, dying, while I search for a Black Tulip that may or may not accept me. But I can't let it go on like this forever. If this plan fails, I'll return here, to Lucentia."

He doesn't realize how personal his threat is. I can do nothing but soberly nod. We should be enemies, but it grows harder and harder to maintain that mindset the longer I'm with him. And that leads me to wondering... if Tatania knew Ikar, would she approve of him? The more I get to know him, the more I respect him. Not many can match his sense of honor. Would she give her permission, her blessing for one of the Black Tulips to bridge with him?

My cheeks heat at the thought of even asking. I know what her answer would be.

I don't want Ikar to die, but neither do the Black Tulips deserve to die again, now or in the future. Apparently, one king deemed worthy turned evil enough to kill the very Tulips he was meant to protect, and it could happen again. But how can doing the right thing, keeping my identity hidden, feel so wrong? I just need to make it a couple more days, just long enough to finish this job, and then I'll leave. *Run away.* Begin my long-dreamed-of plans. *Like a coward.* And forget about Ikar. *Nurse my broken heart.*

Chapter 36

Ikar

"You did it!" Darvy strides forward and gives me a brotherly clap on the back.

I can't stop the grin that forms. He's right. We did it. I have the tulip. I also know I'm worthy. That knowledge alone has healed a festering wound within me. I don't know what made me attempt to speak to her across her field with the path wide open before me, but the words I spoke aloud to her were answered with an overwhelming knowledge that Lucentia finds me *worthy*. I can't explain it. My mark may still be black as ink, but the hole left by years of doubt is now filled with determined confidence. I can feel it in my soul.

Rhosse leans in, squeezing my shoulder. "You're the only one who ever doubted."

I glance at Vera. "Don't know about that."

He follows my gaze. "She'll come around."

He seems so sure, but I truly doubt it, and it does no good to discuss it.

I eye the second sun, close to setting, the third soon behind it. We could probably make it back to the nymphs by the middle of night, but with the gloam as thick as it is...

"We'll camp here and leave in the morning." Everyone seems to relax a bit, and I continue. "That gives us one day and a night to reach the border."

I'm not sure how Lucentia feels about people sleeping within the bounds of her field, but the gloam is so dense outside these fir trees that no one wants to risk sleeping in it. Even from this distance and within the haven of Lucentia's personal garden, I hear the snarls of beasts and woeful howling grow louder as the suns set.

We stay well within the treeline and set out our bedrolls. Rhosse takes Vera into the trees to teach her how to hunt. She looks horrified at the thought, and even appears to look to me to intervene. I say nothing, knowing these skills are vital. I won't always be by her side to ensure she's cared for, so while I want to rescue her from this, I don't—it's time she learns.

They manage to capture a plump rabbit that Vera refuses to clean and prepare, acting as if we made her kill her own pet. Even after it's roasted, she simply picks at the meat. I shake my head and sigh. I look at her once more and find her face still a shade paler than normal. This journey has taken a toll on all of us.

Rupi hops along my thigh, and I reach down to softly stroke her feathers. Without her, I wouldn't have the tulip, and that prompts a burning question. Rupi fit in perfectly with the other birds in Lucentia's field, so much so that I'm left to assume that she's one of them. Not only does she look just like the others, but she was able to drop a tulip in my hands. Suspicion curls within me. Vera knows something about the list, *and* her pet is one of Lucentia's birds? My assumption that her friend is a Tulip seems even more likely.

I try to sound nonchalant, but tension flows through my veins. "Vera, where did you find Rupi?"

Rupi blinks an eye at me innocently at the same time as Vera's eyes widen the smallest bit, and do I catch a flash of fear? "I found her in the forest when I was a child. I got lost, and she helped me get home. She's stuck by my side ever since."

I narrow my eyes slightly, and she ducks her head. I don't sense a lie, but her actions tell me there's more. I let the matter drop, unwilling to push it in front of Rhosse and Darvy who both listen closely, but I'm determined to find a moment to get the answers I need before this journey ends.

The tulip continues to occupy most of the space in my mind as the night deepens, and I can't resist pulling it out once more to look at it. The box opens on silent hinges. Rhosse and Darvy's interest is piqued, and they both lean in to see it closer. Vera eyes me from where she sits.

The stem is long, smooth, and dark green. The petals are velvety black, but I recall seeing hints of deep purple in their depths beneath the light of the suns. It hasn't yet fully bloomed, its petals only lightly unfurled. It's such a small, innocent-looking thing. I hesitate for a moment. My fingers itch to hold it, and my wonder quickly overtakes my worry that I'll do something to damage it as I gently pick it up by the stem. I can smell the honey-musk scent from its petals as I hold it to my nose.

I meet Vera's eyes across the fire to find her still watching with unreadable emotion in her eyes, and I hold her gaze until she dips her head again.

Darvy eyes the flower with curiosity. "How do you use it?"

I turn it between my fingers, slowly, inspecting every perfect petal. "The Black Tulip and I must touch it to bridge. It's all part of a big ceremony. One of Lucentia's demands for the gift of lucent."

Vera is watching again, her eyes glued to the flower in my fingers. Impulsively, I offer it to her. "Would you like to hold it?"

She shakes her head, looking slightly sick. Just as well. Who knows what she'd do with it? If she's protecting a friend, she might even crush it beneath her boot if she gets the chance. I pull the flower back and set it safely in the protective case. I admit, if the roles were reversed, I'd be tempted to do the same. I certainly wouldn't want Vera bridging with Rhosse or Darvy. Just the thought makes me want to punch something. *Is it jealousy, then?*

A new sense of compassion builds simultaneously with the pain of knowing that I can't be with Vera. But no matter how either of us feels, I have a kingdom depending on me, and in order to save it, I have to have answers—I'd bet my enchanted sword she has them.

Darvy looks at Vera. "You know, the four of us make a pretty good team. You sure you don't want to join us for the next part of the search? We could use you."

"I think you'll be just fine," she responds quietly.

The words sound encouraging, but I see the way dread fills her eyes.

Chapter 37

Ikar

We leave the haven of Lucentia's Field of Tulips early, walking back into a world consumed by gloam. It's so thick that my abilities to sense gloam creatures are basically nonexistent. It's everywhere. All over me. So thick that I have no choice but to breathe it and taste its darkness on my tongue.

I pull lucent from the ever-running well of Vera's magic and use it to increase the sensitivity of my hearing, and then I realize how used to having it so readily available I've gotten. I don't know anyone else who can offer lucent like she can, which makes it all the more incredible. I'd offer to hire her as one of my royal originators, but I already know that offer would go up in flames.

I hear distant sounds, but they're difficult to identify. Large and small forest animals, low growls and weak twitters of birds, even the rush of the river ahead—nothing that seems too concerning. I set a brisk pace, mindful that Vera's stride is shorter than ours, but also driven to reach the border before we're left to our own devices. I don't have time to add extra days to an already strenuous journey. I need to find a Black Tulip, my Queen of the Night, *now*. With the flower in my pack, hope has grown, and my drive is renewed. Now if only my wayward magic and my feelings would quit longing for Vera.

The journey down the rock steps is much faster than the way up. We jump off jagged edges and clamber around sharp outcroppings. I almost turn to help Vera once, then pull my hand back when my magic reminds me how much it would like the contact, how aware I am of the flower I carry, and the future woman I need to bridge with. Darvy reaches for her instead, his hands around her waist and hers on his shoulders as he lifts her down. I swiftly turn and tromp down the rest of the hill, irritated. Which makes me the first to see what's ahead.

"What in the blazes?" I mutter to myself as the boat comes into view, surrounded by four looming figures that blend with the gloam almost seamlessly. My stomach fills with dread. Odella warned about a formidable enemy... is it them or some type of gloam creature I've never seen before? And, to make matters worse, I spot three sets of deathstalker eyes through the gloamy mist that tempt me to gaze into their endless depths.

One deathstalker took out most of a patrol I rode just weeks ago; now here are three, along with the figures that stand so still they could merely be dark statues in the forest. The deathstalkers' eyes are magnetizing, but Darvy, Rhosse, and I have enough experience to know that if they catch your gaze, you end up stunned, and stunned soldiers can't fight.

"Don't look in their eyes," I warn Vera, who stands just behind me, a flustered Rupi bobbing her head as she worries a path back and forth across her shoulder. I readjust my grip on my sword as the figures shift ahead of us. It's difficult to watch an enemy you can't truly look at for fear of accidentally meeting its eyes. Instead, I focus on the knife-sharp points that circle the round heads of the deathstalkers, the razor teeth and snakelike skin that covers their bodies, thick and tough. They and the figures stand between us and the boat—our only way to make it back to the nymphs in time.

Darvy grabs his bow and an enchanted arrow, nocking it as Rhosse readies his battle axe. Vera hovers just behind my right shoulder, and I feel the waves of lucent she's already offering. In moments our enchanted weapons glow brightly. I take more lucent, testing how much Vera has to offer as my body fills with magic, my senses heighten, and my muscles fill with strength. Rhosse's shoulders remain tense, belying his worry about the odds of us winning this fight, even with Vera's lucent—it's not something I've seen very often. The odds are not good.

"I have a weapon from Jethonan..." I mutter beneath my breath.

Rhosse scoffs and whispers, "I think that might actually be *more* dangerous."

Before I can reach for it, one of the figures mutters a command, and simultaneously they race forward when the deathstalkers lunge. Faster than I can blink, Darvy sends a glowing lucent arrow flying with a whistle, and it hits one of the figures in the chest, but all I can see are the three deathstalkers still closing the distance between us.

I race forward to meet their attack, putting distance between them and Vera. The moment they reach us is a rush of ear-piercing growls, chill gloam, and snapping jaws. I throw my sword up to block the worst that comes from two that have targeted me, drawing more lucent from Vera to increase my speed in order to avoid their swiping claws and teeth that reach for my neck. I wait for the familiar burning heat of lucent in my veins with the amount I pull, but it doesn't come—no time to think about it now. I spot Rhosse battling the other death-stalker, and Darvy on his own against the three figures, darting between trees and boulders. A quick glance at Vera shows that, so far, her orb keeps them away from her, but I can't believe that a simple lucent orb will prevent the figures from attacking if the rest of us are defeated. We're horribly outnumbered, but I force myself to focus.

A deathstalker lunges toward me, and I jump to the left, moving faster with the lucent, before quickly ducking and stab-bing it through the side. Lucent pulses through its body until it explodes into bits of gloam that float away, but just as my sword is released, another attacks, ramming its head into my left arm. I roar as the knives of its mane pierce the bracer on my forearm and sink into my skin. I wrench my arm away and take advan-tage of the close proximity by swinging my sword up in an attempt to behead it, but it backs off too quickly, and the enchanted steel clangs off its mane again.

All around us are snarls and sounds of battle. A burst of light comes from my left, and the deathstalker retreats farther, momentarily. *Vera.* Another quick glance shows that she's still standing, but how much lucent can one woman offer to three men in a forest void of lucent? I fear she'll end up dead if I continue pulling it at this rate, but she gives me a reassuring look and a nod, and I feel an even greater wave of lucent come toward me—more than I've ever felt. I don't know how she's doing it.

I look over my shoulder to search out my companions and find Darvy battling two figures. The third has fallen to the ground. He's holding his own, but for how long? Rhosse takes a defensive stance as the deathstalker he battles prepares to jump. I know I could beat all of these enemies... if I had time.

But we're outnumbered, and I fear someone is going to end up dead. *Jethonan's weapon.*

The next deathstalker eyes me, crouching low and aiming at my calves as it lunges forward as if intending to drag me to the ground. I jump back in a flash and slice its shoulder, triggering a shrieking growl that leaves my ears ringing as it backs away. I pull the vial from within my vest and yank the cork off with my teeth before dumping some in my hand, hoping it doesn't burn a hole through my body or some such thing. It doesn't, but you never know when it comes to Jethonan. I throw the powder at the deathstalker and take a step back as it implodes in a snarling mass of purple-and-black clouds. Jethonan will be more than pleased to know his creation worked this time. I sprint, pulling more lucent, hoping Vera can handle it without collapsing.

I catch sight of the last deathstalker charging toward Rhosse, head bent to impale him. Still running, I throw the powder in a cloud toward the deathstalker, and as with the last one, as soon as it makes contact, it disappears as if sucked into a black-and-purple portal. Gone.

Rhosse looks my way with surprise.

"Get Vera to the boat!" I call to him over my shoulder as I race to help Darvy with the last two enemies.

As I approach, I see the one that lies unmoving on the ground, gloam seeping from its dead form. Odd, but no time to consider it now.

I lift my sword to block a swing that aims to remove my head from my body. The blade cuts into my armor, uncomfortably close to my neck, but I ignore it and offensively stab at the one to my left. He grunts as if he's a man—their menacing faces within their hoods *appear* to be men, their strength is that of men, but I saw the way gloam seeped from the dead one's body. These are no human men... at least, not any longer.

Out of the corner of my eye, I watch Rhosse and Vera working to slide the boat back into the river, but the gloam soldiers notice too. Darvy's sword slams against the larger sword of the one he battles with with a ring that vibrates in the air around us, but the gloam soldier uses his position and size to shove Darvy back, giving him time to turn and run after Rhosse and Vera. Darvy falters against the jagged rocks beneath our feet with a curse. He quickly gains his footing and sprints after the gloam soldier.

"Rhosse!" Darvy shouts in warning, but Rhosse is already aware.

The distraction works in my favor, the attention of the gloam soldier I'm fighting split, and with a well-timed stab, he falls to my sword. I waste no time racing to the waiting boat, where Rhosse and Vera already wait, as Darvy holds off the last gloam soldier. I jump in, and it rocks dangerously in the water.

"Darvy, now!" I shout.

He quickly jumps over the edge of the boat, but with Rhosse's large frame, struggles to find a seat and nearly falls out as it rocks and swiftly turns into the current when the rope is released. Rhosse grabs the back of Darvy's jacket and pulls him back in, then shoves an oar into his hands, and they straighten the boat out quickly with strong, even strokes.

I glance over my shoulder to find the gloamy figure staring as the river carries us swiftly back toward the nymphs.

"We all know Ikar got the best seat," Darvy complains, breath heaving, as he smashes in beside Rhosse with a scowl and mans the oar with expert precision, his and Rhosse's shoulders hitting each other with the close quarters.

I'll not disagree, but I don't dare say it aloud.

The battle delayed us, but the suns are just past midday, and I'm pleased with the speed of our return—the river's swift current works in our favor. The wind howls around us as if a demon watches our progress in anger, pulling strands of Vera's hair loose from her braid and whipping them about my shoulder and face.

We all made it in one piece.

Relieved silence hovers for a while, but Rhosse and Darvy never slow down. The wind continues to lift my hair and cool the sweat of battle from my body, but I don't let myself completely relax. We aren't safe until we reach the nymphs.

I side-eye Vera, who's pressed against my side. Rupi perches on her shoulder, beak jutting forward as if to hurry us along, her white fluff blown backward by wind with the speed of our travel. But Vera sits still, stiff as one of the glossy boards that make up this boat.

I shift, trying to get more comfortable on the hard seat with the side of the boat digging into my side. Vera's lips remain pursed as our hips and shoulders press closer together until I'm settled.

She raises a brow. "Comfortable?"

I shift my shoulders once more for good measure. "Very."

She scowls, and I look away to hide my smirk. The sound of oars slapping the water and the rush of the river around us is soon the only thing I hear. I consider the next part of the mission. In just a few short days, Vera and I will part ways, likely for good, and I'm to go in search of another woman to share my life and kingdom with. It's a painful thought, one that triggers feelings I don't care to dwell on. Instead, I focus on the moment. Vera's small form pressed to mine, relaxing moment by moment as we continue forward. Other than a soft bump here and there that puts me on guard, we see no river monsters, and soon enough the canyon walls begin rising—an indication that we are close to the nymph border.

I can't help but feel a twinge of relief. But it's doused like a small flame dropped in a bucket of water when something knocks the edge of the boat so violently that, even tucked snuggly between my hips and the boat, Vera almost tumbles out with a scream. Rupi shoots into the air, flying in agitated circles around us. I jump to snatch Vera back, and she ends up half on my lap, breathing heavily, my arm tight around her waist. She remains there in shock for a moment, then two, before I reluctantly release her when she moves to return to her own seat.

"Behind us!" Darvy shouts.

I twist in my seat and glance back to see a glistening black creature rising from the depths of the river. It has a long v-shaped snout with interlocking teeth and eyes that rise just above the surface of the water, followed by a smooth black body which sprouts eight long appendages that twist and flail about like some sort of river demon. But my eyes focus on *one* thing. The gloam soldier, or gloam master, as I suspect it is, standing atop the smooth back of the creature, swimming toward us in a wavelike motion.

I was pleased with our speed moments ago; now it's not fast enough.

"Pick up the pace!" I shout as I watch the enemies behind us.

Rhosse and Darvy push themselves, and it feels as if we fly down the river, but the boat rocks again even more violently than before, and a rush of water flows over the side, drenching Vera and Rhosse. She spits river water from her mouth and wipes wet hair from her face without complaint, lucent still glowing in her hand.

The canyon walls grow taller, draping us in cool shadows,

and I scan the water for the border. It should be ahead. Darvy and Rhosse are already pushing the oars through the water with vicious intensity. *Where is the border?* Another large thump and the boat nearly capsizes.

"Hold on!" I shout at Vera as I scan the water around us.

I can't be worried about her falling out of the boat. I see her reach for the edge, but the glossy wood, now slick with gloamy water, is near impossible to grip, and she looks at me, at a loss.

"Hold to me, then!"

The wind blows her hair across her face, hiding her reaction to my command, but she obeys, wrapping her arms around my waist and holding tight. Just as quickly, she screams, and I look down to find a gray tentacle over the side of the boat, wrapped around her thigh and pulling her toward the water.

I reach out to grab her when she lets go of my waist, but she pulls her sword and slices at the tentacle, forcing the monster beneath the water to retract what is left of it and leaving a limp end twitching at our feet. She's just wrapping her arms around me again when, this time, three tentacles come soaring with a rush of water from the depths of the river. Two target Darvy and Rhosse, forcing them to swap their oars for weapons and allowing the boat to turn and pull more wildly in the force of the river. One swift knock from the right angle, and we'll all be spilled over the side and devoured by the river demon.

I'm turning to help fight off the two appendages going for Darvy and Rhosse when I feel Vera's arms tighten around my waist before they begin to slide off again.

"Ikar!" The way she shouts my name pierces my very soul.

I look down to find another tentacle around her legs, dragging her over the side of the boat. Why does it seem like *she's* the target?

Well, that and my pack. A tentacle wraps around it and

attempts to rip it from my shoulders. I begin to lift from my seat until Darvy jumps forward and chops at the appendage, leaving a second large bit twitching and sliding across the boat.

As soon as I'm free, I waste no time heaving over Vera, who's still being dragged over the side of the boat, to chop the leg off, dropping a third twitching end in the bottom of our boat. At the same time, another two tentacles latch onto my sword arm and attempt to yank me into the river, pulling my weight onto Vera, who wheezes at the impact. I wince, hoping I haven't injured her, while my sword drags beneath the boat with the force of the current. I feel the hilt in my grip become slippery in the water.

I'll not lose my sword.

The slimy chains squeeze my arm, slowing the flow of blood and leaving my grip tingly and weakening. Rhosse swings his axe so close to my arm I feel tingles run across my skin, but the tentacles drop.

I push myself up and help Vera back to sitting, feeling trapped on this tiny boat. We can only be sure of three things if we enter that gloamy water. Either we all get transported to different spots along the river and end up alone and possibly dead before we gain the bank, dragged beneath and eaten by the river demon, or we get captured by the gloam master. None of those options are good.

I search for the border of the nymphs and watch it grow closer. I can see the sparkling lucent part of the river ahead, so close... if we can just get there...

"Almost there!"

I look behind us to find tentacles gliding just beneath the surface, and the mouth of the monster only feet away from the rear of our boat. It waves back and forth as it swims toward us, picking up speed the closer we get to the nymphs. I gauge the distance to the border, where the water begins to shimmer, then look back to the enemy gaining on us. I have only moments to decide.

"When I say three, jump to the border!" I command.

I have a feeling the river demon isn't going to simply let us go. Vera looks at me with wild eyes.

"One!"

"But we're almost there!" Vera shouts.

I can see the blatant refusal in her eyes.

"Two!"

The jaws open wide behind us, casting an even darker shadow, and all eight tentacles rise into the air above us. The distance to the border is iffy for a jump, but it's our only possibility of survival. I ready myself to grab Vera and toss her if I have to.

Chapter 38

Vera

I see the look in his eyes before he says *three*. I already know what he's going to do. I put my hands out to stop him, even as I watch with horror as the slimy tentacles rise in the air behind us and the monster opens its mouth to crash our boat between its teeth.

He swats away my hands, grabs me, and, without hesitation tosses me overboard as he shouts, "three!"

I hear myself screaming, feel the chill air. For a moment, it feels as if I've taken flight with Rupi. I squeeze my eyes shut. How could he have possibly thrown me far enough to evade that monster or the gloam river? Where will I end up, and how will I survive *alone*?

I land with a cold splash, sinking beneath the water while the sounds of the world around me become muted and quiet.

I force my eyes open, terrified I'll be looking straight at the monster that has been attempting to eat us, but all I see are three more large figures splashing into the water around me. Then I realize this water is *clear*. I frantically struggle to kick to the surface, and gasp for air at the top. Ikar surfaces next. I risk drowning faster to splash him with a faceful of water.

"You *threw* me!" My face dips beneath the water again before I resurface.

He wipes the water from his face, easily treading in the water that carries us farther and farther into the safety of the nymph lands, as pieces of our once-beautiful boat float around us. "You're welcome."

I can't tell if he's frustrated or finds it humorous, but it doesn't matter because I can't seem to kick hard enough to stay above the surface, going beneath and sputtering as I come up again.

"I would have jumped on my own," I argue just as my chin dips beneath the surface, and I get a mouthful of water that I have to spit out awkwardly—at least it's not full of gloam.

"You'd pet a deathstalker before you'd jump into gloamy Lucent River," he says with such infuriating surety that if I weren't half-drowning, I would throw more water in his face—buckets of it.

I spit out another mouthful, coughing. My pack floats along somewhere behind us, but the weight of my clothes and my boots are still too much. I've never been much of a swimmer.

I sink below again, and I kick to breach the surface, but I'm beginning to panic. I catch a glimpse of Rhosse and Darvy gathering our packs and making their way toward the bank, and I envy them for their skill in the water as my face goes below again; this time before I have time to take even one proper gasp for breath.

Ikar expertly strokes to where I am, comes up behind me, and wraps an arm firmly around my waist. I come up choking and coughing as my flailing legs tangle with his.

I instinctively attempt to turn around and climb up him for

safety, but he keeps me firmly beneath one arm, my back to his chest.

"Lean back and relax, or you'll drown us both," he growls near my ear.

His deep voice sends warmth through my chilled body and calms me enough to kick-start my logic. I know my odds are exponentially better with his help, so I force myself to relax in his arms, letting my legs drift with the current, as he leans back and begins kicking us toward the bank.

I sink into a surreal sort of daze. The water isn't as cold as the gloam sections of the Lucent River, but it's still cool, and the breeze that hits my exposed cheeks and drenched hair has me savoring the warmth of Ikar's heat against my back. My magic takes the opportunity to scream for me to let it loose, and I'm so tired of it all that I almost do. But I can't. I knot it up and keep it close.

We reach the bank too soon, and Ikar nearly carries me to the soft grass above.

He stops and whispers in my ear, "Darvy told me you're retiring after this job... I think that's probably good because it seems like you need me around."

He practically drops me in a heap, and I glare at him, hating that it's true. Don't ask me how I survived all these years on my own. I'd be dead ten times over without Ikar these past weeks. I sit there, shivering and indignant, and look at the grave expressions on the faces of the three men.

"Who were they?" I ask as my teeth begin to chatter.

"Gloam masters," Ikar and Rhosse answer at the same time.

I'm about to ask what they are, but the name seems to speak for itself, and I saw for myself how they manipulated the gloam creatures.

I look between the two of them. "It can't be that bad, can it? There were only four of them."

"Where there's one, there will be more. Many more," Rhosse says with dreadful promise in his voice.

I frown, even more scared now and wishing I thought Ikar was still a criminal so I could sit beside him, maybe huddle beneath his arm. "Where are they coming from, anyway?"

"They likely entered somewhere here in the Lucent Mountains," Rhosse says as he sharpens a knife. "It's the weakest part of the kingdom now. They were banished hundreds of years ago."

"This is only the beginning." Ikar speaks up, a graveness in his voice that puts me further on edge.

My thoughts turn as I try to make sense of it all. "And they want—"

"The same thing I want." Ikar's smile is bitter. "A Black Tulip, I'm sure. I suppose the high king would be second, to be rid of him. But you're an originator." He looks hard at me for a prolonged moment. "So maybe they were after *me* and the flower I just retrieved." He releases me from his gaze and stares pensively into the forest beyond.

I feel a knife of shock at his words. *Same thing I want. A Black Tulip.* All over again, I struggle with the reality that he's the high king, that *he* is the one who wants the Black Tulips. And apparently, now, so do the Gloam masters. I force my thoughts back to the topic at hand. Something deep in my soul warns me not to ask, but my will is no match for my curiosity.

My voice feels shaky and a bit too high. "Why?"

Ikar looks my way. "Why do they want a Tulip, or why do they want me dead?"

"Both." The answer to the second question is obvious, but I don't want to seem overly interested in the first.

"Same reason I do: to bridge. According to the journal, which holds my grandfather's account of Lucentia from long ago, we know that all of us gained the ability to *use* Lucentia's magic once she gifted it to us... but her Tulips are special. It seems as though they carry a direct link to Lucentia herself. If they bridge with one, it's assumed it could weaken Lucentia enough to defeat her and her lucent."

I swallow tightly as a vivid image of the seer vision comes to mind. *Oh no.*

Chapter 39

Ikar

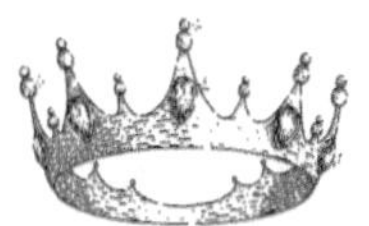

We left the nymphs three days ago, and while I fully expected to be attacked by more gloam masters, all has been quiet—our return trip almost *too* uneventful. It's left me with too much time to dwell on the way my magic reacts to Vera and the fact that we will soon part ways. We busy ourselves separately before the fire, but I can't help catching a glimpse of her every now and then as I try to memorize her features... as if I haven't already.

Rhosse sharpens and cleans his weapons meticulously, and Vera sits a few feet away from him watching Rupi attempt to thwart a spider. From the way she dodges, hops, and her feathers continue to quill up, combined with angry chirps, it appears the spider is winning tonight. Darvy is seated nearby, a bit of charcoal in his hand that is quickly forming what looks to be Rupi in a small book he carries. The tulip, cradled safely in its box and secure in my pack, has occupied my mind since Rupi dropped it in my hands. Vera may not be my biggest supporter, but Rupi adores me. The hope and confidence brought on by having a tulip in my hands has doused further doubts about my ability to save my kingdom. Rupi finds me worthy. If I were to say that aloud, I'd be mocked, but there's something about that tiny bird that seems to *know* things. To me, her opinion counts. And Vera's story about simply finding Rupi in the forest? I'm still not sure I completely believe her. But those details are minor compared to the other information I need from her.

I mentally switch gears from searching out a flower to searching out a Black Tulip. From the look of betrayal in Vera's eyes when Rupi gave me the flower, I don't think she'll be open to me asking about the list again, but I have to. I'm quite aware of the feelings that simmer between us—if my pet gave Vera a flower that would bridge her to another man, I would also feel betrayed.

The thought tightens my chest almost painfully with sorrow. I don't know how I'm supposed to make a life with another woman when the only one I can think about is Vera. But constantly the people of my kingdom weigh on my mind. *Always, duty first.*

If all goes as planned, tomorrow we will find sharp flyers waiting in the field where we began. I have no more time to wait for her to share what she knows... Maybe this isn't the kindest way, but what other choice has she left me?

I pull out the journal, flip to the back where several empty pages remain, and frown at the empty space. It feels wrong to write in my grandfather's journal. I slap it shut.

"Darvy, your charcoal and book?" I reach a hand out toward him.

He finishes a few more sweeps along what is becoming Rupi's back and hands it to me. "You want to draw?" He appears confused—as he should be.

Even Rhosse raises his gaze to see what I'll do. They both know how nonexistent my art skills are.

I smirk, unable to resist goading Darvy. "Maybe if you'd skipped more of your art lessons to practice weapons, like I did, you'd be as good as me."

I pull out my sword the same time Darvy does. We're both up from our seats, our weapons smashing together amidst my laughing... until he nicks my hand, and the laughter dies in my throat. Metal rings in my ears as he blocks my swing. We continue that way, both blocking the other, no one getting the upper hand, until Rhosse calls the fight several minutes later.

"It's a toss-up. Sit down before one of you gets injured," he says gruffly, but I hear the smile in his voice.

I run my forearm across my brow and grin at Darvy, who grins back, breathing heavily.

"We had to settle things," Darvy says matter-of-factly, as he sheathes his sword and heads back to his seat in the dirt, leaning back against a fallen tree trunk, looking pleased with himself.

"Nothing is settled. I still stand by my comment," I argue as I once again take a seat on the fallen log and grab Darvy's book.

Darvy gives a smug smile. "Who got first blood?"

"That's only because I wasn't taking it serious—"

"Men," Vera mutters.

My lips lift in a half-grin at her comment. She would be amazed how quickly problems between soldiers are solved— this was nothing. But I force myself to focus; the journey ends tomorrow.

I open Darvy's book and flip to a blank page, readying the piece of charcoal between my fingertips, and hoping I can write legibly with it well enough.

"On a serious note..." I look between Darvy and Rhosse.

"We all read that list of Tulips. We should have done this sooner, but there's no better time than now. Let's make a list of the names we can remember."

Vera stiffens as she scoops Rupi from her game with the spider and holds her in her lap, stroking her feathers—something I've noticed she does when she needs comfort. My heart begins to soften at the evidence of her stress, but I squash the feeling of compassion. I need answers.

Darvy begins. "There were seven."

I nod, remembering the same, and number the list before me.

"I remember a Patricia, or maybe it was Tetra?"

Rhosse nods. "Petra. I remember that one, as well—it was the first one. And Nova was on the list. It's my aunt's name—it helped me remember."

I nod and scribble the names down. "I remember two, Fina and Maven." I look up at each of them. "Three more."

Four is great. The entire list of seven is better.

"Vera?" Her head jerks up at her name. "Do you remember any?"

She looks at me like she might spit on my boots. "Nope," she says, the p popping a bit with her attitude, matching the disdain in her eyes.

I want to understand her hesitation, but I can't wait any longer.

I plow ahead. "Any others?"

Darvy speaks again. "The only other one I sort of remember was a different type of name, one I haven't heard before. Was it Avanna?" He shuts his eyes, trying to visualize it.

I find myself watching Vera from the corner of my eye. She's statuesque again and pale, stroking Rupi's feathers so hard that she's beginning to quill as Vera's hand passes down her back. But Rupi stays where she is, handling the mindless, anxious stroking like the hardiest of soldiers.

Darvy tries again. "No, that's not right. Avetta?" Now he's frowning with frustration. "It was something like that. It's *right* there in my mind, but I can't quite visualize it. Maybe I'm just thinking that because Vera is with us, and it somehow seems similar. But I know it's a longer name." He laughs and Vera joins him, albeit slightly forced.

"That's alright." I write down the ideas in case it helps us later. "We'll think of them or we'll find someone who can get us another list."

I eye Vera with an accusatory glint. She stares back without an ounce of guilt in her cool gray eyes.

I break the stare between us and look at the page of names. "We aren't the only ones to have had eyes on those names. Someone else compiled it and sold it. I suppose finding out who that was will be our next course of action."

"You don't know who made that list?" Vera asks in a controlled voice.

"I never did tell you where I got it, did I?" I smirk. "No. I don't know who compiled the list."

Darvy folds his arms across his broad chest. "No, he ditched Rhosse and me, and won it fair and square in an illegal fight ring." He looks my way. "I still hold a grudge over that."

Vera's face pales even further. I'm worried she might keel over in a dead faint. Is it concern for me putting myself at risk in a fight? Or the fact that someone else seems to know the names of the Tulips? I'm betting on the latter.

I carefully remove the page from Darvy's book and slowly fold it, pressing the edges into flat creases, wondering what means Vera will resort to this time to destroy it. Will she simply lift it from my pack? Another tea dousing? Or maybe she realizes now that no matter if she destroys it, not only do we remember a few of the names, but there's someone else out there that knows every single one—something she can't change.

Chapter 40

Vera

All this time, it never occurred to me to question where that dratted list had come from. I'd only been worried about destroying it and ensuring the men wouldn't get the names from *me*. I thought it would end here, with me. That if I held my secrets close, they'd stay hidden. It was foolish. Was it one of the Tulips? A betrayal? There *were* only seven names.

I don't realize how heavy my strokes are until Rupi squirms beneath my hand. I lift it to release her, and she affectionately pecks my hand before fluttering into Darvy's lap to observe him sketching her wing. My thoughts return to the list, considering each of the women who appear so scared at every annual meeting—it just doesn't sit right. None of them seems the traitor type. Someone else, then. But who?

Blood rushes in my ears, and I know I need space.

I stand and offer a murmured excuse for needed privacy. Ikar watches me like a hawk as I step into the forest shadows. I start out walking until I'm far enough away, then for a few moments, I run gracelessly through the trees, tripping over large roots and rocks until I finally stumble to a fallen tree and practically curl in on myself, holding my head in my hands and rocking back and forth in an attempt to contain my panic and emotion.

What do I do?

I'd hoped if I tied this job up nice and tidy, I could leave this all behind and pretend it didn't happen. I could simply hide behind my bracelet like I always have. *I was going to fix it.*

"Vera?" Ikar calls from somewhere behind me, his steps so intentionally noisy that I know he's being courteous of my privacy, even though I felt the pull of magic strengthen between us before I heard him approach.

I jump up, roll my shoulders back, brush stray hairs away from my face, contain my magic, and attempt a stony expression. Someone else out there knows about the Tulips, but I certainly won't be making his job of finding one any easier.

I tip my chin in the air, hoping the motion gives me more confidence than I feel. "Yes?"

He takes that as permission to close the last several feet between us, appearing as a panther in the dim moonlight. Stalking like a predator. Half his features are draped in shadow from the angle we stand, and it's difficult to gauge what he's thinking with his eyes veiled in darkness.

I gather a bit of lucent in my hand, just enough to illuminate his face, and I spot Rupi in the shadows near his ear looking as dark as a white ball of fluff can. Suspicion fairly oozes from him, and the line of his brows is hard. My light flickers a bit.

His next words are unexpected, and a hint of sincere concern appears in his eyes. "Are you well?"

I frown, caught off guard. "I'm fine." As fine as a woman can be in circumstances such as these, I suppose.

"It's just... you've looked pale—"

"Did you need something?" I realize immediately it was the wrong thing to ask.

He looks at me for a long moment, his lips tilting into a dangerous half-smile, as if deciding the blunt change of direction in our conversation is acceptable. "Yes. Actually, I do." His voice is low and silky, tempting me to tell him whatever he wants. "I need to know what you know about the Tulips."

He saunters forward until we're a breath apart and looks down at me, holding my gaze. He says it so easily, so directly, as if the Black Tulips haven't worked so hard to keep themselves hidden for centuries now and suddenly our secret has busted out into the open.

"I can't help you."

I expect him to ask why, so I begin formulating an appropriate response. Instead, his next question yanks the air from my lungs in one fell swoop.

"I've wondered why you care so much, why you refuse to trust me... why you *fear* me," he muses, and lets that comment linger a moment, lets my heart rate rise torturously until I fear it's going to stop completely.

When I don't respond, he continues. "You know one of them, don't you? You mentioned a best friend, but you hardly speak of her. You hope to protect her from me. You're terrified I'll find out where she is." His voice is rough now. Accusatory. Assuming.

And sorta right, if I'm being honest.

He stands too close, and I slowly wipe my sweaty palms along my trousers, grappling for words.

"You think I'm a monster," he says darkly, fitting the description he paints of himself.

My heart beats like the hooves of a hundred racing horses.

If I felt panic before, it's nothing compared to this. His guesses are growing too accurate. My breath is shaky, and I hate that he can hear it. And I hate that the only way to throw him off our scent is to hurt him. *Oh, how I hate to lie.*

I gather every ounce of frustration and fear and panic to force anger to ring true in my voice. "You don't know what you're talking about. You want to know what I really think?" I don't wait for him to answer; I forge ahead with sharp spite in my voice. "You are so desperate for the Black Tulips to be real, to believe that you can be the hero, that you have imagined things about me that are wrong to give you a twisted sense of hope. This is all pointless. There's *nothing* you can do."

I feel immediate flames of hot guilt. We stand so still I can't even see his chest move with breath. He doesn't speak, but I glimpse hurt in his eyes for half a second before it's gone. Whatever there was between us extinguishes as quickly as I snuff out the light in my hand, dousing us in darkness.

I begin to walk around him.

"Have you ever trusted anyone in your life?" His voice comes out cold and hard from behind me.

I hesitate. I want to shout that I've trusted Tatania all this time, but have I? What about Mama Tina? My Tulip sisters? Renna? I don't trust any of them with my life, or my deepest secrets, but is that their fault... or mine?

"Thought so. At least it's not just me." He turns and brushes past me, leaving me in the dark with a gaping hole in my heart.

Chapter 41

Vera

My eyes are dry as desert sand this morning from a complete lack of sleep brought on by the horrifying conversation Ikar kicked up about the stupid list of Tulips last night. To hear that they remembered almost half the names is not good. Then they'd almost gotten *mine*, which is also bad. And even worse than that? The conversation that came after.

Something tells me it won't be long until Ikar realizes the secrets I've hidden right under his nose all this time. I don't plan on being anywhere near when he realizes—*if* he realizes. I hate that I feel like a traitor. I know I'll be escaping soon after we land, leaving Ikar to figure this out on his own. I feel both guilt and relief, but I remind myself that this is how the kings wanted it when they killed my sisters, and this is how it will stay.

Now, tears stream from the corners of my eyes with the speed that we return to the kingdom on the sharp flyers. I don't know how long they've been waiting in that field, but they were there when we arrived.

I'm sharing a saddle with Darvy this time, which was a risky choice given the rough start he had on the trip here. Gratefully, though, this time was much smoother, and we left the dreadful Lucent Forest behind. The sharp flyer's powerful wings beat on either side of us, carrying us swiftly back to the high kingdom. Darvy keeps one arm wrapped snug around my waist as if he thinks I might slide off without it.

I smile sadly. I'm going to miss working with these men, but I'm exhausted from all the secrets. Exhausted by my magic constantly reaching for Ikar. I've fought for days to keep my magic to myself, and I'm weary in a way I never knew possible. If ever I was ready to retire, it would be now.

Rest and respite are still out of reach, though, because all I can think is that I must warn Tatania about everything that has transpired. She has to know that we are no longer secret or safe, even if that means spilling all my mistakes over the course of the last few weeks. Discomfort twists my stomach just thinking of it, but it has to be done. Our names are out there, not only between these three men, but whoever created the list in the first place... and what if it was *copied*?

My nerves have been tingling with the urge to reach Tatania before Ikar finds any of us. I know now that if we don't do something different, he will. He's capable, smart, and has every resource available to search us out. It's not a matter of if, but when.

It's only a few more hours before the sharp flyers begin to circle above the castle to land one at a time. A crowd heads in our direction as soon as we're spotted. Apparently, the king was missed. I wrinkle my nose, trying to feign disgust—it doesn't work. Truth is, I feel for them. I miss the king, too, and I haven't even left yet.

Rhosse lands first, Ikar right behind him. He dismounts, jumping to the ground with easy confidence. Rhosse is soon by his side as the groups swarms them. Is this always how it is for him? He did mention having very little personal time when we were stuck in that tree...

I beat the compassion into submission. He's the king; he was raised for this life.

Darvy and I land last, and just like that, the journey is officially over. I try not to glance at Ikar after Darvy helps me off the sharp flyer, but I do. I battle the urge to look at him, to drink in his appearance, knowing I'll likely never see him again... and even though I can't change it or even apologize, I feel horrible about what I said last night.

I risk another quick glance his way to find that he's busy speaking with a group of not only soldiers, but Nadiette, as well. She offers no sign of a friendly gesture forthcoming, and instead turns her attention solely to Ikar. *Surprise, surprise.*

Stable hands come to care for the sharp flyers and lead them away, and without the large form of my friendly flyer, I'm left feeling awkward amidst the busyness of the high king's return. I scoff. Now that I know what he is, it seems so obvious. He so effortlessly leads, commands, decides. The dramatic corner of my heart tempts me to slip away unnoticed, but the logical side isn't leaving without the money I earned.

Darvy catches my eye and ambles closer, offering me a small smile. "When will you open for business?"

Is it me, or do we both feel sad our budding friendship is over so quickly?

I look down and smile, using the toe of my scuffed boot to push some loose dirt back and forth. "Not quite yet. I have some things to do, and I need to visit Mama Tina. But soon."

"Send a message with the name and where you decide to open. I'll stop in."

"When you're not protecting our high king and fighting off gloam monsters?" I smile wryly.

"Yeah." He laughs a little and looks across the field toward Ikar, still surrounded by people. "I can help you get payment, if you're ready to leave. Maybe he'll be done once we finish."

I don't want Darvy to think I *need* to talk to Ikar, so I shrug like it doesn't matter and follow him to the castle. We both know better.

I depart with a heavy purse of coin, Ikar nowhere to be seen. I allow myself a quick glance around as I exit. But of course, no sign of Ikar. It's time for me to leave, and maybe it's best if we don't say goodbye. Goodbyes make it seem like there was something between us. There shouldn't have been.

With my heavy pack resting on my shoulders once again, I weave through the crowded streets of Moneyre and out the city gates. Rupi huddles against my neck, and I'm not sure if she's comforting me or trying to receive comfort. Maybe both.

I lean into her tiny form as the first drops of misty rain moisten the top of my head and shoulders. We're on our own again, and it has never felt so lonely.

I traveled all through the last day and then night, the entire time dreading the upcoming groveling I'll be forced to endure to reclaim my status as one of the Black Tulips. There's no time to waste getting my bracelet back, so though I'd rather skip this part and run straight to Mama Tina's, I force myself to march forward.

The lonely trip has left my mind free to ponder on every-thing I left behind—my new friends Darvy and Rhosse, yes... but mostly Ikar. Guilt and disloyalty swirl within me, because though I seek the protection of the Tulips, I'll never hate Ikar like I'm supposed to. How could I have let this happen to myself?

I refuse to reflect too long on what I feel for him, but it's deep enough to have my heart ache over the loss of him in my life. I try not to worry over the problems he deals with, the worries and the weight he carries. My Tulip sisters have to come first—I promised. *I promised.*

I blink away angry tears at the unfairness of it all. With two of the suns left in the sky, muddy boots, frizzy hair, and a soggy jacket, I stand before the headquarters of the Black Tulips, hoping Tatania or Lillath, her secretary, are here.

Only one way to find out.

Uneven cobblestones lead to the once-grand entrance with tall double doors where a fancy handle is loosely fastened. I'm sure one day it's going to fall off in my hand, but I tug it, and, once again, it holds true. But the door doesn't open. I grab the large metal knocker, damp in my hand, and let it drop a few times. I wait, listening to the drizzling rain drops fall on vegeta-tion, stone, and soil. If no one answers, will I come back?

I begin to turn and step down the first step, an odd sense of relief seeping through me at avoiding this dreaded meeting.

Then the door swings open, startling me so hard I nearly fall off the second step.

"Avenara?"

I turn to find Lillath, her head tilted in confusion.

"I need to speak with Tatania; it's urgent."

She nods with a look that tells me my rebelliousness was

spoken of between them, but I can't gauge how I'll be received from her guarded expression. It fuels my already taut nerves. But she opens the door wider and steps aside so I can enter.

I lift Rupi off my shoulder and onto my finger, quietly whispering, "I better leave you outside this time. Stay close. I'll be out soon."

If a bird could *harrumph* I'm sure I would've heard it. Rupi fluffs her quills like she's offended, but she immediately takes flight.

I step inside and follow Lillath through the familiar building. Down the hallway, I catch a glimpse of the empty ballroom where we hold our annual meetings, but instead of entering its doors, we take another turn. I spot Tatania's office with warm light shining beneath the door.

"Wait here," Lillath instructs. She hustles through the door.

I drop my pack on the floor and lean my back against the wall, uncaring that the state of my clothes has me looking like I just climbed from a river and rolled in the dirt. That awful, lonely, sad feeling is still heavy in my heart, and I can't bring myself to care about my appearance. Another ache stabs my heart, wishing Ikar was still by my side. I've grown used to his steady presence, our banter, teasing him, how safe he makes me feel. The irony—here I am begging for help from the Tulips as I wish myself with the king. I'm a traitor if there ever was one.

A moment later, the door swings open again.

Lillath motions me inside. "Tatania will see you now."

I push off the wall with a tight smile, grab my pack, and enter the room to find a neat desk that is Lillath's, but we don't stop there. She leads me through a connecting door into a larger room with a fancier and larger desk and enormous windows that offer a breathtaking view of the forest beyond.

Tatania stands behind the imposing desk, unnaturally still, eyes hard. "Sit."

I buck at the command, but force myself to sit without argument. I'm supposed to be groveling; apparently, I'm not very good at it.

She takes a seat behind her desk, her gown artfully settling around her, and then she waits.

I swallow, not sure how to begin. "I came to pay the dues... I know they're late." I pull the broken bracelet from my pocket and set it on the desk. "But I have the money, and I'm hoping you can help me get my bracelet replaced."

Her eyes catch on the bracelet with stark disappointment that causes a spike of shame to knife through my chest. "You've endangered not only yourself, but your sisters with your rash actions. What is your excuse for choosing not to pay the dues?"

I curse inwardly. How do I explain a choice that even to me sounds blazing idiotic?

I clear my throat. "I gave Renna the money she needed to secure her safety and took a job that paid well enough I can now pay mine." It's the truth... without the part where I decided I didn't want it anymore.

I'm pretty impressed with myself for wording it so well—makes it sound not quite so bad.

Tatania's expression is stony. "It seems to me you decided you no longer needed the protection of the Tulips. What changed your mind? Why do you find you now need us?"

It sounds horrible when she puts it that way. I see the trap set but can do nothing to avoid it.

"I may have..." *Don't lie.* I swallow. "I *did* come in contact with the high king."

Tatania's eyes widen in alarm.

I rush to spit out the rest. "He doesn't know who I am, but I realize the danger now."

"Hmm." Her displeasure is almost palpable as she leans forward and adjusts the already perfect placement of parchments on her desk. "Though I'm tempted to leave you to your own devices for the danger you put your sisters in, it would leave the rest of us at further risk. I will send a message to the bracelet charmer, but it may be days, or even weeks, before we get it back."

So, no warm welcome back, but she'll get me another bracelet. I should be fine for a few days or weeks, right?

She sits back stiffly, and I cringe at the disapproval in her gaze. "I'll send a message to Mama Tina once it's ready. After hearing of the mercenaries in search of us, I've sent the other Tulips into hiding. I expect the same of you."

Another command that riles me. I sift through my pack and pull out the hefty amount of money needed to pay the dues from my pack, sliding it across the desk with a stiff nod. I take her extended silence to mean she's done with me, and I'm halfway to standing, but I abruptly sit when she speaks again.

"The king," Tatania says, and my eyes jerk to meet hers. "What did you think of him?" Curiosity flashes in her eyes, though she tries to hide it.

I decide to be honest. "He's a good one, from what I know." I hesitate to share the rest, but I figure I should come clean. "He searches for a Black Tulip to bridge with and has the black tulip flower in his possession. It sounds as if he needs one of us to restore lucent for the kingdom."

Her brows raise and eyes widen simultaneously. "He has a black tulip, you say?" Concern knits a fine line between her brows.

I offer a simple nod, because I'm for sure not admitting that I was part of the team to help find it.

"I'm proud that this knowledge didn't sway you, however you came about it, and that you returned for safety. I'll send a message to our fellow Tulips with further warning." She looks at me with an eyebrow quirked. "Though I believe you're the only one who needs it."

I press my lips together to keep the saucy words in my mouth from escaping in response to that. But I can't resist asking, "If one of us doesn't bridge with him, what will happen to lucent... and gloam?"

Tatania waves a dismissive hand. "The kings made their choice when they killed our sisters and chose to elevate originators."

I sit up straighter. "It's just, it seems a little harsh to hold that over *this* king and watch gloam slowly eat away our kingdom and—"

Tatania scoffs. "It seems you didn't escape quite as unaffected as I'd thought. Beware the lies of the kings of Moneyre. I thought I'd warned you enough. You sound as if you spoke with him personally."

She laughs, but when I don't answer, she stops abruptly and narrows her eyes.

No need for her to know the depths I fell to with my wrong choices, but she's right. I'm different because of it, and I'm not sure how I feel about that. At one time, I would've tried to mold myself back into the person the Tulips wanted me to be, but something about that feels wrong now. I've always trusted Tatania, and I believe she truly cares for us. Their protection is all I've wanted these past weeks... and I still want it.

Don't I?

I eye the stack of money on her desk. Money I risked my life for.

"I was only curious," I say, dodging her correct assumption with the most innocent smile I can conjure.

She nods as she slides the money toward her. "As I will inform the other Tulips, take further measures to hide until this settles down. I assume you'll stay under the protection of Mama Tina?"

I nod.

For now.

Chapter 42

Ikar

I sit slouched in my seat at the high table, an elbow on the arm of my chair. The wax and wane of voices and laughter filling the air around me dulls my hearing until my thoughts flow freely. I recall the meeting held soon after we'd landed with several of my highest officers, Nadiette as head of the originators, and Jethonan. Discussions on the gloam masters lasted for far too long; the only solution decided on was to increase patrols and originators. It doesn't seem like enough when I realize the danger of the enemy we face, but until I find a Black Tulip and bridge, there isn't much else we can do.

It wasn't until after the meeting, when I'd gone in search of Vera, that I'd found she'd already left. I think back on the first time we met, her boldness in soaking my hard-earned list of Black Tulip names in tea. Though I was enraged at the time, now a smile twitches about my lips. I never did get the information from her. Stubborn woman. Other memories come to mind, but the one that lingers is our kiss on the dimly lit second floor of Mama Tina's house.

Jethonan's voice pulls me from my thoughts as he leans

closer. "If I were to guess your thoughts, it would be that they center on a woman."

His voice is just above a whisper, but Nadiette, who sits beside Jethonan stiffens, her spoon hitting the rim of her soup bowl before she recovers and takes a dainty sip. I blink as if merely bored.

"There is no woman of that sort in my life." I make no effort to lower my voice, but I can't completely hide the bitter note that tinges my tone. There is one woman I want, and she hates me for being king, which is just as well since nothing can come of the feelings between us anyway.

"But there was, until this morning? Hm?" Jethonan whispers.

A muscle in my jaw ticks, and I realize I'm clenching my teeth. How does he know such things? Blazing observant advisor.

"Your Majesty." Nadiette leans a bit past Jethonan to catch my eye. "Might I have a word with you this evening?"

I incline my head, then take a long swallow of the wine in my glass. Fatigue burns my eyes. Now not only must I speak with Nadiette again, but I must speak with Jethonan about my wayward magic. I sigh and sink a little deeper into my chair. The evening drags on while I wait an appropriate amount of time until I can leave.

It's easy to fall back into memories of Vera, but I catch myself this time. I focus instead on my broken magic. The mental energy to keep it wrapped so tightly the last several days around Vera has drained me. I cautiously loosen my tightly coiled magic just enough for it to move freely through my veins, ensuring I don't offend any ladies in the room. I wait, ready to tug it back, but I find relief in the normalcy of the magic flowing through my body. I continue to relax my grip on it and find that it reaches for... no one.

I wait a few minutes.

Still, nothing.

I try to direct it toward Nadiette, but I find that that part of my magic, for lack of a better term, no longer exists.

Could it have simply returned to normal on its own?

I think back over the past day and realize that after days of having to learn to control it, I have felt no pull or draw since this morning. I need answers.

I take another long swallow and set my glass down hard before I stand and indicate that the meal can continue before I take my leave. Jethonan stands and follows after me. Once we reach his office and the door is securely closed, I turn toward him, frowning.

"There's something wrong with my magic. Or, at least, there *was*."

"Explain so I may understand, Your Majesty."

I start to pace from one side of the room to the other. "I spent days with Vera, and my magic never reacted in any way different. Then, several days before we returned, it did. It draws toward her as you described it should draw toward a Queen of the Night. But just now, at dinner, it's normal. No drawing toward anyone. What could have happened?"

I stop pacing and wait for his answer.

Jethonan leans against his large desk covered in glass vials and bowls of odd-colored liquids and folds his arms. "Could Vera be—"

I scowl and shake my head, frustrated he's asking. I won't hope for something that's not possible. "I already told you that I was with her for days, and my magic never drew toward her like that. I did get injected by velvet widow venom—"

Jethonan shakes his head. "Velvet widow venom has not affected any other's magic, as far as I know."

"How am I to identify a Black Tulip if my magic is drawing toward random women?" I ask angrily.

Jethonan thinks for a moment, then asks, "Is your magic working normally in every other way?"

I nod.

"Has it drawn toward any other woman?"

"No."

Jethonan smirks. "Then the only explanation is that you had a Black Tulip in your hands."

I refuse to consider what he says. "Are there not ways to test my magic?"

Jethonan raises his brows. "May I be honest, Your Majesty?"

"Possibly," I growl.

"You are an observant, intuitive warrior."

I warily accept his compliments with a nod.

He appears to choose his words carefully. "With those gifts... did anything come to your notice that may have seemed *different* about her?"

I rub the back of my neck with a hand as I begin to pace again. "No."

All her differences made sense, sort of.

I shake my head, but then memories begin to show themselves, and I stop. "Have you ever met an originator who never wears white or shows their mark?"

Jethonan shakes his head. "No, but it's believable."

I nod in agreement and continue back across the room. "Animals are drawn to her, but so they are to Rhosse, as well."

Jethonan nods, but the knowing glint in his eye makes me

want to leave his office. There's no possible way Vera is a Black Tulip. It doesn't make sense.

I continue, somewhat warily, this being one of my biggest questions. "What about an originator that also has the magic of a talented healer?"

Jethonan smiles like a smug cat. "Never that."

My gaze whips toward him as the tiniest flicker of hope comes to life in my chest—I extinguish it with a scowl. "But is it possible?"

Jethonan shrugs. "I don't believe so. I've never heard of a person being born with two magical factions." He raises a questioning brow. "Did she heal you?"

"Once, when she believed I was a criminal. I was unaware, but she admitted it when I questioned her later."

"Anything else about her magic?" Jethonan prompts.

I think for a moment, remembering how it felt when I pulled large amounts of lucent and didn't feel like I was going to burst into flames. "It was cooler than I've ever felt, which made it more comfortable to use. I didn't feel as if I were going to burn alive."

Jethonan's eyes are eager now. "And the color of her magic... a hint of yellow as the sun? Or white, like the moon?"

"...like the moon," I say slowly.

I'd forgotten that Jethonan had mentioned something about that at the beginning of all this.

Jethonan retrieves a familiar book from the shelf near the tall windows across the room. The same book he'd shown me before. He opens to a page, then flips a few more, then begins reading and grunting to himself before slapping the book closed. It was hardly enough time for him to have even read anything.

"She's a Black Tulip," he says decisively. "I double-checked for your peace of mind, Your Majesty, as I've known from the moment she left my office the evening before your Lucent Mountain journey. She obliterated the gloam I had planned to use for experimentation, seemingly by *accident*."

I do recall him acting strangely that night, but that's not unusual for Jethonan. What if it just escaped due to her messing with the lid? I find his arguments are convincing, but still, doubts linger.

I stand before one of the windows, fold my arms across my chest, and look out over the tiny bits of glowing light that shine amongst the shops and along the streets in the darkness of night. "Explain to me why my magic didn't recognize her until the middle of our journey."

"There is an explanation; it just has to be found," Jethonan says, sounding overly patient. "Why don't you find her and ask?"

I laugh sardonically. "Another problem I haven't yet mentioned. She saw my mark, and to say she wasn't happy is an understatement. She ran as soon as we returned."

Jethonan moves behind his desk and tinkers with a twisty, curling glass tube as a bright-colored liquid sluggishly moves through."Yet another piece of evidence to indicate our assumption is correct."

He's right. But I can't let go of the question I previously posed, and will again.

"Again, why did my magic not recognize her until two days ago?" Exasperation bleeds through my voice now.

Jethonan gives an overly patient sigh as he flicks a piece of his equipment a few times, and suddenly green liquid begins to pour from a miniscule spout and into a bowl. "My lord, there are ways for a person to hide their magic. It is uncommon, as it is usually quite unnecessary, but surely possible. I can inquire—"

"No." I sigh. "It won't be necessary. You are correct that we have enough evidence to assume she *is* a Black Tulip."

I quit fighting the painful truth. After everything we'd been through together, knowing how much I needed the help of a Black Tulip, still she hid? Told half-truths? Refused to trust me? Betrayal as hot as a knife taken straight from the fire stabs me in the chest.

I run a hand through my hair. "All this time..."

Jethonan stands, giving me his full attention now. "Trust is more easily gained with patience and kindness than anger and retaliation, my lord."

Then my expression has given me away, again. Or maybe it's my fists, now clenched so tightly my knuckles have turned white, but words intended to calm enrage me further.

"She lied to me!" I shout so loudly I can feel the veins in my temple bulge. "She knew, and *still* she lied. Concealed her identity and led me to believe my magic was broken. Refused to give me a tulip from the field," I say through gritted teeth. "Even after she knew I wouldn't kill her."

"Ah, yes. And that right there is the question: *Does* she know that?" Jethonan asks.

Further words of anger boil up, and I'm ready to defend myself. My kingdom is on the brink of destruction and this troublesome, stubborn, beautiful woman may very well lead to my downfall.

"Please release the sword, I have no weapon to protect myself with." Jethonan eyes my hand warily, where I find it wrapped around the hilt tightly.

I look up at him with a glare. I feel justified in my feelings, and I allow my anger to grow, fanning its flames until it's an inferno. I'm ready to stalk from this room and head to the training grounds, sure I'll find someone to battle with to burn off my anger.

But words of pain keep falling from my lips. "She watched me at the Field of Tulips as I waited torturously when she could have given me one all along. She knew..." *My plan.*

The plan where I approach Lucentia. I don't say it aloud because at this point, it may be all that's left for me.

"She knew what?" Jethonan asks, curious.

I shake my head.

Jethonan takes that as permission to continue, warily eyeing my sword. "Keep in mind, their entire magical faction was, at one time, murdered simply for the fact they were Black Tulips. By a king and his originators, no less."

He bends to adjust the heat of a blue flame beneath a tiny pot as bright-green liquid steadily drips, making *tinging* noises that fill the silence.

My first inclination is to argue, but then I remember the look of stark, genuine fear on her face in the velvet widow cave after she'd seen my mark. How it lingered in her gaze ever after. How she reacted when Darvy, Rhosse, and I were trying to remember the list of names. A list of names that likely included hers.

I release my sword hilt and collapse into an overstuffed chair near the windows. The flames of anger still lick at my pride, but mostly all that's left is hurt and weariness.

Haven't I proven myself yet? How much more does Vera require of a mortal man to gain her trust? I clench a fist on the arm of the chair, frustrated for the hundredth time over the fact that the murder of the Tulips ever happened. That was the beginning of the possible downfall of our kingdom. A wrong I intend to right as best I can, and to never allow to happen again, but first I have to convince the Tulips I'm not out to kill them.

"What do I do?" I ask, letting my head fall back against the chair. For just a moment, I want someone to tell me what to do. For someone else to carry the weight of a failing kingdom, to be the leader. Make the decisions. Fight the battles.

"Go find her, of course. And gain her trust." He swirls the small pot and steam in a shade of pink I've never witnessed before begins to rise.

"I already tried that," I mutter.

"Persistence is the path to success, my lord. See it this way: you're still further ahead than you were when you first began. You have the flower, and now you know exactly which Black Tulip you're after."

I consider his words, and, somehow, the perspective *does* improve my outlook. I stare at a small crack in one of the window-panes, likely caused by a minor explosion from one of his experiments, thinking about where I might begin my search. It doesn't take long. *Mama Tina.*

"It appears you have a plan already," Jethonan observes from across the room.

I instinctively catch the vial he tosses at me before it hits my face, and I look at it before raising a brow. "Tell me this is a charm to make a woman trust me."

Jethonan snorts. "Even *I* have limits to my abilities, my lord. There is no such thing as a *trust charm*. I assume you'll be leaving again, and in your hand is the charm I gave you to hide your identity before, in case you decide to use it again."

I toss the vial in the air once before catching it, and stand.

"Better get to work on a trust charm because my record so far is lacking."

"Your self-confidence is inspiring," Jethonan says dryly.

I chuckle as I leave the room, closing the door behind me, but my smile is quickly replaced with a neutral expression when I see Nadiette waiting in the hallway.

"You said we could speak this evening," she reminds me.

I nod, tuck the vial in a pocket, and begin walking down the hall. "Originator business?" I ask as she matches my stride.

"Not quite."

I glance at her, unused to hearing hesitation in her voice. "I have a very long list to—"

She grabs my arm and we stop, facing each other. "Ikar, please reconsider marrying me."

I clench my jaw in frustration. My kingdom is falling apart at my fingertips, and she wants to discuss this again? I step back until her hand falls from my forearm.

"I have a duty to fulfill," I say simply, then turn and continue walking.

"You don't understand!" Her voice rises. "Waylon and the other low kings, they say if we don't marry, they'll mutiny in only two weeks' time. Does *that* not fall under your duties to prevent?"

I pause. "Two weeks?"

"Yes, but if we marry, it will restore peace."

I've never seen Nadiette beg before; it's not a good look.

"If the low kings were on my list of concerns, then maybe I would consider it. They're not." She frowns and opens her mouth to argue again, but I interrupt. "You don't seem to understand that marrying you may restore temporary peace, but it will lead to the eventual downfall of my kingdom. I won't."

I know the words are harsh, but it's the honest truth.

She watches me leave without another word.

***

It's a long time before sleep finds me as I ruminate over the depth of trouble my kingdom remains in. Not only do I feel sorrow for Nadiette and guilt for not feeling as devastated about the ending of our relationship as I should, but the low kings are stirring up trouble behind my back. Their pettiness angers me so much that I find my heart racing even as I lie in the dark of my room. I have to trust that I can accomplish my mission before they act, but even after I calm *those* concerns, snippets of meetings and conversations that were thrust upon me as soon as I returned fight for center stage of my mind... and in the background, distracting as ever, is Vera. Always Vera.

My eyes finally drift closed.

I find Vera beside me, our wrists pressed together as if we've just completed the mate bond in the forest just outside Shift City. We simultaneously pull them apart and eye the bright marks on our wrists as dust specks sparkle and float in the warm air around us. A dream has never felt so real, but if it includes Vera, I'll take it. Her presence, even in a dream, fills the hole she left in my heart when she disappeared.

I look down and meet her gaze with unguarded affection, unhindered by the worries of reality. Here, I'm free.

I brush stray hairs from her face, my fingers grazing the soft skin of her forehead. "Do you intend to torture me by appearing in my dreams now?"

"Gladly." Her voice is quiet.

I can't resist the saucy smirk that turns her lips, so when she tugs me closer, I let her. In a perfect life, it would be like this between us. No titles. No secrets. Nothing to keep us apart... But for now, I'll enjoy this dream as long as it lasts. She tilts her head up in invitation, and I slide my hands up the back of her arms, gently pulling her closer as I lower my head to meet her lips. Our magic mingles intoxicatingly around us...

I wake, arms empty, and staring at the high beams of the ceiling in my room that is barely lit with morning light. I drift on the stark disappointment that it was all a dream, then I slam a fist on my bed angrily and leave my bed for the comfortable sitting chair.

She taunts me. The motion wakes Arrow, who rises from his mat nearby and pads to my side, resting his large face on my thigh. If I don't find Vera... if I don't find a way to gain her trust... somehow I know my heart will never recover enough to love another woman the way it should.

I instinctively place a hand on Arrow's head and rub behind one pointed ear, but I catch sight of the mate bond on my wrist with the motion and hold it up to inspect it closer. It glows as bright as if Vera is right beside me, as bright as it was in the dream... But *why?* And how? It's been dim since she left; in fact, it has always dimmed with any distance between us. Even now, I watch the brightness slowly fade.

When Vera was taken by the Shifters, I used the increasing brightness to track her down. If it's glowing this brightly now... was that dream somehow *real?* Or is it only me wanting Vera's feelings to match my own?

My hand stills, and Arrow nudges my arm with his wet nose to prompt more ear rubs. Likely it was just a dream, and the desires of my heart are bringing her to mind, but the dream fuels my motivation.

Someday, if I can convince her to trust me, maybe things will be that way between us if I don't give up, and that's worth fighting for.

I glance at the light seeping in through the cracks of my drawn drapes. *Time to find my Black Tulip.*

Chapter 43

Ikar

I stand outside Mama Tina's door, several of my men, including Darvy and Rhosse, standing several feet back. No need to scare the woman, though from what I know of her, she doesn't seem to be the kind to fear much of anything.

The door swings open, and Mama Tina's smiling face is before me, but before I can ask for Vera, she pulls me in and wraps me in a tight hug. She makes me feel as if I'm one of the family... and if Vera is truly a Black Tulip and will trust me enough to admit it, maybe soon I will be. With that thought, I step back, nervous about confronting the woman I've come to feel for. I open my mouth to speak, but Mama Tina beats me to it.

"Is Vera with you?" Too short to see over my shoulders, she leans to the side to peek around me and gets a view of my men. She raises her brows with a pleased smile at the sight of them. "We'll have a dinner party. I'll invite some of Vera's friends." She claps her hands together. "How long will you be staying?" She turns and bids me follow her into her home with a wave of her hand.

Nervous roiling in my stomach is replaced with concern. "Vera told my friend she was coming here. Did she return?"

Mama Tina laughs. "Oh, yes, she's been here. She just left for the market with Renna a little while ago. I thought she may have seen you on her way and returned." She flashes me a glittering smile.

I'm about to turn and leave, the itch to find Vera strong, but Mama Tina snags my elbow and draws me farther into her home. The manners stitched into the fabric of my soul bid me to allow her.

"It appears we may have things to discuss, now that I have you here." She wraps a hand around my arm so firmly I'm not sure I could free myself if I tried. Fae are known for their strength, but Mama Tina is on a different level in every way.

My men follow us in and are led to a sitting room that seems too dainty for their large armor-clad forms, where a servant is already heading with a tray of drinks. They stand awkwardly, looking between themselves as if unsure what they should do as I'm led away, deeper into the house.

Mama Tina guides me to another room, this one a small library. She closes the door and turns toward me, more serious than I've ever seen her. "What are your intentions toward my niece?" she asks bluntly.

I take a seat in a small armchair and lean back, embracing a facade of relaxed confidence, with my legs wide and a casual arm resting along the side, giving the idea that I'm completely at ease. I'm not. I didn't expect this conversation right now—seems a bit premature when the woman I plan to marry is currently hiding from me in fear.

"I plan to marry her, if she'll trust me enough to say yes." I flash a dashing smile that hides the doubts, hurt, and pain of Vera's secrets—her betrayal.

Mama Tina smiles wide. "As I thought." I exhale in relief, then she speaks again. "Now, tell me who you *really* are."

My smile wavers. "What do you mean?"

"The charm you use is very similar to fae glamour. Practically undetectable," she murmurs while she squints hard at me as if attempting to peer into my very soul.

I press back into the chair as if that will help evade her searching eyes. "I'm not a criminal, if that's what you ask," I assure her.

She squints a little closer. "Yes, yes. I already know, dear. But you're more than you seem."

"So is Vera."

Mama Tina presses her lips into a flat line and raises a brow. "She'll be angry if I say anything. It's for her to tell."

"How about I guess, and that way you don't have to tell her you told me?" I don't wait for her to agree. "She's a Black Tulip."

Mama Tina's eyes open wide, then her mouth curves into a wide, approving smile. "You should know I wouldn't approve of just *any* criminal for my niece."

"Yes, well..." I clear my throat, and with a somewhat sober tone in my voice, I try to prepare her for my title. "While I'm grateful you think so highly of me, I hope you continue to once you know the full truth."

"Please, tell." She appears overjoyed to be let in on a secret, her eyes shining bright as she leans forward in her chair with her hands clasped tightly.

I begin slowly. "I am not, and never have been, a criminal. Vera arrested me, but the warrant was false. She didn't know who I was until halfway through the mission she contracted with me on."

Her eyes are full of delight at the mystery of it all.

She leans forward even further. "And?"

"I'm Ikar, High King of Moneyre."

Mama Tina's eyes widen. "The high king?"

She throws her head back and laughs so hard that the large bees embroidered on her full skirt bounce with the movement, and I'm concerned she'll fall off her seat.

I sit forward the smallest bit, confused by her reaction, but prepared to catch her if needed.

"Forgive me. It's just... knowing Vera, I can imagine her reaction to all of this." She laughs again, setting her bees to flying a second time.

I sit there with a careful smile on my lips until my patience wears thin. The woman tests me almost as much as Jethonan. Time is ticking.

"Where can I find her?"

She blots at her eyes with her dainty tissue. "You can wait for her here, or go search her out at the fae market. She and Renna planned to spend the day there." She clasps her hands together and tilts her head, more serious than I've ever seen her now. "You should know that I've never approved of a man for Vera, before you. But you have your work cut out for you. I've never been very supportive of the way the Black Tulips have secreted themselves, hiding behind magic bracelets and such—"

"Hiding behind bracelets?"

"Yes." She stands and picks up a small box sitting on a nearby table, muttering something about *wasted money* as she goes. She returns and places it in my hands, waiting for me to open it. I lift the lid, and inside is a bracelet identical to the one that Vera wore—the one that broke.

I think I already know the answer, but I ask to be sure. "What does it do?"

"Hides them from kings, of course." Mama Tina takes the

box back. "This one arrived just last night, and I didn't have the nerve to give it to her before she left this morning. I'll tell her when she returns, and I'm sure she'll put it on." She looks at me with a raised brow. "Unless you can find her and convince her not to. She's been taught to hate you; you'll have to earn her trust."

Something I am highly aware of.

She grabs my hand and squeezes. "Go find her, boy."

I stand, amused by her familiarity and prepared to thank her for her help. Then she adds, "I expect grandchildren right away."

I choke as she pushes me out the door.

Chapter 44

Vera

I wander the fae market, grateful for the busy chaos around me that distracts from the dream I had last night that brought all my locked-up feelings for Ikar back to the surface in the most torturous of ways. The last thing I wanted to do was leave Mama Tina's, but as usual, Renna seemed to sense my inner turmoil and dragged me out shopping.

Now, as the suns warm my face, I'm glad we came. I hold up a glass tea kettle in the sunshine. The light emphasizes the glass etching of intricate leaves, trees, and flowers that climb up its sides. I just *know* it'll sell easily in my future shop. Rupi chirps in approval, shuffling across my shoulder and bobbing her head. She loves the markets as much as I do.

"You already know you'll be buying it," Renna chimes in, impatient. "Hand over the money and let's move on." She eyes another vendor's items down the way eagerly.

The merchant waits to see if I'll purchase it. I bite my lip as I consider the price and finally decide it's worth it. I pull the money from my bag and pay the woman, then use the dainty wood handle to lower it carefully into the leather bag slung across my body. It's already weighed down with several other items I've found this morning, and I'm feeling like a pleased and greedy dragon sitting atop its treasure.

Renna twines her arm with mine and pulls me to the next merchant, chatting happily as we weave through crowds of people who come to the fae for their renowned markets. She gasps, pulling me toward another table. "Look at this ribbon!" She snatches a spool of gray-blue that reminds me of Ikar's eyes and holds it to my face. "It's the perfect complement to your skin tone."

I force myself to laugh. "I've no need of ribbons, Renna. All I ever wear is this." I wave my hand down my body, still attired in the blousy shirt and corset-style vest, to the close-fitting breeches, and tall leather boots I plan to wear for the foreseeable future. Just because I'm retired from my work as an originator doesn't mean I don't reach for the comfortable apparel and my favorite weapons—and I *certainly* have no need of ribbon that reminds me of Ikar.

She returns the spool and reaches for another, but I'm already moving past, my eyes having caught on a shiny copper scale, but just past it... My gaze locks with eyes the color of the ribbon Renna just replaced, and I freeze. The one man I never planned to see again. My eyes widen further when I spot Darvy and Rhosse behind him, and behind *them*, a slew of soldiers and at least one originator.

Rupi chirps with pure joy, her tiny wings brushing my neck, fluttering and bouncing with excitement—it appears she's spotted him as well. There are only three reasons they'd be here: Ikar wants me as an originator, he's determined to get the names on that list from me, or he knows I'm a Tulip and he's here to collect. With the size of his entourage, it's likely one of the last two.

Our eyes stay locked for a moment that feels like forever, and something cracks within me. I know I can't be near him again and still keep my promises. *I can't.* I beat the rebellious part of me that yearns to run to him into submission. I stumble back one step, then two as I ignore Rupi's joyful chirps and flapping wings. Did Mama Tina rat me out? I know how she loves Ikar. I curse my stupidity. I should never have returned to Mama Tina's, at least, not right away. I was just trying to follow the rules for once. Tatania told me to come here, and look where that got me.

"Vera?" Renna asks, frowning and looking around carefully.

I can tell from the way she steps closer that my behavior has scared her.

I don't answer as I hurriedly look right and left, trying to calculate a way to escape the busy market, all the while keeping an eye on Ikar and his soldiers as they make their way through the crowds toward me. His determined eyes never leave mine.

I slip the strap of my bag over my head and, cursing Ikar, shove it toward Renna as Rupi quills up and squawks at my behavior, her quills stabbing my neck. I ignore her. "Take this back to Mama Tina and hide. I'll return when I can. Don't break anything!"

Renna sputters in confusion, but I'm already running. Rupi jumps from my shoulder and takes flight, soaring just above me. I sprint through the market. People jump out of my way, cursing at me as I pass, but I navigate the market as if I designed it myself. My hair, left down today, flows like a sail behind me. I wish I could tie it back, but there's no time. I hear sounds of pursuit, shouting and yelling as Ikar makes his way after me. I use the fear to fuel my pumping legs.

I continue sprinting through the fae city and out the gates, knowing if I can reach the forest I have my best chance at losing him. *Never mind that I almost kissed him in my dream last night—this is different.*

I know this terrain like the back of my hand, so I leave the path and dive into thick trees, darting between them. I hear him shout my name and I shake my head, willing tears to stay at bay. *Keep running.* I hate that I run as a coward, but it's this or face capture and possible execution for treason for all my secrets... or bridging and betraying my sisters.

I jump over fallen trees and large rocks, and push off tree trunks to increase my speed. I smother the yearning in my heart that tells me to stop, to tell him everything, to trust him. But I can't betray my sisters; I made a blazing *oath.* I ignore the scratches across my face from low-hanging branches. But no matter how fast I run, I can feel him behind me.

"Vera, stop!" His voice is closer now.

In my panic and speed, I miscalculate the width of a ravine, and instead of landing firmly on the opposite side, end up sliding down the edge and rolling back down to the bottom. I try to rise, but my body aches, and my lungs have never burned so badly.

Ikar grabs my shoulder, and I pull my knife and arc it toward him, knowing it's useless. In moments, he has my weapon in hand and straddles me with my arms above my head.

"We're back to this?" he asks, voice low.

I hate that I missed the sound of his voice. His hair is mussed as he hovers over me, his blue eyes icy. We both stare at each other, breathing heavily. A drop of sweat slides into my hairline. It feels like the worst sort of deja vu. I could laugh, seeing him atop me in this way again—just like the night I arrested him. But instead of him cuffed, it'll likely be me, because I won't be cooperating.

My mind spins for the right approach, and I quickly decide to play innocent.

"Need another originator?" I ask, still out of breath, my chest heaving and aching with the feelings that attempt to claw their way out with the help of my rebellious magic. "I'm retired now, so you'll have to find another."

He says nothing, just delves into my eyes with his like he's searching for something. I attempt to wipe everything from my expression. *Epitome of innocence.* I fixate on a small scar that marks his ear, but somehow even *that* is handsome because it's on *him,* and I don't need those sort of thoughts at the moment.

"You forgot to tell me something," he growls.

I stop breathing for a full three seconds. I somehow am able to dig up a saucy tone, though I can hardly fill my lungs. "I didn't *forget* anything."

I'm almost positive he's talking about that blasted list again.

Now I hear the raw anger in his voice. "You knew exactly who I was searching for and still—"

"I can't break my promises!" I shout with a frustrated sob as I try to force his weight off me, jerking my wrists held firm in his hands.

"If you had trusted me, we could have—"

"We could have nothing!" I shout, interrupting him again.

The voices of the many people clamoring for my fealty scream and bounce within the walls of my mind. I yank again at my wrists held firm in his grasp. I'm well and fully stuck. Habit has Tatania's warning running clear in my mind—*never trust the kings*—but I shut it down. I don't trust *anyone*

331

anymore. Tatania lied about kings for years; Ikar is nothing like she said he should be. Mama Tina ratted me out. Ikar hid his identity. Rupi, my once-loyal guide, loves Ikar more than any man she's ever met. I feel pulled in every direction, and I don't know which is right.

I just need him to leave because somehow, though his arms hold me captive, they're the only place I want to be, and I *can't*. My emotions turn and twist like the beginnings of a tornado, collecting pain and anger and building strength. All I know is I need space to figure my life out, to figure out what *my* opinions really are, to figure out what is the morally right thing to do. *Protect my sisters or trust Ikar? Because apparently there's no situation where both are safe.* But I can't do that beneath Ikar's weight with his painfully handsome face hovering over mine. I'm also aware that Darvy and Rhosse and their soldiers are not far behind.

Anxiety combines with anger, and all I can think is escape. I can hardly bear to force the rising, harsh words from my mouth, but I need him to leave before I cave to my feelings and make everything worse. I'm about to open my mouth, but I get a reaction I don't expect.

He lowers his face toward mine, until I feel the roughness of half a day's whiskers brush the side of my cheek and the light whisper of his breath near my ear, and my body traitorously reacts. "I will do whatever I have to to earn your tru—"

I hear a sickening thud followed by Ikar's grunt. My eyes widen in horror at the arrow protruding from his shoulder and the blooming dark red stain spreading around it even as his eyes lock on something over my left shoulder. He releases my wrists and stands, pulling his sword from its sheath with his good arm and standing in a protective stance before me while I scramble to standing. I can't consider that even after the way I've treated him, he protects me. With shame, I grab my knife, the only weapon I brought, from the dirt to face whatever it is that is encroaching around us.

My eyes trail up the tall soldiers... a flashback to our travels in the Lucent Mountains reminds me I've seen them before. Hooded cloaks shadow their faces, and loose robes mask their build, but it doesn't dampen the danger that tangibly emanates from them. Gloam masters. Their weapons are larger than Ikar's, and I know his is a force to be reckoned with; what does that mean for theirs? Faster than my eyes can track, four surround Ikar, and two come for me, separating us in moments.

I pull lucent, creating a ball in my hand, and immediately send a torrent toward Ikar who's already immersed in battle. At this point, I don't care if he can discern the difference between the cool of my magic and an actual originator's. We could both die here.

"Who are you?" I demand when they stop several feet before me, trying to focus even as I hear the *clang* of blades on blades behind them, and hope Ikar will be able to fight while injured.

I feel like a trapped rabbit. Why aren't they attacking me? Are they playing some sort of twisted game? I lift my knife higher, widen my stance, and pull more lucent.

A chilling, deep voice comes from within one of the deep hoods. "Isn't *gloam masters* what they call us?" He looks toward his fellow cloaked figure who laughs in a way that has my skin crawling.

"What do you want with us?" My knife trembles in my grip.

"Not *us*." The hooded figure stops not three paces away. "*You*."

Both their hidden, creepy gazes are focused on me. I can

feel it. Do they not realize they have the high king in their grasp? They want *me*? But then Ikar's words as we sat on the bank of the Lucent River after escaping the gloam masters ring in my ears ...*same thing I want. A Black Tulip, I'm sure. I suppose the high king would be second, to be rid of him.*

Oh no.

Ikar's pained shout rings in my ears, and I whip my head in his direction to see one of the figures yank a sword from his midsection. Two lie dead around Ikar, and one falls to the ground as I watch. But dark red blood pours from Ikar's side, and the arrow is still firmly planted in his shoulder. He drops to a knee, and I scream as I watch him fall to the ground.

Darvy and Rhosse and their slew of soldiers scramble down the ravine wall to our right, finally having caught up. I keep up a continual rush of magic for them, hoping it's enough. I forget the gloam masters hovering before me and dart around them, running and landing on my knees beside Ikar, attempting to block him from any further injuries with my body. I ignore the towering, violent figures around us and instead focus on Ikar for our last moments together. I wait for the piercing blade of a sword through my back.

"I'm sorry. I'm so sorry," I whisper near his ear. "Please don't die," I murmur over and over softly, holding his face while warm tears fill my eyes as I will his eyes to open, to meet mine with their stormy depths, even if they *are* still filled with accusation.

I press one hand to his neck and find his pulse, slow and weakening. Rupi lands near his ear and affectionately pecks it, waiting for a response, quilling when he doesn't move. While I wait to die, I intend to do everything I can to save him. I grasp the arrow and pull with so much effort my grunt is almost a war cry. I toss it into the dirt, even more concerned when he offers no reaction. I press both my hands to the injuries and recklessly pull magic, hoping I can do enough to save him. Lucent runs through my veins cool and refreshing, pouring from me and into him. I wait for the killing blow, prepared to pass to the other side of magic with Ikar, even in the midst of my attempt to save his life. He still isn't responding, and I'm panicking.

"Powerful, indeed," the deep-voiced shadow speaks.

He says something indecipherable, and then a large hand reaches toward me, clamps around my neck from behind, and everything goes black as my cheek lands on Ikar's warm, almost-still chest.

Chapter 45

Vera

I wake as a cold hand leaves my neck, my body beginning to thaw with a rush of painful tingles as if it were a solid block of ice—so cold it burns through my veins. My head bounces, and it's difficult to draw breath as I force my frozen lids open. All I get is an eyeful of black cloak and swirling gloam.

"She's waking," says a gritty voice to my right.

Waking? It takes only a moment to realize I'm currently thrown over the shoulder of a large gloam master, and my wrists are wrapped with... *rope*. They swing uncomfortably above my head, and my shoulders ache. Other boots trudge along in my line of vision, but I can't tell how many are here. I try to shift and find a large arm holds me firm around my thighs. I jerk and fight, hitting my fists against his back and hating how weak I feel.

"Put me down, you brute," I mumble with lips that move too slowly from the chill.

Other than a chuckle from one of them, I'm promptly ignored. I decide to save my energy and focus on paying attention to the details around me. I still can't see much with the cloak in my face, but I hear noises around us. Not only the deep voices of men, but also roaring and screeching of creatures I can't identify and that are too far for me to see. We pass tents staked into the dirt, and smoke from smoldering fires burns my eyes. I turn my head to find groups of men who become silent as we walk by, watching as we pass. It's eerie. Signs of life are here, but why does it feel so *dead*?

I pound the brute's back a few more times, but it elicits no reaction. Then, without warning, the man ducks through a doorway, walks down a short hallway, enters another room, and I'm flying off his shoulder, tossed onto a pile of animal pelts that are thrown over one of two surprisingly springy beds, which cushions my fall. I can't help the yelp that escapes my lips at the abrupt action. I awkwardly make my way to my knees, hands still tied, when a man with long dark hair lowers enough to put his face level with mine.

He lifts a gentle finger and brushes stray hairs away from my face as if I'm a delicate treasure. "Careful with my queen."

I forget to jerk away when I meet eyes a shade of blue that my body reacts to. My mind wants to linger there. Why are they achingly familiar? *Do I know him?* My thoughts churn in a frozen whirl that remains just out of reach. And did he say *queen?*

"I'm no queen," I say bluntly.

I mean, it couldn't be more obvious, but I'll say it anyway. I may not remember much at this moment, but I am one hundred percent certain I am not, and never have been, a queen.

"Oh, but you will be." He smiles in a way that should annoy me with its cocky tilt, but instead, my heart stutters at how handsome he is.

What's wrong with me? Apparently, my brain is still a block of ice. This guy emanates darkness—literally. I eye the way gloam whispers out around him, and I don't know if it's coming from within or emanating from without. Either way, I'd consider that a red flag. It's strange and slightly hypnotizing to watch its movement. I look to the tall soldiers who have backed away, but stand silently around the room, watching. Gloam clings to them as well, but perhaps not as strongly as it does to the man before me. Gloam everywhere.

"Do you often lock up the women you plan to marry?" I lift an eyebrow and my cuffed hands simultaneously.

All the attitude fizzles out as quick as a pot of water douses the flame of a matchstick. *Blood.* Caked onto the skin of my hands like it's been there for days. In the creases. My fingernails. Little bits have even flaked off and dust the fabric of my trousers.

"What...?" My breaths begin to come too fast as I stare at the evidence of violence I don't remember.

The visual of my hands triggers memories that claw their way to the frozen surface of my mind and begin to assault me as the room around me blurs into the background. The man before me says something I don't hear for the roar filling my ears, then suddenly the rope is removed from my wrists. I spread my hands slowly before me in horror and see them begin to shake as if I float above my body. My breath comes too quickly to inhale properly. I try to think back, to remember. It takes so much effort that my eyes squeeze shut.

The man mutters something about frail lucent users and shock, but I pay no mind because all I see right now is an image of Ikar above me, looking more handsome than ever. Then a succession of images flashes through my mind. The arrow... the stab wound... Ikar's pulse slowing beneath my fingertips. Me trying to heal him while waiting for us both to die. Then everything froze. I know I didn't have time to finish healing him. I don't even know if I *helped*.

"Avenara," the man nearly shouts. He sounds frustrated, as if he's called my name several times already, but it slices through the fog, and my head snaps up.

"How do you know my name?" I whisper.

Fear and anger and sorrow whirl around me, this man at the center of it all. A level of hatred I've never experienced burns in my core as I stare at him with ringing in my ears, loathing the blue of his eyes. It's as if he killed Ikar and stole them only to taunt me with them as his own—a sort of torture created just for me.

He stands. "It appears you need some time to... clean up and calm yourself. I've brought along someone to help you."

"How do you know my name?" I grind out, still on my knees.

I don't like the position, having him tower over me as if he owns me. I move so quickly it feels as if my cold limbs will crack like the icicles I used to break off the slanted roof of my childhood home in the winter. I awkwardly make my way off the bed and stumble when my feet hit the floor. The man reaches out to steady me, but I slap his hand away with a feral snarl that matches the state of my clothing and hair. He pulls his hand away with a gentlemanly nod, but I find his lack of reaction irritates me further.

I narrow my eyes at him, waiting. I will chase him out of this place like the wild animal I look like if he doesn't answer me. *No one* knows my name except Mr. Edierren and the Tulips. How far did he dig into my life?

"It wasn't that hard to track each of you down." He smiles as if he finds my anger humorous. He moves toward the door.

"Wait!" I impulsively grab his sleeve. He looks down at my

grip with a pleased grin that I hate, but I don't let go. "The others... they're here too?" I hate that my voice sounds so panicked.

"Only one, but if you'd like me to capture another to keep you company..." He lifts a brow as if it would be as easy as snapping his fingers.

"No! No." I pull my hand away as if singed, and step back in alarm.

"Good. I'll send her to... help you." He eyes my hair as if he spots something living in it, and I resist the urge to check.

Who did he find? I nearly groan as I picture each of the Tulips. It's likely not Fina; she's usually not even on the continent unless there's a Tulip meeting. The others... practically helpless in self-defense... or escape. It's hard enough to escape alone, probably impossible with another helpless Tulip in tow. I may not relate well to most of my high-born Tulip sisters, but my loyalty runs deep, and we are bonded by magic. I'm not heartless; I wouldn't be able to leave one behind.

Concern and dread battle with soul-deep sorrow for the forefront of my mind as I watch him walk out. The guards follow him one by one before they close the door that swings so silently on its hinges it's hardly a whisper. The lock turns with a distinct click, then the cracks of the door disappear, leaving only a wall with a handle covered with moving gloam that I assume is meant to seal me in. At least two soldiers are outside, if I count the muffled voices correctly, but I can't see them.

I stare at the wall with pursed lips. I warrant *two* giant sword-wielding guards *and* a gloam-sealed prison? I scoff. For acting like he knows so much about me, the supposed king apparently knows nothing. I'm as harmless as Rupi, maybe even less. *Rupi.* Last I saw her was with Ikar... I can only hope she's found her way back to Mama Tina, but I'd be lying if I said I didn't wish she was here with me.

I sit on the edge of the bed, exhausted. A headache throbs at the base of my head—and I'm about to reach back to massage it out, but then I catch sight of my hands again. Concern for my fellow captured Tulip is overtaken by sorrow that rises like a swelling ocean wave as I stare at them for a long time. Silent tears fill my eyes, then track down my filthy cheeks. Ikar is too strong to be dead, too capable. He's larger than life... unbeatable. But he's also *mortal.* Staring at them sucks me back into the blurry void where nothing around me exists. The image of Ikar dying beneath me drives a knife through my soul, leaving an open wound I fear will never heal.

The first sob feels painful. The second comes more easily. And then I lose count.

My tears fall to my hands, turning the dried blood into pools of red in my palms that only make me cry harder with the visible evidence that he's likely gone.

I continue to swing violently between sorrow and denial for hours. Eventually, I find myself sitting in numb silence, shivering every once in a while, whether from the cool air or shock, I don't know. Thoughts of hope sneak like tempting demons through the numb wall in my mind, reminding me that Darvy showed up before I was taken. He might have been able to help, if the gloam masters didn't kill him and his soldiers too... and they had an originator... but I'm doubtful their originator would have been able to pull enough lucent to heal injuries such as those with the state of lucent.

I lie back, getting lost in thoughts and memories of Ikar's grin. The way his lips felt on mine... how he shoved his hands through his hair when he was upset... the way he rescued me from the shift king... how he had to pull me out from under the tent and unstick the animal heads.

I let out a watery laugh, trying to ingrain everything to memory so I'll never forget. I recall his delicious scent, his muscular frame, and while I'd like to linger on that, my thoughts automatically shift to the mark that stains it. Or, I guess I should say, *stained.*

I squeeze my swollen eyes shut. I had no idea he was a king. It still shocks me. I'm not even happy he's no longer a danger to me or my Tulip sisters. I sit there hour upon hour upon hour, unmoving, knowing deep down that he never really was.

Add to that the immense amount of guilt I feel for how I reacted and behaved since I found out Ikar was the king. Would he be alive if I had followed my gut instead of the fear others instilled in me? It's a sobering thought. I know Tatania meant well, but after everything I've seen these past weeks, the man I know Ikar was... I should have trusted myself.

So what happens to Moneyre now? Ikar doesn't have an heir. Does Lucentia have a plan B in case something like this happens? Something tells me no. I should feel terrified right now, but I'm numb again. Freezing on the outside, already frozen on the inside. A sense of soul-deep mourning, the kind that feels all encompassing, heavy, and everlasting knits into my soul in a way that makes me wonder if I'll ever be free.

Somehow, in this moment, for the first time in my life, I can't make myself care what happens to me. The thought prompts more tears, then I embrace numbness like a blanket that protects me from the excruciating feelings of loss I'm drowning in. I welcome it as it settles into every crack in my heart, and I drift off.

Ikar stands before me, my favorite half-smile on his lips.

I drink up his blue eyes that always look so serious. Wind ruffles his hair, and he looks healthy and strong as ever. Relief washes over me in tingles that rush through my body as my eyes devour his presence. There's a path behind him, and he reaches for my hand as if to pull me along as he traverses it. His warmth calls to me, even from here, and it feels as if my soul begins to thaw simply being in his presence. I stretch my hand out to grasp his, wanting more than anything to feel his hand in mine, but he's just out of reach.

I take a step, and another, and another, but no matter how many I take, I never get any closer. Tears begin to track down my cheeks as the look of frustration and confusion on his face deepens.

"I don't know what's happening..." His voice is distant, muted.

I'm not ruining this dream by telling him he's dead. I let my hand fall to my side and quit trying to reach him. He turns to look over his shoulder at the path.

"Don't do it," I instinctively say, stepping forward even though it doesn't bring me any closer.

I don't know what that path means or where it goes, but I fear if he traverses it without me, I won't ever see him again. Even if the only time I'll ever see him is in my dreams, I'm selfish enough to ask him to stay.

I'm not one to beg, but I'll drop to my knees if I have to.

"Stay with me."

His blue eyes delve into mine, and the half-smile returns. "Always."

Chapter 46

Vera

I wake with eyes so puffy I can hardly see straight, but I spot fresh water and a plate of food nearby. I tear off a chunk of the bread, finding it dry and crumbly between my trembling fingers. I drop it back to the plate—it's been sitting for hours. I have no desire to eat. I simply wanted to have a guess at how long I slept.

I look at the one small window set in the wall, trying to determine if I have the strength to move my body to get there. I stare at it listlessly. The gloam makes it difficult to tell where the suns might be, but I would guess it's late afternoon. I slept an entire day, and if I could keep sleeping, I would. I close my eyes and see the image of Ikar from my dream. I'm tempted to return to sleep, curious if I'll find him again. My burning eyes beg to close, and my lids begin to droop, but before I move to get comfortable and let sleep take me, the gloam around the door disappears, and it swings open to allow a willowy woman to enter.

I blink blearily in disbelief. "Tatania?"

He captured our leader?

She carries two large bowls, and a guard carries a basin of water in behind her.

"Avenara," she says, her brows knitting with concern as she takes in my disheveled appearance. She sets the bowls down and sits on the bed beside me, wrapping me in her arms, not appearing to care about the state of my hair or clothes. She smells of soft mint, and her motherly presence is comforting, something I hadn't known I needed, but no tears come—my numb blanket is secure.

She leans back, but keeps a soft hand on my shoulder. "Are you hurt?"

"No," I croak, cringing at how rough my voice sounds. I feel like a small child in her presence.

"Come." She tugs me by the elbow and leads me to a small dressing table with a mirror. The last thing I want is to see myself in this state, so before I catch sight of my reflection, I snatch the chair and ensure it's facing away.

Tatania drags a small table over to set the bowls of water on, then without asking permission, she gently takes one of my hands and dips it into the warm water. We make no attempt at conversation. I'm grateful she seems to sense I don't want to talk. So I sit here feeling like a traitor as I watch her clean them. The blanket of numbness begins to slip the smallest bit as I watch the way Ikar's blood blooms in a red cloud as she scrubs my skin and nails free. Will I forget him just as easily? I can hardly remember my parents' faces anymore, and I know it will be the same. The thought triggers panic as I dig for memories— his smile, his scent, his strong arms around me, flying so fast through my mind I can hardly revel in them as I try to brand them into my memories forever.

"...clothing to wear to dinner."

Her comment jars me from my thoughts. "What?"

"Renton, he sent clean clothing for you to wear to dinner," she repeats, not seeming to mind that I wasn't listening.

The hoarseness of my voice, combined with the sharp laugh that erupts, sounds like a bark. "I'm not attending *dinner*."

She pauses her washing temporarily and looks at me with a frown, but all I notice is that the cloth she holds suspended above the water drips red. "He's a powerful man, Vera."

My voice comes out flat and hard. "You'd have to make me care."

The numbness descends again.

"Sometimes we must play the game to get what we want." I spot a flash of something in her eyes that disappears with a blink. I don't have the emotional energy to wonder about it further.

What I want is gone.

She pours water from the fresh bowl over my hands. Soon enough they're clean, as if nothing ever happened. I hate it. I don't want to move on. Every minute that passes since he died means one more minute this world will never have him again, and it hurts. I may have run from him, but it doesn't mean that's what my heart wanted.

Tatania dries her hands with a soft cloth. "What happened, my dear, to crush your spirit?"

I'm silent for a long moment, deciding if I have the energy to speak. "*Renton*, as you call him, killed someone I loved."

Possibly killed, the little voice of hope shouts. The numbness claps a hand over its mouth.

She frowns. "What happened?"

I shake my head. It's too complicated. Too tragic to tell her that I fell in love with the very king she warned me away from, only to have him die.

The look she gives me reeks of pity, and I loathe it. "You have suffered great losses in your life, Avenara." She better be going somewhere good with this, or I will lash out with no regret. "But what if you'd given up on life after your parents died?"

She lets the question sit like it's supposed to change my sorrow, motivate me, even. I know she's trying to help, but it's too soon for words like those. Recalling all the pain I've felt only deepens my numbness and feelings of defeat. My fear. What if Mama Tina dies too? And Renna? Rupi? I'll be *alone*.

I want to lie down on these furs and go to sleep forever. Find Ikar in my dreams and be free of worry or care or sadness. It's all too much right now. So I sit silently, without expression, feeling like a shell of myself.

"Think on it, but dinner is any moment now. Give me your clothing and we'll wash it... or perhaps... burn it." She eyes the blood on me distastefully.

"I'll wear them as they are."

She sighs. "Always so stubborn."

Voices outside the door prompt me to find out if my body will move like I want it to. "It's kept me alive this long," I mutter as I climb grudgingly, and ever-so-wearily, to my feet.

Tatania raises a disapproving brow. "Are you *sure* you don't want to change your clothes?"

"I've never been more sure of anything."

I'll carry his blood on my clothing like a battle flag. The rebellion in my heart makes me feel a little more alive. She purses her lips as if she wishes to scold me further, but I see the corners of her eyes soften as she continues to stare at me.

Our attention turns to the door, watching the gloam seep

away before it swings open, revealing a petite woman with streaks of gray in hair that is braided far more intricately than I've ever attempted on my own.

She curtseys so deeply her gray dress pools on the ground. "Avenara." She rises and offers a smile. "My name is Gretta, and I've come to take you to dinner." Then she turns to look at Tatania with a small nod. "Tatania."

I step back from her. "Don't do that." Not to me. I'm not that sort of person.

"Do what?" she asks, as if she's truly confused.

"None of this." I mimic her curtsey, albeit sloppily.

"I was instructed by the king—"

"Just... don't do it when he's not around."

Her eyes are wide, and I can't tell what she thinks of me now, but it's better than the blazing awe in her eyes combined with that horribly deep curtsey. She doesn't agree before she turns and sweeps out the door. "This way."

I'm hardly surprised when two guards split off and follow us, but I *am* surprised when Tatania stays behind.

"Wait, what about Tatania?" I ask Gretta.

"She was not invited. Not tonight."

That doesn't sit well with me, but I don't have enough emotion left to put up a fuss. I end up following quietly while I take in what appears to be a house built entirely of *gloam*. I've never seen anything like it.

"Where are we?"

"The Lucent Mountains."

I'd choke if I had enough spit in my mouth. "How long have you been here?"

"King Renton entered years ago." Gretta doesn't even look at me when she says it, just matter-of-factly marches ahead as if I shouldn't be that surprised.

"And the rest of you?" My voice grows higher with concern.

"Much later. Renton recruited me to his cause years ago, but lucent wasn't weak enough at first for more than one of his soldiers to cross every so often. It was dangerous, and he lost many. But in the past year, he has made much progress."

"The last year...? Recruited...?" I whisper.

Add to that the fact that this woman is a traitor and suddenly I hate her for doubting Ikar, until I remember it doesn't matter anymore, and sorrow descends again.

She looks over her shoulder as she speaks again. "And these last weeks? It seems as if lucent has collapsed altogether. Gloam is thriving now. More of his soldiers arrive every day."

She smiles and waits for my reaction, as if I should be overjoyed the same as she.

Is this why lucent has decayed so quickly in such a short amount of time?

If it's accelerating this fast... will there be a time that even *I* can no longer use it? The thought brings tingles of panic, but what can one lone Tulip do? Ikar was the man for this. *He's* the one who knew the kingdom, the one who knew how to use a sword and command an army, the one with a mark from Lucentia that bound him to his kingdom. What do *I* have to offer? My people hate me, I'm practically useless with a weapon, and soon I may not even be able to lay claim to lucent magic. I don't want to care anymore; it's all too much, and the numbness invites me to dive a little deeper, but I resist. This may be my only chance to get answers, and it seems Gretta is willing to talk.

"He recruited you?"

She nods, leading me down a long, dark hallway. "Yes, there are other recruits here as well. It didn't take much to convince me that his side will win in the end. Just wait, you'll understand soon."

I'd rather eat a plate of live insects for dinner at Mama Tina's than have the conversation she implies, but she's not the one to argue over it with, so I keep my mouth shut. The interior of this building looks like any elegant home would, I guess, except this is the gloam version. Surprise, surprise. I suppose if a gloam master can call a river monster from the depths, then they could create something such as this. Everything moves like it should only be misty gloam... I brush my hand against what *should* be a foggy wall and find that my fingers do, in fact, meet something solid and *cold*. I shiver at the oddity. Gloam creatures are common enough, but I've never seen it used this way, and it's more than concerning. I didn't even know it was possible.

Like the walls, there's nothing to indicate that a floor exists beneath mist that wafts around my boots, but somehow it holds the echo of footfalls on wood. The sensation makes me wonder when I last ate or drank, that maybe I'm not quite right in the mind after what I've been through.

Gretta leads me through a grand, but narrow, hallway with four closed doors on either side and two large open ones ahead. Already I glimpse a dining table and hear the deep voices of a group of men. I straighten my shoulders to prepare myself as I step through in all my blood-covered glory. I stand there, expecting the room to pause. I wait for the gratifying flash of anger at the state of my appearance in his, the supposed king's, home. But he sits at the head of a long gloamy table... and grins.

I didn't realize it was possible for me to scowl any further. Not one person seems bothered that I show up the way I am. In fact, the men who line both sides of his table don't even appear surprised, though they're dressed in what must be their best and cleanest in a camp such as this. One that seems much too permanent.

He stands slowly, the grin never leaving his face. "My future queen, Avenara. A Black Tulip." He says the last part almost reverently.

He gestures my way, as if everyone isn't already looking at me. The weight of their gazes deepens, and I bite my tongue to keep myself from screaming that I am no one's queen.

He swings an arm to the seat at his right that is noticeably empty. "Come, join us."

What did Tatania tell me? *We must play the game if we want to win.* Fine. I'll play the blazing game. And well.

I stride his way, holding eye contact with him even though my instincts scream to look away as the blue of his eyes triggers the sorrow I've so carefully ignored since I left my room. I walk around the back of his chair, and he moves to help me with my seat. I was doing so well, but as soon as I sit and feel his hands behind me, I'm reminded that the last man to help me with my chair was Ikar, and I unintentionally scootch it in almost violently. Can anyone else tell I'm as fragile as a vase full of spider cracks waiting to collapse?

I blink to clear my eyes, and my hands shake as I stare at the feast before me—a feast I should want to devour. Two varieties of perfectly cooked meat, a delectable smelling soup that reminds me of one that Maurine serves in her small bakery back home, and crusty bread with fresh butter and an assortment of root vegetables glisten as if freshly cooked. It's all perfect... except for my distinct lack of appetite. Even *that* reminds me of Ikar, because, for the first time in years, I actually felt like my belt might be getting a little tighter since he kept me so well fed. Guess I'll be back to punching holes in it again. It's fine. Hunger and I are good friends.

Dinner begins, and I sit silently in my chair, doing my best to avoid conversing with anyone. Especially the man to my left. The man to my right laughs and says something to the man beside him about some sort of creature I've never heard of before. I look up to see if I can figure out what he's talking about, my curiosity piqued.

"Avenara," Renton says.

My gaze swings around, and at that moment, I realize my plate is piled with food. *When did that happen?*

"You should eat."

Why? the numbness whispers, but I play the game. I tentatively cradle the gloam fork, which looks as light as dense fog but feels like the cold of silver in my hand as I decide what item on the plate will go down easiest on a stomach that has no desire. I choose one of the vegetables and stab it with my fork. It's not very satisfying. The gloam fork's prongs pierce it easily. I lift it to my lips and chew without any saliva at all. It's while I'm chewing that I realize how hungry I am. And thirsty.

I snatch the goblet like a heathen and drain it, feeling a little life trickle into my limbs. I take another bite. And another. I grow full after several, and I realize how dull my senses had become. For a moment, my mental clarity is back, the numbness fades, and I can think. I allow myself to lean on instinct to fight for my survival, which has always had to be strong, habitual, even. I block out the heavy blackness in my soul that is grieving and focus on Mama Tina and Renna. I know they'd be crushed if I never returned. Can I do this for them... if not for me?

"Who are you?" I ask him quietly, aware of the other dinner attendees and the fact they may try to listen.

"If you're finished, we can discuss this privately." He places his hands on the table and moves to stand.

"I'm not." I shove a large bite of meat in my mouth and force myself to chew.

He watches with a raised brow and lowers himself back to his seat. I don't want to be alone with this gloamy murderer.

"I guess we can begin a formal introduction here, while you... eat."

Gorge myself is what he means. I'll keep eating as long as it takes to avoid being alone with him. I grab a handful of wild berries from a tray near the man to my left, triggering him to look my way with wide eyes and a respectful nod as he shoves the plate closer. I don't have enough feeling left in me to be embarrassed.

"My name is Renton, *King* Renton."

"King Renton of what kingdom?" I ask with my mouth full —don't want him getting any ideas that I might be finished.

"Of Moneyre, of course."

I nearly choke. The audacity. I reject the urge to narrow my eyes and widen them with curiosity instead.

"I'm true heir to the throne of Moneyre. King of a people locked away by Lucentia who are ready to free ourselves and reclaim what is ours. Being banished has lost its... shine," he says with a wry, sarcastic smile. "I've heard us called *gloam masters*, by some."

I frown. "Gloam can't be *mastered*, only destroyed with enchanted weapons and lucent. It's simply a waste product of using lucent, and it eats away like rot at our kingdom," I say bluntly, still certain this guy is a whole other level of crazy. That *is* why enchanted weapons are so expensive.

"Really?" He chuckles, his eyes shining as if he finds me amusing. "Suddenly you're the expert when my people and I have been controlling it for over three hundred years?"

I stare at him, pressing my lips together. *He lies.*

He takes my reaction as permission to continue. "Were you ever told that Lucentia has a brother?"

I stare at him, forgetting to chew. The guy is out of his mind.

"Hm. I didn't think so. Not surprising, but still, disappointing. No one likes to talk about the dark family secrets..." He drifts off a little as he says it. "His name is Gloam, and he is the one who gifted me with the magic. We call it gloam to honor him, of course. Ikar Moneyre, the current... or shall I say *past*... king, is the grandson of my twin brother, Ricard, who was unfairly given the throne." His eyes darken. "I'm the true heir."

The pain his words cause makes it difficult for me to follow his story, and I'm left wondering if my mind is just too far gone to understand or if he's *actually* telling me he's hundreds of years old. "How are you still alive?"

He leans back in his chair as if to relax, but his fingers tense on the armrest. "We were banished, almost died... but gloam saved us. We are no longer captive to the passing of time as mere mortals are."

The man just became twice as terrifying.

Renton glances down the suddenly quiet table and smiles. "It appears we are finished here."

A tactful way to say that we need the very privacy I've been trying to avoid. In a panic, I attempt to grab a few more berries, but he snatches my hand before I get my fingers on them and pulls me firmly, albeit gently, around the table.

What in the blazes am I supposed to do?

"I wasn't quite finished yet," I rasp.

He chuckles as if we're friends and he's known me for years. "You were done ages ago."

He tucks my arm around his and clasps a hand over mine, where it rests on his forearm, then instructs everyone else to continue the meal as he pulls me out a side door and into a shadowy hallway.

I look longingly back at the crowded table that sits silent as their king leaves, but when I see all of them staring after us, I quickly turn back around. This can't be good.

Chapter 47

Vera

We enter a room with tall windows that look out into the encampment. They appear strangely bare without any curtains. An enormous desk with feet in the shape of deathstalker paws fills one half of the space. I startle and sidestep away when I see a live one curled up nearby, taking up a large corner of the room.

Renton pats my hand, and I realize I'm clutching his sleeve. "He only eats those I tell him to, darling."

"Is that supposed to make me feel better?" I avoid looking at it, attempting to pretend it's not there. I wish I could do the same with Renton, but he's far too... *present*.

He chuckles as he pulls a chair closer to the one behind the desk and motions for me to sit. "*You* are our long-awaited queen. No one will harm you."

His gaze gleams with promised violence as he sits back and crosses an ankle over the opposite knee, the epitome of classy ease. But there's scheming in his eyes—the very eyes I avoid for the pain they trigger.

"I'm not fit to be a queen," I say honestly, risking that I'll convince him and he'll end up killing me.

"You are; you just don't see it." He searches my eyes. "Yet."

I hear no noise from outside, and the deathstalker sleeping in the corner? I haven't heard *it* either, but I imagine it'll wake soon, and I'd prefer to be gone.

In an effort to hurry things along, I blurt out, "You said *you* were the heir to the throne."

A smile curls one side of his lips. He's handsome, but the darkness he carries and the fact that my core burns with hatred toward him for murdering Ikar makes his smile worthless to me.

"Why was it given to Ricard?" I'm more intrigued by the story than I should be.

"Our father thought Ricard was more worthy, but he never gave me a chance to truly prove myself." His smile drops. "I attempted to retake the throne and was banished along with my many followers."

"And then...?" I prompt.

"After years of war between us, Ricard approached Lucentia knowing that if she gave them lucent magic it would secure his position on the throne and stop the wars. She did. I, with no other resort but unwilling to give up hope, approached Gloam." He spreads his hands wide. "And as you can see, he gave us gloam, magic of the shadows."

I try to process the information, but he doesn't wait for my mind to catch up.

"Before we could learn to truly manipulate the magic we'd been given in order to fight back, Ricard locked our people away behind a wall of lucent so thick we had no way out for hundreds of years. But suddenly, years ago, it began to *weaken*. We salivated like starving dogs, watching it wear thin, knowing that lucent magic was weakening."

It's quiet between the two of us for a moment.

Then he begins again, quietly this time. "The first time I stepped through that prison wall, through the weak lucent that no longer had power over me, I saw the land I've fought for... *yearned for.*" The distant look in his eyes makes it appear that he's somewhere far away while still sitting before me. "I've traveled it these past few years, you know. Refamiliarized myself with every part of it..."

A bud of compassion sprouts, and I quickly rip its roots from my heart. His story is twisty, and I have difficulty sorting out the wrongs from the rights, but I refuse to let down my walls. Instead of wondering if these people may indeed have a right to our kingdom, I need to figure out his motives, what makes him tick, how far he'll let me push him. I need to figure out the boundaries so I know which ones I can break.

I knowingly test his patience with another assumption.

"In our kingdom, gloam is only thriving because it's like mold, eating away at what's good."

My comment has the opposite effect—a wide smile has his teeth gleaming in the shadows.

"That's simply because no one there has the power to wield it. It only destroys when left to its own devices. Lucentia is the one who started this, you know. Gloam simply tried to make things fair. Gloam, when controlled, can build beauty as you've never seen. I'll show you... soon. Not tonight, but soon."

His way of seeing things has me feeling uncomfortable. That can't be right, can it?

"So if our kingdom leaves lucent behind and begins to use gloam, all will be well?"

Have I just solved our problem?

He chuckles. "Only those gifted the magic of Gloam can use it."

"You plan to kill an entire kingdom of people?" I ask with horror.

"Some may die, and it would be as they deserve for their treatment of my people all these years. But no, I'm much more merciful than that. Those who will peacefully comply will simply be without magic. Absents, as your people would call them. We will make adjustments to care for them." He waves a hand as if it'll be a simple matter. "At this point, lucent is so weak they should hardly have any difficulty adjusting."

Those who peacefully comply? I think of the many people I know whose lives depend on their lucent magic, and those who loved Ikar as king. They would *never* accept this man as their ruler... which means *many* would die.

Including Darvy and Rhosse.

He stands and extends a hand to me. "Come. It's time I show you what my people have been subjected to at the hands of Ricard and his descendants."

I stand on my own, keeping my distance. He smirks, unhurt by my rejection, and leads me out the door. The misty hallways are eerie, and we only pass one servant who quickly bows to both of us on his way toward the dining room we left earlier. It's quiet and lonely, and I don't like it.

We arrive at a large black door with an enormous lock along its edge, covered by gloam so dense I can hardly see through it... and is there sand on the floor? I rub the toe of my boot in it. Sure enough, I feel the grittiness scrape across the hard surface.

I squint to watch closer as Renton waves the gloam away with a hand, then he pulls a set of keys dug from an inner pocket that jingle together and releases the lock with a distinct *click.*

I'm afraid to see what's inside. I step back once, then twice, as if that will keep me from having to enter. My breath continues to puff in front of my face, and my nose is red with cold. I worry I'll never be truly warm again after living in this gloam camp.

Renton pulls the door open and gestures for me to enter through the gloamy opening with a hand. I hesitate, fearing he's about to throw me in a room with some awful creature and slam the door behind me.

I don't miss his heavy sigh. "You won't *die*. What happened to the bounty-hunting adventuress?"

Comforting words if there ever were any. I nearly roll my eyes. The bounty-hunting adventuress died with Ikar. I'll never be the same. I've never wanted to live a solitary life alone in a cozy shop more than in this moment.

I glare at him as I tilt my chin up and gingerly step through, unsure what to expect. But when I feel hot wind tousle my loose hair and my skin begins to tingle as it warms, I almost sigh with relief. Sandy dunes spread before us, soft beneath my boots. I'm tempted to lie on it, just *knowing* it holds the warmth of the suns, but I maintain my dignity and don't move. I do wonder, though, how we are here. There are no deserts in the Lucent Mountains.

"You like it here?" Renton inquires with another handsome smile, watching my reaction.

"It's warm," I admit.

"You just walked through the tear in the lucent wall, into the otherworldly prison that I and my soldiers were locked behind for hundreds of years. It's warm until it's hot. Too hot. Scorching. This is where Ricard banished me. To a desert where no fields can be planted, no clean rivers run, no trees grow for shade. A place where no families followed," he finishes with spite.

I can't help but feel a rush of compassion toward him. Ricard does seem harsh.

He lifts a hand and showcases the scene before us. "Now you see why I fought for so many years to regain the throne. Ricard, the *noble* king, wasn't as perfect as everyone was led to believe. My soldiers suffered here, and many died before we learned how to use gloam to live..." He pauses for a moment, then continues. "Now we've crossed back into Moneyre to build the camp we currently live in as we begin to recover the lives that were stolen from us. Still, compare this to everything Moneyre holds."

He's right. I've struggled to survive for the past several years, but I feel almost guilty for the life I've had compared to what he's had to endure. My mind races with the new information, and I have to remind myself he's my captor, a *murderer*, not a long-lost friend or someone in need of pity. In addition to that, I can't figure out how it involves me, and of even greater concern, that he shares so much with me means it's likely he doesn't intend to release me alive... or at all.

I don't want to hear any more of his heart-wrenching tale.

"Why did you capture me?" I get straight to the point while I savor the warmth bringing my appendages back to life.

He stares at the sandy dunes. "I saved you, actually. And now you can protect yourself by joining my ranks. Gloam is the future of Moneyre."

I narrow my eyes. "I am no traitor."

He scoffs sharply and looks my way. "You still offer your loyalty to them? Even after being forced into hiding and living in secrecy to protect your life? Hearing of the murder of your magical ancestors as if they were evil and being told *you* are evil, as well?"

That arrow hits the target dead center.

"What do you want?" I ask, tired. I simply want to curl up in my cold, eerie room and cry over Ikar.

His eyes light with a hint of desire. "You."

"What for?" I can't hide the exasperation in my voice.

But the pieces are beginning to click together. I know it before he says it, reminded of what Ikar and Rhosse told me about the gloam masters.

He grins. "Bridging."

"It seems like that's all I'm wanted for nowadays," I say with acid in my voice. "But it appears you'll need a new plan because I'm not powerful enough."

Sweat gathers beneath my clothing in the sandy winds now, and I dread re-entering the cold castle and having it freeze on my skin. I swallow so loudly I'm sure he can hear it from where he stands beside me—not my fault my throat is as dry as the sun-baked sand beginning to cover my boots. I need more water.

He laughs deeply. "So you refused the king? What an ironic ending to his reign," he muses, as if to himself.

The arrogant smile on his lips makes me want to throw up. I decline to mention that Ikar never actually asked me... because he didn't know I could... because I'd kept my secrets. *To think that I had a part in all of this.* The meager contents of my stomach roil like they're going to come back up. I swallow slowly as he continues talking.

"You've been told you're not powerful enough?" He doesn't wait for me to respond. "It's a lie, at least in regard to *you*. The others are weak as injured butterflies with those bracelets they think will protect them—I can't gauge their power. I tracked all of you, waiting for years, and you were the only one daring enough to remove it. That alone tells me you're fit to be my queen. The moment we bridge, gloam will grow. It will be an exquisite experience."

He was tracking me? I recall the dark shadows I've been seeing for the past few weeks. How long was I watched and never knew? Along with that, our bracelets don't weaken us... do they? We've *always* been told we aren't strong enough, that the bracelets were merely an extra layer of protection from the kings—

Renton interrupts my thoughts. "Lucentia finally sent a Tulip strong enough to bridge, and it's *you*."

I shake my head. "That can't be true. The other Tulips haven't struggled to pull luc—"

He taps his temple. "Strong doesn't always mean the amount of magic a person has."

I'm still shaking my head in denial. I'm not strong like *that* either. Look where I've gotten myself. *So many mistakes... foolish decisions... and now Ikar is dead...*

"Lucentia apparently felt the recently departed king had redeeming qualities, sending one of you with enough mental fortitude to go against the grain, to bridge with him and save the kingdom. You were her last effort, and he was horrifyingly close. The kings of Moneyre were absolute lunatics. Killing off their power source all those years ago, they've enabled us to return, and now we get to take advantage of Lucentia's gift. You. Her weakness."

"Her weakness...?" I murmur, but I remember Ikar saying something about this, and I'm not sure I want to hear Renton's explanation.

"Yes. You see, that's why she instructed the kings to protect *her tulips* so carefully. You each carry a piece of her within you. When you bridge with me, her plan will come crashing down around her." He eyes my neck as if he can see my mark through my clothing, and I instinctively grab the ends of my sleeves in my fists and pull them snug over my back even though the heat is growing oppressive.

"You don't have to hide it here," he says softly, an understanding compassion in his eyes that makes me want to weep.

What is he doing to me?

"Habit," I say unapologetically, releasing my sleeves and shoving my hands in my pockets so my body language doesn't betray me any more than it already has. "I'm not interested in helping."

He steps closer, eyeing me thoughtfully. "I believe that will change, given time to see everything you've been missing. Our people know how to show true appreciation and respect for the Black Tulips. You'll be worshipped."

I've given enough excuses, but this is the best of them.

The weapon I've kept hidden.

My sharpest sword.

I watch closely for the way his face will fall when he hears it.

"Your efforts are wasted. I can only bridge with a *king*—and the only king where bridging will affect the entire kingdom as a whole is the high king."

"The position has recently opened." I feel his dirtbag smirk from here.

Anger curls my fingers into the fabric of my pockets. I don't even feel guilt for how fiercely protective I feel of the high king. *Please don't be dead.*

"Not happening," I nearly spit.

If I wouldn't bridge with Ikar, I'm sure as blazes not bridging with this creep.

I don't see him move, but suddenly, cold gloam wraps

around my throat, and I find his lips beside my ear. The gloam caresses my neck, riding the line between lover and threat.

"You will, and happily."

Chapter 48

Nadiette

arvy leaves, drenched in sweat, with dark circles like bruises beneath his eyes. He doesn't say it, but I feel a sense of despair about him since it appears we can't pull enough magic to heal Ikar and keep him from the brink of death. He's a mirror of my own fatigue. Out of all the originators, I am one of the most powerful, but it means nothing when there's not enough lucent to *pull*. Lucent continues to weaken, faster than any of us have ever seen. With its decline, gloam is spreading faster, even lingering in the castle and growing about buildings in Moneyre, places where there has never been a sign of it.

I slip my hand into Ikar's, watching his chest closely to see that it is, indeed, still moving beneath the blanket that covers him. He hasn't woken since he was returned to the castle, half-dead, two days ago. If not for his familiar clothing, I'd have thought him another soldier because of the charm he used to disguise his identity to go in search of that *Tulip*—I've heard all about the deranged woman who stole his heart and led him to his near death. I should have warned him further, but I know he wouldn't have listened. I grimace remembering the way he responded to my previous pleas.

Now with the charm neutralized by Jethonan, I stare at Ikar's handsome profile, longing for the days when I saw warmth and affection in his eyes instead of annoyance and frustration. *What must I do to earn it back?*

There's a light knock on the door, and a guard opens it. "Nadiette. Your uncle, low king Waylon, is here to see you."

I nod, but I'm in no mood to deal with my uncle when I can hardly stand. I squeeze Ikar's limp hand once more before I slip out the door that is firmly closed behind me. Two guards stand in the hall, solemnly watching Waylon without expression, as if the mutiny in his mind bleeds out his ears and into the air we breathe, allowing them to sense it.

Waylon uncomfortably clears his throat and motions for me to walk with him. "The dratted soldiers wouldn't allow me, a low king, entrance to his room. Unacceptable." Then, almost beneath his breath, he adds, "But I hear our dear king is about to pass to the other side of magic."

I scowl at the note of barely subdued glee in his voice. "He's not. Who told you that?" I ask vehemently, though I know I lie.

"You know how news spreads of these things; I'm sure the entire kingdom has heard by now." He leans close, lowering his voice again. "It would make things *much* easier, Nadiette."

I step away in disgust. "How dare you!"

"My meddling is no worse than yours."

Shame heats my ears. "I don't want him to *die!*"

He lifts a finger to his lips in a shushing gesture that infuriates me further. "Calm yourself. I promised you a chance to convince him to marry you, and you know I'm a man of my word... I only meant if he passes naturally, he won't have to stand trial and be publicly executed if he refuses to marry you.

At least this way he could pass peacefully and with honor intact."

He acts as if he cares.

I take a very slow breath to diffuse the anger he has ignited.

He continues speaking, his voice as matter-of-fact as if he were discussing the latest shipping schedules for lumber. "I'll return soon. Whether it's for a funeral, a wedding, or an execution. No more than three weeks." He lifts a bushy brow in warning, as if I need reminding.

I watch him walk away as I attempt to wrangle my anger into submission. When it refuses, I decide to funnel it into helping another healer heal Ikar. He must live. I'll wear out every healer and originator in the kingdom if I have to.

Chapter 49

Vera

It's difficult to fall asleep when you're trying as hard as I am. Sleep is a few hours of unconscious escape from the dismal reality that is my current situation. I crave it for one reason: *Ikar*.

I lie on my bed listening to Tatania's quiet, even breaths across the room for one hour... then two. After a bout of panic that I may not rest at all and a fourth round of breathing exercises, I finally sink into restless slumber.

That bright-white light shines from behind Ikar, and I smile widely, almost gleeful. "You came back."

What are the chances I dream of him two nights in a row? He looks good. Really good.

He grins. "Of course I did."

I savor his cocky tone, not allowing myself to be sad when he stands before me, even if he is just a dream. I tentatively reach out this time, attempting to put my hand in his that's outstretched and waiting, but I still

*can't reach him. Curiously, though, his voice sounds
nearer this time.*

*He says something, but even though it's nearer, I can't
hear him—*

"Vera."

I'm yanked from the dream as if a glass of chilled water was poured on me, and I gasp when someone shakes my shoulder.

"It's time for the tour, my lady," Gretta whispers.

Gretta. Curse her, and curse Renton.

I groan. "It's the middle of the night."

I'm feeling great stirrings of hot rage that I was pulled away from the midnight rendezvous with dream Ikar that I worked so hard to sleep for, even if it *was* just a dream. Now I'm left to deal with grief and sorrow until the next night. Numbness descends to protect me.

Gretta ignores my protests. "Believe me, my lady, it's the best time. The creatures thrive in the dark."

Lovely. I sigh heavily.

She holds a long fur-covered cloak in her hands, so long that the length of it pools on the floor. She shakes it impatiently at me while she waits for me to roll out of bed. Tatania sleeps soundly across the room, so I silence any further groans or arguments, snatch the dratted, fancy cloak from her hands, and swing it over my shoulders. It's heavy and drags on the floor as we leave the room.

I blink my tired eyes as we finally leave his... I'm not sure what to call it. It's certainly not majestic enough to be called a castle, but it's much grander than the smaller structures, tents, and smoky fires that we travel through to get to where I'm supposed to meet Renton for a *tour*, as he and Gretta call it.

I look over my shoulder as we leave my prison behind. It's all twisty, swirling gloam, with shadows so deep I can hardly see any details, especially in the dark. The roof is pitched sharply, and two wicked spires stab into the air. I find it to be ridiculously elaborate for an encampment. I would snort, but I'm not in the mood. I can't help but think of the crisp brightness of Ikar's castle, but the numbness doesn't like that thought and devours it before I can consider it further.

Familiar sounds of fires cracking and popping and men conversing fill my ears as we pass groups of them standing near tents or sitting around fires, but it's all interrupted by screeching that spreads goosebumps up my arms. It's some type of gloam monster I can't name, and the eeriness that echoes through the camp tells me I don't want to. There are other sounds of gloam monsters, though more faint, and I can't discern which ones they might be coming from. I fold my arms within the heavy cloak in an act of attempted self-comfort as I glance around warily. Gloam curls and wafts around us as we walk. The childish side of me wants to kick it just to see it swirl around in smoky patterns, but I don't.

I blink blearily again, but it doesn't help clear my vision because everything is so gloamy it appears somewhat fuzzy around the edges, as if my eyes are having difficulty adjusting—it's beginning to bother me. The shadows are deeper, twistier—suffocating. And there's a chill in the air that bites my cheeks and nose. I blink several times. My eyes *are* swollen and dry from crying, but I don't think that's it. I think I've entered a preview of what our kingdom will become if no one is able to stop them. And apparently these people are so confident they've begun to move in... and recruit others, according to Gretta. I shudder, horrified and saddened.

I look up, sensing her before I see her, and it disrupts the numbness I've embraced. Feelings ripple to the surface as Rupi soars through the air, half-quilled as she swoops toward me. She lands amidst the long fur of my cloak, diving through the mess of my braid to reach my earlobe, which she affectionately pecks. I latch onto her presence like never before, choking back a sob as I lean my head against her soft fluff and reaching a trembling hand to stroke her feathers. She huddles into my neck, and for a moment I allow myself to savor the little bit of warmth she offers from her tiny body.

"I don't know how you always find me, but I'm glad you're here," I whisper, blinking back tears.

Her responding chirp, so clear and sharp, is magnified by the muted darkness around us, and it catches Gretta's attention. She abruptly halts her march and turns with a frown, her head tilted as she peers through the literal nest of my hair.

"What is that?"

I keep my expression flat. "My bird." When that answer doesn't wipe the frown from her face, I shrug. "She's harmless."

Rupi quills up, stabbing me in the neck defiantly to prove that she is absolutely *not* harmless, and I mask a wince.

Gretta purses her lips. An indecipherable look is shared between her and the guards that follow us, and one of them nods. I'm almost ready to raise my fists—no one's taking Rupi. I just got her back, and I need her more than ever. But the nod must have been an okay to proceed because Gretta turns without another word, continuing her rigorous pace.

A permanent horrified expression has molded itself to my face.

Renton no longer pays any mind as he gestures proudly toward several creatures. "These are shard beasts."

I've heard of them. I eye the large paddock fashioned of timber and thick strands of gloam that contains them, but I wonder if it's truly enough. The beasts appear to be made of crushed glass, sharp pieces creating a lethal fan around their faces as they crash wildly against their bounds with earsplitting sounds of breaking and scraping glass. It's nightmarish. This, just after we passed a row of pens filled with deathstalkers, gloartawks with wings so large they could span the roof of my childhood home, gloam wolves with spikes down their backs and trailing down their tails, and serpents with eight heads that regrow when chopped off. I saw it myself, unfortunately.

"Only five?" I drawl sarcastically, watching as two of the shard beasts begin to battle and wincing as my ears begin to ring.

He chuckles and leans close to be heard over the fight. "Patience, my queen. As you'll see, it takes much time and energy to create beasts such as these. We simply prepare for battle early, to ensure a swift victory. We want as little violence as possible, which I think you appreciate."

I scoff. *As little violence as possible?* These creatures kill so easily an entire army could be decimated in less than half a day. I curse beneath my breath as the velvety, heavy cloak Renton gave me tangles between my legs. I jerk it away. *Again.* It's completely impractical and looks ridiculous with the state of my clothing underneath. But he insisted—with gloam around my throat when I tried to remove it. Now, that gloam is replaced by fur that is supposed to keep me warm but makes my neck and face itch. I might actually prefer the gloam noose.

When I first arrived, I thought he was crazy. Now I've attended an uncomfortable and delicious dinner, saw every bit of his massive camp earlier this morning, and have now experienced this... eye-opening tour of his gloam beasts that has lasted an entire day. I'm finding he's not only crazy—he's loaded. *One* deathstalker can take out a group of armed men. What will this many do?

We weave around groups of soldiers leaning against fences, who laugh and jest until their king walks by, then everyone falls silent, standing upright and at attention. Those who are training begin to fight even more fiercely. I'm not sure if they fear him or respect him, but his presence certainly keeps them in check. As we pass, I avert my gaze. I don't want to watch them training to kill my people with gloam swirling all around them. It just makes the situation feel more hopeless.

I try to be impressed for my own protection, but Rupi and I are quiet for the rest of the morbid tour. I'm more disturbed by the passion so easily visible within Renton as he tells me about each and every one of his beloved war creatures; gratefully, he doesn't seem to notice when I begin to grow numb and hardly respond.

He wraps my arm around his and pulls me toward a sturdy gloam fence with a burly man at its edge. The fence forms a large circle where gloam whirls in a funnel, thick and wide at its center—it reminds me of the murk that attacked Ikar and me just weeks ago. But when Renton approaches, the gloam calms and stills, leaving what looks like half a creature formed—a scene that turns my stomach.

The man inside the fence approaches and bows before Renton.

Renton claps a hand on his shoulder. "This is Onvid, my best gloam master. Onvid, continue. Let's show our future queen what you can do."

He nods, looking pleased at having the king's attention. "Of course, Your Majesty."

He raises his hands into the air, and the gloam rises with them, first beginning to swirl and then grow. My new cloak whips around me, and my hair flies wildly about my head, so much so that I reach up to clasp Rupi against my neck so she's not swept away in the gusts. But I can't take my eyes off the growing black form before us. Rupi has been silent since Renton joined us, as if she instinctively knows she should be, but I feel her tremble beneath my hand where she has stayed huddled for the entirety of this ghastly experience.

The swirling wind continues for a long time, so long that the chill gusts around me are turning my cheeks and ears red and leaving my skin chapped. Shrieks and roars sound from within the tornado, and dread curls in my chest.

Finally the gusts die down, and the result stands before us, pawing at the ground on pudgy, muscular legs. It's enormous. Three horns line the top of its head, and two sprout from its flatish snout. It stands taller than the man that created it, and is as long as three horses combined... if you include the tail that sparkles with razor-sharp spines.

I'm disgusted imagining Ikar's soldiers fighting against this army and its horrifying monsters. Renton has an unfair advantage. But isn't that why Lucentia gifted magic to our people? We've ruined that—mistakes made on all sides. This dark army surrounding me has me sailing on an ocean of despair.

I momentarily forget to mask my emotion, and Renton takes notice.

"Too much, too soon?" I ignore the concern in his eyes. "You know that gloam can create beauty as well as monsters, right?"

I keep my posture stiff and straight. "I'm not sure I believe you."

He frowns. "Though you are ungrateful, I believe it will help you become more willing when you are reminded what awaits you as my queen."

He wraps my arm beneath his so that my hand rests on his forearm again, and we walk into the forest nearby, away from the noise. He keeps me close, and I'm tired of the forced proximity, but when I attempt to pull my arm from his, he clasps his hand over mine and squeezes my arm against his side.

He tugs me along, deeper into the forest. Through trees, shrubs, and long grass, and into deep shadows. He finally stops when the roars become distant, and the clang of swords and weapons is slight. Then, without warning, gloam begins to spin around us. For a moment I panic. Is he trying to turn *me* into a creature of darkness? I squeeze my eyes shut at the roar of the shadows around me, but then, just as suddenly, it's calm.

I open my eyes and find a kingdom spread before me. Somehow, he created this... *picture* that feels real. I see Moneyre, but the cream stone of the high castle is now a moody, deep gray, the black roofs of the turrets gleam, and gloam is in *everything*. Somehow, though, it's beautiful. Misty and shadowy, yes, but in a way that makes my eyes wide with wonder. This new kingdom spans out before me as if I stand at the top of the world. I'm surprised to see that none of it is dead and decaying like it is now; it looks healthy, in the darkest of ways. I want to hate it. I want it to look dreary and sick and wicked.

Renton pats my hand on his sleeve, and I realize I'm practically clawing him.

"It affects me as well, my queen." His pat turns to a thumb caressing my skin.

I begin to feel the uncomfortable nudge that comes from building tension. It feels as if he expects something. *A kiss?* I immediately release his jacket from my clutches and pull my hand from his arm. He lets me this time—he's safe to assume that I won't be running away into the depths of his beautiful nightmare. At least, for now.

"All this will be yours..." He whispers near my ear as we look over his future kingdom together.

I freeze. Even my heartbeat seems to slow as I truthfully consider his words for a moment. The hurt and battered Black Tulip within me, marked with a flower that is hated, that has been isolated and lectured and constantly hiding, blooms a little as I think of how it would be to embrace this future with the darkly handsome man beside me. I see myself in his arms, wearing an evening gown that matches the black of deep shadows—never white clothing again. My hair intricately braided and curled and pinned up to reveal the mark that has pled for fresh air for years. It's all darkly romantic, heady, and freeing. *Freedom.*

I blink and a single tear tracks down my cheek, leaving a cool streak in its wake. It reminds me that I was never made for this world. My cool magic has felt the barest touch of warmth, and it changed me forever. *Ikar.* I fear, now that he's dead, that I'll be destined to live a life of lukewarm, or even worse, frozen heartache... and it feels as if it's all my fault.

Rupi nudges my neck with her small head, reminding me she's there, and though I want to lean into her affection, I stay still.

Renton's finger gently brushes the chill tear away. He's offering me all I've ever dreamed of. If he'd found me two months ago, I admit it would have been more difficult to say no. A woman who doesn't know warmth wouldn't have been so hard to convince. Two months ago, I didn't know the high king of Moneyre personally. I didn't know he was honorable and good and worthy. I didn't know my magic could call to another's that way. If I was going to bridge with anyone, it would have been Ikar.

The vision around us fades until the forest materializes around us once again. I follow Renton somberly back through the camp, never more grateful for Rupi and her small, steady presence.

Chapter 50

Vera

Renton walks me all the way back to my room, or more correctly said, *my prison*, since I don't get the option to freely come and go. He motions for the guards to leave, and we stand there before the door, just he and I. Rupi lurks behind my braid as if she knows she shouldn't advertise her presence.

He leans a shoulder against the wall and looks hard at me. "You're very quiet."

I shrug. What does he expect me to say?

He doesn't seem to mind the silence between us for several moments. Then he stares at the stains on the fabric of my clothing through the open cloak, and his dark brows pull together in a slight frown. "You loved him."

Suddenly it's so quiet that my breathing seems very loud.

"What?" I play innocent. No need to scream that *I still do, and I will even after death.*

"The stains. That's why you refuse to wear any of my gifts. You fell in love with him, didn't you?"

"I don't fall in love with kings," I say bluntly, forcing a hint of uncaring attitude into my voice though I feel the opposite. *Liar.* I command myself not to cry.

He watches me with his blue eyes—eyes that I avoid looking directly at for the torture they inflict. "And maybe I would believe you if we chose who we fell for, hmm?"

If there's one person I'll tell of my love for Ikar, it will be Ikar. If he died, the knowledge of my love for him will die with me.

"Believe what you want." I shrug. "I said what I said." My voice is so nonchalant that I'm certain, if I tried, I could get a job with one of the traveling groups that performs throughout the kingdom.

A corner of his mouth turns up in a half-smile, and I hate that he knows.

"In time, it will fade."

No.

"We can be happy together, Vera."

I know he's trying to be kind by using the shortened version of my name that I prefer. It's the first time he's said it that way... *and I hate it.* The last man to say my name to me was Ikar.

I simply look down at my dirty boots and try not to shiver.

He straightens, for the first time appearing frustrated at my apparent rejection of his attempt to connect. "You try to hide it, but I know what you felt when I showed you what I have to offer. And if that's not enough, you know I will care for you, protect you, give you everything you could ever want from a man. I know right now it seems too far out of reach, but I *will* have what is mine. And what is mine will be *yours.*"

He's wrong. I don't think it seems too far out of reach. Terror pulses through my veins because it's too *close* to his reach, and I can feel it growing ever closer.

"Some hearts are too broken to love." I look down and pull gently at some of the silky fur on my cloak.

"I'll be patient. I'll help you put it back together, and it will heal." His voice is low and husky. He opens the door, waits for me to enter, and closes it without another word.

I find Tatania within, a pile of parchment and charcoal before her on the dressing table, and a plate of food waiting on a tray on my bed. I realize then that I haven't eaten all day, and I'm *starving*.

She turns in her seat to greet me. "Vera, you're finally back."

Rupi soars from my shoulder, directly to the plate where she begins to peck at the juicy berries that await. I glance toward Tatania to see her frowning deeply. With my life turned upside down, I'd completely forgotten that Tatania doesn't like birds... or any animal, for that matter. Suddenly though, I can't make myself care. I refuse to apologize for my beloved bird, and instead I drop the newly gifted cloak from my shoulders and kick it into the corner before I sit heavily on the bed and begin to pick through the food on the tray with Rupi. The fire crackles and pops as we eat, but it only warms the surface, not my soul in the way it craves.

"How was your time with the king?" Tatania asks, sitting primly in the small chair. Her lips press flat as she observes my fluffy round bird happily sharing my dinner. It feels good to not care.

I don't even try to hide my sarcasm. "Enlightening." I take another bite of meat, then scoot back to lean against the wall and pull one of the warm furs from the bed to wrap around me.

Tonight, Renton offered me everything. I saw it, felt it whispering beneath my fingertips for the shortest and longest of moments. I almost caved to its tantalizing draw. It feels as if I live out the most tragic sort of poem.

I wipe stray strands of hair from my face as I think about Renton's goal in showing me all of that. Was it simply to sway me in his favor? To show me his power and the likelihood that he'll win if he attacks? Was it him simply showing off? To have me willingly agree to become his queen? He practically promised to give me the world. Unfortunately, the scale seems to be tipping in his favor, and it seems that he likely can. To make it worse, he seems to be a decent enough person, besides the fact that he's a gloam monster and his goal is a complete takeover of Moneyre, and I *hate* that.

Tatania nods. "The gloam creatures *are* terrifying."

Rupi reaches for the same berry I do, and I roll it toward her, opting for more of the meat instead. I don't know how much longer the birdseed in my pocket will last, and I don't want her to be hungry.

I take another bite and chew before I speak. "You know what's more terrifying? Renton and his goal to eradicate all lucent and take over the kingdom, killing who-knows-how-many of our people in the process."

"He won't kill those who don't fight him." Tatania gently disagrees.

Is she defending him or attempting to comfort me?

I look her way with a frown. "But what about all the people who *will?*"

I can see Darvy and Rhosse clearly in my mind, leading their soldiers into a battle they can't win without lucent, and further sorrow squeezes my chest.

She sighs. "Vera, you've always had a compassionate heart, but things have to change. People are dying from lack of lucent. What if Renton can fix it?"

My frown deepens. "You can't possibly believe he's our best option."

I begin to feel the first flames of anger. For someone who told me to never trust kings and made me try to hate Ikar, something that ended up leading to his *death*, she's acting suspiciously supportive of a man who, quite literally, seeps *gloam* and seeks the throne. For the first time, I begin to wonder whose side she's on.

"How long have you been here?" I ask carefully. It can't have been too long, since I just paid her to have my bracelet replaced days before my capture. Is it possible she comes and goes?

Her words are careful. "Not much longer than you."

That doesn't mean she's not a recruit, though. Gretta said Renton has been wandering our land for *years*.

"Are you a captive, like me?" I ask bluntly. I've never had a reason to doubt Tatania, but seeing her here now, hearing her opinion...

"Renton believes I'm on his side, so I have a bit more freedom than you do. Like I advised, sometimes you must play the game to get what you want."

"Is it true?" I peer at her.

"Is what true?" She blinks innocently at me.

"Are you on his side?"

She laughs as if my question is ridiculous. "Of course not, it's all strategy, m'dear. How else are we to escape?" She lifts a chastising brow.

Her words and tone are intended to reassure me, but I've never felt *less* assured in my life. I get the sense she actually believes his intentions are good, and that puts me on edge. Even *pretending* to be on his side chafes uncomfortably. Regardless of the power he has, I won't betray my people. I can't. I won't be convinced, even by Tatania. I don't know what Renton will do when I refuse to be his queen, but the offer he presents as a gift comes with a price I'm not willing to pay. His *presentation* does get me thinking, though. I realize now how important the Black Tulips are to maintaining lucent magic. We've been selfish and living in fear, like a large ostrich sticking its head in the sand, ignoring the consequences of our cowardice. Anger and outrage at the treatment of our sisters who were murdered all those years ago yearns to stay rooted in my heart, but I know it's time to start letting it go. Ikar didn't murder them. No one who still lives in Moneyre murdered them. I think of all the hunters I've worked with, my friends among the fae, Mr. Eddieren, Maurine from the bakery... countless people who don't deserve what Renton has in store.

Tatania stares into the fire, absorbed in her own thoughts just as I am in mine, until I break the silence. "One time, I watched a performer from a traveling caravan use shadows to trick the crowd into seeing things they weren't. It was eerily similar to gloam, and he was chased out of town. What Renton did—it was one hundred times worse. It was *real*. He uses gloam in ways I never knew possible, and it's terrifying."

"Yes, I've seen it myself," she agrees quietly.

I admit that as much as I fear the way he uses gloam, I hate that there's part of me that understands Renton's desire to take back what he believes is rightfully his. Wouldn't I feel the same if I were banished? It makes me wonder if perhaps I'm a little evil, too. But that guilt is assuaged when I remember that even though what he wants to give me is tempting, my magic, my soul, and my heart reject it. My mother used to tell me that being tempted doesn't make you who you are; it's the choices we make—I hold the reminder closer than ever.

Tatania picks up the charcoal again and begins working on

a drawing I can't fully see. The light scratches fill the silence, but I know she still listens.

"He wants me to be his queen, Tatania. Can you believe that?" I laugh somewhat sharply, and she chuckles, which I try not to be offended by. I'll be the last to argue that imagining me as a queen is, indeed, laughable. She doesn't meet my eyes, though, keeping hers trained on the parchment beneath her hand.

I continue sharing my thoughts, trying to make sense of it all. "I have to believe I'm choosing right by rejecting Renton's offer. The tour today was all my worst nightmares brought to life. All I could imagine was our people fighting these beasts and dying. Over and over again."

"Admittedly..." she finally speaks, pausing with the charcoal held loosely in her hand, but still not meeting my eyes. "I have also struggled with thoughts like yours."

Tatania? She's always so sure of herself, so matter-of-fact. It's difficult to imagine her struggling over *anything*.

She looks up, as if to gauge my reaction. "I hear Renton killed the king, which means it's only a matter of time until he takes power. I've heard whispers he plans to leave here in just days."

Those words feel like a fresh stab in my heart, a reminder that attempts to send me back into the spiral of numb sorrow. It would be so easy to allow it to engulf me in its painless fog. I feel myself beginning to slip. *Ikar truly died.* Renton said the same, didn't he? Wouldn't he know?

Rupi quits pecking at the berry and stares up at me, head tilted with concern.

"You must escape," Tatania says with finality.

I look up, the numbness temporarily halted at the edges of my mind. "Escape?"

"If he doesn't have you, it will delay him. I'm not sure if it will help much, but we must try."

I nod slowly. "The king... he truly died?"

"I'm sure Renton wouldn't have left him alive," Tatania says sensibly.

I forgive her for not knowing how her response pains me. It's not her fault she doesn't know all my secrets. But I know she's right. The voices of hope within me extinguish so suddenly I stop breathing... and with the last of my hope gone that Ikar survived...

"It doesn't matter anymore," I say flatly. My eyes burn as another round of grief attempts to drown me, but I don't want to fall apart in front of Tatania, so I force a lid on the emotion in my mind that attempts to boil over.

"It *does* matter," she nearly shouts, and I jump, startled.

Tatania is a reserved lady—I've never heard her raise her voice beyond quieting the Tulips before beginning our annual meetings. I stare at her, wide-eyed. She calms herself with a breath before she continues.

"Forgive me, I simply can't watch you bridge with..." She drifts off and swallows while she composes herself, and when she speaks again her voice is more steady. "And while I know you try to hide it, it's obvious you care for the late king."

I can't help but wince at her words.

"If you truly care for him, I would assume you would do everything possible to avoid marrying another so soon."

Her words are an arrow so true it hits the center of my soul. The weary part of me that sorrows edges toward unfeeling numbness that is more tempting than ever to sink into, but I'm nothing if not stubborn and have always had a strong survival instinct. Am I strong enough to grasp that instinct now? If not for myself... can I do this for Ikar? For Mama Tina and Renna? For the other Tulips? Darvy and Rhosse? The kingdom?

A spark of life lights within me. But it's small, and my heart's so bruised it can't seem to handle more.

"I'll think about it," I mumble.

I can tell she wants to argue, but she must sense that I'm done because she presses her lips together and returns to her sketching.

I burrow beneath the furs on my bed and turn to face the wall as Rupi tucks herself beneath my chin and cleans her feathers in rhythmic motions that are soothing and normal, and I'm reminded how much I missed her. Even with Rupi near and my eyes burning with fatigue from being woken so early this morning and kept out all day, I still struggle to sleep. I'm in no mood for further conversation, so I lie there, facing the wall, holding Rupi close until I hear Tatania ready for bed.

Soon the room is quiet, and at some point during the long night, I finally doze off.

Gloam mists around me as if it's waiting until it can completely consume my body. The only thing that breaks the darkness is bright light cutting through the shadows, and I find myself before Ikar again. It feels as if I stare straight at the sun, but I can't pull my eyes away from his face.

He reaches back for my hand, and I stare at it a moment. The last two times I tried to touch him, I was left severely disappointed, but how can I not try? I can feel his heat as I tentatively lift my hand, scared that he'll forever be out of reach... his light and warmth seem to burn away the gloam, and finally, his hand engulfs mine, and then I'm in his arms and my soul begins to thaw. For the first time in days, there's no gloam around me. I instinctively press my ear to his chest as I clutch him tightly, craving the sound of his heart beating strong against my cheek... But it's so weak that I can't tell if I can hear it beating or if it's my own pulse thumping in my ears.

I stiffen in his arms, pausing my own breathing to listen for his as I press my ear harder to his chest, seeking evidence that he might be alive even though this doesn't mean anything in reality.

"Vera?" He tilts his head down to meet my eyes.

"Are you alive?" I whisper.

He frowns, and it seems as if I've just reminded him he's simply a vivid part of my dream. "I... don't know."

"You better be alive," I mumble.

He grins. "Is that an order?"

"Yes." I grip his shirt tighter as I say it. It feels good to boss him around, even if it isn't real.

He draws his thumb gently along my jaw. "Where are you? You're cold."

I shrug as I lean into his hand, soaking up its heat.

"With the gloam masters, somewhere in the Lucent Mountains."

I don't want to think about that right now; I just want to enjoy this moment.

A concerned frown mars his brow. "You should be escaping."

"Shhh. You're ruining my dream."

I rest my cheek against his chest again. I hear his heartbeat... is it stronger? I lift my face away and put it back.

It's more regular. Comforting. I sigh against him. This dream is just getting better.

"Vera?"

"Your heartbeat," I murmur. I must have dreamt it back. His thumb strokes back and forth across my upper back as he holds me.

"I don't know what's happened to me, but I'll come for you. Be ready."

I keep my cheek firmly pressed to his chest. "Dead people... er—" That was insensitive. "People who've passed... you can't make promises."

"The blazes I can't," he growls with his lips against my hair. I close my eyes and relish his nearness. "If I never find you again in reality, I daresay I'll sleep the rest of my life to be with you in my dreams."

He kisses the top of my head and sets me back with his hands still on my shoulders. "Escape."

I revel in his commanding tone, the firmness in his eyes. I've missed it.

His blue eyes delve into mine with unwavering focus. "Promise me you'll try to escape."

I bring my hands up to grasp his wrists with a smile, feeling drunk on happiness just to be near him, even if it's not real. "For you."

Suddenly, I'm awake in the dark, my chest heaving. My arms fall to the bed empty and cold as ice, my breath producing puffs of air before my face. I clap a hand to my chest, clutching the material of my shirt in my fist as if an open wound lies beneath. Mere attraction wouldn't cause an ache such as this. It's love—I love him. I've loved him since I thought he was a

Class A criminal. I still love him, so much so that I know there's no place in my heart for anyone else.

I let the acceptance of my feelings settle in the most right of ways, as if I just pressed a long-lost piece into the last spot of a giant puzzle with a satisfying *click*.

Rupi's head pops up from beneath the furs, her feathers rumpled as she hops to my chest, perches on my hand, and pecks gently at my wrist.

"What is it, girl?"

She hops along my wrist and back to my hand, looking down at it.

"This?"

I turn my wrist and find the mate bond on my wrist glowing brightly in the dark. I frown. *It's glowing. Do mate bonds glow if one person dies?*

I look up at Rupi with wide eyes as she dances across my chest happily, flapping her tiny wings with every hop. Does that mean...? Are Rupi and I simply grasping for a sliver of hope? Maybe. I know she loves Ikar as much as I, but that dream felt real, and the mate bond *is* glowing.

For a moment, I allow myself to ride the wave of hope that, when dashed, could lead to my insanity... What if Ikar is alive? If he is, what *if* I tell him the truth? What *if*... we bridge?

I bite my lip as I consider the ramifications. I see it going two ways. Either I find him alive, convince him to forgive me, bridge with him, and restore lucent to our kingdom and the people are grateful, and I can eventually change their deep-rooted beliefs... or, I bridge with whoever I have to bridge with if Ikar is dead, and the people might still hate us and end up killing me and all my Tulip sisters as they did before. I realize that a lot of it has to do with who is now king. If it's still Ikar, I have to trust him and his ability to sway his people. Anyone else... I'll have to face the sorrow I've shoved into a dark corner of my mind and figure it out, because what's worse than possibly being hunted down and killed in the future by the very people I'm trying to save? Knowing I could have prevented an entire kingdom from being overtaken and not doing anything about it.

I know Renton is after Ikar's throne, but if my king is alive... if I survive the thoughts of escape that begin to form in my mind, I'll tell him somehow. I'll do whatever it takes to be with him. I'll apologize; I'll tell him everything. I will.

My resolve firms as I lie there, his image still fresh in my mind from the dream. I've never shared my secret with anyone outside the Tulips. What am I supposed to do, run into his arms and shout that I'm a Black Tulip? Apologize for lying to him for weeks? Beg him to forgive me for the massive amount of trouble I've put him through? Where do I add in the part where I realized while I was imprisoned by gloam masters that I love him?

I throw an arm over my eyes and groan. I obviously don't know how to do this relationship thing in any normal sort of way.

"Vera?" Tatania calls from across the room, her voice concerned. She must have heard my groan.

"I'm leaving, Tatania. I don't know how I'll do it yet, but you're right—I need to escape. You should too."

She's quiet for a moment. "I'll help. I've been thinking of a plan."

I smile in the darkness, and Rupi twitters softly beneath the furs. My worries about Tatania fade. For the first time, I feel like she and I might actually be sisters.

Chapter 51

Ikar

I wake in my dimly lit room, immediately assaulted by pain. Though it forces a groan from my gravelly throat, for a small moment, I'm grateful for it because it means I'm alive when I doubted that fact while dreaming moments ago. Relief fills me as my heart pounds within my chest.

"Ikar?" Darvy stands and comes toward me from a shadowy corner of my room, relief easing the creases at the corners of his eyes. But I don't miss the dark bags beneath his eyes and the weariness in every line of his face.

"What happened to me?" I grind out. My mind is muddled, and all I can see behind my lids is Vera's face from my dream. Where is she?

"You've been walking the brink of death for the past three days." He laughs without humor as he sinks into a chair near my bed and runs a hand over his face. "Blazing gloam masters," he mutters.

"Three days?" I ask hoarsely.

Darvy nods, and I try to put the pieces together. I

remember the battle, remember the pain of a sword being thrust into my torso...

"They took her, didn't they?" I curse and attempt to sit up, but fire ignites and Darvy pushes me back.

"We've been trying to heal you, but lucent is getting worse. The last originator passed out when we'd barely begun... I can only use Nadiette so many times before she tires, but she's been worried—"

"We have to leave," I interrupt as he offers me a cup filled with water. I painfully lift my head to drink. How am I to find Vera in this state?

"Once you're healed, we'll put together another team—"

"They could kill her!" I nearly shout, and pay for it with another wave of pain that has light dancing behind my eyes.

"You're going to undo all my efforts if you don't calm down. If you want to find her, you have to heal. That means *don't move*," he reprimands me angrily.

"If they let her live... he's going to bridge with her."

Darvy nods grimly and clasps my good shoulder. "We'll work as fast as we can."

I watch as Darvy pushes a needle through my skin, resorting to healing methods most of our people haven't had to use regularly in centuries. I lift my gaze to stare at a small crack in the high ceiling of my personal room. He was able to finish healing my shoulder a day ago, but the originators, even Nadiette, can only offer lucent for moments at a time without fatiguing now. It hasn't been enough to completely heal my side yet, even with the head start Vera offered with her own healing magic—the reason I'm still alive.

"It's good enough," I say after he finishes the last stitch.

Darvy shakes his head. "It's not."

"It has to be." I look down. "It's closed... enough."

"Barely," he mutters.

He finishes, and I wince as he secures a knot, then steps back while I slowly grab a clean shirt and gingerly drop it over my head. I hide all signs of pain and raise my brows in success. I try to hide the fact that I feel weak as a newborn foal. Apparently, it shows.

He offers a slow clap. "Congratulations, Your Majesty, you've put your own shirt on."

I scowl at him, then begin gathering items to fill my pack, frustrated with how carefully I'm forced to move. "I don't know how much longer the mate bond mark will last. They told us six weeks, but it's already been three." *Or has it been four?* The past month has been a whirlwind, and I lost most of last week to injury-induced coma. "We have to go now, or I risk losing not only her, but our kingdom."

I check the underside of my wrist, the small shimmering gold circle my only link to Vera.

Darvy falls into a cushy chair. "What type is it?"

"I don't know. We didn't check, but it's gold and shimmery. We only needed it to prevent another shifter from trying to mate bond with one of us, and all I knew was it wasn't the one labeled *reproduction.*"

Darvy snorts. "You chose the *gold* one while you were searching for a different woman to marry?"

I whip my head around to look at him, blinking away dizziness. "Do you know about mate bonds?"

He shrugs. "A thing or two."

"Well, what is it then?" I'm growing irritated.

"Did you ever wonder *why* it was the most expensive?" He raises a brow, as if I should already know the answer.

"No. The shop was rather... uncomfortable. I just grabbed it."

"Good thing she ended up being a Tulip and you plan to make her your future wife, or you'd have some explaining to do."

"Get on with it already," I growl. He's getting to be as bad as Jethonan about drawing things out.

"It's a connection bond, likely the one labeled *Never Apart.* Some call it the soulmate bond."

I still for a moment, confused. "Never Apart?"

"I assume so. It's the only one I've ever used—er, seen." Darvy rubs the back of his neck.

"What does it do?" I stare at the gold circle, dim now.

He appears to consider his words carefully. "If it's the one I've *heard* about, then it connects you in reality... *and* in dreams when you're apart. Have you... dreamt of Vera?"

"Wait. The dreams—are you telling me those were *real?*" I freeze as a rush of emotion runs through me, and I try to wrap my mind around the fact that my suspicions all those days ago were correct.

He smirks. "It's a dangerous thing, buying a mate bond without knowing what it is first, especially when it comes to dreams where we often feel uninhibited. Might you have some explaining to do?"

"What? No." I shake my head, grateful I kept my head on straight. And why does Darvy act like he knows from experience? It's something I intend to ask about later.

"So if I go to sleep right now, I'll be able to talk to her?" Hope blooms in my chest.

"If she's *also* asleep."

I look out the window to see the third sun setting.

"Kissing her in your dreams will be quite helpful in the current situation," Darvy drawls sarcastically.

I scowl at him. Unfortunately, no kissing happened in the dreams.

"Like you said, it connects us in life as well... I used it to find her when the shift king imprisoned her. Led me right to her tent. It glows brighter the nearer you are."

"What about your magic and hers, they draw together, don't they?" He lifts a questioning brow.

"Yes, but only within a certain distance, which is too far in this case to be helpful. If I'm able to dream with her, I'll tell her we're coming. She doesn't know they're real, but I'll try to convince her."

"You really should wait a few more da—"

"We leave tomorrow." Nothing will sway my decision.

"Tomorrow?" Darvy sputters, and I feel a twinge of guilt. He's worked hard to keep me alive this week, and here I am, barely healed enough to leave my bed, heading out on a dangerous rescue mission. Even *I* feel a twinge of unease. But the stitches will need to be enough, for now. I shove the worry aside. There is no time to wait. Who knows what they've done to Vera. I intend to make them pay.

"We can heal it more again in the morning before we leave, if you have enough energy. It'll be enough," I say firmly.

From the look on Darvy's face, he doesn't agree.

"Tomorrow. Tell Rhosse."

He throws his hands in the air in exasperation, then turns and stalks out of the room, muttering something about me beneath his breath. I don't hold back a small chuckle, even though it triggers another wince.

Now, time to dream.

Chapter 52

Vera

Renton seems to be confident enough in the death of Ikar that he's not worried about a rescue attempt, and leaves only one guard at my door now. Unfortunately, I believe the same. I still battle emotional swings, ranging from sorrow that Ikar is likely dead to heady determination to make my way out of here. I focus on escaping so that I don't cry. Or scream. It doesn't help that I dreamed of Ikar *again* last night, and this time instead of tender hugs and letting me listen to his heartbeat, he spent the entire time attempting to convince me that he was coming to get me, using our glowing mate bond to *prove* it was all real. It was the worst sort of nightmare—the type that waved all my broken dreams in front of my face like a feast placed just out of reach before a starving beggar. Painful enough that when Tatania shook me from sleep and told me to wait for a signal, I was relieved to be awake. Before I could ask what *type* of signal, she was whisked away by a guard and hasn't returned.

I'm left by myself for one hour after the next, waiting for a signal I hope I'll recognize. I end up sitting against the wall on my bed, wrapped in furs to keep warm while Rupi pecks birdseed gently from my palm. I ruminate about the dreams of Ikar. I'm dangerously drawn to thoughts I shouldn't even consider. *Could he have survived?* I go round and round, trying to pick out any further details I may have forgotten or missed, but all that sticks out is how pale his face was, how much blood poured from him, how slow his pulse was beneath my fingertips. Is it possible I healed him enough before I blacked out? Maybe, but likely not. Tatania certainly doesn't think so.

If I did, if he lives, wouldn't he have come for me by now? Immediately I scoff, and the fur near my face blows out and back with my breath, tickling my skin. He wouldn't come for me. I cringe at the way I ran from him, the hurt I caused, the mountain of trouble I've dragged him through these last weeks.

I jump up from the bed with the furs wrapped around my shoulders, pacing. I force the thoughts away and, instead, attempt to prepare myself for what's to come. What will the signal be? Will I recognize it? What will I have to do to get away? The thoughts have me sweating, but they distract me from the dreams. I can't go back to those.

After a morning filled with anxious pacing and my focus solely on escape, I'm in no mood for Renton when he shoulders through the door around noon with a single tray of food. I stand, unmoving, while he throws out a large bear fur on the gloamy floor as if he's preparing for a lengthy, too-intimate lunch before the crackling fire. He wastes no time sprawling out as if he hasn't a care in the world, lying on his side and supporting himself with one strong arm, the strength of which strains the fabric of his shirt until I fear it may tear.

He pats the fur. "Join me."

It's a command. I almost refuse, but then the reminder that Tatania and I will attempt to escape this very day urges me to maintain the facade of peace. *Play the game to get what you want.*

I pull my furs tighter and lower myself to the floor, opposite where he lays, sitting on my knees. I refuse to make it the romantic meal I can tell he intends, so I snatch food in bits and pieces like a greedy squirrel. He merely grins and watches me as he chews casually, in no hurry to finish. He eyes the last berry on the tray before he lifts it with two fingers, and I find it waiting before my lips. My eyes meet his as I press my lips shut. Not happening.

"It's apparent you love berries, so either you're full... or you refuse to take it because it's from *me*." Chill gloam slithers around my neck. "Why won't you give me a chance?"

I'm swinging between confusion and defiance. How dare he ask it so innocently while I have gloam around my throat. It tightens when I refuse to respond. The berry waits tantalizingly against my lips. Will I truly choose to die over a berry? It's getting difficult to breathe now.

I finally open my mouth, and as soon as the berry hits my tongue, I snap my teeth shut, hoping to get his finger. But he's fast. Faster than should be possible. He chuckles as his eyes sparkle with what I must be mistaking for adoration. The man is as twisty as the gloam tendrils that linger about him. The gloam noose evaporates, but I refuse to pull my clothing up to warm the skin of my neck and show him how much it affected me.

Renton doesn't try to feed me again, but he stays a torturously long time chatting about annoyingly normal things while I sit silent and nervous that Tatania will unexpectedly bust in the door with her escape plan and it will go up in flames because *he's still here*. I'm relieved when he finally pulls the door shut behind him, but I'm more eager than ever to escape. I have no choice but to wait, antsy and pacing my room to manage my nerves for several more hours. *Where are you, Tatania?*

Chapter 53

Ikar

I've watched the mate bond mark closely the last several hours, making adjustments as needed and watching as it brightens and dims to know which direction we should travel after we landed the sharp flyers a half day's journey from the nymphs this morning. Now it's nearing the end of the day, the second sun about to set, when Rhosse, Darvy, and I find the encampment we search for.

We stealthily make our way through the forest, the gloam so thick I almost resist the urge to breathe as the mate bond on my wrist continues to grow brighter the closer we get. My side aches as we climb a small hill, but it's forgotten when we see what's on the other side. A full army makes camp. Smoke from hundreds, if not thousands, of fires permeates the air, filling the spaces between tents that spread into the distance as far as we can see. A mix of roaring, growling, and the easily recognizable sound of screeching and breaking glass fills the air—a sound I'd hoped to never hear again.

"Shard beast," Darvy mutters with dread.

"Five of them," Rhosse adds.

I clench my jaw, remembering the last shard beast I fought and very nearly lost to—I have a scar to prove it. With the weakness of lucent magic, five would decimate my entire army.

"Let's find out what else they've got," I mutter.

"You have a death wish?" Darvy scoffs.

"A kingdom to protect and a Tulip to rescue," I growl, then begin leading the way around the edge of the encampment to get a closer look at the gloam beasts. It takes longer than I like, crouching painfully behind large dead bushes and scraggly trees that hardly help hide us from groups of soldiers that pass every so often. The awful sound of the shard beasts growing louder tells me we're traveling in the right direction. One particular roar is so loud that Rhosse curses.

Between the scraping glass and my ears ringing, Darvy whispers to Rhosse, "What do you bet I could tame one of those?" Darvy gestures with his chin toward the shard beasts.

Rhosse considers the beasts with narrowed eyes. "I'll bet a month's pay you die within three minutes of trying."

Darvy appears truly offended, but I speak before he can argue because his foolish bet has given me an idea.

"I have a plan," I say, still counting gloam beasts trapped within gated, gloam-wreathed pens below us.

"Every time you say that I end up almost dying," Darvy whispers.

"We simply need to set them all loose. Cause a big enough distraction that I can find a way through the camp." And hopefully find Vera unharmed. I point far past the many tents and a smattering of smaller buildings to a large house, designed to be more imposing and indicative of status. "I assume she's there."

The tightness in my chest at the thought of what they could have done to her solidifies my decision. We need to move quickly. Rhosse frowns as he stares across the wide expanse of tents and penned beasts that block the way.

Darvy appears just as doubtful. "How do you know she's there? What if she's in one of the thousands of tents?"

"You like to gamble," I remind Darvy. "Think of it like that."

"Except it's our lives instead of money," Rhosse mutters darkly.

Darvy ignores Rhosse, his eyes brightening with interest. "I'll bet you six months' pay and my second-best enchanted sword I can set half of them loose."

Rhosse shakes his head and challenges the glint in Darvy's eyes. "Your confidence is terrifying. What happens if we're unsuccessful, which is likely?"

Darvy offers a bitter smile. "Honorable death. Living on the other side of magic, preferably with the beautiful goddess, Lucentia."

Rhosse scowls.

Darvy turns toward me, serious now. "As your healer, I strongly advise you to stay here. Rhosse or I can get Vera."

The suggestion irritates me. "I'll not hide in the bushes," I growl. "Set the beasts loose and run. We're not here to battle an army with only the three of us. I just need enough chaos to reach that house undetected. I'll circle around in the forest that way." I point to our right. "We'll leave from there as well—meet there as soon as you release the beasts."

Rhosse and Darvy both nod, taking the official order as well as any top commanders would.

I unsheathe my sword. "Let's go."

Chapter 54

Vera

As the middle of night approaches, Rupi and I are jolted from half-sleep by a thud against the wall of our prison that leaves the gloamy walls shaking. She tumbles from my shoulder to the furs on the bed, and quickly hops up, as flustered and wide-eyed as me. I scramble away from the wall where I fell asleep upright and realize that, even through the walls, I can clearly hear sounds of chaos outside. Is *this* the signal?

I scoop Rupi up and place her on my shoulder before tentatively walking to the door and pressing my ear to the splintered wood. I don't hear the voices of guards outside, but that doesn't mean they aren't there. I stew for a moment. I already know I can zap gloam; I did it to Jethonan's experiment, and I've also used lucent orbs to ward off gloam monsters. Can I do something with this as well?

I lift a finger and pull lucent, never more grateful for its cool and familiar feel, and touch my finger against the gloam surrounding the door. To my delight, it begins to disperse. I pull a little more power and push it through my finger. I'd sit and wonder at the sight before me, still as in awe now as I was when I first realized I could do this, but suddenly the lock clicks, and I quickly backstep to avoid being hit with the door as it swings open forcefully. My mind is already spinning some sort of excuse together as I expect the large form of a guard to be standing there, questioning me about the missing gloam. Instead it reveals Tatania, appearing agitated. Dirt stains her gown and strands of hair blow about her face as if she just ran here... And is that a tear in her sleeve?

I stand there blinking at her, feeling caught even though I'm not the one who just unlocked the door. She slips into the room as I let relief calm my anxiety that, somehow, I'd botched my escape before I'd even begun.

"Where have you been?" I whisper at her, almost angry. I know it's not her fault that Renton behaves the way he does, but now that I've decided to escape, I no longer want to wait around for another moment such as the one that happened at lunch.

"I'm not free to roam the camp, my dear," Tatania scolds, reminding me she's a captive too.

Escape. Mama Tina and Renna wait on the other side of it, and there's a heck of a lot of sorrow to be faced, but I know for sure I don't want to bridge with Renton and make his takeover easier.

"The plan?" I whisper.

"I've... taken care of the guard." She wiggles a key in her finger before grabbing my hand. "Come with me."

I run with her through the hall and out the front door of Renton's house, but I immediately pull back when I catch sight of the utter chaos before me. "You released the gloam monsters?" I nearly shout in panic.

What sort of plan is this? I'm more likely to die than escape now.

She shakes her head. "I don't know how that happened, but we'll take advantage of the distraction. It's better than we could have ever asked for."

I have an opinion to share about that, but I keep my lips pressed shut.

"Renton has already arrived, and if you don't leave now, you never will. You must run."

Three massive shard beasts trample through the large encampment, roaring so loudly it raises the hair on my arms, and it feels as if glass punctures my eardrums. I scan the devastation and spot roaming gloam wolves, deathstalkers, and other beasts that I have no name for. Fire licks up many of the tents, spreading quickly as it grows into an inferno. Gloam soldiers are running and shouting, attempting to control the beasts, and above them, large birds with talons so long they could stab me straight through swoop and dive at the soldiers. It's a scene I certainly don't want to run into. The sounds alone have me clapping my hands over my ears and instinctively shrinking back toward the shelter of my prison.

Tatania grabs my forearm and tugs. "Run, Vera!"

"What about you?" I ask, confused, as she grows impatient and begins pushing me along the shadows of the house somewhat roughly.

"I'll be along. Don't worry about me. Ensure he can't find you. And *hide*," she warns.

"But—"

"Go!" she shouts, a vein in her forehead throbbing and her eyes wide.

"Take care of yourself." I reach for her hand and squeeze it once, wondering if this is the last time I'll see her. I don't have time to argue with her.

She nods sharply. I don't know what lies on the other side of this gloam camp, but I can't stay here. I send up a prayer to Lucentia and run hunched over, making myself as small as I can, toward the shadows of the next half-burnt building.

I glance back at my prison through hazy air, wondering if I would've burned alive if not for Tatania releasing me, and I shiver. Rupi's quilled feathers begin to prick into my neck, reminding me to focus, and I tear my gaze away. I dart around the licking flames, startling violently when a loud pop and a crack come from within and the roof falls in. Sweat beads on my forehead from the heat, but I welcome it because the light from the flames helps me see where I need to go next.

I get braver the farther I go, darting between buildings without recognition as the chaos rages around me. I crouch down and sprint to a small group of tents, hiding beside one that hasn't begun to burn yet as I warily watch a pack of death-stalkers pass by several feet away. I breathe a sigh of relief when they don't seem to notice me... until I turn my head and come face to face with one of the hypnotizing creatures with spikes framing its gruesome face. All the air leaves my lungs.

I instinctively stand up straighter and back up, remembering that Ikar told me to never stare into their eyes, but my distraction has me tripping over one of the blazing tent stakes. I crash to the ground painfully. Sparks from one of the burning tents burst nearby, a few of them floating down to singe my clothing and highlighting the magnetism of the deathstalker before me as it places a large clawed paw into my boot.

Oh no.

I pull a lucent orb just as it lunges, raising my arm up

defensively in front of my face, waiting for its weight to crush me, for its jaw to snap around my neck. But when I look up... only wisps of gloam raining down around me and disappearing into the air remain. My eyes widen, and I look at my little lucent orb with a new level of respect.

"Did you see that, girl?" I whisper with awe. Rupi tugs my earlobe painfully, urging me on. Her quills poke painfully into my neck, drawing blood now. "I'm going, I'm going."

I allow the lucent orb to snuff out and scramble to my feet, searching carefully around me to figure out the best way to escape into the forest. I can continue sneaking through this chaotic, burning camp, or... I eye the wide-open space that leads to the thick treeline... I can run for it and hope the flying creatures above don't take advantage of my prime bait status. I have only moments to make a decision.

I look over my shoulder before I run and spot Renton with another group of gloam masters, working magic furiously to contain all the monsters that broke out... or were they let loose? They already have two shard beasts captured beneath what look like large nets made of gloam. He works fast, and I know if I don't take this chance, I might not get one again. So with one last glance at Renton, who seems to look up and meet my eyes even though there's no possible way with the distance and chaos between us, I shake off the chill in my soul, crouch down, and run across the open expanse toward the treeline. The screeching of the enormous creatures flying above me remind me to stay low. I wait to feel talons rake across my back as I run, and as I get closer, I swear I feel the beat of wings behind me. But even worse than fearing the gloartawks above? The eerie sense that Renton watches me the entire time. It motivates me to run faster.

It's too dark to truly *see* anything, and it's impossible to dodge the bare, dead tree branches that scrape at my face and arms. So I run recklessly, as fast as I can, keeping up with Rupi who darts and swoops around branches and trees alongside me, uncaring about the lack of grace in my movements. Until, suddenly, I smash into something hard and scream before a hand claps over my mouth, and I'm pulled back against the solid chest of my captor. *Renton found me.*

"It's me," Ikar whispers in my ear.

Immediately, I freeze, my hands clutching at his arm around me like a literal lifeline, as I feel my magic react to his proximity, and my knees go weak. Shock vibrates through my body. *He's alive? He's here?* I worry I'm dreaming again. Panic-induced, maybe? Or the excitement and stress of my escape has created a brilliant hallucination that will ruin me when it's past. All I know is that for the first time in days, I feel *warmth* at my back. My magic bursts with pleasure, and tears burn my eyes as I grip his arm tighter.

When he loosens his hold, I spin and wrap my arms around his waist, holding him tighter than I've ever held anyone in my life. The force of my affection seems to catch him off guard, but after only a moment his arms come around me. I press my cheek against his chest and nearly sob when I hear how strong his heart beats, even from beneath the leather of his armor that smells so familiar. *And it's not a dream.*

The dark forest around us disappears, the horrid memories from the past week fade away, the cold thaws. *No more secrets.* I won't waste the chance to be with him again. I begin to formulate the words. Nerves, or maybe shock, have my hands and feet tingling. How do I say it?

Before I can, though, I realize he has other ideas—none of which include spilling my deepest secrets or reveling in this incredible embrace. He tugs my arms from around him and sets me back, appearing to search for injuries.

"Are you hurt?" he asks.

"I'm okay, just my boot..."

His eyes grow dark with anger as he looks over my shoulder. "Their leader, or one of the soldiers?" One hand gravitates toward his sword as if he's going to charge into Renton's camp and kill every one of them this very night.

"Gloam beast."

"One and the same," he mutters.

The sounds of monsters grow closer, and with the smoke mixing with gloam in the air and seeping into the treeline, I can't tell if I just saw shadowed figures or if it's simply my adrenaline-fueled imagination seeing things.

"We have to go," Rhosse whispers from somewhere behind us.

Ikar is still looking toward the camp, eyes dark and a muscle in his jaw tight as if he truly considers going to battle this very moment. I snag his hand and tug him along after me, diverting him from his murderous intentions without another word. He lets me, though he mutters something I can't quite catch but sounds horribly violent beneath his breath as he follows.

We run to catch up, but I can hardly keep track of Darvy and Rhosse ahead of us. They're so quiet—like wraiths moving silently amongst the trees. I don't say anything, content to follow their lead, and more relieved than anything to be reunited with my friends and not traversing this forest on my own.

I nearly fall several times, tripping over crooked branches I'm positive lift from the forest floor just to drag me down, bushes clawing at my trousers and scratching my boots, and shadows that play with my vision, but always, Ikar is there.

Our gazes lock for moments at a time, and the intensity of those looks and the questions that beg to be answered between us weave a thick awareness. There are so many things I need to say, so many questions to ask. While we've shared a kiss-and-a-half and attraction is strung tight between us... after the things I did, the secrets I've kept, I have no idea where we stand. Did his honor drive him to come for me... or his heart?

I refuse to hope for more when it could be crushed. *Just be grateful they came.*

I fight to keep my eyes on the ground ahead of me, but like my magic, all they want is Ikar. I still wonder, as waves of disbelief wash over me, if I'm hallucinating, seeing him beside me. When we finally take a longer break from our steady jog to walk a few minutes, through the patches of moonlight that snake through the spindly trees, I notice he looks exhausted and sweat dots his brow.

Darvy drops back and quietly asks him something, but Ikar merely shakes his head... and why is his arm pressed to his side like that? I frown. Is he not fully recovered, or has it just been a very long day? I don't think I've ever seen him look so... weary.

Rupi coasts to his shoulder and he greets her, stroking her feathers gently. She leans into his touch, appearing perfectly content to have her favorite perch back. I envy my bird and the attention she receives from him, but I let her enjoy it. She did, after all, endure captivity with me—she deserves it.

Darvy retakes the lead with Rhosse, and I might not have time to tell Ikar everything I need to right now, but I have to say *something.*

I work up all my courage and finally whisper words that have never been more true. "I'm glad you're alive."

It seems too small an offering—not enough. The emotion

and feelings I feel are so much more, but here in this forest, on the run...

Ikar's eyes delve into mine, and I hate how guarded they are. "Saved me, even after you ran."

I don't blame him for being confused; I would be too. I can sense the question in his statement, as if he's as unsure of where we stand as I am, and the only one to blame is *me*. Guilt tightens my lungs. How can he not know how much I care for him? Didn't my reaction to finding him in the forest hint at my feelings? Maybe, maybe not. I've been sending mixed messages for weeks. All the hurtful things I've said to him seem to echo in my head, and I inwardly cringe at the way I ran from him, refused to trust him, lied to him... led him to injury. It feels as if I swallow a rock, but I intend to fix the pain I've caused the best I can, and that starts now.

"I'd do it again." I keep my voice low, but my tone is firm, bold even, as I force myself to maintain unwavering eye contact in the weak light.

One corner of his mouth lifts, hinting at the smile I crave, and the guarded look in his eyes softens the smallest bit—I savor the gift that it is. I glance at Rhosse and Darvy, getting farther ahead as they begin jogging again. All the words I want to say urge me to spit them out. I told myself I'd tell him everything, and right now I feel ready. He has to know I don't fear him— the opposite, actually.

I take a breath and open my mouth, but Ikar's attention is now trained ahead, his focus back on the danger that could be behind and around us.

He watches their disappearing forms ahead of us. "We need to catch up."

The words clog in my throat.

He begins jogging, motioning for me to follow. I imagine

running after him and catching his hand and forcing him to listen to me, but I don't. I don't think any of us are in any condition to wrangle with gloam monsters tonight if we've been tracked. My courage has been squashed for the night, anyway; it drains away like fine sand in a timer.

I sigh and grit my teeth as I begin to run.

Chapter 55

Vera

"You look... tired," Ikar says carefully, as if he's afraid he'll offend me as he looks down at my stained clothing, messy hair, and mangled boot.

"And you look like you were dragged through a deathstalker den," I respond with a sassy smirk, only half-joking.

Really, though, he's as handsome as ever, but he looks terrible.

"Feels like it too," he mutters. His eyes linger on the stains covering my clothing before he meets my eyes again. "Did he not offer you anything else to wear?"

I feel my cheeks heat, but I lift my nose the smallest bit. "I refused them."

There's an unreadable look in his eyes, and I'm terrified he's going to ask why. Am I supposed to admit that I planned to wear these blood-stained trousers forevermore in his memory? I don't feel ready to tell him I love him, but somehow, this feels like a silent declaration.

I watch him carefully from the corner of my eye as we walk, on edge, waiting to have to explain myself. But something tells me he might already understand. He doesn't mention it again, just walks beside me. Pensive.

After thinking it was likely he was dead for over a week, every detail about him stands out to me now. I wouldn't have thought it possible, but he's grown even more handsome since I saw him last. My fingers twitch with the urge to grab his hand. It feels too forward. Too risky. He needs a Tulip, but is it a business deal? Or is it possible I can still salvage a romantic relationship and rebuild trust?

I want him to make the first move, but how many times can I expect that of him? I know it's my turn now. I shut down my thoughts, and instead, I simply act. I slip my hand into his larger one, and if I surprise him, he doesn't show it. His thumb moves across the skin of my hand with familiarity, leaving a trail of heat before he twines his fingers even tighter with mine. My heart skips a beat with how natural and right it feels.

We walk hand in hand until we reach the familiar entrance that leads to the nymph's slice of still-lucent mountain heaven. We travel it until warm sunshine beckons from ahead, streaming through the ceiling of the cave, indicating that we've reached the end. Just as before, as soon as we tread beneath it, the guards step from their places in the cave walls, their weapons drawn. A familiar but still unnerving sight.

Ikar releases my hand, hands Rupi over to me, and steps forward. I frown when I watch how carefully he removes his leather armor—I've never seen him this way. When it's gone, all that's left is the white shirt he wears beneath, a portion of it drenched in a dark red stain. I stare at it until my eyes burn and my vision grows fuzzy. We've been running and walking for *hours*. Why didn't he ask me to heal it? Why not Darvy?

I fuzzily notice him pull aside the shoulder of his shirt to show his mark, which this time, seems to satisfy the guards well enough without entirely removing it, and they grant us entrance. I'm not sure who else they think would be tromping through this forgotten, gloam-drenched forest but us anyway.

The same nymph we met our first time here, with the flower petal clothing, leads us through the forest to Odella. Rupi wastes no time launching into the air and into the safe treetops, but I find I don't share her same lighthearted joy. All I can think is that I want to yank Ikar aside and have an angry conversation about why he isn't healed yet, but he and Darvy speak ahead of me in muted tones so low I can't decipher what they say. It doesn't feel right to interrupt, but I intend to find out.

I drop back to speak with Rhosse. "Why isn't he healed yet?" I keep my voice low so Ikar doesn't overhear.

"Not enough lucent. Darvy's been working on it for days. We're just glad he woke up."

I'm almost afraid to ask. "...Woke up?"

"He entered the sleep of death—almost died. I've never seen Darvy so exhausted trying to bring him back; the originators couldn't keep up with him."

I swallow tightly, letting the information soak in and feeling guilt so heavy it feels as if it might strangle me for being the cause of such injuries. If I hadn't run when I saw him at the market... *stop*. I shake my head to ward off the useless thoughts. All I can do is try to right my wrongs.

We are led through sunset-warmed forest, just as beautiful and dreamy as last time, but I hardly notice it. Mixed with guilt are thoughts whirling with the fact that lucent is worse than I've ever imagined, Ikar is *alive*, and I have to somehow figure out the words to tell him all my secrets soon. I remind myself that I *want* to while simultaneously swallowing a hard lump of anxiety, and also fanning irritation that he's still so injured. I admit I'm an emotional mess, and lack of sleep isn't helping. We follow the winding and twisting path, traverse the vine bridge, and finally reach Odella's throne—the four of us looking worse for wear.

"You've returned," Odella states, but I see curiosity in her eyes.

Ikar speaks, his voice sounding stronger than he looks. "We ask to rest here for a time, to recover and prepare for the return journey to Moneyre."

He's the high king. He could command her to give him what he wants, but instead, he asks. I take note. One more way he's unlike the kings I was told of.

Her eyes drop to his shirt. "You're injured."

"Looks worse than it is," he states simply, his face void of emotion.

Of course he says that. I almost roll my eyes. He would say the same thing if he was bleeding out and coherent enough to speak.

Odella inclines her head. "As always, King Ikar, you are welcome here. Please rest."

She motions to a nymph so short and fragile-looking that I'm worried if I breathe too hard, it will lift her by her dandelion-seed dress and spin her through the air. She dances ahead of us with four keys that seem giant in her tiny hands, and leads us through forest that is now familiar. And *warm.* I find myself searching out spots of sunlight that sneak past the thick canopy of trees, walking in a way that I'll pass through them to feel the heat of the sun. I'll not take warmth for granted ever again. And while there may be barriers of my own making between Ikar and I, I've never felt safer than I have with these three men and amidst the land of the nymphs.

I fully expect to be led back to our rooms with the

hammocks, but this time, we're led within the largest tree trunk I've ever seen, even surpassing the size of some of the fae homes, which are quite grand. I realize quickly that this must be Odella's home—her castle, of sorts.

There's a grand entrance with beautiful wood-grain floors, and hallways made of strong branches reach far from the trunk. Nymphs of all sorts busy themselves going quietly to and fro, all bowing to Ikar as the dandelion nymph guides us through. Hardwood stairs, complete with a railing that I very much appreciate, are set against the rounded side of the trunk. They lead us upward, and we pass three more landings. On the fourth landing, we're led down one of the hallways made within a hollowed branch. Then about midway down its shadowy depths, we climb a shorter set of stairs, and she opens a door that leads to the outside of the branch. Another bridge made of thick vines leads to another wider branch where a row of small rooms has been built atop. They are drenched in green-cry, soft moss, and beautiful flowering vines, enough to distract me from the dizzying height as we cross the expanse from branch to branch.

"Here we are." She hands us each a key, each with a different flower that matches those growing on the small huts.

I hear her say something to Ikar about us meeting Odella for dinner after we've cleaned up, but I'm too busy heading toward the hut with the light-blue flowers that match my key to pay much attention.

"Vera." Ikar's voice stops me in my tracks.

I turn back, hope springing up inside me at the same time as a rush of nerves as I wonder if this is the moment we'll be able to talk.

"May we come in and talk for a moment?" I don't miss the

we in his question, and I sigh. His expression is all business as he awaits my response.

I nod. I figured they'd want to know all the nitty-gritty details sooner rather than later. I resign myself to recounting the chill tale as the three men enter after me, crowding into my cramped room.

Ikar eyes a small chair by the wall warily before he carefully settles his large frame into it. Seeing that it holds his weight, he relaxes against the back with his legs sprawled wide. "Can you tell us what happened?"

I take a seat on the edge of the bed, leaving a somewhat tiny stool for Darvy to take. Rhosse stays standing, leaning against the wall near the door. Everyone appears weary, but they're alert. I resist the urge to fidget—it's uncomfortable with the three of them staring at me so intently.

"What do you want to know?" Just thinking about the last week has goosebumps rising along my skin as I remember the chill of gloam and Renton's cold eyes on me.

"Everything," Ikar says.

My mind races—I don't know where to start.

He seems to sense the overwhelm that washes over me and offers me a place to begin. "Who's the leader?"

I can answer that. "A man named Renton—apparently, a long-lost uncle of yours. He said your grandfather was Ricard, his twin."

"It's as we assumed, then." He looks between Rhosse and Darvy.

"They knocked me out, and I woke up in a house made of gloam. I spent most of my time there locked in my room with Tatania—"

"Tatania?" Rhosse asks.

I nod. "She's my... friend. He still has her captive."

"Go on," Ikar urges.

"Renton believes he's the rightful heir to the throne, and told me he's been waiting over three hundred years for lucent to weaken enough for them to return and battle for it."

"What else did he tell you?" Ikar's gaze has darkened, and I hesitate to share the rest.

That he wanted to marry me. "That gloam isn't bad."

"And?"

That I would be worshipped. "That he wouldn't kill all your people."

"That's mighty kind of him," Ikar growls.

"Why did he capture *you* when he had the high king in his hands?" Rhosse speaks from the wall where he leans.

Suspicion oozes in the room, but I'm not spilling all my deepest secrets in front of a crowd. I look at Ikar again, and he seems to sense my discomfort because he changes the subject while giving me a look that promises we'll be talking later. I swallow. It's what I want, but that doesn't mean the thought of it isn't terrifying. I still don't know how to tell him.

Darvy speaks next. "Did he say when he plans to attack?"

I think back carefully. "No, but I don't think it'll be long. You saw his army... his beasts."

I look around the room at their sober expressions. It's not a good sign.

"Did he hurt you?" Darvy glances at my torn boot.

I shake my head. "A deathstalker claw tore my boot, is all." I stretch it out in front of me, inspecting the once-beautiful leather with a frown. "But Tatania is still there..." Unless she happened to escape after I did.

"We can't go back for her right now," Rhosse says, with an apologetic note in his voice. "But hopefully we can defeat Renton soon, and she'll be free."

I look down at my boots and nod. I understand, but it doesn't stop the worry that she'll be in even deeper trouble once Renton learns she helped me escape.

"Anything else we should know?" Ikar asks.

My gaze returns to his. *Besides the truth?* "No."

He winces as he stands, and I try not to stare at the stained blood on his shirt, but it's hard when it's a stark reminder of how close he came to dying.

"We're heading to the bathing pool. Will you be alright?" he asks.

I nod. "I'll be down soon."

We share a prolonged look, then he nods firmly and follows Darvy and Rhosse.

"Shout before entering," Darvy calls over his shoulder. "... Or don't," he adds just before they disappear from view.

The comment brings a smile to my lips, and Ikar looks my way with a brow raised.

"Shout," he warns seriously, as if I actually need to be told.

"We'll see," I respond tartly, irked by the assumption even though he might be correct.

I think I catch the merest hint of a tired smile as he turns.

Chapter 56

Vera

"Everyone decent?" I call around the privacy hedge.

I waited for what felt like forever and a day before I worked up the dignity to come down. I hear one of them laugh, and Ikar gives the okay, but I still hesitantly peek around, ensuring I'm not intruding. All I get is an eyeful of damp-haired, bare-torsoed warriors that many a woman would fight for. I can't stop the hot blush that stains my cheeks, but I ignore it and try to act unaffected as I drop my bundle of clothing away from the edge of the bathing pool and make my way over to the shore made of smooth, polished stone, where Ikar sits before the water. He's washed, and smells of mountain springs and pine. A clean bandage is wrapped around his torso. I also notice the way his clean trousers hug his long legs that stretch out before him. I find that suddenly my mouth is much too dry. Maybe it was a mistake to come here. I should have just waited until they returned.

Ikar looks up with a grin, appearing more relaxed now. "Here to kick us out?" He puts on a good front, looks as handsome as ever, but even after bathing and cleaning up, I can tell he's unwell.

I recall the way he twined his fingers with mine when I held his hand, and I pull on that to give me confidence to risk sitting close beside him. He doesn't shift away—I take it as a win.

Now I eye the bandage, raising a reproachful brow. "How come it's not healed yet?"

He watches the waves lapping at the shore. "In Moneyre, there's only enough lucent available to speed the healing process, not entirely heal it. Darvy was working on it before we left, but it was taking too long, and we needed to find you. Even though there's more lucent here, it still takes a lot of energy to heal—especially more serious wounds, and I've pushed him to the brink of his abilities the past few days. Darvy won't admit it, but he's tired. It'll probably take another day or two."

I force myself to shove down the strong habitual urge to hide my magical gifts. Things are different now, and I have to trust him if I want things to change. If I want him to forgive me... eventually.

Before I change my mind, I blurt out, "Can I? Heal it, I mean."

Fear seizes my tongue, and the words come out in an awkward jumble. I want to dive into the pool to escape, but I sit there and endure it. *Courage.*

He looks at me doubtfully. "I thought you didn't like blood."

He suffered because he thought *I didn't like blood?* It's the sweetest and most anger-inducing thing I've ever heard. It gets ten times worse when I remember he's only injured because of *me.* He's in this horrendous forest again because of *me.*

For a moment, I begin to doubt that he could ever feel more for me than basic responsibility for a former business partner.

"I don't, but I want to. I... owe you." *I love you.*

His brows draw together the smallest bit as his intense blue eyes search mine... for what? Sincerity? I don't yet have words to describe my feelings for him, so I dip my head like a coward while I slip my knife from my boot. He acquiesces and lifts his arm so I can slice the gauzy material away.

I try not to look too hard at the wound; my stomach already roils and turns seeing the irritated, puckered skin, still festering—Darvy's even stitches holding it all together. Red streaks travel outward. It's nowhere near healed; in fact, it looks infected and only barely closed. I'm cringing before I realize he's watching me.

He lowers his arm, intentionally blocking the sight from my eyes. "You don't have to. Darvy is capable. I'll be fine." His tone is decisive, and he grabs the bandage to cover it.

I maneuver onto my knees, determined—it's the least I can do. "No. Let me."

He reluctantly allows me to push his arm away, and the skin contact sends my magic into pleasant sparks that I instinctively keep close. Maybe if I release it, it'll give me away, and I won't have to tell him the uncomfortable way with words and awkward apologies. A coward's wish. I keep it wrapped up tight. I intend to do this properly.

I hover my hand over the wound and pull lucent. He tenses up, then sets his jaw and prepares himself for the coming burn that goes hand in hand with usual healing magic—but not so for mine. I watch his expression as he eyes my hand, feeling the lucent as it runs through my body and into his. I can visibly see him relax as the magic works to heal him, soothing and comfortable. He watches with amazement as the skin knits painlessly together, the stitches fall uselessly to the stones beneath us, the red streaks reverse, and the swelling and redness fade until only a white scar surrounded by healthy skin is left. Another scar to match the others that are scattered across his body.

I drop my hand and sit back on my heels.

"It didn't burn." His voice is controlled, but I see his awe in the way he touches the new scar.

I shrug and smile. "One of my secrets."

"When are you going to tell me the rest of them?" He looks up at me, where I still kneel beside him, placing my eyes directly in front of his very serious ones. It catches me off guard.

Now. Say it now.

I pick at a loose thread on my trousers and swallow tightly. "That would take a lifetime."

"I'm here for it." His voice is deep and a little rough and entirely too convincing.

My breath turns shaky. This is the moment I'm supposed to share it all. My third chance. My lashes flutter in time with my heart beneath his intense focus. My thoughts scatter with the adrenaline of knowing what I'm about to do. How much do I share? Is he meaning that as a friend... or more?

I drop my eyes to get a reprieve from his soul-searching, patient gaze, only to get an eyeful of his impressive chest and almost fall over as I scramble to look elsewhere. Looking elsewhere, meaning searching for a shirt I can toss at him so I can behave properly. I don't see one nearby, but I manage to make it back to sitting beside him without embarrassing myself too badly. I end up a little closer than before, our legs only a hair's width from touching.

So much change in so little time has me reeling. I thought I was prepared for this—in my mind I can clearly *see* myself sharing everything with him. I imagine how it would feel to just say it, to let him take the weight of my secrets in his capable hands and heal my broken places. That is, if he forgives me.

Ikar looks at the new scar on his torso again, and I follow his eyes, which is a mistake because... still no shirt. I've never felt less disciplined in my life.

"Thank you for this," he says.

I nod and look back down at the pesky thread. "It's me that should be thanking you. And also offering an apology. The things I said on the journey, the way I ran... I didn't know who to trust."

"And now?"

I meet his gaze. "I think that's obvious."

"Is it?" He offers a frustrated sort of smile before he rests his arms on his knees and turns his attention to Rupi, who hops through the shallow water and wet rock, cleaning her feathers happily.

His comment is a little icy, and I don't blame him. We both know there are too many secrets between us still—mostly mine. Still, he doesn't force an answer from me.

I watch Darvy and Rhosse climb steep cliffs beside the waterfall, engaged in some sort of dangerous competition men are drawn to, I suppose. I smile at their bickering, and then Ikar's bare torso steals my attention again, but this time it's his mark. I trace the scrolling ribbons that travel down the upper part of his chest and arm with my eyes, and watch how it trails down to his mid back, curling and turning. Most of it is stark black against his skin, but I see small portions at the ends of the scrollings that shine almost white.

"Tell me about it?" I ask, gesturing toward his mark with my chin, feeling vulnerable and unsure. How does he feel about talking about it?

He looks at me for a long moment. I almost begin to apologize for asking at all. We both know it's my turn to share, and I can't blame him if he decides to say no.

"What do you want to know?" His expression is guarded as he looks out over the water. He's so still he could be a gorgeous statue in some rich lady's courtyard.

"I've heard every new heir is born with his part of the mark added on, but I didn't know it was two colors."

"Every generation adds to the mark. The first started here." He shifts to a position where he points to the uppermost part of his collarbone and shoulder so I can better see. "And here is where magic really began suffering." He points to scrolling parts of the mark that go from lucent to black. "It's a history of our people and magic, of sorts."

"And is this your part?" My finger brushes against a few scrolling ends at his mid-back, not yet completely black. His skin is warm to the touch. After a week of icy cold, it draws me more than ever. It's only when he stiffens and goosebumps spread across his skin that I realize I probably shouldn't have touched him. My magic runs wild within my veins. *I definitely shouldn't have touched him.*

We both freeze, awareness a heady fog between us.

"Yeah, that's my part," he finally answers, his voice low and deep.

I pull my hand away and squeeze it between my knees to better keep it off him.

Ikar swallows and looks back over the pool.

"So it turns black if lucent is weak while you're king?" I ask.

"Yeah."

"Yours is still gold—that's a good sign."

"Some of it." He breathes out, and with it, his shoulders seem to drop beneath invisible weight.

"What will happen if it *does* turn all black?"

He shrugs a shoulder. "My father had an heir at my age already to add more gold by the time his turned black, to *carry the kingdom forward*, if you will. If I don't fix this and I don't have an heir..."

Heir—the word brings a horrid image of me forever keeping my dratted secrets and living my life alone with a flock of white fluffy birds while Ikar marries another Tulip and has a brood of gorgeous children. I feel a little like a lusty everwisp right now with jealousy running like hot lava through my veins.

"No," I breathe out.

The image I'd just created brings almost tangible pain, and I find myself clutching the fabric of my trousers with a white-knuckled fist. One of the reasons I worked up the courage to escape Renton was so I didn't lose Ikar to another Tulip, or to *anyone*. If I ever want a chance to see what could be between us, now's the time to fight for him.

My quiet exclamation catches Ikar's attention, and he appears slightly confused. I would find it incredibly endearing if I didn't have to spill my deepest secrets in the next moment.

Chapter 57

Vera

"Ikar."

I currently feel like I'm going to hyperventilate or barf—both maybe. I just know if I hold my hand up, it'll be shaking like a leaf in a violent storm. The words I'd made an oath to never share, and that have been trying to fight their way out, feel stuck in my throat—locked behind the promise I made to never tell anyone, *especially* a king. But then... that image of him with another Tulip pops into my head again—motivation enough.

"I'm a Black Tulip." It comes out sort of strangled, quiet, and shaky.

He smiles in a way that makes my heart beat faster than it should, looking more warm and pleased than ever. I'm not sure what I expected his reaction to be, but it isn't this.

"Finally," he breathes.

I merely blink at him in obvious confusion.

He speaks again, this time softer. "Thanks for trusting me. I know that took a lot." He holds my gaze steadily, and my eyes begin to tear up when I realize the depth of his sincerity, and more so as I bask in the relief of sharing everything with him.

I told him.

"How long have you known?" I mumble in shock.

"Why d'you think I was chasing you through that fae market like a mad man?" He laughs. "Thank the blazes I had that identity charm, or people would think their king had lost his mind."

He chooses another stone and tosses it expertly across the surface of the pool. I watch as it skips several times, then disappears.

He searches for more stones. "Jethonan helped me figure it out. I would've realized it sooner, except for that innocent-looking *friendship bracelet*. Blazing thing threw me off." He tosses another rock that soars close enough past Rupi that her feathers blow in its wake. She fluffs her wings up indignantly and casts a scolding look our way before she resumes her playful bathing.

"I thought you wanted the names on the list..." I say slowly as the pieces begin to click together. I never let him speak more than three words without interrupting once he caught me that day... then we got attacked, and that has a way of ending a conversation rather quickly. Did I honestly think he would have chased me down just because he needed my help as an originator all this time? Or he needed names on a list? I feel foolish. Still, it was I who needed to tell him. He needs to know I trust him if we're to make anything of our relationship, and that prompts the question of... what are we?

I bite my lip as he throws another stone. There are a few moments of silence between us where I try to catch up with the fact that Ikar knows everything. *I don't have to hide anymore.*

He's known for days. The bracelet that was a tangible reminder of my promises is long gone, but all this time, I admit, there's been an inward bracelet locking up parts of me just as tightly, and it feels good to finally be free.

"So we can fix this, right?" I ask, almost scared it's too late.

He looks down at me. "Yeah. We can fix this, with you as my queen."

A corner of his lips lifts into the handsome half-smile I dreamed about for the last week. Hope looks good on him.

"I don't know how to be a queen," I warn, trying to hide the terror I feel when I consider the position I'll be taking but haven't been prepared for.

"You know how to be a Black Tulip, and that's exactly what our kingdom needs. The rest will come." He truly seems unconcerned about my lack of queenly training. I wish I could be, as well. *Do* I know how to be a Black Tulip? Will I know how to bridge when the time comes? Do I have to do anything to make it all work? I was never taught any of that, and it's scary to say *I don't know* when an entire kingdom of people is relying on me, but I try to draw on Ikar's confidence and tamp down the instinct to panic.

I recline on my hands beside him again, trying to be present—content. He's alive and well, we're getting along, we seem to be friends again, and he says we can fix things now. Shouldn't I be ecstatic? This is all I dreamed of while imprisoned in Renton's camp, but it's hard to be content when I imagine there could have been a kiss accompanying that moment where he told me we could fix this together, and there most definitely wasn't. Besides holding my hand yesterday, he's hardly touched me since that single beautiful kiss at Mama Tina's weeks ago. I've caused monumental trouble for him, and I should be happy that he's even willing to sit here and be friendly with me. I should be satisfied... but I'm not.

I know that with bridging comes marriage. Does he see the rest of our lives like a well-written contract? Will we simply be powerful magic friends who wed out of necessity? My nose wrinkles in response to that thought. I need to know, or I'll drive myself batty.

I mentally prepare myself to ask, to be okay with whatever comes of my inquiry. I will not sob in front of him, but how to word it so I don't sound overeager? My palms begin to sweat on the smooth rocks.

"Ikar?" It comes out all breathless and lover-like. Dratted nerves. This is not going according to plan. He looks my way. *Here's my moment.* I swallow, and my tongue seems to grow three sizes. "Can you forgive me? Can we be—er, are we... *friends?*" I nearly choke on that last word since it's *anything* but friendship that I feel for him.

He lifts a brow at my struggle to spit the words out, a smooth stone in his frozen hand—there's a beat of silence between us.

"I don't generally kiss my friends," he says wryly.

"Well, I don't either," I argue, blushing hotly now, and stare hard at a spotted stone that has suddenly captured my attention. "But it's been a while since... y'know... and I've caused a lot of trouble, and I don't expect you—"

He places a finger beneath my chin and lifts my gaze to his. "Is that what you want to be?" He's as direct as always, and it's terrifying to a person who loves to beat around the bush— rather, hide behind it.

I swallow, and I'm sure he can hear it. I can't read him; his eyes are guarded again. He doesn't sound angry, though there *is* a small crease between his brows I fixate on. Is he exasperated? Frustrated? I bite my lip.

"Is that what you want to be?" he asks again, softer now, beginning to pull his finger back. My chin follows it, begging him not to distance himself, and do I spy a hint of disappointment in his eyes, or is it a figment of my overactive imagination?

This is where I'm meant to declare my love, where I fight for him, and all my feelings rise up in a great symphony, ready to sing out in strong vulnerability—instead, all that comes out is a shaky, "Do *you* want to be friends?"

I can hardly meet his eyes. Friends is so much less than I'd dreamed of having with him, but better than nothing at all.

His eyes darken and his lips turn up in a roguish grin. "I've never wanted to be friends with you, Vera."

My eyes shoot up to meet his, wondering if he means what I think he means—can he really feel the same as I?

"That's awfully rude to say," I whisper as he chuckles deeply and leans close.

He draws a thumb slowly along my jaw. I tilt my head up, and our lips brush so lightly it could have been a gentle breeze. Then I lean closer, feeling bold, and meet his lips again, and he responds... firm, gentle, intoxicating as his warm hand cradles my face, and his thumb moves across my skin in a gentle caress. His clean scent hovers around us as our magic twines, warm and content. Suddenly, I can't get enough of him. I find myself on raised knees beside him, his hands now at my waist tugging me closer and mine sliding from his strong shoulders to the back of his neck in a close embrace as our kiss deepens. All my senses are set afire as the world around us disappears, leaving just he and I and the magic swirling around us.

"King Ikar."

Ikar's head jerks up almost violently, and I'm left severely disappointed as we both turn to find a squat nymph covered in skin of rich brown bark and hair of orange leaves bowing lightly before us—I swear I hear cracking like a tree bending too far in the wind.

He straightens. "I've been sent to invite you and your entourage to a celebration thrown by Queen Odella this evening."

Ikar nods and clears his throat, but the roughness of his voice sends heat through my entire body. "We'll be there. Please send Odella our thanks."

The man nods sharply and waltzes out the open gate, oblivious to what he interrupted.

For a moment, I wonder if maybe we can revisit that kiss, but Ikar reaches an arm around me, and I sit down as he pulls me into his warm side. I lean into him, soaking up his nearness.

"So... does this mean you forgive me for all the trouble I've caused you?" I ask.

He looks down at me with a slight frown turning his brows, and I worry I've ruined the moment by bringing it all up again. I open my mouth to say something to fill the silence, but he chooses that moment to continue, so I close my mouth with an audible click of my teeth.

"The day I realized that you were what I had been searching for, and you knew it and chose not to trust me, I was angry."

I thought I was prepared for this conversation, but the pain that tightens my chest tells me I could never be ready.

"And hurt. More than I've ever been. I thought I'd done everything I could possibly do to earn your trust."

I look down and my eyes burn again. I refuse to cry and make this about me. No words of defense come to mind.

"I wasn't sure I'd ever be able to."

That's where he's wrong, and I'm about to tell him so, but then he speaks again and I've interrupted him enough over the past several weeks, so I stay quiet. Trying to be patient. It's his turn now. I take small breaths since that's all my lungs will allow.

"So, yes, I was upset, but I'm not now, and... there's nothing to forgive, Vera."

I sit there staring at the rocks beneath us blurrily while his words echo in my head at least three times.

"That's not true," I say almost angrily.

His eyes soften, and he grabs my hand in his, rubbing a thumb across my skin, leaving it tingly and warm.

"I may have been angry, but I've had time to reconcile that. I understand. You stayed true to promises you believed needed to be kept, thought you were protecting people you cared for—that's an honorable thing—though I must say with the extent of your loyalty, I'm glad you're on my side now." He chuckles. "No forgiveness needed from me... it seems it's you who needs to forgive yourself for not knowing any different."

Forgive *myself*? That's something I've never thought of before. It feels odd to consider.

"Ikar, don't you think it's about time to let Vera use the pool?" Darvy stands nearby, smirking as he eyes the way Ikar's arm presses me close to his side. There's a towel in his hand that he must have used to dry his short hair that currently sticks up like the quills of a threatened porcupine.

Ikar nods, speaking to both Rhosse and Darvy. "We've been invited to a celebration tonight."

"We could skip it," I suggest with a whisper, prompting a chuckle from Ikar.

I don't want to go to a party. I want to stay right here with him, just like this, for the rest of my life as I feel his broad chest expanding beside me with even breaths. He's alive, he knows what I am, we're to be married, I don't have to hide anymore, and from the conversation and the heady kiss we just shared, I *think* we might be more than friends.

"We should go. Queen Odella has been good to us." Ikar plants a soft kiss on the top of my head. I can hardly believe I'm the recipient of his affection, and this time... *it's not a dream.*

Chapter 58

Vera

I'd hoped to see Ikar before dinner, but all is quiet when I reach my room after bathing. I didn't have time to wash and dry my clothing, as I have nothing else to wear, and now that I know Ikar is alive and well, I loathe donning my blood-stained apparel—especially for dinner, where I know it'll garner attention.

Rupi soars into the room as I open the door, and I gasp when the first thing I see is a pile of deep-purple flower petals strewn across my bed. My first thought is that it might be a romantic gesture of some sort from Ikar, but when I pick up one petal... others follow, and I realize it's a *dress*.

"What...?" I pull the entire dress up until it hangs in front of me from shoulders to toes.

"I made it for you."

My head whips to the side to see the little nymph in the flower petal dress sitting on the squat stool, swinging her legs and grinning somewhat shyly. I should've figured she made it; it's almost an exact match for the miniature version she wears.

"Thank you. It's beautiful," I say sincerely.

Rupi chirps in agreement from her perch on the bedpost.

"It's for dinner tonight. I thought purple might be nice." The nymph continues kicking her small feet.

I nod, looking down at the dress again. The back dips quite low, but if I leave my hair down...

"Do you truly like it?" she asks.

I look straight into her sparkling, innocent eyes, and shove my doubts aside. "I love it."

She rewards my answer with a bright smile and hops down. "I'll help you dress."

"Oh, that's okay, I'm sure—"

Her face falls. "Do you not plan to wear it?"

I sputter for a moment, looking down at the dress. It simply doesn't seem as if there's enough *substance* to wear it. What happens if the wind blows? I have concerns.

But the look on her face.

I smother a groan and force a wide smile. "Help would be nice."

Within minutes, my clothing has been replaced with the petal dress as the tiny nymph uses vines in a corset fashion to tie the back while I slip a pair of velvety soft leaves fashioned into slippers onto my feet. I wiggle my toes, reveling at the softness. I may need a pair of these to take home.

The little nymph finishes tying and skips to stand before me while eyeing me carefully. She narrows her eyes, then darts forward and plucks a petal from the dress in one spot, then another.

I block her from snatching another and laugh nervously. "I need all the petals I can get."

She ignores me and plucks one more. I'm about to snatch her in my hands to keep her from removing any others, but she finally steps back, appearing pleased.

I look down. I have to admit, the dress is stunning. The petals are a gorgeous shade of purple, wide and round, sewn together in layers that cascade down my body. A row of petals make up the straps over my shoulders, the bodice has a sweetheart neckline that I'm pleased to see doesn't plunge too deep, and the bottom is full enough to walk normally, but not too big. With no mirror available, I can't see the back. I can tell it's not *low*, but it's low enough that my mark will show.

"Now for your hair." She eyes my somewhat damp, frizzy hair, and drags the stool over to me before she plucks a flower from the nearby table. "I'd hoped to use this." She blinks at me as she spins it slowly in her hand.

These nymphs are more dangerous than they look, getting whatever they want from me with a simple, sad look. *They're as bad as Rupi.*

"As long as you leave it down." I lift a brow in warning.

I've already told Ikar what I am; I don't *need* to hide it... it's simply habit and comfort to keep it covered. I remind myself that years' worth of instinct and fear won't be erased in a day. If I feel ready to show him tonight, I will. But it'll be on my terms.

She pulls me down to the stool. I acquiesce with a sigh, knowing if I don't like the style, I can simply change it before I leave. The scent of flower petals on my skin and the gentle fluttering of her fingers with the lightest pulls and tugs in my hair has me so relaxed I nearly topple off the stool when she steps back.

"All finished." She clasps her hands before her, appearing pleased with her work.

I reach a hand up gently to touch my long brown hair now hanging in smooth, silky waves around my shoulders, and the purple flower has been artfully tucked above my left ear. I may not be able to see it, but I can tell it's beautiful.

"Thank you," I say quietly.

I stand, and Rupi perches near my neck, greedily eying the thin strap of purple petals on my shoulder. "No eating the petals. I can't afford to lose anymore." I narrow my eyes as she shuffles nearer, side-eyeing me as if waiting for me to look away before snatching one. "I mean it. This dress has to last the entire evening," I warn her. It's already so fragile I worry that a strong breeze will blow away the bulk of it.

She blinks innocently at me.

"Time to go," the little nymph says brightly, almost bouncing with impatience.

She grabs my hand, and I laugh as I let her tug me out the door.

Chapter 59

Ikar

I sit at the head of a long wood table settled in the middle of a small meadow amidst tall grass and wildflowers as if it was planted and grown here like everything else. Matching chairs line its sides, filled with at least forty people. Vera is seated to my left, Odella on my right, and Darvy and Rhosse appear comfortable farther down. Vines with tiny flowers wrap around the thick table legs and creep up and over the edges of the surface, and an artful mix of pinecones, pine boughs, and wildflowers grace the center of the table. It's all beautiful, but it's nothing compared to Vera. The dress she wears, one made entirely of petals, is perfection on her frame, the purple a flawless complement to gray eyes that are so open and warm I can hardly believe I'm the recipient of their attention.

I'm forced to drag my gaze from hers when wood bowls are set before us, filled with fresh, dark berries interspersed with a variety of seeds and nuts, topped with sweet tree sap and fresh mint. They're accompanied by enormous leaves full of perfectly cooked fish, a pile of something that looks suspiciously like some sort of insect's eggs, and wild carrots. I notice none of the nymphs who dine with us have fish or insect eggs in their leaves—apparently they don't eat meat. I sort of wish I don't either at this moment.

Odella stands, and immediately the table grows quiet. "We celebrate the success of our king in finding not only the Field of Tulips and being found worthy to take one, but also in that he found a Queen of the Night herself."

There's a round of celebration that sounds like rushing wind and water and creaking branches as everyone's eyes turn to the two of us. I grin broadly at Vera, who blushes at the attention, but she offers a small smile.

Odella begins the meal, and we dig in. I find that the food of the nymphs is similar to the fae, so I'm not surprised when Vera takes a bite of insect eggs without hesitation. I eat those first, forcing them down between bites of delicious fish to ease the gag. No one would know I thought the meal anything other than normal. I've been raised for this. I smother a smile as she takes another graceful bite. Vera was made to be queen; she just doesn't know it yet. The fact that I have years to show her just how perfect she is brings a rush of contentment.

From my right, Odella asks, "What comes next, King?"

With practiced swallowing, another bite of insect eggs goes down. "We return to Moneyre where we will marry and bridge." I take a sip of the orange liquid in my cup that tastes like some sort of tangy nectar.

"The gloam masters," Odella states.

"What about them?" I ask.

"Will they be destroyed by you and Vera bridging? Or will you have to banish them behind lucent again?"

I pause. I don't actually know how any of it works. Jethonan never explained that part to me. "That's something I intend to find out."

She directs her attention to Vera over the low rumble of nature sounds and voices. "Does Renton know who you are?"

Vera nods. "He knows I'm a Black Tulip and plans to bridge with me."

I find my hand fisting on my leg beneath the table.

She looks at me. "But he won't be able to if I bridge with someone else first." She realizes a second too late what she said before the crowd, and I see her sink into her chair, her knee pressing against my thigh with the motion.

But even with her embarrassment, her eyes meet mine with so much invitation I barely manage to stay seated. I'm ready to leave tonight, retrieve the flower I left in Moneyre, marry, and bridge. The words are practical to everyone else, but to me, they hold promise. When Vera meets my eyes, her cheeks warm even more.

The meal continues with the low hum of conversation. Plates are cleared, the night grows late, and still conversations continue. I watch Vera talk and laugh with a nymph the color of a blushing rose, but she must feel my gaze on her because she glances my way and tilts her head with a question in her eyes. I simply quirk my lips in a half-smile as an overwhelming rush of affection runs through me. I sit back, for the first time feeling like I can fix things for my people. At times I can still hardly believe I found a Black Tulip—not only found one, but fell in love with her too. My heart was vulnerable to Vera from the moment I met her—I felt it. The fear, the knowledge, that I'd fall for her before I could distance myself was there from the beginning. I smile as I realize the woman I thought I could never have... is the only one I ever needed.

The night is quiet around us as we walk hand in hand up wide leaf stairs, the noise of celebration behind us gradually replaced with soft chirping from crickets and the rustle of leaves in the warm breeze. It feels surreal to hold her hand in mine without the weight of secrets between us, our magic twisting and curling together, natural and free. We don't speak, but the warm tension between us is heady. I hesitate to speak and disrupt it, but I have one question that simmers in my mind.

"You never told me what Odella showed you."

"Is that you asking?" Vera smirks, but I see a hint of worry as her brows draw together.

"Sort of." I offer a casual smile to hide the fact that it's been killing me not knowing.

"I never saw the original seer vision, but the one she showed me matched the one I've heard about... a Tulip bridging with a being of darkness. Someone like Renton—the same thing they saw hundreds of years ago." Fear glimmers in her eyes. "I don't want to be that person."

"You won't." I squeeze her hand, attempting to reassure her.

"I'll believe you once we've bridged." She smiles wryly as we reach the landing that leads to our rooms.

"That day can't come soon enough."

She looks up and meets my eyes with a smile on her lips that's so tempting it takes everything within me to not pull her to me and claim her mouth with my own. I resist leaving her at her door like I know I should. She appears reluctant to end the evening as well, but when she slips her hand from mine, I quickly shutter my disappointment. I expect her to say good-night and enter her room. Instead, she holds my gaze as she pulls the length of her hair forward, letting it fall over the front of her shoulder before she slowly turns and rests her palms lightly on the dainty wood railing overlooking the forest beneath us. The three moons and flickering tiny lights amidst the trees offer a warm glow, and in the distance, I can still hear the nymph party, but right now all I can focus on is the small tulip mark at the base of her neck.

I hesitate to move, or even breathe. She's always been too intentional about hiding her mark for this to be anything other than her gifting me every last remnant of her trust. My eyes rove the lines of her mark, so small, so stark against her fair skin. I step forward, fearing if I touch her, she'll run. I take the risk and slowly slide my hands down her upper arms, watching for any sign that she doesn't want my touch.

She turns her head to look over her shoulder, standing so still I hardly see her shoulders rise and fall with the movement of even breath. I still, giving her a moment to step away, to turn around, to run if that's what she wants... but she stays, unmoving, as if waiting for me to make the next move.

I slowly lift a finger and reverently trace the outline of her mark, not missing the way her breath catches... the warmth that begins to burn between us.

Chapter 60

Vera

My heart races, but I remain still as his warm finger grazes my skin and gently traces the mark I've kept hidden for a lifetime, leaving a warm, tingling trail. I battle the instinctive urge to spin around, to continue hiding like I always have, but I impulsively offered an invitation... and he took it. The only thing that moves are the petals of my dress gently fluttering in the lightest of warm breezes. I rally the confidence gained from the conversation we shared earlier, long looks shared across the table over dinner, and the low light from the moons shining on us... my walls are defenseless against him.

His hand slides from my arm to my waist, and a moment later, my breath hitches as he leans down and kisses my mark so gently my eyes begin to burn. Tingles race across my skin as the light scratch of a day's worth of scruff on his jaw brushes the warm curve between my shoulder and neck, where he leaves another slow, soft kiss that sends heat running down my arm. Another stilted breath when his lips brush my skin again as he makes his way toward my shoulder... I can't resist any longer.

All at once, I turn, and his arms come around me as his lips claim mine, firm and warm. My lower back presses lightly against the railing as I cling to his solid waist, and our magic twists and curls around us, mixed with his incredible scent and the strength beneath my hands as they move from his waist to his back.

Our kiss deepens as one of his hands slowly slides from my back and up into my hair, and with it, I let the years of hiding, weeks of wanting, and days of fearing he was gone pour out of me as I pull him closer, all of it replaced with a warmth and confidence I never knew possible. Here in Ikar's arms, I feel whole for the first time. Safe. *Free.*

His other hand cups my cheek, caressing, even as he begins to pull away. In a desperate attempt to match his retreat, I rise to my tiptoes, but he laughs low and rough as he breaks our heady kiss.

"I intend to be a gentleman."

I know exactly what he means. Those words are both comforting and infuriating when all I want is him. Instead of backing away and leaving as I fear he'll do, he enfolds me in his arms and rests his chin gently on my head. I place my cheek against his chest, pleased to hear that his heart beats as rapidly as mine.

"I love you," I whisper. I know he'll hear it. Maybe I should've looked in his eyes or said it louder, but the words have already left my lips.

"I love you too." He kisses my hair, his lips lingering for a moment.

Just to be facetious, I add, "Would you love me if I weren't a Tulip?"

I feel the growl in his chest. "I already did before I knew you were, and it nearly broke me, imagining living my life with another woman when the only one I wanted was *you*. My magic wasn't the only thing you captured with that cuff; you took my heart as well."

His words remind me of my time in Renton's camp. "That was a motivation, you know."

"What was?"

"To escape from Renton. You're so blasted noble that I knew you'd find another Tulip if you had to... if you lived. The thought of another woman in your arms, just like this, made me sick."

"It wasn't the dreams?" he asks, stepping back slightly and ducking his head to find my face in the moonlight.

"The dreams?" My eyes grow wide. "Those were really *you*?"

My cheeks grow hot as I try to recall if I did anything untoward.

"I didn't know until the third one, when you asked if I was alive..."

I nod, indicating he should continue.

"But Darvy told me it's a bond called *Never Apart*. Some even call it the soulmate bond because of how strong the connection is. It helps you find each other, both in reality and in sleep. Did you ever notice the gold mark is brightest when we're together?"

He releases one of my arms and tugs my marked wrist from around his waist. I decide to be mature and let him. We hold our wrists up and see the gold shining as bright as ever.

"I'd thought it was some sort of tracking charm... but it's a *soulmate* bond?"

"It does work for tracking. I've used it to find you, but we didn't know about the dreams because, for a while, we never spent a night far apart. The days when I was injured—"

"I couldn't touch you." *He almost died.*

He nods. "Until the one that woke me from what soldiers call the sleep of death, one where many pass to the other side of lucent after an injury such as that. I believe you saved me."

I'm quiet for a long moment as worry builds. It all seems too good to be true; is this the moment it falls apart?

"What happens when it wears off?" I can't help the tremor in my voice, and I wish for more confidence. Will he feel the same for me? Did the bond mess with *my* feelings? As I think back to that mate bond shop, I remember I already felt for Ikar in ways that had me ready to attempt to convince a criminal to marry me. I'm not worried about *mine.*

Ikar watches my expression carefully, sensing my concern. "I feel more for you than any mate bond could ever offer, Vera. Watch it wear off, and I'll show you."

There's a challenge in his deep voice. A promise. It has chills racing lightly across my skin as I look up and meet his eyes. He seems utterly secure in my feelings for him, but I say it anyway with a bit of sass. "Back when you were my bounty, I already loved you so much I was going to wait for you to get out of jail. Help you reform your criminal tendencies. I wouldn't do that for just *any* criminal." I raise a brow.

"Such devotion," he says wryly. He pulls me tighter against his chest and plants another kiss in my hair.

"You'll always be my criminal."

"I'm not a criminal."

I snicker into his shirt and squeeze him a little tighter. All is right in my world for the first time in my life.

Chapter 61

Vera

The thought of arriving in Moneyre has me nervous. My heart picks up in pace as the terrifying thoughts I've ignored since I told Ikar everything rise to the surface now that we exit the cave of the nymphs and enter into gloamy lucent forest. I don't know how to be a queen. For that matter, I don't even really know how to be a Black Tulip. Will I know how to bridge when it's time? And how will people receive me once they know what I am? It's all beginning to feel very real.

Ikar squeezes my hand, and it breaks me from the fearful thoughts. It's then I realize how hard I've been clutching him.

He raises a brow. "Are you okay?"

"Just thinking about what's next." I try to sound confident, but I know he'll see straight through it.

His eyes soften with understanding. "We landed closer this time, about half a day's journey to the sharp flyers, so we should reach them anytime now. When we return to Moneyre we'll need to marry quickly so we can bridge." His brow furrows with an unspoken apology. "There isn't time for lengthy planning for the ceremony."

That doesn't bother me. I don't need a fancy ceremony, I just need Ikar. But I *am* curious about one thing.

"Can you bridge without being married?" I ask.

Ikar pauses. "I've read nothing that says you *can't*."

"So we could bridge right now?" I know I sound overeager, but I need answers. If we can fix this right now, why don't we?

He smirks. "If I had the tulip, I suppose. It's in Moneyre. Both the king and Tulip have to touch it to bridge, but traditionally marriage comes first. In our case, I feel it's even more important that our people see us marry to present a united front and build their confidence with a Black Tulip as queen once again."

At my concerned look, he adds, "They'll be hesitant at first, but they'll come around once they get to know you."

"Sounds wonderful," I whisper.

He chuckles. We walk in comfortable silence, hand in hand, until Ikar speaks again.

"Will you tell me about the rest of the Tulips now?"

"What do you want to know?"

"Everything."

I laugh, feeling almost giddy that I can finally share this part of my life with him. "There are eight of us. Tatania is our leader, but acts more like a mother. Renna, my best friend, she's a Tulip too—"

"So I *was* right," he interrupts with a cocky smile.

"About what?"

"I guessed you didn't want to tell me about the list because your friend was on it. I thought you were just jealous."

"I would've been," I say, unashamed. Feeling a little bold, I add, "The only Tulip you can ever have in your arms is *me*."

And we'll be married in days.

The roguish half-smile on his lips sparks a fire within me. "As you command, my lady. I am yours alone."

The blush on my cheeks deepens at the look of warm promise in his gaze, but he takes mercy on me a moment later and redirects the conversation. "You were telling me about the Tulips?"

"Oh. Er—Yes..." I stumble over my words as I try to get my mind off the thought of Ikar's arms around me, his lips on mine... "I mentioned Tatania and Renna, and there's also Fina, who I've always looked up to. She's—"

"They're gone!" Darvy shouts from ahead.

Rhosse curses.

"Hold that thought." Ikar squeezes my hand, then releases it and jogs ahead.

I grumble to myself as I watch him go, imagining the long trek we have back to Moneyre without the sharp flyers to help. Now it will be even longer before we can wed—not that I'm impatient at all. But I can almost tangibly feel my mood darkening the more I think about it.

Rupi's warning chirps sound from the treetops just before I hear swords clash through the thickening chill gloam encroaching around us. Dread snakes through my body as my steps slow, and Rupi shoots to my neck, quilling up on my shoulder. Her feathers prick into my neck hard enough to draw blood, but I ignore it as I run forward, pulling lucent and sending it farther than I've ever tried in order to reach the men ahead.

I catch sight of Ikar through the shadows, and he meets my eyes. I don't know what to think of the unfamiliar expression on his face, a mix of panic and fury, as he attempts to get back to me. He yanks his sword from a gloam soldier and kicks him to the ground before he sprints to reach me, only to have two more soldiers corner him. He roars in frustration as he blocks their swings with expert precision.

The look on his face and the presence of gloam soldiers can only mean—

The unmistakable chill of the horribly familiar gloam noose snakes around my neck, and when he whispers near my ear, I'm not even surprised. *Renton.*

"Miss me, my queen?"

Fury grows so hot in my chest it feels as if I might combust. I finally have hope and happiness in my grasp, and he shows up to snatch it away. I throw my elbow back in an attempt to take him off guard, but he grabs it and twists it behind my back, while tightening the noose around my neck, leaving me choking for air and gasping from pain. I've never hated anyone so much in my life.

Amidst the sharp pain in my twisted shoulder, my thoughts spin. Renton said the bracelet weakened the Tulip's power... I *did* destroy a deathstalker with a simple lucent orb. Can I do that to this noose? Can I free myself, maybe even kill Renton?

I draw lucent into my free hand and clap it around my neck. The noose bursts into dark, misty ashes that seems to surprise Renton as much as I. He loosens his grip on my elbow momentarily and I spin, pulling lucent and shoving it at him. I don't know what I expected, ideally him exploding... at least *something.* Instead he shouts at me, as if it merely pained him, and trades the gloam noose for his own arm around my neck, pulling me back roughly against his chest.

"Stop, or she suffers," Renton shouts.

Ikar blocks one more swing, pushes the gloam soldier's sword away from him and steps back, breathing heavily, a look so dark crossing his features that even *I* feel afraid of him for a moment.

Rhosse and Darvy pull back from the fight as well. Renton forces me forward, and I find we're surrounded by at least thirty cloaked figures. I try to swallow, but it feels like shards of ice scrape my throat with how tightly his arm wraps around my neck. I feel the freezing gloam waiting to knock me out, hovering just above my skin. *I can't be the one who ruins our kingdom.*

Ikar, Darvy, and Rhosse stand tall, their arms pulled painfully tight behind their backs as they face us, and tension fills the space.

"I've come to your rescue," Renton drawls near my ear. "It appears my timing was impeccable." He brushes the back of a finger along my jawline. "Can't have you marrying anyone but me. We have plans... remember?" he finishes with a raspy whisper.

My body tenses as I try to jerk away, but he tightens his arm, and I end up choking on a painful shout instead.

He hands me off to one of his soldiers, then spins toward Ikar, Darvy, and Rhosse as he laughs. "I wondered how it would feel to meet my long-lost nephew in person. Ironic that we desire the same woman, isn't it?" He turns his gaze to Darvy and Rhosse. "Lowly knights of Moneyre, meet Renton, King of the Shadows and true heir to the throne of Moneyre. Soon to be your liege." He lowers into a dramatic bow.

Ikar's face is a mask of hard granite, no emotion shown besides furious anger in the depths of his eyes. He offers no response to Renton's taunting. Darvy and Rhosse stare at Renton with condescension, but hide it well. I'm sure mine is written all over my face, as usual.

How does he always find me?

"No honor at my introduction?" Renton asks the two men, his brows raising with mock offense. They stare at him, stoic and silent.

He pulls out a knife with a blade black as night faster than my eyes can track and holds it at Darvy's neck. "You will bow before me," he commands.

Darvy's jaw tightens. "I've sworn my sword and magic to Ikar, High King of Moneyre. He is the only liege I kneel to."

The knife presses deeper and a trickle of blood trails down Darvy's neck. A scream builds as I fear the worst will happen, then Renton whisks it away, sheathing it. "I cannot fault honor or your loyalty, as they will serve me well when it's me you're bound to."

"The tulip," he calls, waving his fingers.

One of the gloam soldiers steps forward with the special case that holds the tulip Rupi gifted Ikar, and a strangled gasp escapes my throat. Renton plucks the perfectly formed flower from its protective depths and sways it beneath his nose, inhaling as if it's the oxygen he needs to survive. I suppose he does, in a way. I don't miss the surprised anger on Ikar's face before he swiftly masks it.

This is not good.

"Did Lucentia find you worthy, then?" Sarcasm laces Ikar's voice.

Renton lifts a derisive brow as he rolls the stem of the flower between his fingers. "No, but someone else did." He grins with satisfaction. "I traded this in exchange for the lives of you and your two friends—a trade much in my favor." He chuckles. "The Field of Tulips has evaded me for years. Not only have you delivered a tulip into my hands, albeit inadvertently, but also our Queen of the Night." He throws a look of censure toward Ikar. "You really should choose your friends... or should I say *lovers*, more wisely."

He steps up to Ikar, a hand's width from his chest, twirling the tulip beneath his nose. "Does it look as perfect to you as it does to me?" But he turns to look at me.

Ikar's jaw clenches, and I see a vein in his neck throb. I've never seen him this angry.

Renton drifts to my side, a soft smile about his lips. "All that is left is to marry and bridge, and Moneyre will be beneath my rule, as it was always meant to be." He turns his head to ensure Ikar will hear. "Our wedding night will be divine," he whispers loudly, drawing out the last word.

Ikar snaps, and I send a torrent of lucent magic to him, Darvy, and Rhosse. He easily breaks free of the grasp of the cloaked soldier who held him, forcefully throwing an elbow back and catching the man in the throat, dropping him to the ground. He tears his enchanted sword from its sheath, but I can't see much else as spots begin to sprinkle my vision. I try to keep lucent flowing, but air is also required, and there's not enough with the gloam soldier squeezing the life from me. All thirty of the cloaked figures charge with shouts toward the three men as lucent lessens to a trickle through my body.

My vision blackens for a moment, my body growing limp from lack of air. All I hear is fuzzy shouting, and then... the gloam lifts, and I gasp for air, coughing and heaving violently. I successfully draw a full lungful of air only to find Ikar, Darvy, and Rhosse once again captured and forced to their knees with their hands behind their heads.

"I thought you cared for her." Renton shakes his head, testing the blade of the wicked black sword he has yet to use with his fingers, and looking at Ikar as if he's a despicable being.

"You won't kill her," Ikar growls.

It sounds more like a warning than a statement.

"Don't kill them. Please," I beg, still panting, my voice rough.

Renton looks at me, somewhat disappointed, as he purses his lips. "I already promised their lives, darling. I'm a man of my word. Besides, it will endear the people of the kingdom to me if I'm not the one to kill their beloved, *weak* king and his lowly commanders. I'll let them do it themselves."

"His people won't kill him," I hiss.

He laughs, sheathing the blade. "Oh, but they will."

I try to spit at him, but it has never been one of my talents, and it lands far short of his annoying billowy cloak and shiny boots. A dirty hand claps quickly over my mouth, making breathing difficult once again.

He smiles with apparent approval. "The flower is blooming."

I meet Ikar's eyes across the distance, fighting despair. Something in his gaze bolsters me, reminds me to stay strong. *But how?*

Renton turns and signals with a nod to the three men holding Ikar, Darvy, and Rhosse. In tandem, they raise the pommels of their swords and slam them down. The three men fall to the ground. I scream beneath the hand over my mouth, writhing until my throat feels as if it's collapsing beneath the pressure of the man's arm. He squeezes tightly, sending gloam colder than sheets of ice through me as dots dance before my eyes, and then it's all black.

Chapter 62

Ikar

I wake in the back of a wagon. The distinct lack of fresh air moving about me tells me it's enclosed, but with my eyes covered and my hands and legs bound, it's difficult to properly scope out the situation. My head throbs, and I muffle a groan as I attempt to move. I lay still and think back to the last thing I can remember... the nymphs... that kiss with Vera. *Vera.*

An image of her with Renton flashes in my mind, reminding me what got me here, and immediately my chest tightens with a mixture of rage and concern. Where did he take her? I have to trust that Renton truly does want her to bridge, and that he won't hurt her. It'll at least give me a chance to get her back.

"Darvy? Rhosse?" I whisper.

A swift kick in the ribs forces a surprised shout from my lips as my head slams against the ground.

A man's harsh voice barks from my left. "No talking."

I suppress another groan. Can I not go a day without an injury?

It's not long before the large wheels bump across cobble-stone streets, which indicates we're in a larger town or city. I continue to listen carefully, preparing for escape. A heavy breath sounds from beside me, followed by another from my other side a few moments later. I have no doubt it's Darvy and Rhosse signaling their awareness, and it's enough to buoy me as I prepare myself to fight with no weapon. We've been through worse; we can do it again.

The wheels roll to a stop, and the neighing of a disgruntled horse sounds from outside the wagon. Then the wagon door swings open with a loud *creak,* and the familiar smell of a stable washes over me. Anticipation thrums in my veins as the binding around my feet is cut. I'm roughly yanked from the wagon, and I expect some sort of fight, words... something. But I'm left alone, still blindfolded and wrists tied.

I attune my senses, testing the amount of lucent available... listen for my brothers. I hear the scuffle of boots, followed by a door moving on oiled hinges, and then, a familiar voice.

"Ikar?"

Nadiette?

I stand there, confused. She rushes closer, and her fingers fumble with the ropes until I'm free. I immediately pull the tie over my head to see her freeing Darvy and Rhosse... *in my own stable.*

"What's going on?" I ask slowly, frowning as she comes my way.

She throws her arms around me. "You're safe."

I remain stiff and unmoving.

Her eyes scan over me. "Did they hurt you? Renton promised he wouldn't. I know this doesn't make sense, but I had to do it for your safety and our kingdom." She hardly takes a breath before continuing. "Waylon is on his way with his and the other low king's armies. We must marry, or there will be *war*. You returned just in time, but be assured, preparations are already underway."

"Unbelievable," Rhosse mutters from behind me.

"Preparations?" I pry her arms from around me and set her back, and her brows drop in disappointment.

"For our wedding. So there's no *war*." She says it slower this time, appearing to grow irritated that I didn't listen closer the first time. "We must hurry." She reaches for my hand, and I step back.

Did she truly plan a wedding I told her I'd never participate in? I shake my head in disbelief. I was *that* close to finally bridging with Vera. To finally healing our kingdom of the disease of gloam and preventing our enemies from taking my kingdom. Now I'm here, Vera is captured again, and the flower is gone.

Anger grows so hot within me I'm surprised flames don't erupt from my body.

She opens and shuts her mouth, then begins again. "He required it in exchange for your life, and the others—" She looks at Darvy and Rhosse.

"You have *no idea* how badly you've ruined everything." I push past her, giving orders to Darvy and Rhosse. "Get weapons, and meet me in Jethonan's office."

Nadiette's face morphs into several different expressions: confusion, hurt, anger. But still, she follows me out the stable doors and all the way across exquisite gardens that are filled with flowers and garden tents that only further confirm the truth of her words. I cringe seeing the evidence of her scheming around us as I stomp past.

"Ikar, wait! How can you say that?" Nadiette asks with disbelief, sounding as frustrated as I feel with her hands fisted at her sides. "Waylon will be here in hours, or less. All you have to do is marry me, and he will stop *all* of this."

I whip around. "You are confused to think I view Waylon as a threat." My voice is cold. "I know my enemies better than you ever will. Don't think to act for me again."

Fear and hurt flash across her eyes, and she steps back. "You'd rather have *war* than marry me?"

"We will have much more than war if I marry you." I turn and make my way toward a private side door where two of my soldiers stand, waiting. Now that I'm home, I need to find Jethonan and figure out how to fix this mess.

"Ikar—"

The guards offer sharp salutes before opening the door, and I step inside, leaving Nadiette behind. I don't have time to process the fact that she has been working directly with my greatest enemy behind my back. I lock up the betrayal I feel. I'll deal with her later. Now, more than ever, I'm grateful I didn't marry the blazing traitor.

***

I find Jethonan's rooms empty and clean. I would smirk at the sight, knowing he's been too busy with the work *I* usually handle to have time for his experiments, but I don't. Instead, I rush to my office. The guard spots me and hastily jerks to attention, stepping out of the way as I throw the door open.

Jethonan jumps in my chair, and a loose piece of parchment floats off the front of the desk. "Your Majesty!"

"Did Nadiette inform you Waylon is about to attempt to take my throne?"

Jethonan straightens a few of the scattered parchments.

"Of course she did. She's been flitting about like an anxious hen since you left."

His unwavering confidence in me is a balm after finding out Nadiette appears to believe I'm incapable of handling a job I was raised for.

"I know I just returned, but I must leave. I don't have time to share everything, but I need every weapon you've ever made or tested for me. Quickly." I don't have a plan, but I figure more weapons won't hurt.

Jethonan's eyes widen with excitement at my interest in his concoctions. "Yes, Your Majesty. Come with me." He sweeps around the side of the desk and back into the hallway with his robes floating around him.

We reach his personal office, and I watch without patience as he rummages through a cupboard, haphazardly placing a variety of small and large vials on his large desk nearby, one by one.

I eye the vials carefully, prepared to commit the instructions to memory. "Tell me how to use them, the best you can."

"How to say this in the short version?" he mutters to himself. "Let's begin with this one here—" He grabs a vial filled with bright-blue powder and holds it up, pinched between his forefinger and thumb, as if he's a teacher about to give a lengthy lecture. I motion him to continue with an impatient hand and raised brows.

He begins. "This one—"

The door behind us bursts open with a loud *bang* as it smacks against the wall, and a large group of soldiers wearing Waylon's patches spills in. I reach for one of my weapons before remembering I don't have one. Renton took *everything*. This day continues to grow worse.

Waylon struts in behind them like a blasted peacock as they

encircle Jethonan and I. I inch toward Jethonan's desk, ready to snatch one of the vials, willing to risk all our lives by using it in these close quarters, but before I reach it, Waylon's soldiers surround me.

"What is this?" I look at the men, but they deliberately avoid my gaze.

"Bind him," Waylon commands as he pulls a folded paper from his pocket. He snaps it open and begins reading, "Due to the lack of consideration for the safety of the kingdom of Moneyre, three of the four low kings have voted in favor of placing the High King, Ikar Moneyre, under arrest. He will voluntarily abdicate the throne to King Waylon, and the kingdom will be divided amongst the four low kings..."

I scoff beneath my breath and wonder which one wasn't willing to go along with this sham. I'm pulling the small bit of lucent magic available, ready to fight my way out even without a weapon—I'm relatively sure I can make it from the room alive. Before I can move, though, my arms are forced behind me. I jerk against the soldiers' grips while Jethonan shouts indignantly as he receives the same treatment. I don't hear what else Waylon reads of his fraudulent arrest warrant as my ears buzz with hot fury. I'm pushed roughly past Waylon and his cocksure smirk and led to the dungeon beneath my castle in silence.

Jethonan and I are thrown into adjoining cells. The doors slam shut, and we're left in darkness—the only light coming from two tiny cracks that are considered windows.

Jethonan groans dramatically as he picks himself up from the floor. "This is terribly inconvenient, my lord, but see it this way: I now have time to educate you on the weapons."

I slide to the floor against the cold block wall, and rest my forearms across my knees. "If you hurry, you might finish before Renton arrives."

I thought I felt hopeless at the beginning of this journey, but that was nothing compared to now. I run my fingers through my hair, pulling at the strands roughly. The low kings have taken my throne, Renton has Vera *and* the tulip, I'm imprisoned and likely on my way to a public execution, and I can guarantee Renton will be marching his army here soon. Waylon is no match for him, which means my kingdom will be lost.

I lean my head back against the cold stone and listen to Jethonan begin a history-book-length lesson on how he created the weapon made of blue powder. His words become mere buzzing as my thoughts drift to Vera. Is Renton capable of having feelings for her? The way he choked her—hurt her—implies not. But there was something about the way he looked at her... The memory sparks an inferno of rage. Would he have killed her if I hadn't dropped my weapon? I don't know, but I wasn't willing to risk it. If I die and he takes my kingdom and my queen... My chest tightens to the point I can hardly draw breath.

"Sire?" Jethonan asks, concern pulling his brows together.

I look up to see his face pressed against the bars between our cells. It would be comical if my life weren't in ruins. "Yes?"

"Are you alright?"

I can't bring myself to answer. I've never been less alright than I am right now. I dodge his question with one of my own. "Renton is my long-lost uncle. I know he and my grandfather were twins, but he believes he's the rightful heir. Do you know anything about his claim?"

Jethonan clasps his hands behind his back and paces a few steps in both directions within his small cell. "Rightful heir?"

"So he says," I drawl.

"In my study of Lucentia, she gifted magic to Ricard, your

grandfather, because she believed him worthy, which we take to mean she agrees he was the true king. Ultimately, though, it was their father who decided years before then. According to our record, Ricard was honorable. Renton was a strong fighter, popular with the people, but proud and bloodthirsty. I believe the king chose right between his sons. Not that my opinion matters." He continues to pace, avoiding a puddle of murky water growing steadily wider from the slow drip coming from above, each one echoing ominously off the cold stone walls.

"Renton wants a Black Tulip," I say, my voice void of emotion. Numb.

Jethonan stops pacing, his back turned to me, and holds a finger in the air as if pleased he finally knows an answer. "Yes, he'll want one to destroy Lucentia with their magic. It's vital to ensure he doesn't find one."

I lean my head back against the slimy wall. "He has Vera," I growl.

Jethonan makes a strangled sound, and his eyes grow wide as saucers as he turns around to look at me, his long hair swinging widely around his shoulders with the movement. If I wasn't filled with complete and utter despair, I may have laughed. This is the first time I've seen his feathers ruffled, and I can't even enjoy it.

He seems to have trouble gathering his thoughts upon hearing my upsetting revelation. He opens and closes his mouth before he clears his throat and grabs one of the iron bars to steady himself, his knuckles white.

"If you remember, Lucentia said it was very important that her Tulips were protected by the kings. Why do you think that was?" His voice lowers. "Because they are filled with parts of her own magic. If Vera's power is directly linked to Lucentia and she bridges with gloam, three things could happen. Either the lucent and gloam will mix into some unusual combination, the lucent will overtake the gloam, or... the gloam will take advantage of that direct link to Lucentia and weaken her so that she's easier to destroy. You know she has a brother, don't you? Gloam."

"Yes, I remember our discussion." I sigh, weary. Lucentia is our only chance of winning this... if Renton bridges with Vera, lucent magic could be extinguished forever, and gloam would grow unchecked.

"If I were able to escape my imminent death and somehow find and bridge with Vera... what happens to the gloam masters?" I ask.

Jethonan appears slightly lost without one of his ancient tomes to reference. "Well, my lord, that has not yet occurred in history, so I have no way of knowing. I only have assumptions and my own logic to go on, but I've wondered if their banishment was an act of mercy on Ricard's part. Couldn't stand to kill his twin, maybe? Either way, I assume if..." He catches sight of my glare. "Er... *when* you bridge, they'll either be killed, or you'll need to find a way to banish them again like your grandfather did. But to still be alive after this long indicates they're no longer fully mortal, so if gloam is destroyed... it's likely they will be too."

I groan. My ancestors had broken the rules, refusing to bridge with Tulips like Lucentia instructed, and now we're paying for it.

Chapter 63

Nadiette

I shove through the doors to the throne room, not waiting for Waylon's permission or the guards to allow me entrance. He has ignored my request to speak with him for two days, but no longer.

"He had but moments to decide if he wanted to marry me," I state as I stride toward him, my skirts twisting about my ankles, cheeks hot with anger. This has gotten out of hand.

Waylon turns from a hushed conversation with one of his personal guards and settles more deeply into his seat. "It fits me nicely, does it not?"

I stop before the steps leading to the throne, hands fisted, eyeing the slightly smaller throne beside the larger one that was intended for me—until now.

"The deadline for our marriage was not yet up before you imprisoned him," I seethe.

"It is now."

"We had an agreement!" I hide my fists within my skirt to conceal their shaking.

"You had weeks, my dear. 'Tis not my fault he's not interested. The guards say he rejected you quite quickly upon his return." He inspects the gold edging along the left arm of the chair, rubbing it with his thumb. "But as agreed, you'll maintain a high position within my court."

"What of the other low kings?" I ask.

"We are no longer *low*. Do not use that word again." He narrows his eyes at me. "We are now The Four Kings, and this portion of the kingdom is mine."

"And what of you ignoring me these past days? Is that how you will treat your head originator?"

"You may go. Resume your duties as normal." He waves his hand at me as if I am a nuisance.

"But—"

"*Now*."

Two guards step forward, and I quickly spin away in order to avoid their grasp on my arms. I silently curse my uncle and wonder how to fix the things I've done. Or rather, undone. There must be a way.

The guards corral me toward a door set in the far wall that will take me toward my office. I stand in the hallway, fuming as they close it behind them, and I listen as their footsteps fade. I turn to leave, but upon hearing the throne room doors once more slam open on the other side of the door, I pause. I risk cracking the door open the tiniest bit, and the ring of swords being swiftly drawn within the throne room sounds at the same time as Waylon raises his voice.

"Renton. What is this? You've already been paid."

I turn and peek through the crack when I hear the tread of many boots cross the marble floor.

"I'm The King of Shadows, here to reclaim my throne." He glances all around the throne room as if letting the long-awaited glory of it settle in his vision. "The kingdom of Moneyre is rightfully mine."

Waylon laughs, loud and low. "You are a simple mercenary. I've never heard of what you speak. *Shadows?*" he asks mockingly.

Even from my secreted space, I feel the tension seep from the throne room into the hallway where I hide. Dread pools in my belly. *The King of Shadows?*

"Arrest them," Waylon commands, his voice cold.

I open the door a little wider, just enough to see what's happening, when a burst of black engulfs the room. Its smoky, wispy edges begin to crawl swiftly toward me in the hallway like writhing snakes, weaving amidst the shouting of guards. Then there's a strangled shout—louder than the rest—and a gurgling choke. As the darkness clears, I gasp to see Waylon slumped over one side of the throne. Gray... and very *dead.*

A whimper begs to escape, but I clap a hand over my mouth and remain still.

Renton speaks, his black-clad entourage of soldiers unmoving. "I am King of Moneyre. You answer to me now. If you don't, you'll be as dead as he."

The guards look between each other, then sheathe their weapons, one by one.

"Good." Renton nods as he smoothly climbs the steps and tosses Waylon from the throne with a sickening thud before taking the seat. "Arrest all originators, and prepare the Tulip."

Arrest us? And the Tulip? Breath refuses to come fully as I realize the consequences of my actions are bigger than I ever could have imagined. Shadow King? Renton?

I press a hand to my head, feeling faint for the first time in my life, as my thoughts spin. *I did this.* My stomach turns as if to heave its contents, and I resist the urge to sink to the floor. Those wisps of gloam are growing thicker now, slithering along the crevices and smooth stone walls around me. I step away from them in horror. Ikar is the only one who can fix this... All at once his anger over my actions hits me with painful understanding. The betrayal on his face... I cover my mouth with a shaky hand as the thud of Waylon's body hitting the floor echoes in my ears.

I can't fix what I've already done, but maybe I can still help. *Drade.*

I lift my dress above my ankles and run, the words to a message already running through my mind.

Chapter 64

Vera

I wake from the icy darkness I never wanted to experience again, shivering at the tingles that run through my veins as my blood reheats. I open my eyes to find myself in what I can only describe as a room fit for a royal. I lie there, staring at the ceiling and the strong, wide beams that run across it, while the memories of what brought me here begin to unfurl.

I remember the battle, and I remember with horror the way Ikar, Rhosse, and Darvy were knocked out... but I don't remember getting *here. Here,* on a bed so large I could probably roll across its expanse five times.

I sit up and swing my legs over the edge, but it's so tall my feet dangle in the air. I face lofty windows, framed with drapes so long they leave elegant puddles on the expensive rug that spans the entire room. My eyes drift to an exquisitely crafted table with an enormous mirror and an array of feminine jars and bottles in neat rows on its surface. It's all very light and bright, and dread brews as I consider where I might be.

I scootch off the large bed, the thump of my boots on the ground muted by the thick rug, and push aside a heavy drape to peek out one of the large windows that overlooks... the south side of Moneyre. My guess was correct. *Ikar's castle.*

My breath catches. Is it possible that Ikar, Darvy, and Rhosse are here too? And where is Rupi?

It's then I notice a second door in the room, and I swallow tightly. Is this... the *queen's* chamber? I stare at it for a moment. In the next day or two, I'll be married to one of two kings. My heart and soul yearn for Ikar. I can't bear to think what will happen if it's Renton—to see that door opening with his face behind it. I find my breath grows shallow at the sickening thought. I'd rather try to escape and die than marry a man who will leave me frozen and dark while he ruins my kingdom and my people.

The suns are setting, the dwindling light heading toward darkness. It's disconcerting to realize I have no idea what day it is because I don't know how long I was in that frozen, sleeping state. But even as my room darkens, I resist lighting the candles or stoking the embers in the fire, and I'm certainly not climbing back on that bed. I'm not ready to sleep again. My body thrums with energy—the type that leads to impulsive and reckless decisions. I've got to find a way out of here.

I glance at the door to check for gloam, but there's none. I'd bet the sword Ikar gave me it's locked. *What a way to begin a marriage.* I blow a strand of loose hair out of my face and check the door anyway. The knob doesn't move.

I curse even though I'm not surprised.

I turn to head toward the other door, dreading what I risk finding behind it, but I stop when I hear a familiar voice in the hall. It's muffled, but I would recognize it anywhere.

Two firm knocks sound.

I approach the closed door. "Tatania?" I whisper.

My response appears to be permission enough to open it for the guards.

It swings open, and I rush forward. "Tatania!" I hug her tightly with relief. "You're alive!" I step back, my words rushing out. "I'm so sorry I didn't come back for you—"

She shushes me as she glances over her shoulder at the door as if reminding me there's a guard listening as she steps further into my room. She closes the door behind her. "I've come to get you out. It's about time you finally woke. This is the third time I've come to check; the guards wouldn't let me in without you awake."

I frown at the scolding in her voice. How was I to know? Not my fault Renton froze me. Something feels off. But my entire life is off right now, so I squash the thought.

"Are any other Tulips here?" I ask.

"No. Just you and I. They're all safe. We must go now." She grabs my hand. "There's no time for questions. You should have stayed hidden." Her voice is tinged with a mix of chastisement and sorrow.

I sputter a bit. "I didn't even have time to hide," I whisper in an attempt to defend myself.

She throws a censuring look over her shoulder, and I press my lips together as she pulls me out the door and past the guard who says nothing as he watches us go. Has she gained so much trust in this short time? I tuck my questions away; I'll have time aplenty to learn about her clandestine methods after we're away. Then another thought, one I can't ignore, has me pulling back on her hand as soon as we're out of sight.

"I need to find the tulip first," I whisper.

"There's no time." She shakes her head, growing more agitated and impatient than I've ever seen her. "Even if there was, there's no chance of that when Renton keeps it with him at all times."

I let her pull me forward again, deciding it doesn't matter now—especially if both of us are escaping this time. I just need to get out so I can figure out how to fix this mess. If I have to trek all the way back to the Field of Tulips to get another, I'll do it. I'm not sure how she plans to get us both out of here, but I don't ask; I simply follow. She had a plan last time and it worked, didn't it?

My confidence grows as we leave the hall behind and run down several flights of stairs. Hope burgeons as we enter the weapons area and not one of the soldiers or servants we see on our way stops us. What must Tatania have sacrificed to gain this sort of status with Renton? I remind myself that with her beauty and natural air of authority, it makes sense that Tatania would excel at subterfuge. I temper the concern again—I must focus.

Here, in the weapons area, we're alone. We sneak past walls filled with all varieties of weapons. I'm tempted to snatch one, but most of them are obviously crafted for warriors, if their size alone is any indication. I eye them closely for one that's a bit smaller and spot a row of daggers and a selection of short swords nearby. *Perfect.* I stop only long enough to snatch one off the wall. At the same time, I hear the ring of a sword behind me. Panic races through my veins until I remember Tatania is here. She'll be able to talk us out of this.

I spin around, prepared to face whatever gloam soldier has caught me, but it's only her. My shoulders sag in relief. It appears she had the same idea I did—better to escape with a weapon than without.

I laugh sharply. "The stress is getting to me. I thou—"
She lunges.

"What?!" I yelp as I dodge to the side. "Tatania!"

"All he ever talks about..." She stabs again. "...is *you*."

"Me?" I jump to the side again, wishing I'd grabbed an actual sword instead of a dagger.

"He knows I'm as powerful as you, and still he wants an ill-mannered, filthy urchin," she spits.

Ok, that hurts a little, but I don't have time to let it sink in. With every dodge of her swings, I've made it close enough to snatch one of the short swords. All the practice Ikar and Rhosse forced on me suddenly becomes worth it as our blades meet with a ring—loud in the enclosed room. The vibrations run up my arms. Where did Tatania learn to use a sword?

"If I kill you, he'll have no choice but to choose me," she grinds out as she prepares to swing again.

"I think we can come up with a better solution than that," I offer, panting. "I don't want him."

And I don't want to kill the woman who I always trusted to keep me safe.

She roars in the most unladylike way I've ever seen as she swings again; it would be comical if the blade wasn't coming toward *me*. With both hands on the hilt, I bring mine up to block hers, but I'm pushed back into the wall of weapons with the force of it.

I try to get past the crazed look in her eyes, help her see sense. This isn't what she really wants, is it?

"Look. I'm in love with someone else. Help me get away, and Renton will *have* to choose you!"

Sweat rolls between the crease of my shoulder blades as she leans her weight against the swords, pressing them closer to me. I know exactly what I should do next—my training thrums in my muscles, but I resist. Tatania has never said anything like this. She's just traumatized; she can't really feel this way.

"Please," I gasp, struggling to keep hold with my sweaty grip.

But her eyes are cold and hard, unreachable. As determined as a bantha stalking its prey. In that moment, I realize she means it. She won't stop. It's her or me, and if it's me, I'm not going out begging for my life.

"I tried asking nicely, Avenara. I asked you to *hide* so Renton couldn't find you, and I wouldn't have to kill you. Then I was patient enough to help you escape after he caught you. But you *constantly* rebel. You're caught *again*, and now you'll die because of it. Renton is mine."

I risk ducking and pushing my sword up simultaneously, causing Tatania's blade to slip off mine. It sends her crashing into the weapons behind me as I scuttle away and regroup. I gasp when she turns around. A gnarly gash is openly bleeding, stretching from her cheekbone through her once-perfect lips. If eyes could be fire, that's what hers would be.

"Your name wasn't on that list." Pieces begin to come together.

"Of course not. I'm the one who created it." The blood is flowing in rivulets down her pale cheek and dripping onto her blouse. It's making me sort of queasy.

She doesn't seem to notice it, her eyes full of indescribable hate. "What better way to encourage the rest of you to *hide?* Or perhaps be caught and killed by a mercenary so I didn't have to do it? I didn't *intend* to kill any of you. *You* just insist on continually being difficult."

Rage builds in my veins. "I got to know Renton pretty well in his gloam camp." Her eyes burn brighter in a way I didn't know possible. "And while I'll do everything to stop him, I think he wants a woman with loyalty, and you'll never have that."

Her lips turn in a bloody sneer as she swings again.

I lived with a hollow belly, dirt-poor and half-starved, taking dangerous jobs because *she* claimed we needed to be protected and pay exorbitant amounts of money for worthless bracelets. Now she wants to murder me? Not happening.

I block her swings with relative ease. My breath is speeding up with the effort, but not as bad as hers.

But I have to know one last thing. "Tell me, were the dues *really* for the charmer?"

She grins wickedly. "Of course. I'm not heartless. I gave the charmer half." Her tone is cocky, and it distracts her enough that I'm able to gather my strength.

I use our crossed blades to shove her sword back with a war cry, and don't let myself think as I switch the angle of my weapon and push the blade through her.

She stumbles back before she falls to the ground in a heap, appearing surprised that I actually did it. I look down at her with growing horror, but I see none of the love I imagined in her eyes all these years. Even as she dies, she stares at me with hatred. A moment later, her breath stops.

I killed Tatania.

Sorrow tears a gaping hole in my heart as I stare at her in shock. The woman I thought of as a sort of mother... one I trusted all these years... she wanted Renton? This is all too much at once.

My hands begin to tingle, and the sword drops from my hand with a loud clatter as my hands turn clammy and cold. I clutch my stomach as I feel its contents begin to rebel and a single horrified sob that doesn't sound like my own rips from my throat.

I jump when I hear a deep chuckle to my right, near the entrance of the weapon room. I turn, slightly dizzy, to find

Renton, one shoulder against the door frame in a relaxed manner, as though he watched simply for entertainment.

A pleased grin turns his lips. "I knew you had it in you." He taps his temple. "Like I said, you're stronger than the others."

"You stood there and... watched?" My stomach still roils with revulsion over what I've done.

Amusement shines in his eyes. He lifts a hand, and I watch tendrils of black gloam swirl around his fingertips. "I wouldn't have let her kill you."

I'm not sure what he expects. Is he waiting for me to run into his arms bursting with gratitude that he stood here, ready, *just in case?* I'm surrounded by lunatics.

"Further proof you will make an excellent shadow queen," he adds.

I think it's meant to be a compliment, but I hate it. I just killed the woman I've always trusted to keep me safe, second only to Mama Tina. Tatania tried to *murder* me. How long has she hated me? I feel oddly numb as Renton wraps an arm around my shoulders, and a wave of chill rushes over me while I stand amidst the gloam that swirls around him. He leads me back toward the room I thought I'd escaped, and I listlessly allow him as my thoughts sluggishly churn.

He chats the entire way, reassuring me that the shock will pass, and I will be stronger for it. He mentions something about how he hates to rush our wedding, but it must take place tomorrow, and that I must get some sleep. It's odd how normal he seems at times. I don't say a word, but it doesn't ruffle him—as usual. We've quickly returned to our previous status, and as he tucks me into bed, I numbly accept that this is soon to be my life.

Chapter 65

Ikar

The surprise in Vera's expression matches what I feel when I see her standing before me. I step forward to take her in my arms and she quite literally falls into them, clinging to me as I wrap her tightly in my embrace.

"You're alive," she whispers with relief. "Where are you?"

"In the dungeon of my own castle." I can't help the bit of sardonic anger that colors my tone.

"I apparently don't dream of you when Renton knocks me out... but I didn't know, and I was worried—"

"I'm fine," I reassure her, not sharing that I feared the same when I slept the past two nights and didn't dream of her.

The relief of having her in my arms washes over me, but she still seems... off. Hurt somehow.

"Did he hurt you?" I force myself to stay calm as I wait for her answer.

"No."

She doesn't say anything else and appears content to

have my arms around her, so I let her be, sensing she needs it.

After several long moments, she mumbles into my shirt, "I killed someone." She says it so flatly I know she's still in shock. Suddenly I understand her behavior.

"Renton?"

"No."

"Who?"

"Tatania," she whispers.

I don't say anything for a moment as I try to put the pieces together, but I'm lost without more detail.

She continues, her arms tightening around me. "She tried to murder me, told me she was the one who created the list... that she wanted Renton for herself, and she grabbed a sword, and—"

"And you protected yourself," I say firmly.

She nods, but I can feel her silent tears wetting my shirt. I simply hold her, rubbing a hand along her back. I know she's hurting, but this might be my only chance for answers.

"Vera, has Renton told you his plans?"

If possible, her voice is even flatter than before. "He plans to marry me tomorrow."

There's silence between us, and I can tell she's listening to my heartbeat, a sound that may be absent after my trial, and which has picked up pace with the controlled rage that flows through my veins.

"Tell me you have a plan," she says, her cheek still pressed to my chest.

I swallow roughly. There is no plan this time. "Jethonan is in prison with me, and he's a genius. We'll figure it out." I force confidence into my voice.

We both sense the lie and pretend we don't.

"I love you." I place a lingering kiss on her soft hair.

"Are you saying goodbye?" She lifts her head and looks up at me with red-rimmed eyes.

"Whether in reality or in dreams, I'll always come back for you." A promise I intend to keep whether I live or die.

I'll not allow Renton to live happily ever after with the woman intended to be my wife.

"The mate bond is about to end." She looks at her wrist with a frown.

"The absence of a mate bond won't keep me from you." I hold her tighter, inhale the sweet scent of her...

I wake in the dungeon, where the scent of the musty, wet stone is ten times worse for just being with Vera. I eye Jethonan lightly snoring in the corner of his own cell and assume something or *someone* must have woken her. I fist and refist my hands, feeling more helpless than I've ever felt in my life.

Chapter 66

Vera

The dress is made of the lightest fabric, similar to the spider silk the fae use, and the off-the-shoulder design has me concerned that it will simply fall off in a puddle if I move wrong. I look down its black length. A slit in the fabric is intended to bare my left leg to mid-thigh—a height I am more than uncomfortable with, but no longer. With needle and thread snatched in an act of revenge from the seamstress who woke me early this morning from my dream with Ikar, I knot the last stitch. The extent of my sewing skills is replacing the buttons on my jackets, and it shows. The stitches are uneven and loose, the slit still shows a bit if I look close, but it'll do. I rise and test its strength, confident that if I walk carefully, the stitches will hold.

Now the suns are setting, and I have nothing to distract myself with. So I sit and worry. I imagined my first time in Ikar's home would be by his side, not waking up from frozen-induced sleep, imprisoned by a horrid gloam king. I press my fingers together and touch my chin as I think. I cannot bridge with Renton. *I can't.* The entire kingdom is at stake. Can he force me? Unfortunately, I don't know. I blow out a breath.

I jump when two hard raps at the door jolt me from my thoughts. I attempt to compose myself as I stand, my clammy hands at my sides. The door swings open and Renton strolls in as if it's just another day. As if he's not about to attempt to take over a kingdom and kill innocents. As if he's not about to force a woman to bridge with and marry him. I stand so still I fear I'll pass out as he drags his eyes over my appearance.

"You look ravishing." He lifts an approving brow, and I feel gloam caress the bare skin of my shoulders, lingering over my mark. So different from the warmth and trust between Ikar and me, when he touched it just days ago. The sorrow must show on my face because he stops before me and stares straight into my eyes.

"Remember, darling, you'll be worshipped." He looks toward the window, then back to me. "Not only by them, but by me." He lifts my wrist and kisses the inside softly, but the only lips I want on my skin are Ikar's, and I tug my arm away. His eyes darken. "In time you'll see that I can love you better than he ever could."

I keep my expression flat. I refuse to argue with an ancient narcissist.

He wraps my limp hand around his arm and guides me from the room, but instead of the throne room where I expect this to take place, I'm led to the main steps of the castle. I hardly have time to prepare myself before we step through the enormous doors, and I find myself before a crowd of people so large I can't number them. *So many people.* The low kings stand sullenly in a line to our left, watching. For a moment I try to catch Drade's eye; he wouldn't let me marry this deranged gloam monster, would he? But he refuses to look my way. Are all of the kings... all of these people... being forced to see their new king wed and bridged? Or did they choose to be here? When the people see me on Renton's arm, a wave of murmurs spread. I don't miss the heated glares, the jeers, the cursing, until gloam guards begin to weed the disruptive citizens out and drag them away.

My cheeks heat with shame. What must these people think of me?

My heart drops even further at the scene to my right. Upon a hastily erected platform is a crowd of dull white. At least twenty originators are cuffed and silent. Cloaked soldiers with swords ready stand guard, prepared to end them at a moment's notice. Their stark white clothing is streaked with blood and covered with dirt, proving the struggle to capture them. I spot Nadiette near the front, still and stoic.

"How the mighty have fallen," Renton says near my ear, being careful to stick to the shadows of the castle walls.

"You're not going to kill them, are you?" I ask quietly, nearly shaking.

"What better gift could I give you?" Renton asks, affronted. "You should be pleased. They are the ones who murdered the Black Tulips for their own gain, forcing you into a life of fear and hiding. It's a necessary message. That behavior will not be accepted under our rule."

I can't breathe. This is never what I wanted.

Soon, there's silence. I look over the people, wanting to shout that I didn't choose this, but the only eyes I meet are filled with judgment and mourning. No understanding, no mercy. I wonder then if this is how it would have been either way, whether it was Ikar I would be bridging with or Renton. I admit that, even with Ikar by my side, they may have been afraid, but I had hope that we could change things. With Renton? There's none. I'll be seen as one who took over a kingdom, one who fulfilled a dreaded seer vision they've feared for hundreds of years.

I swallow as the scene Odella showed me replays in my head. Though it's not my choice to be by his side, I'm feeling as wicked as they believe me to be. Has it always been my fate to destroy my own kingdom?

My eyes burn, and I look down to blink away the moisture, only to find the perfect Tulip lying on an intricately crafted black iron table beside me. I remember the day Rupi dropped it in Ikar's hands clearly. Has he already been tried and found guilty? Executed while I was locked in my room? I stare at the flower. Never will I know his magic bound with mine, his warm to my cool. For the smallest moment, it seemed as if I held everything I ever wanted in my hands... and in the next moment, it was torn away.

The flower taunts me. Dark, mysterious, beautiful. I reach out and twist its stem. It doesn't seem wilted, even days after being plucked.

"I have an eager bride." Renton smiles.

I don't correct him, because what's the use?

"Do you plan to remain in the shadows the entirety of your rule?" I ask, the judgment of his courage obvious in my voice.

He merely offers a lazy grin, unbothered, his focus some-where else.

I follow his gaze to a procession of cloaked soldiers who lead two men out of a side door and toward the wood stage built across the distance. My stomach heaves. *No.*

Chapter 67

Ikar

Jethonan and I are pulled from our cells and cuffed before we're led from the depths of my castle and out to the main entrance, now filled with my own citizens and soldiers. I keep my gaze forward as we pass the crowds who've come to witness my farce of a trial and the marriage between Vera and Renton, ignoring gasps and shouts as I pass. I can't tell if they're angry at me or Renton or even the low kings who I see from the corner of my eye, but the exclamations don't sound pleased.

Beneath the dim light of the third sun setting, we step up the short set of rickety wood stairs of an execution platform to find over twenty of my best originators chained in rows behind where they lead me. I clench my jaw when my shirt is torn from my body, and I'm forced to my knees on the rough wood planks. My wrists are locked in short chains that are bolted to the ground, forcing me to bend forward at an awkward angle. A stone chopping block lies ahead of me. I swallow amidst the wave of gasps and murmuring arising from the crowd.

Two of the gloam masters comment between themselves behind me, and chuckle. "Rumors are true, the mark is completely black. The last of the weak kings. If we weren't killing him today, he'd die on his own soon anyway."

I would correct them, as there is a very, *very* small piece of gold left on the end of the longest scroll that trails down my back, but that small part seems a joke now. Useless.

Jethonan grumbles as he's pushed down roughly and chained beside me, though his clothing is left intact. Seems they took my shirt intending to use my mark to make a spectacle of my family history, ensuring the people's opinions are swayed against me. The black mark, if anything, will do it.

Though it's awkward in my bent-over state, I lift my head, only to find Vera upon the castle steps dressed in a daring black dress, staring across the distance between us, hands fisted at her sides. Sorrow and dread roil in my gut at the despair on her face. Renton leans close and says something in her ear, grabbing one of her fisted hands and twining his fingers with hers before he kisses the back of it.

I jerk at the chains, my body thrumming to fight. Vera does nothing, just stands straight as an arrow, her eyes locked on me.

I hang my head down. I can say without regret that I truly did as much as I could to save my people, but that doesn't ease the knife of failure that slips between my ribs, robbing me of air.

Jethonan speaks, resignation in his voice. "My lord, it's been a pleasure working with you."

"You'll not escape me for long, Jethonan, I'll see you on the other side." I force a half-hearted grin his way.

Jethonan doesn't deserve this. Another knife of failure between my ribs.

A sob behind me has me glancing over my shoulder. Nadiette is chained among the other originators. Another knife. So many dying because of my inability to restore lucent.

My worst fears are coming to pass before my eyes.

Chapter 68

Vera

I resist the urge to shrink away from Renton's nose beside my ear. "It wasn't *I* that ordered it, I'll have you know. You can blame the low kings for that."

He smiles the smile of one who believes he's gained everything he wants, and fiery rage builds in my chest because it appears he has, and I'm helpless to stop it. Here he stands, whispering in my ear, attempting to convince me that I shouldn't hold this against him.

He eyes the flower. "We'll wed, first. You may choose to leave after that. You'll soon see that I can, indeed, be merciful."

Merciful? Does he mean he won't force me to watch the man I love be executed?

I grit my teeth as he rounds the table. "I think we have different ideas about what mercy is."

His eyes darken. "I could make you stay and watch. Is that what you'd prefer?"

He doesn't wait for me to respond as he steps forward, leaving the shadows and entering into view of the crowd of people and soldiers spread before us. It grows quiet all around us. "My people." He gestures to me with a gallant hand. "Here, our precious Tulip, who will restore the gloam masters to their rightful rule. Fortunately for me, you discarded the power you were given years ago when you chose to raise up originators to save your kingdom. But I see the treasure in your midst and will restore the Black Tulips to their intended glory."

Silence covers the crowd, so deafening that my eardrums buzz. Already his magic stirs in the air between us, dancing around me with wispy threads. It's cold, not offering the pleasant balance that Ikar's heat brings. Instead, the longer his lingers around me, the colder my magic seems to grow. If I bridge with him, I will be forced to grow used to icicles within me for the rest of my life.

"Shall we begin, my flower?" Renton asks as if he truly cares for me. When I fail to respond, he looks over the crowd of people as he brings a wisp of gloam to his hand. "Did anyone tell you how quickly King Waylon died on his throne?"

The wisps flutter around his fingertips, and I know he's threatening those who watch, those who would become his people—if they survive. But for all the fear he's instilling in me, I can't pull my eyes from Ikar, who watches with an indecipherable expression. A hot tear tracks down my cheek. I would never have guessed that life as I knew it would end in unimaginable betrayal. But if I don't do what he asks, all these people... I know he'll kill them, one by one until I comply.

I stare at Ikar until Renton guides my chin toward him with a gentle thumb. "This way, my dear."

Moments later, I speak forced vows with him. Vows that, with every word, rip my heart to shreds with poisoned knives I know will leave eternal scars. Within minutes, we're married. Sealed with a firm, chilled kiss that would've gone on had I not broken it off early. I feel as if I've died and left my body empty of the soul that gave it life. I stare across the crowd toward Ikar again, only to see his head hanging low, looking more defeated than I've ever seen.

Chest-crushing betrayal threatens to suffocate me, so heavy that I can't draw a proper breath, and I stumble when dots blur my vision. The crowd before us remains silent. Mournful. Gray clouds churn on the horizon as night falls, and a lonely breeze gusts and stirs through the crowds. I battle for control of my body—my head wants to preserve my life, but my battered heart aches to kill.

Renton slips an obsidian ring onto my limp finger, then places my hand over the stem of the tulip. My fingers stay flat against its smooth surface, and rage grows within me—pushed too far. This flower wasn't intended for him.

"Hold it," he growls.

Have I finally found the end of his patience?

The wisp of magic leaves his fingers and snakes smoothly toward the people at the forefront of the crowd. "Now, my dear."

How many people would I be willing to watch die?

None.

My trembling fingers twitch, but I pause, attempting to sift and reason through muddled thoughts. Can Renton even bridge with me if he's not an official king of Moneyre? If I don't try to bridge, Renton will begin killing innocents... If I do, Ikar will be killed, and all of us will be subject to his rule, but they might all die anyway.

How do I win?

My heart breaks, and another tear escapes the corner of my eye. It appears I can't, but if I bridge now, these people might survive... and maybe I can save them somehow later. It's a depressing thought. My life will never be my own again. All I wanted was freedom; now I have less than ever before.

"I love you, Ikar," I whisper almost silently, attempting to send the words on a streak of lucent that I highly doubt, but hope he will hear all that distance away.

Feeling like a blazing traitor, my fingers curl around the thin stem, and immediately the ends of my magic unravel in answer, ready to officially bridge with another's. But before either Renton or I can react, a fluffy white ball flashes by, and the tulip slips from my fingers. I stare at my hand, flat upon the cool iron-etched table, no tulip to be found.

"Shoot it!" Renton shouts.

My eyes lift to find Rupi soaring through the dark sky, tulip within her tiny grasp, small wings pumping hard to gain higher elevation. Arrows fly toward her, then gloam hawks shoot from Renton's side and speed toward her. They'll eat her in one bite. A muffled scream followed by choking comes from within the silent crowd, and a sob erupts from my throat. The cold. The death. I panic as I watch Rupi struggle amidst a cloud of gloam, dodging weapons and gloam hawks until she drops the tulip, and it flutters and twirls back to the ground, landing some-where on the platform. Renton's going to take her away from me too.

I lunge toward him, grabbing his arm as I scream for him not to kill Rupi, but her daring seems to trigger a cascade. I watch with horror as one of the cloaked soldiers lifts his sword overhead and slams it toward Ikar, but instead of killing him, the chains break with a spray of sparks. A wisp of hope rushes through me. Simultaneously, Drade and Renton shout orders to their soldiers, and suddenly chaos unfolds as citizens attempt to escape, screaming amidst gloam and soldiers at battle. Renton shouts more orders even as the rogue guard on the platform frees Jethonan, who proceeds to catch a weapon tossed his way. The cloaked man pushes the hood back to reveal his face. *Rhosse.* I nearly collapse with relief. That is, until I hear the screeching of glass that can mean only one thing. *Shard beasts.*

Rhosse tosses Ikar an enchanted sword, and they jump into battle, fighting through gloam soldiers swarming toward the platform. Darvy works to release the originators, who immediately race to battle with soldiers who already rally around Ikar. Then gloam spreads from Renton in thick waves, spreading like a black ocean as soldiers from both kings pull swords on the other.

All around me the sounds of battle ensue.

I can clearly see Darvy and Rhosse battling side by side. Then there's Nadiette and her originators sending any bit of lucent magic they can, which is a dreadfully small amount. But I can't catch sight of Ikar, and a wave of panic engulfs me as small flashes of lucent light mix with clouds of gloam until I can hardly see past the steps. Gloam monster's roars and screams from the crowd overwhelm me until I'm tempted to clap my hands over my ears to escape it.

But I don't have time for escape or hiding. I don't allow myself to overthink the great advantage Renton still has. I waste no time helping in any way I can. With a lunge that rips out every painstaking stitch I sewed into the slit of my dress I ram my shoulder into Renton's, hoping to distract him from the focus he's put into his gloam creatures and the awful streams of it leaching from him that slither toward his soldiers, fueling them.

When my shove hardly budges his large frame, I pull the lucent magic that still makes me who I am, shove my hands toward him, and push my magic and all its light into him, hoping that, like the deathstalker in his camp, he'll simply explode into gloam bits.

No such luck. He roars in pain and backhands me so hard that I fall to the ground, seeing spots and fuzzy edges of blackness in my vision.

"Bridge with me now, or I kill them all. The tulip did enough of its job."

"You are *not* the rightful heir," I grind out. "It won't work."

"It appears I *am*," he snarls.

His magic comes at me so forcefully that my arms shake as they hold me up from collapsing on the cold stone. It violently travels my body, searching for the waiting edges of my magic, forcing his to complete mine. My body grows so cold my teeth chatter, but I hold the edges of my magic to my soul, unwilling.

He grabs my hair and yanks my face up to his. "*Now*."

A dark form charges up the steps to my left, and Renton is forced to form his own sword of gloam, black as the deathstalkers snarling within the crowds. Drade appears, swinging a blood-soaked fae sword in an invitation to fight, and I'm reminded all over again how Drade secured his throne. The eager violence in his eyes is chilling when he sees the way Renton grips my hair. Fae soldiers surround him, protecting his back as Renton releases me and prepares to fight.

I scoot back, dragging the fabric of my dress with me as I attempt to gain my footing and escape as more gloam soldiers race up the steps, straight for Drade. I scan the gloamy chaos for Ikar, but he's no longer on the platform and worry tightens my chest. *He has no armor.*

I bite my lip so hard I taste blood. Jethonan leaps from the platform and into the crowd, and my energy drains from me as Renton's cold envelops me—desperate and vicious. His magic clings like a pest, searching for all the places it needs to connect, each wisp more painful and cold than the last. The gloam darkens around us as Renton gains strength from our growing bond, faster than I expected.

I fall into frozen darkness until I feel a single spark of warmth my magic craves, pulling me from the gloam that attempts to consume my soul. My magic searches it out, eager— a magic I thought I'd never feel again. *Ikar.* I can't see him yet, but he's close. Somehow. Or my mind has finally broken for good, and I'm officially insane because it doesn't seem possible that he made it from the platform and across the heavy battle beneath us in this short a time.

Renton must sense it as well because he returns to where I shakily hold myself on the ground and grabs one of my arms roughly, dragging me backward with him before he drops me in a heap near the castle wall and steps forward with his gloam sprouting out around him like thick, weaving snakes. He appears agitated, more than ever.

He grips the hilt of his black sword, and with a wicked grin, shouts, "You've come to meet my *wife?*" He swings his sword back and forth, preparing for the fight. "I've never seen a woman so eager to say yes."

I ignore his barbed lies. My body and every sense attune to the large form that is obscured by clouds of gloam that surround us. *Could it be?* But who else would Renton taunt like that? I peer through the deep shadows as a man strikes toward Renton, and Renton roars with anger. *Ikar.* Pure, unadulterated joy runs through me like a spark of lightning—the same as the horror of my new marriage grows. I may not be able to help much in this fight, and I may have wed Ikar's greatest enemy, but even if it means my death, I intend to help.

So much gloam and so many gloam soldiers swarm around the castle that, at first, I don't see Jethonan running up the castle steps, the somewhat crushed tulip in hand, his long hair swinging and sweat running down his temples as he dodges outreaching hands and swinging blades.

The tulip.

I shout when a gloam master stabs the point of his sword through Jethonan's battered robes, pinning the fabric to the steps and forcing him to his knees. But Drade appears and forces the gloam master back as Jethonan clambers up, reaching for the tulip at the same time as another gloam master. Before either can reach it, Rupi dives from above and snatches it once more. She comes barreling toward me, and I prepare myself to grab it from her small grasp, but instead, she aims for Ikar. I hope Jethonan can hold his own as sparks of magic begin belching from his hands toward the gloam soldiers surrounding him, and I wonder for half a second what kind of magic he even has. Beyond him, I see the shard beasts and other gloam monsters wreaking havoc, screaming and shouting... How long before they kill us all?

I force my shaking legs to stand and grip the edge of the cold table as I work to break Renton's bridging away from my magic. With every tear my energy drains away, but I have to reach Ikar—we both must hold the tulip. I send every bit of lucent magic I can muster to Ikar and his soldiers who battle below us. Rupi returns, flowerless, and flaps about my head. I understand what she wants.

"I'm trying!" I shout, but how do I interrupt a sword fight between two powerful men to get to the dratted flower?

I scuttle around the side of their duel, aware that if I get too close, I could be killed on the spot. I ignore the fear that guts through me at the thought of being stabbed, and force myself to focus. When I get as close as I can, I summon more lucent than I've ever attempted to pull, so much that I begin to fear the power I hold in my hands, and push it toward Renton's chest, catching him off guard.

He staggers back with the force, shouting in anger and pain, and my eyes widen as his chest seeps clouds of gloam. For a moment, I even wonder if it'll kill him.

Ikar looks my way with determination in the set of his jaw. Faster than I can believe possible, he pulls the crumpled and limp flower from the pocket in his trousers where, apparently, he stuffed it after Rupi's delivery—hopefully it'll still do the job. He extends it to me, and I grasp it firmly, my fingers enclosed in his, meeting his eyes.

"Only ever you," I say.

My words trigger that deadly half-smile.

Renton lunges forward with hot rage in his eyes. "Wrong target, *wife*," he growls, swinging his sword toward Ikar.

Ikar releases the flower into my grasp, stepping in front of me protectively, already bringing his sword up to block his blow. The ring of their swords meeting vibrates through my body, and my face scrunches in a wince as I hitch my dress up and quickly backstep until my shoulders meet the cold stone of the castle several feet away. I wait to feel Ikar's magic reaching for me, *willing* the abused flower to work, even as I return with rabid focus to tearing Renton's magic from mine. Does my link have to be completely broken with Renton first? Even with most of it undone now, still all I sense is Renton's to bridge with. *No.* Panic begins to tighten my chest, but it only prompts me to free myself more fiercely while also leaving questions that sting the hope I'm clutching. Is the flower too broken? A one-time use?

I curse when gloam soldiers and a mix of deathstalkers and gloam wolves begin to climb the stairs in waves. Then, from within the swirling shadows a distance away, I faintly hear

Drade rally the fae and soon the sounds of battle are even louder through the thickening gloom. I look down to find the crushed tulip hanging limply in my hand—it looks about how I feel right now as despair and dark whispers of failure begin to fill my ears. How many will die? Did I ruin everything by touching the flower with Renton?

Darvy and Rhosse jump from the crowd and join Drade in pulling their forces together to attempt to stop the wave heading up the stairs toward Ikar and me, but the shard beasts catch sight of the growing battle, and their screeching roars increase as they charge. I don't watch them long, my attention drawn by a pained shout from Renton who now seeps gloam heavily from his left arm and upper leg, but my vision locks on a grisly cut to Ikar's ribs and another on his shoulder, leaving blood trailing down his skin in dark rivulets. I force myself to look away in order to focus, my heart pounding in my ears as the kingdom teeters and sways between the two kings, and things appear to fall apart below us.

Even amidst the chaos, my battered magic, and the weakness in my limbs, I finally manage to tear away the last of Renton's link and look up in utter surprise. *I actually did it.* I have the urge to throw a victorious fist in the air, but the men's swords meet and hold between them, pressing and battling for the upper hand, and through the crossed blades Renton's eyes meet mine. I *know* he feels the stark absence of the bridge. He roars in anger, and I resist the urge to shrink back against the stone of the castle. Instead I tip my chin up and narrow my eyes in challenge even though I know if he gets the chance, it won't be bridging that he seeks with me next—it'll be a violent death for my guiltless betrayal.

Ikar pushes Renton back, the playing field now evened with neither of them bridged with my power, freeing their crossed blades. The fight continues with an intensity I've never before witnessed. Renton's magic still hovers near, sporadic and hungry for mine... but where is Ikar's? The whispers of doubt rise again, and I look at the ruined tulip in my fist. Petals are missing, and another dangles precariously. I fight the despair, not waiting for Ikar's to search out mine; instead, I push my magic outward, seeking his.

It has to work.

"Finish it, Ikar! Bridge!"

Both their magic rushes me, hot and cold and overwhelming.

Chapter 69

Ikar

My mark burns as if the left half of my body has caught fire, a clear sign that gloam is growing, and I'm on the verge of losing my kingdom. Renton's gloam grows, and my strength dwindles, slipping between my fingers like sand. How long will Vera be able to send lucent once Renton bridges with her? Can it be undone?

All I know is if I give up, my kingdom falls. Only intense focus on the battle with a capable opponent keeps me from screaming in agony on my knees as another wave of fire runs the lengths and twists of my mark. Then Vera's voice calls me from the deep depths of driven focus, and the cool of her magic dances around me, calling my heat like a siren. I instinctively react. Unraveled ends of magic twist and turn between us, beginning to weave into one continuous, perfect strand. The burn in my mark stops, turns to tingling... and as I block another of Renton's swings, which grow weaker by the minute, the rush of cool magic fills every twist and curl of my mark.

But I don't miss the way Vera cries out behind us, almost

painfully—the hint of distraction in Renton's almost crazed eyes tells me I'm not the only one still trying to bridge.

My sword meets flesh and leaves more gloam seeping from Renton's side, but he masks the pain with an evil smirk that doesn't hide the rasp in his voice. "You're supposed to marry first. I still have the advantage."

I can't help but smirk. "Vera prefers the unconventional."

With every connection, every link, set in the bridge between Vera and I, my strength and energy grow so rapidly that Renton is merely blocking my swings now, fighting his dwindling speed as the gloam around us dissipates and weakens, evaporating like morning mist beneath the warm rays of the sun. My sword finally finds its mark in Renton's chest, and there's a beat of silence between us as he stares at me with hate-filled eyes. Lucent stronger than I've ever seen pulses through my sword as I mercilessly pull magic that comes freely to me now, and he drops to the ground with a lifeless thud.

I pull my sword from his disintegrating figure and immediately turn and reach for Vera, who's already coming forward, taking her into my arms. I hold her close as our magic continues to link and become whole, until the last wisps connect, so strong and so bright that my mark, all at once, emits blinding white light that shines from its scrolls and twists, forcing the soldiers below to cover their eyes. In that moment comes a shared vision, merely a flash, of a field of tulips, white birds flying overhead... and Lucentia smiling with approval. In a blink, the vivid picture is gone.

"Did you see that too?" Vera whispers.

I nod, soaring on a moment that feels too surreal to fully comprehend.

Vera watches from within my arms, wide-eyed, as the gloam around us disappears and lucent overtakes the cracks and crevices where darkness hid for too long. The screeching and growling fade as monsters burst into gloamy bits before disappearing completely, and scattered shouts sound as the gloam soldiers watch the weapons within their hands evaporate and their bodies follow after. Their powerful forms dissipate and blow away like mere smoke in wind.

"It's not finished yet," I mutter as I gently set Vera back and step in front of her, facing the soldiers, originators, and others that wait below.

I stand at the top of the steps, sword in hand, ignoring the blood that trickles down my body and soaks my trousers. My mark shimmers brilliantly in the twilight, no speck of black within its scrolls and twists. A flash of Lucentia's approving smile once again comes to mind, and never before have I felt so sure of my purpose.

"Call me your king, and I will take mercy." I hold my sword strong and steady, ready at any moment to continue the fight. "Kneel and swear your fealty. If you don't, the battle continues. There will be no other king on my throne."

Without hesitation, Darvy and Rhosse kneel, then Jethonan and Nadiette, and a wave of soldiers and originators follow after them. The only ones left standing are the low kings. Midon drops to a knee rather quickly. Then Farlow. I wait for Drade. One moment, then two. I meet Drade's challenging, hard eyes as a muscle in his jaw flexes and he finally kneels, his frame stiff and proud. I know how much it must wound his pride, but relief washes through me. I don't know that Vera would forgive either of us if we were to continue the fight.

It's silent in the near-darkness now as I turn and reach out to Vera, pulling her toward me and wrapping an arm around her waist. "Stand and honor the Black Tulip who has restored lucent and saved our kingdom." I'm pleased when my command is followed by the crowd rising in a wave and cheering so loudly I'm sure my ears will hear its echoes forever.

A rush of pride and warm affection fills my chest when she nods to herself, takes a deep breath, and keeps her chin held high, when I know from past experience all she'd like to do is step behind me. She doesn't know it yet, but she was made to be queen.

Nadiette launches lucent magic in the shape of a bouquet of tulips into the darkening sky, and the other originators follow suit, savoring the free-flowing lucent and sending it into the air in bright, sparkling designs and patterns that draw citizens from Moneyre through the castle gates in excited droves.

With sparkling magic raining down around us, I turn to one thing that has been driving me to the brink of insanity. I lift Vera's left hand from my chest, pulling her attention from the show of lucent, and inspect the glittering obsidian ring on her finger with a growl, feeling violent again.

"I'm not sorry for killing your husband." I've never spoken anything more true. "The only ring that will ever be here is mine."

She grins wryly. "Yes, Your Majesty."

My eyes lift to meet hers, taken back to that moment in the forest where she first used my title. Then, there was fear in her gaze, even disgust. Now...

She watches my face intently as I turn my attention to pulling it from her finger, then she steps closer and slides her arms slowly around my neck with a soft grin that has me wishing even more we were already married. My hands find the curve of her waist as I dip my head, and the touch of her warm lips moving against my own, her scent, the way her heart races in time with mine... it sends me sailing on a current of heady warmth and anticipation for the future I've never allowed myself to embrace until now.

The brush of feathers and Rupi's small wings flapping against Vera's neck force us to reluctantly break our kiss. Rupi perches on Vera's shoulder with her chest puffed proudly, one wing drenched in red and tucked carefully by her side—a battle wound. I frown with concern.

"You saved the day, girl," Vera whispers as she lifts a hand up, and Rupi hops into her palm. It only takes a moment for Vera to heal her wing, then she lifts her to her cheek affectionately.

"Always my loyal guide. I should have listened better," Vera admits.

Rupi fluffs up with pleasure, chirping in agreement and offering a cheeky side-eye.

"You don't need to rub it in," Vera mutters.

My attention turns to Jethonan who straggles up the stairs, his robes in tatters, a lock of his hair cut away much shorter than the rest, and sweat-soaked.

"We've done it, Your Majesty," he gasps.

I chuckle and give him a brotherly hug, clapping him on the back so firmly he grunts. I step back, scanning the still-churning crowds of people below us. "Have you seen Darvy? Rhosse?"

He nods. "They've sustained minor injuries, but should be fine. Darvy is already busy tending the wounded with the healers. Rhosse and the other commanders are gathering your troops. Now I must ensure that my office is in order." He marches away and continues to mutter, "Don't know what those soldiers may have done to it after I got arrested. *Me*, arrested. Of all people." He shakes his head and disappears through the large doors.

I look down to find Vera with an amused grin on her lips that matches my own.

I pull her closer to my side where we stand at the top of the steps together and watch as the chaos becomes organized before us. *It's over.* Disbelief and shock mingle in my veins as I take a moment to let it sink in. For so many years, my people suffered and died as the gloam continued to grow. I watched, and felt, my mark darken torturously. The years-long struggle to believe I was worthy as I watched the lands of my kingdom sicken and die before my eyes. Faces of soldiers I fought the gloam with flash through my mind, making the back of my eyes burn. Memories of pain and struggle invite me to slip further into the past, but Vera appears to sense my feelings as she squeezes my waist tighter for a moment, returning me to the present. The present that is absent the chill of lurking gloam... with plentiful lucent still lighting the sky above us in glowing bursts, and those below us watching Vera with open curiosity and wonder.

I take a moment to truly feel and savor the way our bond twists and curls between us with pleasure and strength, the way my mark thrums with cool power that is a relief after years of pain.

Vera's voice is soft when she breaks the comfortable silence between us. "I was worried I wouldn't know how to bridge, how to be a Black Tulip, but this is the most natural thing I've ever experienced. The kingdom... it's as if I know the entire span of it, every detail, every person and their need for lucent." She looks up at me. "Is this how it always is for you?"

"It's clearer now. Stronger."

She looks down at her hand engulfed in mine, then peers at my mark shining brilliant white and smiles.

"We broke the rules and bridged first," she whispers.

I chuckle and turn toward her, offering her my full attention and lowering my voice. "I wouldn't have expected it any
other way from you." I draw a gentle finger along her jaw, and
she tilts her chin upward with the motion. "I finally found my
Queen of the Night."

She tugs me closer. "Only ever yours."

Epilogue
Vera

The sweet scent of black tulips lingers in the air, and a warm breeze blows through the open balcony doors, cooling the heat of my skin brought on by an evening of dancing. Couples fill the ballroom floor, twirling beneath lucent orbs of light to the music of a small orchestra. I itch to snag Ikar's arm and drag him back to the dance floor, but the well-wishers lined up to our left wait patiently for their turn to offer congratulations. Rupi perches on my shoulder, chest puffed proudly, as if *she* was also crowned queen this morning. I pat her soft feathers with a grin.

To my left, Ikar speaks to an official from another country I've never heard of before, and I use the opportunity to admire how dashing he is in his royal uniform—so much so, I've been unable to keep my eyes off him the entire day. Their words turn to a buzz as I remind myself again... *we're married*. Butterflies dance in my stomach at the thought. Since we spoke vows this morning in a beautiful chapel, I've had to continually remind myself it's all real.

Lucent was restored just weeks ago, but Ikar insisted we

have a beautiful wedding and that we celebrate with the kingdom to build a strong relationship between the people and me. I think the fact that I helped save them from gloam was enough, but I didn't argue. So far, all who've greeted me have seemed kind, some curious. And with my hair up and the intentional design of my wedding gown, the mark on my back is showing for all to see.

The originators keep their distance, but I sense no hostility from them, and it gives me hope that maybe, just maybe, I can help mend what is broken in time. Nadiette is noticeably absent from their ranks, having chosen to step down as head originator. Because of her help during the battle, she avoided a trial for treason. I've been told she has taken a position in her cousin, Rosten Waylon's, low kingdom.

"Come here, my girl."

I'm pulled from my thoughts by a familiar voice, and my eyes immediately brighten. "Mama Tina."

Finally, a familiar face.

She wraps me in her outstretched arms, and I remember a second too late that I'm not sure this is how a queen should act. But when I glance at Ikar, all I see is warmth in his eyes. I step back and he nods to Mama Tina, appearing dignified until she yanks him into a tight hug that leaves him smiling.

Mama Tina steps back and leans toward me. "I knew he loved you when you showed up at my door wearing that atrocious animal dress."

"Did you now?" Obvious unbelief colors my tone.

She gives me a knowing look. "Any man willing to travel the kingdom with a woman in that monstrosity has to love her."

Rupi chirps in agreement from my shoulder, her feathers half-quilled—she never did like that dress. Ikar chuckles, wraps an arm around me, and pulls me into his side before he whispers in my ear, "She's right."

Mama Tina's eyes grow watery, and I know she intends her next words to be on a more serious note as she grabs one of my hands between her own.

"Never stop trusting yourself, my girl."

I nod, my eyes beginning to tear up as well. Mama Tina motions Ikar closer and whispers something in his ear that leaves him smiling as he straightens. "Come, Rupi. The fruit awaits," Mama Tina calls. Rupi pecks my earlobe affectionately once more and flaps to Mama Tina's shoulder eagerly, even as Mama Tina shoots Ikar one last look with a raised brow and struts away.

"What was that about?" I whisper.

"She was just reminding me of something."

"What was that?"

A smile twitches about his lips. "She expects little ones soon."

His smile grows roguish at the blush heating my cheeks, but the next person in line has already stepped up and throws her arms around me.

"You actually did it." Renna hugs me tightly. "Queen of Moneyre."

She steps back, and I don't miss the hint of sadness in her eyes that matches my own. Things are different now. We're still Tulip sisters, but the rest of our lives will never be the same, including the fact that we'll no longer share a home.

She squeezes my hand. "I'll be staying with Mama Tina for now, until I figure out what's next for me."

I nod. "Just, don't get into trouble with the fae," I warn.

She rolls her eyes. "You worry too much."

"I'll have Drade check in—"

Her eyes widen and she shakes her head, but before she can speak, a deep, cold voice behind her says, "Congratulations."

Drade steps up, and Renna pales as she sidesteps closer to me. For a moment, I wonder if they could ever develop feelings for each other... I care deeply for both of my friends, but I'm positive I just felt Renna tremble beside me, so I brush the fanciful thought away. Drade is like a prowling, sleek panther; Renna, the gentlest of doves. Certainly not two who I would ever imagine together.

Drade meets Ikar's eyes for an intense moment, and I frown when I sense the challenge rising between them. But I'll not be having a brawl in the middle of my wedding celebration, and Ikar and I are married now; fighting over it won't solve anything. I place a hand on Drade's arm to grab his attention.

"Thank you for coming, Drade." I offer a soft smile, one of friendship.

"How could I miss it?" he drawls lazily. We all know he was forced to be here.

"You remember Renna?" I gesture to her at my side where she seems to be entranced by the swirl of marble on the flooring.

"Of course." Drade merely sounds bored now.

"She'll be staying with Mama Tina... you know humans must be careful with the fae..."

"I'll be fine, Vera," Renna mutters beside me, sounding embarrassed.

Drade interrupts before I can say anything else. "It's an honor to have one of the Black Tulips residing within the fae kingdom. Do let me know if you need anything." He bows slightly, turns on the heel of one of his sleek shoes, and abruptly crosses the room and exits through one of the side doors—I know he's leaving.

"He's a terrifying man," Renna whispers to me.

"But handsome, you have to admit." I bump her shoulder.

She shakes her head, but I know her well enough to know that she agrees. Before I can continue to tease her about it, a young man who bows before her and asks her to dance claims her attention. She looks back once more with a smile and a wave of her fingers.

Just past her, I spy Darvy dancing with Petra, one of my Tulip sisters, and Rhosse stands against a wall surrounded by three women, though it seems he was trying to hide in the first place. A smile turns my lips. After years of struggle, it feels surreal to be here, our friends safe and lucent restored—some parts of our kingdom healed quickly, others will take time. Admittedly, as news of the Black Tulips has spread, so have rumors. We have a ways to go in gaining the trust of the kingdom, but hope grows as I observe the sense of genuine celebration over Ikar's and my marriage.

The final dance is announced and Ikar draws me away from my thoughts, stepping before me and executing a perfect bow before taking my hand in his and kissing it so softly that tingles race up my arm as the crowd quiets and watches in silence.

"Dance with me, my queen?" The bit of unfettered desire in his eyes as the last word leaves his lips leaves me so breathless I can hardly respond, but somehow I'm able to perform the expected, somewhat graceful curtsey without falling over. I allow him to lead me onto the cleared dance floor as the music strikes up in the background. With Ikar's solid presence before me, one strong hand at my waist, and the other holding my hand as he leads me through the steps, I find that suddenly... the crowd blurs into the background.

Warm air brushes the bare skin of my back as we dance, and I'm reminded how visible my mark is. But here in Ikar's arms, as the bridge of our magic flows whole between us, made stronger by the love we share, there is no fear. All my life I thought freedom was not paying Tulip dues and hiding away with my secrets in a quaint shop... and while I haven't given up on the dream of my own shop—even as the new Queen of Moneyre—*this* is freedom in a way I never imagined possible.

The sound of Ikar's deep voice draws my eyes up to his. "I've never told you, but—" He continues leading through steps I can hardly recall, distracted as I am, before he continues. "I'm glad you're good at breaking rules." My eyes widen, and he grins as we make another turn, my dress floating out around us. "And I can't believe I'm saying this." He pauses as he leads me into a spin, and then his hand lands firmly on my waist before he tugs me close and lowers his voice. "But thank you for arresting me."

Heat runs the length of my body at the look in his eyes. I don't even notice we've stopped dancing or that the other couples have joined us on the dance floor, spinning all around us. The only thing I see is Ikar and the look in his eyes that mirrors mine. Soon, it will be just he and I. He must be thinking the same as he eyes the doors that will lead us away from the celebration soon.

"Just so you know," I begin with a mischievous whisper that prompts his gaze to return to mine. "You're my favorite criminal."

His gaze darkens, and his lips turn up in a roguish half-smile as his hands tighten around my waist with protective affection. "I better be your *only* criminal."

I laugh with genuine surprise at his reaction. "No denial?" I raise a curious brow.

"It's useless. Besides—" He growls and steps closer, his lips brushing my ear and sending a rush of tingles down my body. "If you're the captor, it's the only thing I want to be."

I smile just before his lips meet mine, and I'm struck anew that the king I was hiding from, the one I was taught to fear... is the one I love, and the one who set me free.

THE END OF
The first duology in The Black Tulip Chronicles

The story will continue with a new romance between two of our favorite characters in the second duology

SIGN UP FOR MY AUTHOR NEWSLETTER...

...to get access to a ***bonus epilogue*** for Queen of the Night!

As a subscriber you'll also be the first to learn about updates on current and future projects, get early art and chapter reveals, and receive other exclusive bonus content.

I'd love to have you join me!

https://www.kayleejarvis.com/newsletter

Acknowledgments

My first thank you will always be to my husband who offers me endless support and encouragement through the ups *and* the downs.

A special thank you to my early readers: Madelyn Smith, Terri Brown, Curtis Brown, and Jeremy Jarvis for their time and help in bringing the story to the next level with their incredible feedback and support.

And of course, I want to thank my kids. Even with my busy schedule they encourage me to keep writing. And also, thank you to the many sweet friends who support me.

You all make this possible, and even better, you make it fulfilling.

And last, but not least, I'd like to thank the professionals who were part of preparing Queen of the Night for publishing. First, Dragana, my cover designer, tied this beautiful cover in with Bounty Hunter's perfectly. Also, Caitlin Miller, my line editor, and Alicia Whitaker, my proofreader, both have an eye for detail that is truly incredible. They helped polish and bring my manuscript to the next level. I will be forever grateful to have found such an amazing team to work with.

About the Author

Kaylee Jarvis loves telling stories filled with fantasy, romance, adventure, and humor. She enjoys writing no-spice, sizzling romantic chemistry, creating complex and relatable characters, and bringing it all to life in unique worlds.

She is originally from Southern Utah. Now, as an active duty military spouse, she makes home wherever the military takes her—and as a bonus, she gets to see her handsome husband in uniform almost every day of the week. She's mom to four rowdy boys and one sweet girl who is the caboose of their family, and pet mom to their much-loved family dog. When she's not writing or reading, you'll find her buying more plants, lifting weights at the gym, and eating dark chocolate (which she believes is its own sort of magic).

www.kayleejarvis.com

Find her on Instagram, TikTok, Facebook, and Amazon
@kayleejarvis.author